THE MESSAGE

THE MESSAGE

MAI JIA

TRANSLATED BY

OLIVIA MILBURN

First published in China in 2007 by Nanhai Publishing Company
First published in the UK in 2020 by Head of Zeus Ltd
This paperback edition first published in 2020 by Head of Zeus Ltd

Published in agreement with the author c/o The Grayhawk Agency Ltd, through Georgina Capel Associates Ltd

9 7 5 3 1 2 4 6 8

A catalogue record for this book is available from the British Library.

ISBN (PB): 9781789543032
ISBN (E): 9781789543001

Typeset by Siliconchips Services Ltd UK

Printed and bound in Great Britain by
CPI Group (UK) Ltd, Croydon CR0 4YY

Head of Zeus Ltd
5–8 Hardwick Street
London EC1R 4RG

WWW.HEADOFZEUS.COM

PART ONE

The Wind from the East

ONE

1

My story is set in 1941, during the Japanese occupation, just as spring turned to summer. The location is West Lake in the city of Hangzhou, a famous beauty spot in east China, in the province of Zhejiang.

In the 1930s and 1940s, Hangzhou was less than a fifth of its present size, but the heart of the city – West Lake – was no smaller than it is now and had just as many beautiful vistas and historic sites in and around it as it has today. Extending across the lake was the causeway built in the name of the Tang-dynasty poet Bai Juyi and the causeway constructed by the Song-dynasty poet and essayist Su Dongpo; dotted along these were the Broken Bridge, the Bridge of Gazing at the Immortals, Brocade Belt Bridge, Jade Belt Bridge and Linked Waves Bridge. There were also the Three Pools Mirroring the Moon, the famous vista known as the Moon Over Peaceful Lake in Autumn, and at the head of Xiling Bridge the tomb of the lovely but ill-fated fifth-century courtesan Su Xiaoxiao. There was the vista called Orioles Singing in the Willow Trees and the temple commemorating the Qian kings who made Hangzhou their capital in the tenth century. On Gushan Island there was the tomb of the revolutionary martyr and feminist Qiu Jin, executed in 1907, and the famous Louwailou restaurant. Tucked away in the hills surrounding the lake were the White Cloud Nunnery, the seven-storey Baochu Pagoda, Precious Stone Hill Floating in the Rosy Cloud, and the temple commemorating the patriotic Song-dynasty martyr General Yue Fei. And so on. They were all there, as they are still – the hills and the pools, the causeways and the pagodas, the temples and the bridges, the artificial islands and the scenic sites – left quite untouched by the Japanese.

In August 1937 Hangzhou was quite heavily bombed by the Japanese. I am told that, even now, more than seven decades on, unexploded ordnance is regularly uncovered along the Qiantang River, with the manufacturer's marks fully legible. Bombs fell from the sky, scaring people half to death even when they didn't explode, and most of them did. Explosions rent the heavens and shook the earth; they opened great chasms in the ground and unleashed infernos that caused countless deaths and injuries. The inhabitants of Hangzhou all fled. West Lake would no doubt have run away too if it could have, but since that was impossible, it had to stay and take what was coming.

As it happened, however, West Lake was amazingly lucky. Several hundred planes flew dozens of sorties and bombed Hangzhou itself into a wasteland, but West Lake and its many vistas and historic sites were entirely unaffected, as if protected by the gods. Only the temple dedicated to General Yue Fei seemed to have fallen outside this charmed circle, sustaining a small amount of bomb damage.

In those days, if you exited the Temple of General Yue Fei and turned in the direction of the Baochu Pagoda, along what is now Beishan Road, you would have seen quite a number of grand houses and estates. Of course, these were the homes of rich and powerful people. The rich and powerful have much better access to information than ordinary people, and so, long before the Japanese began their bombing campaign, they upped sticks and left. Once the Japanese had established their puppet government in Nanjing and the situation in Hangzhou had stabilized, as if by magic they reappeared. In some cases they sent their servants instead, to look after their properties and make sure that no one from the occupying regime requisitioned them.

One such property was a mansion that stood with its back to the mountains and its face to the lake; its owner was a man named Tan, a one-time gangster who'd taken advantage of the chaotic wartime situation to leave his criminal past behind him. He bought the land and built a house, which soon became famous far and wide; people called it the Tan Estate. Maybe it was just too attractive, just too well known, because during the occupation it was swiftly requisitioned and then handed over to the puppet regime's newly created East China Counter-insurgency Corps, the ECCC. And so its buildings were put to new use.

In the front courtyard was a three-storey building that Mr Tan had designed as a teahouse and restaurant. This was now transformed into an ECCC officers' club cum pleasure dome where every fleshly desire could be satisfied; anything went, and the place swarmed with prostitutes. Behind it, within a forest of bamboo, stood a C-shaped building that had originally been the servants' quarters but was now used as office space. If you kept on walking, you reached the rear courtyard, where a pair of small Western-style houses stood facing one another. The one to the west became the private residence of the ECCC's commander, Qian Huyi, while the one to the east was where he met his visitors and accommodated a handful of his cronies and aides. Since these buildings had once been the residences of Mr Tan and his family, they were beautifully appointed and very luxurious; when Qian Huyi moved in, he realized how right he had been to throw in his lot with the Japanese.

At this time, the political situation in China was extremely complicated. In the north-east there was Manchukuo, while in the south-east there was the Reorganized National Government, based in Nanjing and led by the collaborationist Chinese official Wang Jingwei. Both of these areas were under Japanese control; they were puppet regimes of the Japanese state and were entirely dependent on the Japanese for protection, so naturally they did what they were told.

There were also two anti-Japanese regimes centred elsewhere in the country. The Nationalist Kuomintang or KMT government was based in Chongqing, in the south-west, and was headed by Chiang Kai-shek; while the Communist government was based in Yan'an, in the north-west, and was headed by Mao Zedong. The Nationalists and the Communists both considered resisting Japanese aggression to be in the national interest, so they established a united front to fight the enemy together. But they also had their own antithetical preoccupations and aims, and their apparently united front actually concealed deep rifts; in reality, each side acted entirely out of self-interest, cutting the ground from beneath the other's feet. This complex political situation meant that the whole country was in chaos, and the lives of many of its people became unbearably difficult.

In Hangzhou, Japanese military control was relatively weak at this point, and the city also had good transport links with nearby Shanghai and Nanjing. Both the Nationalists and the Communists exploited this to their advantage and Hangzhou became a focus for underground operations conducted by both sides: the Nationalist agents were providing intelligence for the Bureau of Military Statistics, while the Communist agents were running covert missions on behalf of their Yan'an headquarters. As a result, the city's anti-Japanese resistance movement had strengthened considerably. Which was why Wang Jingwei's puppet regime established the East China Counterinsurgency Corps and put Commander Qian Huyi in charge.

Qian Huyi vowed to wipe out these resistance organizations. He had at one time been an officer in the Nationalist Party's National Revolutionary Army, but his desire for wealth and status had made him easy prey for the Japanese and he became a collaborator, a henchman of the invaders (people called him Qian-the-Dog). He was very much aware of the deep divisions that existed between the Nationalists and the Communists, for all that they appeared to be united in their resistance efforts, and he skilfully drove a wedge between them, causing enormous damage to the underground movements on both sides. For their part, both the Communists and the Nationalists were desperate to infiltrate his anti-insurgency ECCC, to secretly sabotage his efforts and turn the tide against him.

In the summer of 1940, ECCC commander Qian Huyi's crimes finally caught up with him and he was murdered, along with his entire family. In the middle of the night, someone managed to get into the rear courtyard of the Tan Estate and kill every single person in those two little Western-style buildings. Male and female, young and old – no one was spared.

The two buildings had remained empty ever since; that is, for the past nine months or so.

You might think that any number of people would have jumped at the chance to move into such a beautiful pair of buildings in such a lovely location, or that if no one wanted to live in them, they could at least have been put to some other use. In fact, the sort of people powerful enough to pull the necessary strings to allow them to live there were bothered by the murders and didn't dare move in, while the sort of people who weren't bothered were just too insignificant. So the two houses remained empty, right up until one evening nearly a year later, in 1941, just as spring was turning into summer.

Late that evening, on a cloudless night so bright from the moon that the stars were barely visible, two groups of people turned up at the Tan Estate, one shortly after the other, and moved into the two empty buildings.

2

The first of the two groups went into the eastern building. There were a great many of them, a whole truckload, and when they assembled on the terrace in front of the house, they filled it completely. In the dark it was hard to count, but there must have been a couple of dozen people in total. The majority were young soldiers; some of them were shouldering guns and others were carrying various bits of equipment. In charge was a fat little man with a revolver and a short sword stuck in his belt. He was a staff officer in the secret-police unit attached to the military base: his surname was Jiang, but his personal name doesn't seem to have been recorded. As soon as he'd unlocked the door to the building, those people carrying equipment entered in single file. The others, the soldiers carrying guns, stayed where they were until Staff Officer Jiang came out of the building again, then followed him as he walked off into the darkness.

About an hour later the second group of people arrived, and they went to the west building. There were five of them, three men and two women, all military officers, all of them in the East China Counterinsurgency Corps, all of them formerly under the command of the late ECCC boss Qian Huyi.

Wu Zhiguo was the highest ranking. At the beginning of the year he had commanded a very successful attack against a small guerrilla group of insurgents active in Huzhou, north of Hangzhou, removing them in one fell swoop. He was highly regarded by the new ECCC boss, Commander Zhang Yiting, and had thus been promoted two grades, to the position of Chief of Staff at headquarters. He was now responsible for all training and combat across the entire region; effectively, he was the Chief of Staff. He had just taken office and things were going very well for him; he walked with a spring in his step and his future seemed bright.

The second member of the group was Jin Shenghuo, Section Chief in charge of the office responsible for military security and confidential matters. The third was a woman, the cryptographer Li Ningyu, in charge of the unit that deciphered top-secret documents. Bai Xiaonian was the fourth member of the group, but his name could equally well have been cited first, because he was Commander Zhang's aide-de-camp and private secretary; this put him right at the heart of whatever was going on. Although his official rank was not very high (he was a mere captain), his powers were almost limitless. Gu Xiaomeng, the second woman, was one of Li Ningyu's subordinates. She was young and very pretty. With her tall stature and striking good looks, she attracted attention even in the dark.

These five people arrived in a Nissan jeep and under cover of darkness were driven through the secluded Tan Estate to the rear courtyard. The houses that had already seen so much death, so many brutal murders, were about to become a place of terror once again; with the ECCC officers' arrival, it was like putting a knife into the hands of a murderer.

There was much more to what was going on than met the eye: even the people who were caught up in it had no notion of the conspiracy that had them in its grip. All five had been asleep in their beds when Secretary Bai had been woken by a phone call from Commander Zhang. Following that call, Secretary Bai had roused the other four and they'd all then been brought together as quickly as possible, hurried into the car and whisked off to the Tan Estate. Nobody had any idea why they were there, and that included Secretary Bai.

The person in charge was the local Chief of the Secret

Police, Wang Tianxiang. Only once he'd seen each of them settled into their rooms in the west building did he offer the tiniest hint as to what was going on.

'Commander Zhang asked me to inform you that you have been selected for a special mission,' he said enigmatically. 'You won't be getting much sleep over the next couple of days, so you should make the most of tonight. The Commander will come and see you at the earliest opportunity tomorrow.'

He was obviously relishing the mysterious nature of the whole enterprise and he made it plain that bringing them there was just one of many things he needed to organize that night. So, having given them this message, he said goodbye.

Gu Xiaomeng found this enigmatic high-handedness deeply irritating. Sticking her exquisite little nose in the air, she muttered contemptuously, 'Pah! That son of a bitch, who does he think he is!'

Though she hadn't spoken at all loudly, her comments were enough to make her colleagues stare nervously at their feet. As the local Chief of the Secret Police, Wang Tianxiang had special powers, which made him untouchable. Even Commander Zhang tiptoed around him.

The secret police occupy a special position, they are like Janus: there's the face you can see, but also the one that you can't. You never know quite whose side they're on. Officially, Police Chief Wang's activities came under Commander Zhang's jurisdiction, but his covert duties included spying on the Commander. Every month Wang Tianxiang had to submit a report to the Shanghai branch of the Japanese secret police, detailing any important activities or conversations on the part of every senior officer in his district, including the Commander.

Under the circumstances, it wasn't surprising that he was arrogant. Who would dare say anything about a man like that? Absolutely no way would you criticize him to his face, and even behind his back you'd still have to be careful, because if someone reported it you could find yourself in serious trouble. So to hear Gu Xiaomeng come right out with it like that was a shock. The others therefore acted as if they hadn't heard her and each went their separate ways.

They went their separate ways only to reconvene elsewhere.

They came together in Chief of Staff Wu Zhiguo's room, all of them with the same question on their lips: why had the Commander dragged them out of bed in the middle of the night?

They'd all been quite sure that someone would know the answer, but it transpired that nobody did. Since nobody knew, all they could do was guess. Everyone proffered at least a couple of ideas, but that merely proved that they didn't have a clue. Even so, nobody seemed to be prepared to give up; they wanted to continue discussing it. The only exception was Wu Zhiguo: he'd been inspecting the forces under his command that day and there'd been a banquet in the evening – he was tired, he'd drunk a lot of alcohol and now he really wanted to sleep.

'Go to bed, go to bed.' He was trying to get everyone out of his room. 'There's no point trying to guess what's going on. Unless you have some special insight into what the boss is up to, you're just wasting your time.' Then he changed tack. 'And talking of bosses, do you know whose bed this was?' He looked up and grinned. 'Our old boss's – Commander Qian Huyi's. He was murdered in this very bed!'

Gu Xiaomeng leapt off the bed with a screech.

Wu Zhiguo laughed. 'What are you so scared of, Xiaomeng? If I was as jumpy as you, I'd never be able to sleep at night. Now if Qian Huyi were still alive, you might have cause – everyone says he didn't take no for an answer where women were concerned.'

'What are you talking about, Chief of Staff Wu?' Gu Xiaomeng shot back.

'He's just being nice,' Section Chief Jin chipped in. 'He's complimenting you on your looks.'

Wu Zhiguo saw that Xiaomeng was about to say something, so he shushed her with his hand. 'Do you know who killed Commander Qian? It was someone from this very estate! This place used to belong to some big gangster – they say he'd laid up enough cash to buy the whole of West Lake and that all of his gold bars are somewhere in this house, or in the grounds at least. That's why the estate's changed hands so many times: everyone wants to find the stash, and that included Commander Qian, but nobody's had any luck – so far.'

Everybody had heard the story before.

Chief of Staff Wu stood up. 'Go to bed, everyone. There's nothing more to discuss. If you want to waste your time on pointless speculation, then try and work out where the old gangster hid his cash.' He laughed. 'Go to bed, go to bed – see how late it is. Tomorrow, when Commander Zhang arrives, we'll find out what's going on.'

Everyone went to their rooms. By that time it was already well past 1 a.m.

3

The following day, just as the sun was rising and before the mists that veiled West Lake had dispersed, Commander Zhang's black car was already bumping its way along the shoreside road.

Commander Zhang Yiting had been born into an ordinary family in Anhui province, but from a very early age it was clear that he was unusually intelligent. At eighteen he took first place in the provincial examinations for the imperial bureaucracy and seemed destined for a prestigious job in the civil service of the Qing dynasty. But, like a bolt from the blue, the Revolution of 1911 destroyed his dreams, and for many years afterwards nothing went right for him. He was ambitious to serve his country but condemned to remain on the sidelines. Too often he was treated with contempt by others; too often he found himself at the mercy of misfortunes he'd done nothing to deserve. This situation lasted until the Japanese installed their treasured collaborator Wang Jingwei in Nanjing. Only then, when Zhang Yiting was in his fifties, the hair at his temples already turning white, did his future began to look bright. He became Qian Huyi's deputy: Vice-Commander of the ECCC.

But what kind of future lay in store for him? A year earlier, when he'd returned home to attend his mother's funeral, one of the villagers had poured a bucket of shit over him. He was so furious that he grabbed a gun off a subordinate and fired at the villager. He didn't kill him – the man just lost a bit of skin off his leg – but for Zhang Yiting this marked the end of an era. He understood that he would never be able to go home again, and he decided to carry on down the path he'd chosen with redoubled determination. So when his boss Qian Huyi was murdered and the rumours flying around were such that none of his colleagues dared step into the role, he accepted the promotion, exhibiting surprising courage and boldness.

That was almost a year ago now, and he'd never regretted his decision, not least because he had no other choice. Now, as he thought about all that had happened the previous night, and all that was about to happen at the Tan Estate, he had exactly the same feeling: he had no other choice.

The black car skirted the lake, followed the road up to the Tan Estate and after a few blasts on the horn came to a halt at a high wall. Sentries shouldering guns stood to attention outside the main gate and the guards ushered the Commander through. It was 7.30 a.m. – he had indeed come at the earliest possible opportunity.

Before him was a T-shaped grey-brick building with a black-tiled roof, very much in the traditional style, and a pretty but not at all practical grille door that was nowhere near high enough to stop a determined person from climbing over. It was here that the Tan family had quite brazenly installed a brothel. The sign that now hung over the door said it was an officers' club, which was pretty much the same thing.

The car traced a circle round the large open space in front of the officers' club and then turned right, in the direction of the rear courtyard. It drove through an area densely planted with phoenix-tail bamboo and on down a narrow road between stands of imperial zhennan trees. Commander Zhang caught a glimpse of the two buildings to the east and west, and then, as the car passed an ornate rockery overgrown with weeds and a wisteria-covered pergola, he saw that Secret-Police Chief Wang Tianxiang was waiting respectfully on the terrace of the western building.

Standing to attention behind the Police Chief was a sentry with a Mauser pistol at his hip, and behind the sentry was a wooden signboard, newly erected, which read: 'Military Area. No Admittance for Unauthorized Personnel.' There was also a freshly painted white line demarcating the area. This had all been put in place by Police Chief Wang during the night.

Since everyone had gone to bed very late the night before and hadn't expected Commander Zhang to arrive so early, the five ECCC officers had all got up late. Indeed, Gu Xiaomeng was still in bed when he turned up. To have the Commander arrive at such an early hour was kind of flattering, but it brought home the seriousness of their mission. Even more so when they came out of the house to go to breakfast and saw the sentries standing to attention and the white line encircling the building.

The dining room was in the officers' club in the front courtyard. Police Chief Wang appeared to have been waiting for them and he escorted them the whole way. Although he hadn't slept at all the night before, he was evidently fully alert and seemed very pleased with himself. He was acting as if they were a group of VIPs who'd travelled extremely long distances and this too made everyone feel like they were engaged in something significant, because ordinarily he never behaved like that.

Once everyone had vacated the west building, two people dressed in plain clothes and carrying toolboxes slipped across from the east building. The fat little Staff Officer Jiang led the way. They looked over the whole house inside and out, from the loft to the cellars, as if they were inspecting the wiring. Commander Zhang had already had his breakfast, so he joined the workmen in their search of the house.

4

It was a classic little Western-style house: two storeys and an attic. The attic, however, had already been sealed off.

There were four bedrooms upstairs, but one of them was locked, leaving three. Section Chief Jin Shenghuo had been given the small room at the end of the corridor, and the two women, Gu Xiaomeng and Li Ningyu, had been allocated the next room along, which was arranged like a normal guest bedroom with two single beds, a pair of wickerwork chairs and a desk. This had previously been Commander Qian Huyi's study; the rack for drying calligraphy brushes still hung outside the window. Opposite that was another guest room, currently locked. Beyond the stairwell was the main bedroom, given over to Chief of Staff Wu Zhiguo, which stretched the width of the building. It was very luxurious, with a little balcony at the front, and a huge terrace at the back complete with marble pillars and a grapevine growing up the trellis.

A few years earlier, Commander Zhang had accompanied his then boss, Qian Huyi, on a visit here and the place had been in a real mess, with the floorboards taken up, the furniture all topsy-turvy, cracks in the walls and holes in the ceiling. It was a house that had been through the wars. Even so, he'd been shocked by the extravagance of the place: the floorboards were made of sandalwood, the furniture of mahogany, there was a European-style sofa and chaise longue, chandeliers of crystal, glazed floor tiles, a flush toilet... Everything was of top quality and really expensive. Qian Huyi had it all repaired and it really was lovely, even better than the general's suite at the officers' club. After Qian Huyi's death, people kept urging Commander Zhang to move in there, and he did seriously consider it. But there were reasons to hesitate and in the end he decided against it.

A few months ago, he'd sent some people to remove as many of the expensive fixtures and fittings as they could, after which the two buildings were turned over to the officers' club. They were told to outfit the rooms for guests and to start using them.

There were two reasons why Commander Zhang had made these arrangements. One was that he thought it a shame to leave the buildings empty. The other was that he was very unhappy about the disgusting goings-on at the officers' club in the front courtyard. Unlike Qian Huyi, Commander Zhang was a well-educated man and he simply couldn't condone such activities. He was worried that someone else might find it equally abhorrent and make a formal complaint to his superiors, in which case he would lose his job. But he was also worried that if he closed the club down, he would annoy some other bigwig in the

Imperial Japanese Army, which would result in him losing his job anyway.

It was much more exhausting for him to be a commander, a puppet of the Japanese, than it had been for Qian Huyi, and this was all thanks to his past as a young intellectual in the imperial era. It was like a burden permanently strapped to his back: the weight of history continually grinding him down. But he couldn't bear to give up the power and wealth he'd acquired under the new regime, so he had to put up with the problems that came with it. He either had to close his eyes to the things he found unacceptable, or, if they represented a real threat to his present advantages, he had to try and resolve them, talk people round to his way of thinking.

He had the two buildings redecorated with a view to moving the brothel, and the foul activities associated with it, to the rear part of the estate. This would get it out of plain sight without getting rid of it altogether; surely no bigwig was going to object to that! It seemed to be the best of both worlds.

It was a good idea, but it failed. The prostitutes who'd been working in the front part of the estate when the murders happened were scared witless; they were familiar with the rear courtyard and had seen for themselves the scene of the crime. But the girls who'd arrived after the murders were even more scared: they had to listen to the others talking about it, and that was truly horrifying. Fear is catching, and like a malignant growth, each teller made the story worse. It got to the point where nobody dared so much as go for a walk in the rear courtyard, not even in broad daylight. It had happened right there, and not so long ago either, and the ghosts of the dead were still wandering through the bamboo forests, unappeased. The girls weren't taking any chances. No way were they moving – they would rather quit than move!

Commander Zhang decided to get rid of that group of girls and bring in some new ones, but that turned out to be harder than recruiting an entire division of troops. In the end, his plans came to naught. The buildings were left empty and he was left out of pocket. This made him so angry, he would have happily pulled them down brick by brick.

Yesterday evening, when he'd discovered what was afoot and realized he'd have to find somewhere to accommodate his five ECCC employees, he'd immediately thought of the Tan Estate. Finally, he could put the place to good use! And now that he was on site, he was even more delighted with his arrangements.

There were two buildings and two groups of people, each doing their own completely separate thing – yes, very nice. But why had Police Chief Wang arranged the rooms the way he had? Since there were four bedrooms upstairs, he'd assumed each person would have their own room. He didn't know why one room was locked, obliging Gu Xiaomeng and Li Ningyu to share.

Secretary Bai had been given one of the two smaller downstairs rooms and the sentries had the other. The third, bigger downstairs room had been arranged as a conference room by pushing some tables together; it looked very nice, but, again, Commander Zhang wondered why the Police Chief had gone to so much effort when the sitting room, on the other side of the house, would have made a perfectly good meeting room, with its cane chairs and coffee tables. He didn't understand what Wang Tianxiang was up to, but he was impressed nonetheless. Actually, this was very much the Commander's everyday approach to the man; he usually tried to think well of the Police Chief and avoided quarrelling with him.

He sat down at the head of the conference table, pulled some papers out of his briefcase and began to flick through them, ready for the coming meeting. A sarcastic smile flitted across his face. There was a hint of contempt in there too.

5

Police Chief Wang Tianxiang presided over the meeting, but Commander Zhang was the principal speaker. He opened with some platitudes about their present campaign against Communist insurgents. He stressed that there were new trends in the insurgency and that the attacks by the Communist underground were more numerous, more violent and more difficult to deal with than the situation with the Nationalists, which was at least open warfare.

The Communists and the Nationalists were also fighting among themselves – to the amusement of the puppet government. The repercussions from the Wannan Incident had not yet died down: even now, several months later, the sound of gunfire and the smell of blood seemed to hang in the air. In the Wannan Incident, a crack division of anti-Japanese troops consisting of nine thousand Communists had been turned by the Nationalists into several thousand corpses and more than two thousand stragglers in the space of just a couple of days. Some Communist soldiers had escaped, however, infiltrating Japanese-held areas around Hangzhou and making contact with the underground there; others had gone their own way, launching guerrilla-style attacks and spreading the scope of resistance activities.

As the Commander spoke, everyone could see that he was in an unusually good mood: even though he could hardly be pleased about his subject matter (which must have been a huge headache for him), there was a smile on his face and his tone of voice was cheerful. 'As you all know,' he continued, 'yesterday afternoon our bosses in Nanjing sent us a top-secret message informing us that a senior Communist known as "K" has set out from Xi'an and will arrive in Hangzhou within the next few days. We know he's coming here to plot against us. We've seen a lot of Communist Party conspiracies, so that in itself is no surprise, but this time they're up to something big and they're being very careful to keep it all secret, so we have to take this very seriously indeed.'

The Commander paused to emphasize his point. The group were to be left in no doubt about the gravity of the situation and the importance of their mission, whatever that turned out to be.

'K has been dispatched by Zhou Enlai himself to preside as his representative over a meeting of all the leaders of the Communist underground here in Zhejiang province. That meeting is to be held at 11 p.m. on the 29th of this month at the Agate Belvedere Inn on Mount Fenghuang. Just four days from now.' He straightened his back and raised his voice slightly. 'Let us be clear: four days from now, the Communists are going to hold a meeting with the express aim of coordinating their resistance activities. If this meeting goes ahead, they'll be able to band together, those scattered guerrillas will become a unified force, and instead of the minor inconveniences we've had to deal with so far, we'll be up against a powerful army. Quashing this insurgency will become a lot more difficult. So we're lucky indeed to have got this intelligence.'

He looked around at his ECCC officers. 'As the saying goes, good luck comes in twos, and yesterday was my lucky day – and a lucky day for all of you sitting round this table. In the afternoon we received the all-important telegram from Nanjing. Then in the evening—' here, he pointed at Wang Tianxiang '—Police Chief Wang brought me another present. And what was that…?'

He picked up a fat dictionary and showed it to the assembled company.

'It's right here.'

The book was filthy, as if it had been dragged through the mud.

'What is this? It's the recently published *Comprehensive Dictionary of the Chinese Language* – maybe you have a copy yourselves at home. You may well be thinking, what sort of present is that? I thought the same to begin with. But then Police Chief Wang explained that this was no ordinary dictionary and that a huge secret was concealed within it. Which was why an unlucky Communist agent threw it out of the window just moments before he was arrested, hoping to destroy the evidence.'

He turned to Wang Tianxiang. 'That's right, is it not, Police Chief Wang?'

Wang Tianxiang nodded, and picked up the story. 'This

Communist agent was living in one of the staff apartments at Qingchun Middle School. His rooms were up on the second floor and had a window at the back, so I posted a guard outside in case he tried to escape that way. In the end he didn't get away, there wasn't time, but he threw this book out. All he cared about was getting rid of this dictionary, so I knew there was something important here.'

'Yes, I thought exactly the same,' Commander Zhang interjected. 'So I examined the dictionary really carefully. I checked every single page, read it through until my head was spinning, but I didn't find a thing. There was nothing written anywhere, nothing out of the ordinary.'

He flicked through the fat dictionary with a theatrical flourish, brandishing it in front of the bemused ECCC officers.

'Eventually, I went out for a walk, setting down the cup of tea I'd been holding before I left. I didn't even notice that I'd put the cup down on the dictionary, but when I came back, a miracle had occurred – some blurred writing had appeared on the flyleaf! The heat of the teacup had revealed a series of Arabic numerals in a little circle, like a stamp. That really was a stroke of luck. I immediately understood that with the application of more heat, more would appear. So I fetched a hot-water bottle and look what happened!'

He held the dictionary open at the flypaper. Its coarse yellowish paper was covered with white Arabic numerals, arranged as if in a telegram, in row after row. Although the numbers weren't very clear, they could still be read:

120 3201 009 2117 477 1461...
741 8816 187 5661 273 4215...

There were dozens of lines like that.

Commander Zhang jabbed his finger at the group and asked, 'What is this?'

He answered his own question. 'You know as well as I do: this is an encrypted message. Or to put it another way, it's a cypher-text. Why encrypt it? Because it contains important intelligence. The Communists were afraid that it might fall into our hands – so afraid, in fact, that the agent didn't care if he got killed, providing he could stop us from getting hold of it. Which means that the intelligence hidden here must also be extremely important for us, would you not agree?'

Again he glanced at the faces around the table, and again he answered his question himself. 'I'm sure that by now you've all realized why I dragged you out of bed in the middle of the night and brought you here.'

He raised his eyebrows and waited expectantly. No one moved a muscle.

'I want you to decipher this message.'

Everyone looked a bit shocked, and Gu Xiaomeng appeared to mumble something.

But Commander Zhang ploughed on. Heaving a deep sigh, he said, 'Heaven really is on our side,' and then he got up and started pacing the floor. 'Now I need you to help me too,' he said as he circled the table. 'With that one stroke of luck we got on to this thing, but that's not enough. I want to know what's going on, I want to find out what it is that they've gone to such trouble to conceal. It's my guess that this has something to do with the agent code-named K. If that is correct—' here, he stopped his pacing and faced them directly, his tone more aggressive now '—then there is a great deal at stake here, and you must decipher it!'

Perhaps because he'd been through so much in his life, the former scholar was a moody, bad-tempered man; furthermore, he'd been in a position of power for several years now and could be nasty when he had to be. Because of this, his subordinates were scared of him. Just now, when his voice had changed, they'd lowered their eyes. But today he was in a good mood and didn't want to terrorize his staff, so he went no further. Noting how quiet and serious they all were, he smiled and sat back down again, speaking in as kindly a voice as he could muster.

'As the saying goes, you train your troops for a thousand days to use them for an hour. Right now, I need you more than ever. Although none of you have experience in cracking the cyphers used by the Communist military, I'm sure you won't let me down. I think that... how to explain? Well, first of all, I doubt the code can be that difficult, because otherwise that agent wouldn't have risked his life to get rid of it – if it was going to be impossible to decipher, he could just have left it where it was. Secondly, you all have your own areas of expertise. Chief of Staff Wu here—' he nodded at his highest-ranking member of staff '—knows the Communists like the back of his hand – you could call him a living encyclopaedia when it comes to their strongholds and positions.'

Chief of Staff Wu sat very still, determined not to show how pleased he was at this very public vote of confidence from his boss.

'Section Chief Jin and Unit Chief Li are both old hands at this kind of work,' Commander Zhang continued. 'They must have deciphered tens of thousands of encrypted telegrams in their time. And Staff Officer Gu is a bright young woman, she knows how to use her brain and she's prepared to speak out.'

He flashed them each a cool smile. 'As the saying goes, three regular guys can beat a genius when they put their minds to it, so I reckon that the four of you should have no problem doing the work of one professional cryptographer. In short, I have full confidence in you.'

Leaning forward now, Commander Zhang pressed both palms on the table. No one dared catch his eye. 'I should also tell you that no less a personage than General Matsui is taking this very seriously. So much so that he's sending an expert to help with the decipherment. This expert is already on his way and will be here this afternoon. Of course, I'm hoping that my people will be able to decipher the message themselves – by which I mean you. This is a wonderful opportunity for you to show your loyalty to me, and for me to show my loyalty to General Matsui and the Imperial Japanese Army. I want you to concentrate all your efforts on deciphering this secret message. It is by success and failure that we measure heroes. I really hope that you are all going to be heroes, that you will help our forces to triumph, and that in doing so you will pave the way to better futures for yourselves.'

Commander Zhang's words left the ECCC officers feeling quite bewildered. Why had he singled out the four of them in particular? None of them had any experience decrypting enemy cyphers – their job was to decipher their own side's messages and that was all. So why entrust them with such an important task? On the other hand, if this job really was as simple as he implied, why give them such an easy opportunity for promotion? And then there was the Commander's uncharacteristic behaviour: by turns frightening and friendly, it was as if the things he'd talked about were not really what he wanted to say. There was an atmosphere of smoke and mirrors; it seemed obvious that something else was going on.

But it appeared the Commander had nothing more to tell them. He merely instructed Secretary Bai and Police Chief Wang to look after the group and make sure they were comfortable, then he shook hands all round, got in his car and drove away.

Wu Zhiguo, Jin Shenghuo, Li Ningyu and Gu Xiaomeng were left feeling lost. They had the strangest sensation that the ground beneath their feet was crumbling away.

Half an hour later, when they had deciphered the dictionary message with perfect ease, that earlier sense of bemusement was replaced by an all-consuming, paralysing terror. It was as if they'd been flayed, as if they'd been stripped of their surface equilibrium and reduced to raw emotion.

6

Just as Commander Zhang had said, the encrypted message was not at all difficult to decipher. In fact, it was as unsophisticated as it gets – so easy you could hardly call it a cypher; anyone with basic literacy could have worked it out.

In truth it was just a word game that Commander Zhang

was playing with them. This so-called cypher was simply a list of numbers indicating the page, the line and the word so that you could pick them out of the dictionary: such-and-such a page, such-and-such a line, such-and-such a word. Thus the very first word they obtained was 'This'.

On to the next, and the one after that, until they had the complete message:

This message is a fake,
But there is a real plot, at West Lake.
If you want people not to see,
Do not show them what you be.

Right here at our heart there lies,
A Communist agent in disguise.
Wu, Jin, Gu and Li,
Which of you can it be?

Confess now or be denounced,
Before your sentence is pronounced.
When it is all over, do not rue
That you did not believe our offer was true.

Maybe only someone who'd been through the old education system would have thought of showing off their learning in this way and attacking his enemy in verse. Though, in truth, it was a pretty poor piece of doggerel: the lines didn't even scan properly. All those years in the military may have dimmed the Commander's poetry-writing skills, but as a way of getting to the heart of the matter and laying it all out there, it was unquestionably a masterpiece.

Quite apart from the effect it had on the 'Wu, Jin, Gu and Li' identified in the poem, even Secretary Bai, who hadn't been named, felt as though every word was a knife. A cold wind was blowing in from all sides and shivers ran down everybody's spines.

TWO

1

It was impossible to relax.

Everyone was on tenterhooks.

Early that afternoon, Commander Zhang's car returned, but this time it pulled up outside the east building. As it came to a halt, the Commander himself jumped out and raced round to open the rear door, bowing to the man inside as he got out.

The man was wearing an ordinary scholar's gown, in a dark colour, with narrow sleeves. His choice of dress made him seem like a character from Chinese history, like a gentleman from the Tang or Song dynasty. He was not quite forty years of age, short, with pale skin and a friendly expression – there was also something feminine about his movements. Commander Zhang was old enough to be his father, but he was so respectful towards the younger man, it was as if he were his junior. Even though the man wasn't in uniform, and even though he didn't have the usual little moustache, there was no hiding his identity: he was Japanese.

He was Japanese and his name was Hihara Ryūsen. However, he was different from other Japanese soldiers in China in that he had grown up in the Japanese Concession in Shanghai and had then spent many years in China as a secret agent. He was completely fluent in Chinese, and even if you tried speaking to him in Zhejiang or Shanghainese dialect, he'd be able to understand eighty to ninety per cent. Earlier in his career he'd been the personal interpreter to General Matsui Iwane, when Matsui was Commander-in-Chief of Japan's invading Shanghai Expeditionary Army. A year ago he'd been appointed head of Matsui's secret police and now he was in charge of counter-espionage across Jiangsu, Zhejiang and Jiangxi provinces. He was General Matsui's most trusted agent and gave orders to Police Chief Wang Tianxiang and many others like him. He had arrived direct from Shanghai and had with him secret orders from General Matsui to supervise the investigations at the Tan Estate.

Police Chief Wang Tianxiang came rushing out to welcome his boss, and Colonel Hihara immediately queried the arrangements he'd made. 'Why have you put these people here? They're wandering in and out just as they please.' Though his manner was respectful and his voice soft, this was unquestionably a reprimand.

Commander Zhang spoke first. 'Police Chief Wang thought that we might be able to trick them into blowing their cover.'

'That's right, Colonel. I chose this place—' Wang Tianxiang waved his hand in a big circle, encompassing half the estate '—with a view to tricking the Communists into coming out of hiding, so that we can get them all at once.'

Hihara looked at him in silence.

'If we kept the suspects under really tight guard,' Wang Tianxiang continued, 'so that nobody else could get close to them, we'd have no hope of arresting the others. I thought it would be a good idea to leave a few holes, let them think it might be worth trying to make contact. Whatever happens, if someone does show up, whether openly or in secret, we'll know about it. There's a listening device in every room – we can track them wherever they go – and I've got men everywhere. Whenever they leave the building, they'll be watched, and the people in the dining hall are also my men. There's absolutely nothing to worry about there.'

Here, Commander Zhang put in a flattering word. 'Colonel Hihara, don't you worry about a thing, a good general always makes fine soldiers of the men under him – your people are sure to know what they're doing.'

Hihara decided to use bureaucratic jargon to sidestep the compliment. 'Excuse me, Commander Zhang, but Tianxiang is one of your subordinates. Since when did he become one of my people?'

Commander Zhang could only paste an ingratiating smile on his face and say, 'We both serve in the Imperial Japanese Army, do we not? And so does he…'

Police Chief Wang Tianxiang, walking in front of Colonel Hihara, now said warmly, 'Yes of course, we all know how loyal Commander Zhang is to the Imperial Army.' Perhaps his intention had been to say something nice, but neither of his superiors was pleased.

The three men entered the building.

2

The eastern building stood on much higher ground than the western one – on that side the mountain sloped more steeply, and the foundations of the house had been built up to allow for a rise of three steps. Viewed from the front, the two buildings appeared identical: both faced south and were designed on an east–west axis, and both had two storeys and an attic, a red-tiled roof, and white walls with courses of grey brick at the top, middle and bottom. Once inside, however, you could see that the eastern building was actually a lot smaller, and much more ordinary. Everything in it was functional and of unexceptional quality. At first glance you might assume the owner had run out of money and been obliged to skimp on this building, making it a bit smaller and simpler. But if that's what you thought, you'd be wrong.

According to those who'd worked on the construction of the Tan Estate or were involved in its management afterwards, the eastern building was only put up as a kind of temporary measure after the western building was almost complete, and it owed its existence to a passing comment by a visiting feng shui master. The master came from Manchuria and on his way through Hangzhou visited West Lake to admire its famous views. As he walked around, he happened upon the Tan Estate, then under construction, and seemed drawn to it by some mysterious force. He circled it three times, inspecting everything very carefully, and just as he was about to leave, muttered the following: 'There is a dragon and a phoenix here, there is good luck and bad; trouble is brewing and it will come from the east.'

When Mr Tan heard this, he mobilized all the forces at his command to search Hangzhou for this feng shui master. Although he knew it would be like looking for a leaf in the forest, he was determined to try and find him, and he did. He treated the master as the most honoured of guests, held a banquet for him at West Lake's celebrated Louwailou restaurant and asked for his advice.

The master went out for another look. Eventually, he took up position on the spot where the foundations of the eastern building would later be laid and sat there the whole night, listening to the wind and watching the clouds. He then advised old Mr Tan to construct a second building in order to prevent the disaster from the east from reaching the other house. Since it was to be defensive, it would have to be tall, which was why it was constructed further up the slope and on higher foundations. It would not be appropriate to skimp on the exterior and so, from the outside, the two buildings appeared very much the same. But the interior didn't matter.

That was why the place looked the way it did.

3

Police Chief Wang led Colonel Hihara and Commander Zhang upstairs.

There were three guest bedrooms and a bathroom. The Police Chief himself was staying in the first bedroom and the second had been allocated to Colonel Hihara. They had put a large decorative screen in the Colonel's room, symbolically dividing it in two: the inner part contained the bed, the outer part had tables and chairs, for Hihara to entertain his visitors.

Police Chief Wang was aware that Colonel Hihara liked to lie in bed reading late into the night, so he had specially organized for him to have a lamp next to his bed, and a very fine one at that: it had been borrowed from the general's suite at the officers' club. And, since summer was on its way, he'd also had an electric fan installed. Fruit and flowers had been placed in the outer part of the room. They had arranged a branch of late-flowering white plum blossom from high in the mountains next to a branch of red plum blossom just about to bloom; the red and the white complemented one another perfectly and filled the otherwise ordinary little room with a delicious perfume, bringing it to life.

When Colonel Hihara entered the room, he immediately noticed the white plum blossom. He inhaled appreciatively. 'Look how artistic that is!' he said to his two companions. 'With no green leaves to set it off, the flowers stand proud of the bare branch as they unfurl their petals. Just as the poem says, their scent fills the air, arousing much admiration.'

Commander Zhang, having received a traditional education, had memorized many poems and was just about to recite something himself. But before he'd even opened his mouth, a woman's angry voice suddenly broke in on them. It appeared to be coming from the large third bedroom at the end of the corridor.

'I want to see Commander Zhang!'

It was Gu Xiaomeng's voice.

Despite having travelled along the wires and through the microphone, her voice retained all its anger, sharpness and rudeness: it seemed to hang in the air of the room. Just as Wang Tianxiang had said, they'd secreted listening equipment throughout the western building, and you could hear every word as clear as day.

Colonel Hihara left admiring the flowers for later and walked down to the large room, listening as he did so to the conversation being transmitted from the other building:

Secretary Bai: Why do you want to see Commander Zhang?

Gu Xiaomeng: Why...? That's what I want to ask you – why are you doing this to me?

Secretary Bai: I don't need to tell you again, you know perfectly well.

Gu Xiaomeng: I am not a Communist!

Secretary Bai: Then prove it! Anyone can just say they aren't.

Gu Xiaomeng: Go to hell! Bai Xiaonian, how dare you speak to me like that! Just you wait...

Hihara listened with interest to the angry clip of Gu Xiaomeng's heels retreating into the distance. When he could no longer hear them, he turned to Commander Zhang. 'Who is she? She seems to have a very high opinion of herself.'

'Have you heard of a man called Gu Minzhang? Very rich – involved in armaments.'

Hihara thought for a moment. 'The one who gave President Wang Jingwei an aeroplane last year when he visited Wuhan?'

'Yes, that's him. And she's his daughter. Given how powerful her old man is, she thinks she can throw her weight around.'

Hihara nodded thoughtfully as he walked over to inspect the listening equipment. It was all laid out on a large table that had been fashioned from a bedstead: a pair of amplifiers, a speaker, two sets of headphones, a microphone, a tape recorder with a voice-activated switch and so on. There were also two pairs of German-made binoculars. He picked up one of them, went over to the window and focused on the building opposite, muttering, 'She'd be the one in the middle room upstairs... Oh, very young and very pretty. What was the name...? Gu Xiaomeng. Oh, she does look cross. She has a temper, that one.'

Commander Zhang picked up the other pair of binoculars and stood next to Colonel Hihara, focusing in the same direction, counting off the occupants one by one. Gu Xiaomeng was sitting on her bed, looking furious; Li Ningyu was combing her hair; Chief of Staff Wu Zhiguo was sitting all by himself on the sofa smoking a cigarette...

He could see everything with the binoculars, even the mole next to Section Chief Jin Shenghuo's eyebrow and the curl of smoke rising from Wu Zhiguo's cigarette. He suddenly realized why Police Chief Wang had arranged the rooms as he had. One of the rooms had been locked so that Li Ningyu and Gu Xiaomeng had to share, because only these three rooms were in the direct line of sight of the east building.

The two men watched for a while, then Hihara put down his binoculars and patted Commander Zhang on the shoulder. 'Let's go over there. She was desperate to talk to you.'

4

There was a nasty stench permeating the western building: the smell of death, corruption and fear. It was as if there'd been a repeat performance of the previous year's murders.

Police Chief Wang Tianxiang showed Commander Zhang and Colonel Hihara in, and Secretary Bai rushed out of the conference room to greet them. Perhaps the latter was upset on account of the shouting match he'd just had with Gu Xiaomeng; certainly, he made a mess of his greetings. Having shaken hands with Colonel Hihara, he then went over to shake hands with Commander Zhang.

Commander Zhang glared at him. 'What is wrong with you? Has this run-in with the Communists addled your brain? Why are you trying to shake hands with me?'

Secretary Bai withdrew his hand and laughed idiotically. 'No... not at all... I—'

Commander Zhang cut him short. 'Go and get the others. We're having a meeting.'

The meeting was worse than a funeral. Everyone kept their eyes lowered, not daring to look up, as if afraid they might disclose something.

> Wu, Jin, Gu and Li,
> Which of you can it be?

Commander Zhang's ditty had set everyone on edge. Fears and suspicions swirled, unvoiced, crowding the thoughts of the ECCC officers, overlapping, contradictory, angry, scared.

Was it the most senior among them – Chief of Staff Wu Zhiguo – or was it the oldest, Section Chief Jin Shenghuo? Was it the young and pretty Gu Xiaomeng, who came from such a powerful and famous family, or could it be Li Ningyu? Was one person involved or was it two? Did they even suspect three? Was this a new agent or had they been working for the Communists for years? Was this person anti the Nationalists or in favour of a Communist alliance with them? Why were the bosses so sure there was a Communist among them? Had someone stolen a top-secret message or had they killed someone? Were they doing it for money? Had someone turned traitor to escape the death penalty? Had someone made a silly mistake or had the ECCC been infiltrated long ago? Did they know who they were looking for or was everyone under suspicion? Was this a big fish or just some poor devil who'd be got rid of and that would be the end of it? Would whoever it was turn themselves in or would they be denounced by someone else?

Wu, Jin, Gu and Li,
Which of you can it be?

Damn this! What the hell is this? This is a grenade! A pile of shit! A nightmare! It's as if we've been stripped naked or have fallen among pirates; as if we've met a ghost or have taken poison; as if we're in a torture chamber.

Damn this!

In this horrible situation, no one had any idea what they should do or what they should say. Whatever they said would be wrong. Whatever they did would be wrong. It would be wrong to swear, but not swearing would also be wrong. It would be wrong to cry. It would be wrong to smile. It would be wrong to stand up, wrong to sit down, wrong to walk out, wrong to stay put. It would be wrong to look, wrong to shut your eyes. Wrong! Every single damn thing would be wrong, but doing nothing would also be wrong.

No one knew who to believe.

No one had a clue how to get out of this.

Commander Zhang invited Colonel Hihara to take the seat at the head of the table. Hihara refused and sat down instead in the first seat to the left. Then he very politely requested that everyone else be seated.

Once they had taken their places, Secretary Bai padded over to Commander Zhang's side, whispered something in his ear and slipped him a piece of paper.

The Commander looked at it and laughed, then handed it on to Hihara. 'Have a look at this, Colonel. This is the message I gave them.'

Hihara slowly read it aloud.

'This message is a fake,
But there is a real plot, at West Lake.
If you want people not to see,
Do not show them what you be.

'Right here at our heart there lies,
A Communist agent in disguise.
Wu, Jin, Gu and Li,
Which of you can it be?

'Confess now or be denounced,
Before your sentence is pronounced.
When it is all over, do not rue
That you did not believe our offer was true.'

When he'd finished, Commander Zhang applauded. Then he said to Wu, Jin, Gu and Li, 'I knew that you would all make great cryptographers: you got my original message absolutely right, not a single word wrong. However, this is just the beginning. I composed it to keep you occupied while we were waiting for Colonel Hihara to arrive. The real reason you are here—'

Hihara interrupted. Gesturing at the piece of paper, he said, 'The real reason is this: "Wu, Jin, Gu and Li, which of you can it be?" Am I not right, Commander Zhang?'

Commander Zhang laughed. 'You are absolutely right. That's the real code we need to crack. It would be best if you gave me the answer yourselves, but if you're not prepared to do that, it doesn't matter, since our Colonel Hihara is an expert at that kind of thing and has been sent by General Matsui to help us.'

'Well, I wouldn't really call myself an expert, I just like this kind of work.' Colonel Hihara and Commander Zhang were definitely singing to the same tune. 'So when Commander Zhang asked me to come as soon as possible, I was happy to oblige.'

Commander Zhang opened his briefcase and took out a piece of paper. 'To decrypt this particular code you need some more information. Here we have a telegram… Come, Section Chief Jin, you read it.'

Jin Shenghuo picked up the message and read it out in a feeble voice.

```
'Telegram from Nanjing:
According to reliable intelligence, Zhou
Enlai has already dispatched a special
envoy, code-named K, to Hangzhou. At 11
p.m. on the 29th of this month he will meet
with leaders of the resistance movement in
Zhejiang province at the Agate Belvedere
Inn on Mount Fenghuang to plot further
joint guerrilla activities. This—'
```

Commander Zhang cut him short. 'That's enough, Section Chief Jin. This isn't the first time you have read that message, right?'

Jin Shenghuo silently shook his head.

5

Jin Shenghuo had first read the message at about three o'clock the previous afternoon. The message had come in at half past two, when Gu Xiaomeng was on duty in the decryption office. She saw that it bore the very highest level of security, 'top secret', and immediately started to decipher it. She couldn't do it. She just got a random string of characters. This was very intriguing, but it also made her nervous, so she went to ask Li Ningyu what she should do.

Li Ningyu had worked as a cryptographer for a long time, she was extremely experienced, and whenever one of her subordinates had a telegram they couldn't decipher, they would ask her for help. She looked at the telegram, looked at the string of characters Gu Xiaomeng had produced and realized that it must have been encrypted twice.

As you will understand, messages in cypher are intended to be secret: in a plain telegram, when you see 1234 or abcd then it means 1234 or abcd; you go to your international code book and then transcribe the corresponding text. But in an encrypted message, when you see 1234 or abcd, that's not at all what it means – it could be anything else, but not that. There are thousands, tens of thousands, millions, even countless possibilities. So how do you work it out? You need the key to the cypher. Without that, an encrypted message is impossible to read. But if you have the key, even an untrained operative can decipher it and read it off. It's very simple, like looking for words in a dictionary – you check them off one at a time.

When a message is top secret, however, yet another level of encryption is added at the final stage, in case the key is known to the enemy. Because this second level of encryption is added at the very last moment, it's quite weak; for example, in the case of the numbers 0 to 9, or the twenty-six letters of the English alphabet, you might move one place or you might move several. In that case, 0 would actually represent 1, 1 would represent 2 and so on. Or 0 might represent 3, in which case 1 would actually be 4, and so forth. It's very simple but can sometimes prove quite useful; on this occasion, Gu Xiaomeng had been floored by it. So if this message had fallen into the hands of a third party, even if they'd had the key to the cypher (having cracked it or because they'd stolen it), or if it had ended up with a novice cryptographer like Gu Xiaomeng, they might have been floored by it too.

In such cases, a weak level of encryption suddenly becomes very important; it might even delude the enemy into imagining that a new cypher has been used. After all, when things go wrong, people tend to think of complicated explanations for it. This was not the case for Li Ningyu: first of all, she knew perfectly well that the same cypher was still in use, so she wasn't going to make that mistake. Secondly, she'd seen plenty such messages before, so she worked through the possibilities and very quickly discovered how they'd done it, whereupon she began decrypting the telegram.

Once the text had been written out in plain language, Gu Xiaomeng did as protocol required and handed it over to Section Chief Jin. He then passed it on to Commander Zhang. Which meant that before it reached the Commander, it had already passed through three people's hands: Jin Shenghuo, Li Ningyu and Gu Xiaomeng. The three had already admitted as much.

As his next question, Commander Zhang asked Jin Shenghuo, Li Ningyu and Gu Xiaomeng whether any of them had mentioned the contents of this top-secret message to anyone else between the time it was decrypted and the middle of the night when they were brought to the estate. In fact, he'd already asked each of them this the previous evening, on the phone. But this time his tone was much more searching.

Section Chief Jin swore that he had not.

Gu Xiaomeng also said very firmly that she had not.

Li Ningyu glanced at Wu Zhiguo and then said with an embarrassed air, 'I am very sorry, Chief of Staff Wu, but I feel I ought to tell the truth.'

'What?'

Li Ningyu said that she'd told Chief of Staff Wu about it.

The Commander noted that they all repeated exactly what they'd said the night before on the phone, only this time with greater conviction. What he had not expected, however, was that when Li Ningyu spoke, Wu Zhiguo would spring up from his chair and shout at her in a thunderous voice, 'When the hell did you mention it to me?'

Commander Zhang asked Li Ningyu to be more specific. And did she have any witnesses?

Li Ningyu said that yesterday afternoon, just after they'd finished decrypting the message and while Gu Xiaomeng was still in the office writing out the text for their superiors, Chief of Staff Wu had suddenly come in to look at some files. Since this was a top-secret telegram and nobody without the right security clearance was supposed to know what it said, Gu Xiaomeng was worried that he might read it, so she quickly covered the message with a newspaper.

'I guess that made Chief of Staff Wu curious,' Li Ningyu said. 'He asked Gu Xiaomeng what the message was and why she was being so secretive about it. Gu Xiaomeng tried to make a joke of it. "You'd better go away," she told him. "It's top secret." And he replied, also jokily, "I'm not going anywhere. I want to know what it says, and what are you going to do about it?" The two of them were just bantering, nothing serious. But when he'd finished reading through the papers that he'd come in for, he said he wanted to talk to me, so I took him to my office—'

Again Wu Zhiguo leapt to his feet and shouted, 'You're lying! When have I ever set foot in your office?'

Commander Zhang ordered him to sit down. 'Let her speak, and then it will be your turn.'

Li Ningyu continued in a calm voice, each word clearly articulated. 'When we got to my office, he asked me what the telegram was about. I said I couldn't tell him. He asked if it was about some new appointment or whether someone had been dismissed. I said no. He kept on at me, and in the end, although I knew that the rules said I shouldn't tell him, I thought he'd have to know sooner or later anyway, seeing as he's in charge of dealing with Communist activities, so I told him.'

Wu Zhiguo was about to explode again, but he was pinned to his seat by a glare from Commander Zhang.

Commander Zhang asked Gu Xiaomeng whether Li Ningyu had spoken the truth. She said she could vouch for the first part of Li Ningyu's story, but as to whether Chief of Staff Wu had then gone into Li Ningyu's office, she shook her head. 'I have no idea. I can't see round corners, so I don't know where they went. I was focused on getting the message written out. Of course, if I'd realized that it was going to be important, I would have got up and had a look—'

Commander Zhang quickly understood that Gu Xiaomeng was trying it on. 'That's enough!' he said. 'I get the picture.' He turned to Wu Zhiguo. 'Now it's your turn. You say you didn't go into her office, but is there someone who can corroborate that?'

'Well...' This was a problem for Wu Zhiguo. He had no witnesses, so he could only swear by this and that that he hadn't gone anywhere near Li Ningyu's office.

Commander Zhang thumped the table impatiently. 'She says you went to her office and you say that you didn't – who am I to believe? If you don't have any proof, I don't want to hear it.' He paused and clarified his thoughts. 'Actually, it doesn't matter either way – knowing what the message said isn't what's at issue here. Wouldn't you agree, Colonel Hihara? You must have a pretty good idea of what happened, right?'

Hihara smiled and nodded.

'It's this that's the real problem.' Commander Zhang took a packet of Pioneer cigarettes out of his briefcase and handed it to Colonel Hihara. 'Police Chief Wang obtained this from a Communist agent, and there's something very important indeed inside it.'

There were a dozen cigarettes inside the packet. Hihara tipped them out, and then a single crushed cigarette rolled out from the bottom. He picked it up and stared at it as if he'd hit upon a great secret, then used the very tips of his fingers to gently extract a tiny ball of paper. Someone had taken the tobacco out of the cigarette and hidden a slip of paper inside.

He uttered a very deliberate 'Ah' of surprise, and then said, 'You're quite right, this is very important.' He unrolled the strip of paper and read it out:

'Tell Tiger that 201's special representative has been spotted. Call off the Gathering of Heroes.

Ghost.

For immediate dispatch.'

When he'd finished, Colonel Hihara raised his head and looked straight at Commander Zhang. 'Here we have another secret message.'

'Let me explain,' Commander Zhang said rather smugly. 'This so-called "Tiger" is the head of the Communist underground here in Hangzhou; he's the boss. We've been looking for him for the last two months, but he's a slippery customer. We've nearly had him on more than one occasion, but he always manages to get away.'

'How could he fail to get away?' Colonel Hihara said. 'Ghost was right by your side: even an idiot could have done it.'

'Yes.' Commander Zhang nodded. '"201" refers to Zhou Enlai. It's a cypher used by the Communist headquarters up at Yan'an – there's a different number for each member of the Communist Party's top brass. The Gathering of Heroes is the meeting on Mount Fenghuang.' He snorted sarcastically. 'A few insurgents get together and they call it a "Gathering of Heroes" – who the hell do they think they are?'

Hihara laughed and then said with a sigh, 'So we have a ghost in our midst. Someone inside the ECCC read the top-secret message from Nanjing and attempted to warn the insurgents of its contents.' He very deliberately looked up, then with fake bonhomie addressed the four people in front of him. 'Which one of you is Ghost? Wu, Jin, Gu and

Li, which of you can it be?' His voice was soft and slightly muffled, as if his mouth were watering.

6

The four reacted to this new twist in the drama as if they'd just woken from a dream. But this was a nightmare: the devil was among them and they didn't even know where. Even worse, any one of them could at any moment find themselves the innocent scapegoat, sacrificed by the demon in their midst. They sat in silence, too scared to speak out, just looking at one another, hoping against hope that this might help them understand what was happening.

Commander Zhang didn't like this silence at all; he wanted them to start talking, either to confess or to denounce someone else. He tried offering inducements, and he also tried threats, but still nobody confessed, and nobody denounced anyone else.

There was one person who wanted to make a denunciation, and that was Chief of Staff Wu Zhiguo. Later on, he consistently held to the view that Li Ningyu was Ghost. But right then, in that nightmarish situation, he just sat there stunned, unable to speak, the words frozen in his throat. The circumstances were too horrifying – everyone was petrified.

They would have to wait, give everyone time to get over the shock.

The silence was broken by the sound of hurrying footsteps coming closer; evidently someone had something urgent to report.

It was the fat Staff Officer named Jiang. He whispered something in Commander Zhang's ear. The latter got up from his chair, thumped the table violently, and shouted, 'So you don't want to speak! Well, when you have something to say, go and find Colonel Hihara. I don't have any more time to waste on you.' As he strode out of the room, he yelled, 'I am sure that one of you is this Ghost. Until you tell me who it is, none of you are leaving this place. If you want to get out of here, tell me who Ghost is!'

Colonel Hihara had also stood up but made no move to leave. Instead, he said with an amiable smile, 'I agree with what Commander Zhang just said. However, there is another point I want to make, which is that you cannot all be Ghost. Some of you are innocent; in fact, the majority of you are innocent. The problem is who? Which of you has done nothing wrong? We don't know the answer to that, but you do. So, as the saying goes, only the hand that tied the knot can loosen the tiger's bell.' His voice was unnervingly soft, his diction refined.

'Right now we don't have any choice: we have to keep you all here, under observation and under lock and key. You're just going to have to put up with the humiliation for a few days. As I am sure you understand, we have to do this – we cannot afford not to. Of course, if you want to leave, all you have to do is tell us who Ghost is. Either confess or make a denunciation, we don't mind which, and then we can all go home.'

Commander Zhang had been standing by the doorway listening to Colonel Hihara. Now he came back into the room, walked over to the table and rapped on it. 'Remember, you have until the 29th. You've got four days to get yourselves out of this – out of here. After that, you'll have only yourselves to blame for what happens to you.'

'Yes,' Hihara said. 'After the 29th, it won't matter what any one of you does or says, innocent or guilty. If Ghost hasn't been unmasked by then, you'll all be in the same boat. And what boat is that? What will determine your fate?'

He took out a sealed envelope and patted it.

'This will. General Matsui gave me this before I set out. As to what instructions it contains, I don't even know myself.' He laughed. 'Ladies and gentlemen, this is a secret message. A secret set of instructions. Depending on what happens, I may simply burn it, in which case the contents will remain a secret forever. Or I may have to open it and carry out General Matsui's commands. Once you've forced me to read it, nothing you can do will change the outcome – neither Commander Zhang nor I will be able to save you. It is entirely up to the four of you whether I burn it or whether I read it. So I want you to take this situation very seriously, because it is your own lives that are at stake.'

He spoke quite calmly, as if he were offering them friendly, heartfelt advice. Afterwards he walked round the table, saying a few polite words to each one of them.

Even so, for Wu Zhiguo, Jin Shenghuo, Li Ningyu and Gu Xiaomeng, it was as if their worlds had come crashing down around their ears. They were in a state of total shock. Their eyes had gone dark, their legs were trembling, and their minds were blank, as if half their heads had been blown away. Their hearts were pounding. They were engulfed in blind, boundless panic.

THREE

1

Who was Ghost?

Who the hell was Ghost?

That afternoon the sky was blue, the flowers were fragrant, and the pretty young whores at the officers' club in the front courtyard sat in front of their mirrors as usual, getting ready for the men who would visit that night. In other words, time that afternoon passed as usual, minute by minute, tick-tock, tick-tock, on and on, as the hands of the clock moved on relentlessly, towards the coming night. But in the western building, time seemed to have gone backwards, back many months, to the night when all those people had been murdered there: former ECCC commander Qian Huyi, his wife, his children and his many members of staff. Yet again, the fates of those holed up in the west building were in the hands of an unknown individual, a murderer, a demon who was controlling the situation, had its hands around their throats, was squeezing their jugulars.

Commander Zhang had been called back to his office, so Colonel Hihara and Police Chief Wang Tianxiang escorted him to his car. Once he'd gone, Wang Tianxiang began heading back to the west building, but Hihara waved him over. 'Leave them to stew for a bit. Come with me – there's something I wanted to ask you.'

Hihara strode purposefully towards the front courtyard and the entrance to the Tan Estate, following in the wake of Commander Zhang's car. As they walked, Hihara posed his question. 'Where did that message in the cigarette packet come from?'

'From a Communist agent code-named Turtle.'

2

Turtle was a poor old man, aged about sixty, very thin and with unusually long legs. As he walked, he kept his upper body upright, but his legs swayed quite noticeably, making him look like a praying mantis. The previous winter, he'd begun collecting rubbish on the military base in Hangzhou. In the daytime, he was one of the cleaners at the main office building on the base, then in the evenings he collected household rubbish from the family quarters.

The previous week, the ECCC had arrested and turned a Nationalist agent, and a couple of days ago that agent had spotted Turtle while he was having lunch in the canteen and recognized him as a known former Communist agent. Although no one was sure of Turtle's current status, his presence at the base certainly looked suspicious. So suspicious that Police Chief Wang Tianxiang placed him under surveillance.

For two days Turtle made no contact with anyone and

did nothing unusual; he just cleaned the main office building as normal, then collected the rubbish from each household. The previous evening he'd left the base at about five and headed off to the dump with his three-wheeled dustcart, making no contact with anyone the whole way there. On his way back, however, he did something odd: he went to Lute Tower Park.

In the evenings, hawkers gathered in the park to sell snacks and knick-knacks. Turtle parked his dustcart next to a girl selling flowers, then hung a portable display case of cigarettes around his neck and started selling them. Very soon, a woman sitting in a rickshaw called him over and bought a packet. She was very young and extremely fashionably dressed in an emerald-green silk qipao – with the cigarette in her mouth, she looked like a whore. There was nothing out of the ordinary about a whore buying cigarettes, but what was strange was that she handed over a large note to pay for them and then didn't wait for the change. For his part, Turtle just took the money and showed no sign of being pleased at having made such a big profit; in fact, he reacted as if that were normal.

'How could that possibly be normal?' Wang Tianxiang said. 'A whore would care about losing her hard-earned cash. And a guy like that, with a case of cigarettes slung round his neck, ought to be pleased when he gets to keep the change.'

Hihara nodded his agreement and kept on walking, his eyes fixed on a distant point as if he were in a hurry. By this time they had exited the Tan Estate and reached West Lake. They began walking along Su Dongpo's causeway, which stretched before them as straight as an arrow, extending right the way across the lake. The Su Causeway is famous for its flowering plums and the trees sparkled before their eyes, the blossom set off by the fresh green leaves, the air full of their strong perfume. It was as if the entire length of the causeway were enveloped in a pink mist, and the powerful scent wafted out across the waves. If this had been peacetime, the place would have been packed with tourists come to enjoy the blossom, but as it was there was hardly anyone around, so it was fine for the two men to stroll along discussing military secrets.

Police Chief Wang was coming to the end of his account. 'So my surveillance team set off in pursuit and arrested the whore. When they searched her, they found that slip of paper in the cigarette packet.'

'You arrested her?' Hihara stopped abruptly, as if he had missed his footing. 'Why did you arrest her so quickly? You should have quietly had her followed. For all you know, she might have led you straight to Tiger.'

'Exactly.' Wang Tianxiang seemed as upset about this as Colonel Hihara. 'I couldn't agree more, such a wonderful opportunity. But... well, I wasn't there myself and things got a bit out of control.'

At least they hadn't arrested Turtle; he was still under surveillance. If Turtle as well as the whore and Ghost had all disappeared at the same time, their comrades would immediately have assumed that their cover had been blown.

'The arrests of the whore and the ECCC suspects have to be kept completely secret,' Hihara said. 'Where there is suspicion, there is fear, and when there is fear, everyone keeps their heads down – just the rippling of the breeze in the grass can be enough to set off alarm bells.' He shot the Police Chief a stern look. 'The moment they suspect that Ghost is being held for interrogation, we're going to come out of this empty-handed. Turtle must be watched carefully. And we need to think of a way to deal with the whore, to make sure her accomplices don't know that she's been arrested. After all, Turtle passed her a piece of intelligence and might report that to his superiors. We need to confuse the enemy, so we must begin by plugging any holes in our story.'

Would Ghost be able to let people know he or she was being held? No. However, it was vital that information about what had happened should be closed down: Ghost's comrades must not know about the incarceration at the Tan Estate, nor even suspect it. Hihara wracked his brains and began sharing his thoughts out loud.

'We'll tell everyone that the ECCC officers have been brought here on official duties... to undertake an important mission. Which was why we rounded them up in the middle of the night and so on.' He nodded as a smile crept across his face. 'Yes, that's it. That's what everyone is to say from now on.'

He came to a standstill beside a cluster of willow trees and gazed absent-mindedly at the flashes of orange carp in the water beneath Crossing the Rainbow Bridge. 'You need to find a way to pass this disinformation to Turtle as soon as possible. I want everyone to be told it – in fact, the more people, the better – so tell the same thing to their families, their superior officers back on the base, their colleagues and so on. If you can keep all of them in the dark, then you can keep the Communist Party in the dark too: that's the only way we're going to be able to net K, and then we'll haul in all the small fry with him.'

His attention was drawn by the shimmer and swerve of a large mottled carp as it disappeared beneath the bridge. 'You know, Turtle is going to be crucial here – he's going to make the difference. Give Turtle the disinformation that Ghost is off working on an important mission for the ECCC and he'll do all the hard work for you; he'll report to his organization that Ghost is neither being interrogated nor under house arrest but that he or she is in fact safe and sound.'

'That's easily organized.' Wang Tianxiang patted his chest. 'I'll see to it immediately.'

3

Colonel Hihara's eyes followed Police Chief Wang as he headed off down the causeway and towards the shore. The edge of a red roof atop a buff-coloured wall entered his field of vision: this was West Lake's famous Louwailou on Gushan Island, his favourite restaurant. He immediately decided to go there for dinner that evening. It was ages since his last visit; he wondered whether Master Jiulong was still working there.

At an earlier stage in his career, Hihara had often come to Hangzhou, and on every occasion he would make a point of going to Louwailou to sample Master Jiulong's dishes. Now that he'd called fat old Master Jiulong to mind, he was even more determined to go there that evening for dinner. But who would join him? Various special guests came into his head, then suddenly he shouted 'Hey! Hey!' to Wang Tianxiang, who by now was already quite a distance away. He told him to get in touch with Commander Zhang and tell him that he would be hosting a banquet that evening at Louwailou and hoped that the Commander would be able to attend.

'Who are you going to invite?'

Hihara smiled. 'Their families.'

Wang Tianxiang looked nonplussed.

'Do their families know that you've brought the ECCC officers out here?' Hihara asked.

Wang Tianxiang shook his head.

'What on earth were you thinking? You have them all shut up out here, forbidden from going out, not allowed to phone their families – you might as well shout from the rooftops that something's wrong! So we're going to rectify that. We're going to invite their families to a nice meal, to show them that we appreciate the sacrifices they're making.' He laughed. 'Isn't that the least we could do?'

Police Chief Wang Tianxiang was not a stupid man and he immediately grasped Colonel Hihara's idea. Everyone said that the Reds were just like rats: they came in nests. Hihara was concerned that Ghost's family might also be members of the Communist underground, so he wanted to invite them to dinner and feed them the same disinformation. That way, they would report the same message back to K and Tiger. Clever! Very, very clever!

Fat old Master Jiulong did them proud: there was his signature West Lake fish in sweet-sour sauce, a dish of locally famous Dongpo pork that had been braised to perfection, and – Hihara's favourite – fried shrimps with Dragon Well tea.

After dinner, Hihara introduced some little improvisations to his plan, designed to make the whole thing even more convincing. When they left Louwailou, he escorted the various family members up to the officers' club on the Tan Estate and then had the cars drive round to the rear courtyard. The cars came to a halt in front of the eastern building, from where the families had a clear view of their relatives in a brightly lit conference room in the western building directly opposite; they were all seated around a table and engaged in solemn discussion, as if they were in the middle of an important meeting.

Seeing is believing: how could they fail to believe what was right before their eyes? Everyone was filled with pride at the sight of their own family members sitting there, surrounded by guards because they were undertaking top-secret work of vital importance; they were being treated like kings, and they were completely safe. They were right there in front of them, but they might as well have been on the other side of the world: the relatives couldn't get close, they were only allowed to look, though that in itself was very flattering.

There was, however, one fly in the ointment. Gu Xiaomeng wasn't married, didn't have her own family, and her extremely wealthy father seemed to think Commander Zhang's invitation beneath him so did not come in person; he just sent the housekeeper. There was some logic to that; the housekeeper had brought up Gu Xiaomeng after her mother died. Nevertheless, it didn't seem quite right to put the woman in with the others' families, which might undermine the prestigiousness of the occasion. So, even though she had come all that way specially, they didn't let her attend the banquet. Instead, there was a private meeting at which the situation was explained, then she was given a few token gifts and sent on her way. Afterwards, Colonel Hihara decided that it didn't matter: the housekeeper would report what they had told her to her master, and the same disinformation would then be circulated among the other servants. Which was exactly what they wanted. They wanted the Communists to take the shadow for the substance, to find themselves trapped in this web of lies.

In fact, if Colonel Hihara had had to eliminate one person from his enquiries at that point, he would have chosen Gu Xiaomeng, for the simple reason that the wrong person had come from her family. It was too odd. It stood out like a sore thumb. If Gu Xiaomeng were Ghost, there would be other Communist Party members within her family circle and they would never have sent the housekeeper.

Of course, the fact that there were no accomplices in her family didn't necessarily mean that Gu Xiaomeng wasn't Ghost. But right now Hihara wasn't prepared to play a guessing game about who was and was not the enemy agent. They were just setting the scene. The overture – the banquet that evening – had gone very well and he was now looking forward to the next stage. Let the show begin!

4

Police Chief Wang Tianxiang felt the same way. Although it was not appropriate for him to appear at the restaurant, he'd been fully involved in the events of the afternoon. His task had been to go back to headquarters and arrange for Turtle to get the message they'd prepared for him. This was the work of moments – he simply arranged for a few people to discuss the whole episode just where Turtle could hear what they were saying. Covering up the arrest of the prostitute, on the other hand, was going to be much more difficult; he would have to question her, find out where she lived and who she spent time with, and then think up some way of cobbling together a story to feed them that would explain her disappearance.

As the whore had been arrested the night before, by rights Wang Tianxiang should already have interrogated her. But finding that slip of paper had come as a bolt from the blue and since then he'd been busy dealing with Ghost; he simply hadn't had time to think about anything else, let alone go back to headquarters and question the woman. However, the moment he clapped eyes on her that afternoon, he felt as though a new planet had come into his orbit. Despite all the changes, despite the fact that the erstwhile refined, upper-class lady was now dressed as a whore, Wang Tianxiang recognized her immediately: it was former ECCC commander Qian Huyi's concubine who stood before him.

Sometimes the world really is very small and coincidences do happen. The moment the concubine entered the equation, Wang Tianxiang understood exactly whom Qian Huyi had to thank for his horrible fate. His concubine must have fingered him to his killers. He knew that Qian Huyi had fallen in love with her at first sight; who would have imagined that she would turn out to be a Communist? This unexpected discovery meant that Wang Tianxiang spent a very happy, if busy, afternoon. It was a strange kind of joy, too, as if he were a lost mariner and had suddenly spotted land on the distant horizon.

Given that Qian Huyi's entire family had been killed, how was it that the man's concubine had survived?

There was a reason: the concubine had never been formally accepted as part of the family, so she had never lived on the Tan Estate. Newly promoted into the role of regional commander, Qian Huyi had been very concerned about his image, so when he moved his household into the Tan Estate, he didn't bring his concubine. Wang Tianxiang wondered whether the young woman had hated him for that. Since she wasn't living there when they were all murdered, nobody had suspected her. Now it seemed all too obvious: it was the concubine who'd sent Commander Qian and every single member of his family down to the Yellow Springs, to the Realm of the Dead.

Having recognized who she really was, there were lots of questions that Police Chief Wang no longer needed to ask her, like where she lived, who she spent time with; he knew all of that, and none of it mattered any more. The crucial thing was that she had been Qian Huyi's woman – that was quite enough to account for him having had her arrested.

Although there was no proof that she'd been involved in the murders, what was wrong with saying there was? So Wang Tianxiang called up a couple of policemen, rushed round to the concubine's bijou residence and searched it from top to bottom, scaring the old servants out of their wits.

Reporters were on the scent right away – of course, their

information had come from Wang Tianxiang himself – and within moments there was a swarm of them there. He was quite happy to answer their questions; there was going to be a lot of publicity in this.

Right enough, that very evening, the concubine's photograph was on the front page of two local evening papers, with huge headlines letting everyone in Hangzhou know that the truth about the murder of Commander Qian and his family had finally come out and that the guilty party had been dragged off to prison in chains. Of course, once she was in prison there was no way she'd be able to contact her comrades in the underground.

Wang Tianxiang had really done an excellent job of providing a cover story, and Colonel Hihara praised him highly.

When people are praised, they often come up with other good ideas. Wang Tianxiang now thought of something else he could do that might bring Ghost out of the woodwork and earn him even more credit. So while Hihara was entertaining his guests at Louwailou, he decided, off his own bat, to move the concubine out to the Tan Estate in secret, so that she might be brought face to face with each of the suspects individually, right there in the conference room.

What for?

An identity parade.

To see if she could pick out Ghost!

He had promised the young woman all kinds of things – so long as she was able to say the word 'Him!' Or, of course, 'Her!'

He had no idea whether the concubine was playing him for an idiot or if she really didn't know, but to every inducement and promise she simply said, 'I can't help you.' Whatever he said, she stuck to the same line. 'No comment.' His nice little scheme went west, and there was not a single thing he could do about it. It was a complete mess. All that effort for nothing. Well, what kind of woman was this concubine? She had had the late Commander butchered, she was hardly likely to crack at the first couple of little questions. Wang Tianxiang had set up his little kangaroo court, wanting to get the whole thing over and done with, but clearly he had been overhasty. Pride comes before a fall.

When he was told that Colonel Hihara was on his way back from Louwailou and was bringing the relatives so that they could see what was going on, he had to get the whole conference-room scene set up in a hurry. The concubine was sent back to the city, Wu Zhiguo was told to take the seat of honour (quite naturally, as he was Chief of Staff), and Wang Tianxiang himself retreated to the sidelines. His own scheme hadn't worked, but perhaps Colonel Hihara's would. In Hihara's scenario, Police Chief Wang wasn't to be seen to be in charge of anything, he was meant to be merely providing security at the conference table.

As soon as the relatives left, Wang rushed out to find Colonel Hihara, who had gone back into the eastern building to collect something. When he re-emerged, it was clear he had no intention of going over to the western building but was instead heading towards the front courtyard. Wang Tianxiang was surprised; he ran after him and told him that the foursome was waiting for him in the conference room, ready to start the meeting.

'What meeting?' Hihara said. 'I'm busy. It will have to wait until tomorrow.'

When Wang Tianxiang asked what was up, Hihara ignored him and simply said, 'Come with me.' He was carrying a bag but wouldn't say anything further, other than, 'Let's go.'

So they went. They walked out of the estate and headed for West Lake. It was dark by then, but the moon had not yet risen: the contrast with the bright lights of the Nanshan and Hubin roads made the lake seem even darker. The water was pitch black – it didn't seem like a lake but rather an enormous piece of black cloth that had been spread across the ground, stretching out to the horizon, rippling in the breeze. Police Chief Wang almost had to run to keep up with Colonel Hihara as he strode at speed into the darkness. He seemed like a spectre, walking a familiar route through the night.

After about a kilometre, Hihara stopped in front of a tomb mound. It was right beside the lake. With the water lapping at its base, the tomb almost seemed to be moving – it was quite frightening. Hihara appeared to be entirely familiar with the place: he walked round the mound, patting it here and there, pulling up a few stray weeds. Then he took a few things out of his bag: some joss-paper spirit money and a pair of candlesticks with candles.

'You're going to have a memorial ceremony?' Wang Tianxiang couldn't keep silent any longer.

'Uh-huh.'

'Whose grave is this?'

'A young woman called Yoshiko.'

'A friend of yours?'

Hihara was silent for a long time. Then he said coldly, 'You ask too many questions.'

After they left the gravesite, Colonel Hihara seemed depressed – he didn't say a word on the way back. When they got to the Tan Estate and passed the officers' club, he suggested going in for a drink.

It wasn't until several hours later that they emerged; it was late by now and they were very drunk. The ground sparkled in the moonlight, lovely and pure, almost as if there'd been a frost. Hihara was so drunk that for a moment he couldn't tell which it was. Through the fug of alcohol clouding his brain, he thought to himself, it doesn't matter if it's frost or if it's moonlight, tomorrow will be a lovely day.

5

Sure enough, they had lovely weather the next day. As the rising sun rested on the Qiantang River, it shone with a pale light, almost like the moon. Its rays pierced the gaps in the curtains and probed Colonel Hihara's blankets, rousing him from his sleep, even though he'd gone to bed late. He felt weak and didn't want to get up; he'd clearly drunk far too much the night before. He couldn't even remember whether he'd been with a whore or not. As he lay there, he began thinking about the many things that had happened in that very place several years back. For Colonel Hihara was in fact all too familiar with the Tan Estate. A few years earlier, he... But that was his secret and he wasn't going to discuss it with anyone, and that included Wang Tianxiang.

Wang Tianxiang was up even earlier and had been listening out for signs of movement from Hihara's room next door. While he was waiting for him to wake up, he read through the transcript of the previous night's conversations – several times over. The transcript didn't even fill a single piece of paper. In other words, the ECCC officers had said almost nothing. Nevertheless, he noticed two things in particular.

Firstly, after the meeting (that is, the 'conference' he had stage-managed for their relatives), Chief of Staff Wu Zhiguo had called Gu Xiaomeng to his room on her own and asked her to remember everything she could. Of course, what he really wanted was for her to testify on his behalf and say that he'd gone nowhere near Li Ningyu's office. But it didn't work. According to the transcript, Gu Xiaomeng had simply said, rather self-righteously, 'Trust me, Chief of Staff Wu, I will report the facts truthfully to our superiors.'

Secondly, a short time later (the transcript indicated one minute and forty-one seconds), Gu Xiaomeng went back to her room and recounted to Li Ningyu exactly what Wu Zhiguo had just said. Police Chief Wang would have expected some reaction from Li Ningyu, but the transcript simply carried the notation: 'Li said nothing.' On being questioned further, the wiretap operative on duty explained that she had merely said 'Uh-huh' and then changed the subject, telling Gu Xiaomeng to go and have a wash. She didn't even thank her.

There was clearly something more to all this. The wiretap operative suspected the two women had some kind of agreement, in which case there'd be no need for either of them to say anything: they'd be able to sense what the other one wanted. But, mindful of Li Ningyu's detached, arrogant personality, Wang Tianxiang thought it premature to come to that conclusion.

They all worked in the same building, they saw each other every day, so Police Chief Wang knew all the ECCC officers very well. Particularly Li Ningyu. He had fallen out with her once, and he was only too aware of her so-called upright character. It had happened some years ago, and it seemed laughable now. One day he and Li Ningyu had shared a car – she'd been buying some stationery for the office and he had helped her load it into the car and had then helped himself to a notebook. It was such a little thing, right? The two of them had gone off to get this stuff and he got something out of it. She should just have let it go, it wasn't worth making a fuss about. But Li Ningyu hadn't just let it go – she was unreasonable like that – which had put him in a very embarrassing position.

Objectively speaking, before they fell out over the notebook, Wang Tianxiang would have said that he quite liked Li Ningyu, or at least that he liked her more than he disliked her. Afterwards, he started to really dislike her and would often tell other people that he thought she was a hypocrite. Even so, if he were to have been asked right then to make a decision regarding her guilt based on such insubstantial material, he wouldn't have dared. There was only one thing he was certain about, and that was that Gu Xiaomeng was very fond of Li Ningyu, very fond indeed.

He decided to report what had happened to Colonel Hihara and let him analyse it.

Hihara listened to Police Chief Wang's first couple of sentences and then waved his hand to silence him. He wasn't interested in any of that. 'Listen to me,' he said, 'and do what I tell you.'

There were three things that he wanted done. Firstly, he wanted Wang Tianxiang to go over to the west building immediately and take the group to breakfast; secondly, he was to inform them that Hihara had gone back to the city the night before and that no one knew when he'd be back; and thirdly, after breakfast he was to have Secretary Bai interview each suspect individually in the conference room.

'I don't care whether they confess or whether they denounce someone else, but I want every single one of them to tell me who they think Ghost is.' He just wanted them to start talking. 'They don't have to have a particular reason for their opinion, and it doesn't matter if they get it wrong, we're not going to include it in their records – though we don't want them passing on gossip or settling scores. They just have to say something; the important thing at this point is not what they say but how they say it. We want to see how they deal with the challenge.'

Of course, while Secretary Bai was sitting behind the desk and asking the questions, Colonel Hihara would be lurking in the shadows, watching the proceedings and secretly listening in on every word.

FOUR

1

Ghost couldn't sleep. The situation was too tense. It was impossible to switch off. Lying there listening to the sound of the wind, Ghost kept picturing Warrior's eyes in the darkness, blazing through the night like searchlights. It made Ghost feel dizzy and frightened, as if they themselves had been transformed into a ray of light, to be blown out by the wind.

Warrior was the concubine. The moment Police Chief Wang had brought her into the conference room, Ghost had understood exactly what had happened. Ghost wasn't worried that the concubine would be able to make an identification – that was quite impossible. Even if it had been, Warrior would never betray her comrades. Ghost had heard other comrades praise Warrior on many occasions for her commitment to the Revolution and the anti-Japanese resistance movement; she was unconcerned about her personal circumstances, money and fame meant less than nothing to her, and she was quite prepared to sacrifice her own reputation. In short, she was a good comrade who put the needs of the Revolution above everything else.

Warrior wasn't the problem – the problem for Ghost was how to get out of there, how to get a message out. That problem hung there, in mid-air, like Warrior's eyes in the darkness, impossible to ignore.

That was how Ghost spent the long night, and when dawn started to brighten the skies and filter through the windows, a depressing thought came to mind: there might well be another long, long day ahead.

2

Chief of Staff Wu Zhiguo was the first to be summoned into the conference room for the post-breakfast chat with Secretary Bai. He didn't know he was being recorded (and nor did Secretary Bai), so he began by cursing everyone left, right and centre, in particular Li Ningyu, the Reds, and Commander Zhang. The fact that Commander Zhang had so little faith in him had been deeply hurtful, so it wasn't surprising he had a lot to say on the subject, but who could be sure that he wasn't putting it all on? Fortunately, Commander Zhang was not present and didn't have to listen to it.

Colonel Hihara and Police Chief Wang, however, could hear every word. The sun was shining, there wasn't a breath of wind and the line didn't have the slightest kink: every sound floated along it clear as a bell. This ensured that these two dangerous men, the master and his servant, one

Japanese and the other serving the puppet regime, felt as if they were standing right there in the room, even though they were more than a hundred metres away.

Secretary Bai responded with lots of soothing words and Wu Zhiguo eventually calmed down. He began to describe what had happened that afternoon in great detail – how he had exited the room with Li Ningyu, leaving Gu Xiaomeng behind; how he had discussed something with her out in the corridor (a completely unimportant matter); and how he had then left, without ever setting foot in her office. And so on.

'So how can she have told me about this top-secret telegram? She's made the whole thing up. It's a lie! That's proof enough for me – she's making false accusations, so she must be the Communist. It's obvious she's trying to muddy the waters and get herself out of trouble.'

Hearing this, Colonel Hihara said rather pompously to Wang Tianxiang, who was standing at his side, 'He has a point. If he can find someone to testify that he never went near Li Ningyu's office, then we can be sure that she is Ghost.'

'But he hasn't found a witness yet,' Police Chief Wang replied straight away, almost as if he were afraid that his boss might have forgotten this.

'Exactly,' Hihara said. 'So everything else he has said is worthless.'

Ah, so his boss was being sarcastic… Wang Tianxiang giggled. 'Including him swearing at Commander Zhang.'

Colonel Hihara gave a hearty laugh. 'Yes. And let me remind you, none of this is to go any further.'

3

Compared to the building opposite, with its chatter and laughter, the western building was like a tomb. Chief of Staff Wu Zhiguo stomped out of the conference room in a rage, to be replaced by a silent Jin Shenghuo.

Section Chief Jin Shenghuo looked like a pig: he had a low forehead, a wide mouth, tiny little eyes, a bulbous nose and a huge beer belly. His looks did not lie – the man was a pig. But as the saying goes, appearances can be deceptive; even if the man looked like a pig, he might still be highly intelligent.

He was the oldest of the four suspects, being already in his fifties, and the most experienced. In the ECCC office back at base, he was considered one of the most senior officers. In light of which, a certain snobbishness towards those in subordinate positions was understandable. He was always profoundly respectful and admiring of his superiors, and ordinarily got on perfectly well with everyone, not least because he was so polite. However, the moment he came into the room, he started to complain to Secretary Bai.

Jin Shenghuo: Oh my God, I don't know what I've done to deserve this! I'm obviously not going to be a Section Chief for much longer...

Secretary Bai: Not necessarily. If you can get Ghost to come out of the woodwork for us, it'll be a great achievement. There'll be a reward for that and maybe even a promotion.

Jin Shenghuo: Tell me, Secretary Bai, which one is the Communist agent – do you have any clues?

Secretary Bai: That's what I wanted to ask you.

Jin Shenghuo: Oh my God, I... I'm not in any position to know that kind of thing.

Secretary Bai: You're quite wrong, Mr Jin. This has nothing to do with position or rank – this is about being aware of what's going on right under your nose. There are four people here, one of whom is yourself and two of whom are your subordinates. You must know what's going on!

Jin Shenghuo: So you don't trust me?

Secretary Bai: This isn't about whether I trust you or not. You have to face facts, the situation is what it is, and they want you to name someone.

Jin Shenghuo: I wish they didn't. Secretary Bai, if I knew who it was, I'd be giving them to you on a plate, but the problem is...

Hihara could hear the man violently shaking his head.

He was shaking his head because the situation was impossible. Faced with Secretary Bai's question – Who is Ghost? – his mind had gone completely blank. He was reduced to grinning inanely, to muttering and mumbling; he didn't say a word and he didn't give a name. He even went so far as to burst into tears, in the hope that Secretary Bai might feel sorry for him and help him through this.

In actual fact, both Secretary Bai, watching him, and Police Chief Wang Tianxiang, listening to his sobs at the other end of the wire, were hoping that he wasn't Ghost. They wanted him to pass this test. In order to pass it, assuming he didn't confess to being Ghost, he had to point the finger at one of the other three, even if that were a complete guess. Those were the rules that had been laid down by Colonel Hihara, and that was why Secretary Bai now said, 'Okay, Section Chief Jin, you have to pick one of the three. Just make your choice and that'll be it.'

It was in these circumstances, with no other option, that Jin Shenghuo chose Gu Xiaomeng. His reasoning was that she'd often said things that might be considered pro-Communist and that she regularly went off base.

Secretary Bai wanted him to give details: dates, places, examples. Jin Shenghuo furrowed his brow, thought long and hard, and then began to stammer out his answers.

'The rules say that unmarried personnel aren't ordinarily allowed off base, but she goes quite regularly without permission from anyone...

'Sometimes she says things – I hardly dare to listen, it makes me so nervous...

'Once in the office she was cursing the Imperial Japanese Army. She called them "Japanese bastards", and she used swear words too...

'She isn't serious about her work – last year she forgot all about a telegram that came in concerning an anti-insurgency campaign: it nearly ruined the whole exercise...

'If she is the Communist, that's a really terrifying prospect; she's been going to meet senior officials in Nanjing quite regularly with her father. I've heard she's even been to President Wang Jingwei's house...'

Colonel Hihara found listening to this man bloody exhausting. He stammered and kept going off the point; like a child, he'd start a sentence but wouldn't finish it, or he'd come to a conclusion without any context, or he'd make a statement without considering its implications. As a result, having listened right through to the end, Hihara decided that he'd heard nothing of significance; he simply pushed the Section Chief's comments to one side with a smile.

4

Next, it was Li Ningyu's turn.

Maybe it was because Chief of Staff Wu had already accused her directly, but Hihara felt that Secretary Bai was unusually firm with her; he was sure the man must have a self-satisfied smile fixed on his face.

Secretary Bai: You're a clever woman, so you must know why I've summoned you here.

Li Ningyu: ...

Secretary Bai: You're an experienced cryptographer and you've deciphered a lot of encrypted telegrams. Yesterday, when you all cracked the dictionary code so quickly, I imagine you played an important role. I hope you'll be able to solve today's puzzle, the issue of Ghost's identity, equally quickly.

Li Ningyu: ...

Secretary Bai: What's going on here? Are you refusing to speak, or is it just that you haven't decided what to say yet?

Li Ningyu: ...

Secretary Bai: I know you're not a talker – I've heard people say that nature intended you for a cryptographer of classified documents, since you don't ever speak to anyone. Right now, though, you're not a cryptographer but one of four people suspected of being Ghost. You can't keep silent any longer. You have to talk.

Li Ningyu: ...

Secretary Bai: Come on, Li Ningyu! It doesn't matter whether you accuse someone else or whether you confess, you just have to say something.

All the while that Secretary Bai was questioning her, the microphones didn't pick up the sound of her voice at all, but there was a continuous rhythmic hissing, almost as if he were talking to a pendulum clock.

'What's that noise?' Hihara asked.

'I don't know,' Police Chief Wang replied.

It was the sound of hair being combed. Li Ningyu wasn't answering Secretary Bai's questions because she was too busy combing her hair. What a way to behave!

Secretary Bai had had enough of this. 'Li Ningyu!' he shouted. 'I can tell you that other people have already said they believe it's you that's Ghost. If you sit there in silence, does that mean you admit it?'

Finally, Li Ningyu raised her head and looked straight at Secretary Bai. She spoke quite calmly. 'Let me remind you, Secretary Bai, that fifteen years ago my father was beaten to death by the Red Spears, and that six years ago my older brother was murdered by that bald Nationalist bastard Chiang Kai-shek.'

Secretary Bai: What are you trying to say?

Li Ningyu: I am not a Communist insurgent and nor am I working for the Nationalists.

Secretary Bai: If you're neither a Communist nor with the Nationalists, why are you lying about Chief of Staff Wu?

Li Ningyu: If I am lying, then I must be psychic.
Secretary Bai: What on earth are you talking about?

Colonel Hihara and Wang Tianxiang, listening in the shadows, were similarly bemused.

She began by asking Secretary Bai whether on the evening before last he'd had any idea why they'd all been brought to the Tan Estate.

Of course he hadn't. Nobody knew that.

'You didn't know,' Li Ningyu said, 'and nor did I. So just think about it: if I had no idea what I was here for, how could I have already invented false accusations to tell Commander Zhang when he phoned us all before we were brought here?'

The fact was that nobody had known why Commander Zhang had summoned them, so it was unthinkable that Li Ningyu could have invented a false accusation against someone; not unless it had been prearranged with the Commander. But that... Surely that was impossible! Secretary Bai obviously saw her point, because as Hihara and Wang Tianxiang listened in on the line, they could hear that both his language and his tone of voice had become more friendly.

Secretary Bai: So you're saying it's Chief of Staff Wu that's lying.
Li Ningyu: Of course he's lying.
Secretary Bai: So do you think he's Ghost?
Li Ningyu: Who?
Secretary Bai: Chief of Staff Wu.
Li Ningyu: I have no idea.

Secretary Bai: What do you mean, you have no idea? You've just said he's lying!

Li Ningyu: He is lying, but that doesn't necessarily mean he's Ghost.

Secretary Bai: What?

Li Ningyu: Asking about the contents of an encrypted telegram is against the rules, even if he was only interested in staff appointments. It would be really embarrassing for him to have to confess that to his superiors, so he's lying and refusing to admit what he's done. That's entirely possible.

Secretary Bai: So who do you think is Ghost?

Li Ningyu: Right now, I really wouldn't like to say.

Secretary Bai: You may not like it, but you have to give me a name.

Li Ningyu remained silent. The silence lasted a long time. It was the silence of a statue. No matter what encouragement Secretary Bai offered or how much he tried to provoke her, she completely ignored him. This made Secretary Bai furious and anxious, to the point where he said, 'Have you been struck dumb? Li Ningyu, I'm talking to you!'

At that, Li Ningyu leapt to her feet and shouted, 'I'm not saying anything because I don't know! If you think I'm going to play guessing games about this kind of thing, you're a fool.' And she grabbed her comb and stalked off, leaving Secretary Bai so shocked his mouth hung open.

Wang Tianxiang was amused by this. 'Bai Xiaonian has really annoyed her.' He turned to face Colonel Hihara. 'That's the kind of person Li Ningyu is – she's got a nasty temper. Normally, she doesn't have much to do with anyone; she's happiest in her own company – it must be a boring life. But if you annoy her, she can get really angry, and she'll make life absolutely miserable for you, no question about it.'

It was his opinion that the reason Li Ningyu dared to openly disrespect Secretary Bai like that (and indeed the reason she was disrespectful to Wang Tianxiang himself) was because of her close personal connection with Commander Zhang. Some years back, Li Ningyu had been a military nurse while Commander Zhang was exterminating the Red Army in Jiangxi province; the Commander had been bitten by a poisonous snake and so, with no doctor nor any medicine available, Li Ningyu had sucked the poison from his wound and saved his life. As you might imagine, the two of them were very close.

Colonel Hihara listened to this but expressed no opinion on the subject.

5

Gu Xiaomeng was the last to be interviewed.

She got straight to the point the moment she entered the room. 'Don't imagine that I'm going to let you interrogate me, Secretary Bai. All I have to say is that I don't know anything about it. I'm not Ghost and I don't know who is, so you're going to have to ask the others.'

Even though they couldn't see her, Colonel Hihara and Police Chief Wang could easily picture the arrogant, impassive expression on her face. But Hihara soon found himself fascinated.

Secretary Bai: I'm asking the same question of everyone. They've all said their piece and now you must say yours.

Gu Xiaomeng: I've already told you that I don't know whether any of the others are Communists – all I know is that I'm not.

Secretary Bai: And how are you going to prove that you're not?

Gu Xiaomeng: How are you going to prove that I am?

Secretary Bai: There's at least a one in four chance that you are.

Gu Xiaomeng: Well then, how about you kill one fourth of me – head or leg, whatever you like.

Secretary Bai: Gu Xiaomeng! All you're achieving by this is annoying Commander Zhang and Colonel Hihara. No good will come of it.

Gu Xiaomeng: I can tell you for nothing, Bai Xiaonian, that you'd better kill me right here and now. Otherwise, if I get out of here, it'll be your head on the block.

Secretary Bai: Miss Gu, I know who your father is... [A conciliatory laugh] It's my job to ask these questions, and I'm hoping that you'll help us out here.

Gu Xiaomeng: I really have no idea whether any of the others are Communists or not, and I don't think it's right to just guess.

Secretary Bai: How to put this, Miss Gu... Section Chief Jin and Unit Chief Li are both your superior officers, so you must know them well. If you had to choose one of them, which would it be?

Gu Xiaomeng: I have no idea.

Secretary Bai: You have to choose someone.

Gu Xiaomeng: Well, in that case I choose myself, okay?

Hihara could hear the clip of Gu Xiaomeng's shoes as she walked away. Everyone had passed the test – he hadn't expected that. He'd assumed that they'd all be scared witless, that all he'd have to do would be to utter a few empty threats and they'd turn on each other, ripping each other to shreds until everything came out. He'd even thought that this one round of questioning would be enough.

His many years of experience had told him that whether he was dealing with Communists or Nationalists, none of them could withstand much; a bullet or a slash of the sword would reduce them to a heap – it was really quite laughable. He often said that the reason he was always so cheerful was that he'd seen too many laughable things in the way that Chinese people behaved, and so he was endlessly amused. Sometimes he simply couldn't help himself, he just had to laugh out loud. But these interviews hadn't given him the laugh he'd been expecting, so he couldn't help but feel a little disappointed.

However, he remained convinced he'd be able to winkle Ghost out. He still had a really lethal manoeuvre up his sleeve – his trump card. Police Chief Wang, on the other hand, was looking and sounding panicky as he speculated on who Ghost might be.

Hihara tried to cheer him up as he headed out of the listening room. 'Don't be in such a hurry – you don't have to try and guess who it is. You need to have faith. Ghost is under our control now, and whoever it is, they're not going anywhere. Just wait patiently and all will be revealed.'

Wang Tianxiang followed him out. 'That's right,' he replied ingratiatingly, 'Ghost won't be going anywhere. With Colonel Hihara here, no matter how tricky this Ghost is, they won't get away.'

Hihara retired to his room for a cup of tea. 'You say that Ghost is tricky,' he said to Wang Tianxiang. 'Well, that's fine by me – it'll make this so much more interesting. If the four of them had given us the name today, where would be the fun in that? There'd be no sense of accomplishment. The whole fun of the thing is in the process by which you are victorious, not in the victory itself.'

He was drinking Dragon Well tea, grown locally in Hangzhou, a tea of the highest quality; the leaves were shaped like swords, and the tea itself was a clear light green and intensely aromatic. In an instant the room was filled with a perfume so deliciously pure and fresh, it was almost as if the leaves were still growing on the bush.

FIVE

1

What does it mean to have each day feel like a year? Right then, every day felt like a year to Ghost. As the minutes ticked by, so Ghost's chances of keeping K and the others safe trickled away. Ghost was trapped, unable to do a thing about it. Outside the window there was the sky, and from time to time a sentry passed in complete silence, but in Ghost's heart there was only darkness and despair.

Ghost knew how carefully the comrades would have planned each detail of K's journey. Ghost kept urging them, 'Call off the Gathering of Heroes! Call it off now!' But the only person who heard the shouts was Ghost. It was the worst possible punishment. As another comrade had once said, for people in their line of work, operating as undercover agents, the absolute worst thing was that they sometimes had no option but to stand by and watch while their own comrades were killed by the enemy. Ghost had been afraid that this might happen, and now it seemed unavoidable.

It was much harder to bear than Ghost could have

imagined. Ghost kept asking the same question, over and over – How can I get my message out? – as if this might in some way lessen the pain, when in fact all it did was make it worse.

2

Who is Ghost?

That afternoon one of the sentries brought important news to Colonel Hihara, pointing the finger of suspicion at Gu Xiaomeng.

It happened like this: by the time Secretary Bai had finished interviewing everyone, it was almost time for lunch. According to the rules, if the group was going to eat or if one of them wanted the toilet, they had to be accompanied by Police Chief Wang. However, this particular mealtime, Wang Tianxiang couldn't go with them. Because Colonel Hihara couldn't appear (being supposedly back in the city), Wang Tianxiang was going to have lunch with him. Hence it fell to the fat staff officer to take them instead.

Gu Xiaomeng promptly made herself difficult. She wasn't hungry and didn't want any lunch.

The situation was delicate. Staff Officer Jiang wasn't at all sure whether he should allow that or not. If he denied her, he would have to drag her out by force, since Gu Xiaomeng was lying in bed and refusing to get up. What could he do? Nothing! But what if something happened to her? He left a sentry on guard to watch her.

He had no idea that that was exactly what Gu Xiaomeng was hoping for.

When Colonel Hihara and Police Chief Wang noticed that she was missing from the group going to lunch, Hihara wondered if she was pretending to be ill.

'If she were to say she's sick, what would you do – would you let her leave the estate?' Hihara put this to Wang Tianxiang as they watched through the window, almost as if he were testing him.

'If she was pretending, I wouldn't pay any attention,' Wang Tianxiang said. 'But if she really was unwell, I'd call a doctor. Either way, I wouldn't let her leave.' His answer was careful and considered, as if he'd prepared it in advance.

'That sounds nice and easy,' Hihara said, 'but how would you know if she was faking or not? She's a woman; if she said it was some kind of gynaecological problem, how would you decide? And if you did get a doctor in, what would happen if he worked out what's really going on here and then went off and told everyone he met?'

That was a good question. If Gu Xiaomeng were to pull that kind of stunt, there might be all sorts of ramifications.

Fortunately, Gu Xiaomeng did nothing of the kind. However, she did cause Wang Tianxiang a lot of extra work and worry, so much so that he couldn't even eat his lunch in peace. It was a very nice lunch they'd been sent too, and he'd been looking forward to sharing it with his boss. It was a rare opportunity to sit there one on one, just chatting, almost like old friends. But before they'd had time to exchange more than a couple of words, before he'd taken more than a mouthful or two of his lunch, one of the sentries knocked hurriedly on the door and came in to announce that something was up.

Something was indeed up.

It turned out that once Secretary Bai and the others had left for the dining hall, Gu Xiaomeng had gone downstairs to try and make friends with the sentry. She'd begun by chatting about this and that, mainly with a view to making sure that he knew of her special status, and then she'd explained what it was she really wanted. And what was that? She wanted the sentry to phone someone for her and tell them to come immediately to the Tan Estate because she had something really important to tell them. Of course, she wasn't expecting the sentry to help her for nothing – she promised to show her gratitude properly later on. As to who she wanted to contact, the sentry said that it was someone called Jian, a Mr Jian, and that there was a phone number. That was all he knew.

3

Who would this Mr Jian turn out to be and why was Gu Xiaomeng in such a hurry to see him? Was he part of the conspiracy or was this about trying to divert attention? Hihara stood looking out of the window, lost in thought. After a long pause he turned round and gave instructions to the sentry. 'Go back and tell her that you made the call but nobody answered.'

Hihara then requested the transcript of Gu Xiaomeng's conversation with Secretary Bai. 'What do you get from this?' he asked Wang Tianxiang. It appeared to be a rhetorical question. 'What I get from this is two quite different Gu Xiaomengs. One is a spoilt young woman who uses her position to bully people, who does just what she feels like, and who is afraid of nothing and nobody because she is Daddy's Little Girl; the other is the highly experienced, brave and intelligent Ghost who has successfully confused us all along with her daring and counter-intuitive actions.'

That was very deep. Wang Tianxiang was left speechless.

'We've already decided that she's been behaving like this just to be annoying – throwing her weight around,' Hihara explained. 'But if she wasn't so rude to everyone, she'd be in the frame for being Ghost. What if she really is Ghost? She's actually confessed – she's admitted her guilt – but in such a way that we immediately discounted it. That's very clever, very courageous. Isn't there a story about that kind of thing from the Song dynasty?'

He paused and looked over at the Police Chief, as if waiting for confirmation. None came.

He elaborated. 'A thief broke into the house of a rich man, but even though he rifled through the trunks and searched the cupboards, he didn't find any treasures. It turned out that the man had hidden his riches in his storehouse, suspended from the roof beams among his hams and sacks of dried chillies. It was a counter-intuitive move, a kind of dirty trick, something that nobody would expect, and that's why it worked.'

Wang Tianxiang could see that his boss was pleased as he said these astonishing things. He was clearly preparing to embark on a new phase of his investigation, and he was getting up his confidence and looking very excited. Since excessive excitement had rendered his own mind totally blank, he couldn't think of anything worthwhile to say, so he just mentioned courteously, 'Earlier, Section Chief Jin Shenghuo did say she was a Communist.'

'I wouldn't normally believe a word that Jin Shenghuo says,' Hihara said darkly, 'but when applied to the Gu Xiaomeng we have before us today – someone who is desperate to make contact with the outside world – we need to take it seriously.'

He told Wang Tianxiang to call up this Mr Jian immediately. 'Tell him that Gu Xiaomeng is too busy at work to be able to get away but that she's asked you to take him a present, and that you want to meet him.'

Mr Jian was absolutely thrilled when all this was communicated to him. He obviously had no idea it was a trap, and it was the work of moments to decide when and where they should meet.

Of course, the meeting needed to happen as soon as possible – Wang Tianxiang would set out straight away. As to where, well, at the man's home would be best; that way he couldn't escape.

Now they had the problem of what to take him. The item itself wasn't so important, but it needed to somehow force Gu Xiaomeng and Mr Jian into revealing their true identities. It was Colonel Hihara's view that if Gu Xiaomeng was indeed Ghost, then there was every chance that Mr Jian was another agent, either her superior or one of her juniors, and that the reason she was desperate to see him was undoubtedly to get a message out. In line with this theory, Hihara planned to secrete into whatever was chosen as a gift a slip of paper asking Mr Jian to go to a specific location to collect some equipment for Ghost.

In the end they decided on a tin of biscuits that Hihara had brought with him from Shanghai. The slip of paper was carefully placed right at the bottom, underneath all the biscuits, so that it wouldn't be discovered by accident – you would find it only if you were looking for it.

4

Mr Jian was a northerner, a tall man who spoke standard Chinese, had a long scarf wrapped round his neck and wore glasses. There was, however, something odd about him. Given his height and build, he could have been a marine, and he was clearly very strong, but he also had the air of a scholar, thanks to his refined manners and polite way of speaking. As soon as he saw him, Wang Tianxiang was sure that he recognized this Mr Jian, and it soon became evident why. It transpired that Mr Jian was famous in Hangzhou; he was an actor and at the start of the year he'd had the lead role in a play about Sino-Japanese friendship, so posters with his face on it had been plastered all over the city. There'd even been a special performance put on for Police Chief Wang's division at headquarters, so it was no wonder he remembered the face.

Mr Jian was living in a hotel, in a suite on the second floor. On the nightstand in his bedroom there was a cabinet photograph of Gu Xiaomeng, so the two of them were obviously very close – quite possibly he was even her boyfriend. The photograph had been tinted: her lips were red, her eyebrows black, and her cheeks peach-pink, a blush floating on chalk-white skin. At first glance, it didn't look much like Gu Xiaomeng, but when you examined it more closely, it was an excellent likeness.

The other room in the suite was a sitting room cum

library. Wang Tianxiang sat down on the sofa there, smoking a cigarette and chatting with Mr Jian. It was his considered opinion that Mr Jian seemed quite normal. He certainly didn't appear nervous or suggest in any way that he was up to something, and their conversation was perfectly pleasant. He really didn't look like a member of the Communist underground. However, the book that he'd left on the sofa was somewhat concerning; it was the latest work by the famous avant-garde writer Ba Jin, *Autumn*, which had been published the year before, in July 1940. Police Chief Wang looked at the bookcases and saw that they contained lots of Ba Jin's other writings: *The Family*; *Spring*; *Destruction* and so on – all of his novels, in fact. He also noticed a lot of other works by left-wing writers such as Lu Xun, Mao Dun, Ding Ling, Jiang Guangci, Xiao Jun and Rou Shi. There were an awful lot of them. Did that mean that when he performed for the Imperial Japanese Army, it was all an act?

When Colonel Hihara was given this news over the phone, he ordered Police Chief Wang to keep Mr Jian under surveillance and arrest him the moment he went to the meeting place they'd identified on the slip of paper.

However, Mr Jian didn't go anywhere, or at least not straight away. Having said goodbye to Wang Tianxiang, he went to the theatre and didn't come out again. Wang Tianxiang remained on guard for two hours and by the end of it was very bored and irritable. When it began to get dark, he had a soldier take over while he went back to report to Colonel Hihara.

⋆

Yet again, things hadn't worked out the way they'd hoped. Should they allow the situation to evolve naturally or should they stir things up with a big stick? Colonel Hihara favoured the second option. But how and with what sort of big stick?

Then Wang Tianxiang happened to mention that Gu Xiaomeng was a real gourmet, which immediately gave Colonel Hihara an idea.

'Well, in that case we'll organize a banquet and trap her that way!'

He could never have anticipated that it would be Li Ningyu who would draw all eyes upon her at dinner that evening.

5

Colonel Hihara himself joined them for their banquet, which he hosted in a private room in the dining hall. The food had been carefully selected; there was fish, chicken and very strong Daqu liquor. Hihara wanted them to drink as much as possible – to drink until they were drunk, to drink until they started turning on each other, to drink until they told him the truth.

So as soon as they got there, he poured them all a large glass of wine, right to the brim, then raised his own glass in the first toast. 'Come on, everyone, raise your glasses. This is the first time I've been able to join you here for dinner, and I hope it'll be the last.'

However, Li Ningyu refused to raise her glass. She was very sensitive to alcohol, she said, and never drank it.

Hihara asked the others whether this was true, and they all said that they didn't know. Since Li Ningyu never had anything to do with anyone else, nobody had ever had a meal with her before.

'Clearly, Unit Chief Li here was very well brought up,' Hihara said.

Li Ningyu remained stony-faced. 'Of course I was. Were you hoping otherwise, Colonel Hihara?'

Hihara laughed heartily at this. 'Do you really think that one glass of wine would make you a fallen woman? What about having just have a sip?'

But Li Ningyu wouldn't budge. Her refusal to join in ruined everyone else's mood and made them feel uncomfortable about drinking, which was very annoying for Hihara. He studied Li Ningyu's cold face, saw how determined she was to set herself apart and couldn't help but wonder: is she afraid of getting drunk and revealing the truth? What followed, however, was rather more dramatic.

A quarrel broke out between Li Ningyu and Chief of Staff Wu Zhiguo about halfway through the dinner. This was bound to happen sooner or later: the two of them had come out as enemies very early on, and they'd both been spoiling for a fight. From the moment they took their seats, Wu Zhiguo had been glaring angrily at Li Ningyu, and at one point he actually balled his fist and shook it at her. When they'd finished eating and the toasts began, he said all kinds of strange things, some of which were barely veiled threats and others that were just pointedly sarcastic. Li Ningyu didn't say a word. She just put up with it, pretending that she hadn't heard. She was obviously a woman who could hold her nerve, but by letting him get away with it, she was also showing weakness. Finally, as if he'd suddenly thought of the idea, Wu Zhiguo demanded that she repeat everything she'd said the other day about her office and the contents of the top-secret telegram.

'If she changes her story in any way,' he said to Colonel Hihara, 'that'll prove that she's been lying.'

'But if I don't,' Li Ningyu said, 'won't that prove that you are Ghost?'

'If you repeat it word for word,' Wu Zhiguo said, 'that just means you're a really slippery customer, if you can even remember your own lies.'

'In that case I'm not saying anything. Whatever I say, I'm going to end up in the wrong.'

'You just don't dare. You don't even dare have a glass of wine in case you slip up and reveal that you are Ghost—'

Before he'd even finished speaking, Li Ningyu had grabbed a glass and hurled the contents at him. The wine hit him full in the face.

That caused absolute chaos. Fortunately, there were plenty of people present, and they were quick to separate the two of them, otherwise Li Ningyu would have been on the receiving end of some nasty kicks and punches. That was the kind of person Chief of Staff Wu Zhiguo was – he was a military man, he beat people up for a living, and he was used to using his fists and his feet. Li Ningyu might have been frosty and austere, but being a woman, when it came to trading punches, she was definitely at a disadvantage.

*

Hihara's banquet-as-trap plan had been ruined. As he watched them file out of the room, his gaze was focused on one person: Li Ningyu. In his opinion, her behaviour that evening had served to tip her hand. She was a clever woman, but she'd made a clever person's mistake.

She'd been so patient, putting up with all those insults Wu Zhiguo had hurled at her to begin with, so why did she suddenly snap? Had what he said really been so insulting? No, it had not. What he'd said had been perfectly straightforward, no swear words at all – no 'fuck you' or abuse about her family; at worst it was an unpleasant personal comment. Was that worth getting so angry about? The more he thought about it, the more Hihara felt there was something not quite right about it. Had she launched her sudden attack to avoid having to answer Wu Zhiguo's challenge – because she was genuinely afraid that her story wouldn't hold together? Which would mean she was actually lying. Which would mean…

It was becoming more and more complicated.

The strange thing was that Colonel Hihara wasn't annoyed at this development – not at all. In fact, he seemed to be pleased. Perhaps in his heart of hearts he didn't want Gu Xiaomeng to be Ghost. After all, her father was an important supporter of the puppet government; Nanjing had given him a lot of publicity, and he was regarded as a key figure, a model of cooperation. If his daughter had to be executed as a traitor, that would be really bad, for the government and for the army. The puppet regime had enough problems as it was; they didn't need yet another scandal in its upper echelons.

Of course, no matter how much he might hope for a

particular outcome, the facts were the facts, and it was still far too soon to come to a conclusion. They would just have to wait and see.

6

See what?

Police Chief Wang Tianxiang suggested analysing the group's handwriting.

This was a good idea; Hihara had considered it himself. The only problem was that, in his experience, if targets were warned in advance, handwriting tests rarely worked. And these targets were already on edge, so if they were suddenly summoned to copy something out, how could they not smell a rat? Also, he already had the guilty party right where he wanted them, so why go to all that extra effort?

However, the situation was not as simple as he'd originally thought. He'd tried talking nicely to them, he'd tried threatening them, he'd tried tricking them, but all to no avail. Given the circumstances, then, he didn't mind putting in a bit of extra effort. He decided to test their handwriting.

Colonel Hihara prided himself on his problem-solving abilities. It was very important to him that other people appreciated his intelligence and he hated it when he was caught off guard and made to look foolish. The fact that he wasn't immediately able to come up with a plan for the handwriting test didn't mean one wouldn't come to mind shortly. Maybe he should go for a walk, go to sleep, dream – maybe the very thing that he was missing would emerge from nothing, from emptiness, from the darkness. Hadn't these people's ancestors always said that everything was born from emptiness?

Police Chief Wang thought it would be really easy to test everyone's handwriting. 'Just get them to copy out what Ghost wrote in that note in the cigarette packet. You read it out and order them to write it down.'

It would have been perfectly simple to do that, but very difficult to get a result. In order to make sure of achieving a result, Hihara was determined to make the whole thing enormously complicated. He put a lot of thought into his plan, and Wang Tianxiang and Secretary Bai were also required to wrack their brains.

Eventually, he decided that he would make the four of them – Wu, Jin, Gu and Li – write a letter home. The letter would say that although their duties had called them away, they wanted their families to know that they were safe and well. This letter was to be about a hundred characters long.

What was so difficult about that?

The difficulty lay in making the contents sound natural, because the letter had to contain every word in the note from Ghost. This was like trying to dance in chains or rake leaves into a pile on a windy day. Fortunately, Secretary Bai turned out to be very creative and on the ball, so the letter that he produced was not only worded with impressive elegance, it was also done quickly. When Hihara read it, he gave him full marks.

This would allow the handwriting test to proceed without the targets realizing what was going on. Why couldn't they just write their own notes to their families? Because they might phrase them badly, inadvertently revealing the fact of their secret incarceration. That was a good enough explanation if you didn't think too much about it. At the very least it would confuse them, and so this plan would achieve its primary aim in keeping them paralysed with fear.

Secretary Bai took charge of proceedings. The atmosphere in the western building was already dark and treacherous, and the row at dinner had made it even worse. The tests were designed in such a way as to impress upon the four that this affair was by no means over, not at all; in fact, it was only just getting started.

The four were kept isolated from each other and were called downstairs separately, one at a time, to trick them into thinking that they were the only one involved. Once the individual was seated in the conference room, Secretary Bai dictated the letter to their family on the spot, as if he were making it up as he went along. That way, they were obliged to write just one phrase at a time.

When the individual emerged from the conference room, they were taken to the sitting room, where Police Chief Wang made them copy out the message from Ghost three times:

Tell Tiger that 201's special representative has been spotted.

Call off the Gathering of Heroes.

Ghost.

For immediate dispatch.

This time they were allowed to know what it was they were doing. There was the real test and the fake test, to make sure they remained in the dark.

Copying out Ghost's message in triplicate took roughly the same amount of time as writing out the letter to their family, so it was possible to streamline the process. The first suspect was called downstairs, went into the conference room for Secretary Bai's dictation, and then went through to the sitting room to copy out Ghost's message; meanwhile, the next person had been called into the conference room and was writing out their letter. Wu, Jin, Gu and Li were moved up- and downstairs, into one room and out of another, writing letters and copying messages, keeping the whole building busy.

Right at that moment, Commander Zhang arrived, adding to the confusion. He had come specially to show Colonel Hihara a telegram that had just been received.

Over the past two days the Wireless Communications Division had been in frequent contact with Nanjing; just yesterday, six telegrams had been exchanged during their five periods of contact. These mainly concerned the precise whereabouts of K, and General Matsui's instructions regarding the matter. An hour ago, having finished dinner and having nothing much else to do, Commander Zhang had happened to look in on the Wireless Division. By chance, they had received a very important message just moments before, which read as follows:

```
For immediate attention!
According to reliable information, K
has already arrived in Shanghai. It is
```

```
estimated that he could arrive in Hangzhou
this evening. You must act according to
plan; do not do anything rash.
```

Commander Zhang had thought this telegram so important that he'd brought it round in person.

Hihara worked out the timings: if K had left Xi'an the morning of the day before yesterday, then he might well have arrived in Shanghai a whole day earlier than originally anticipated, assuming he'd gone by train and hadn't stayed overnight in Wuhan.

Commander Zhang said that he'd come to the same conclusion and so, before coming to the estate, he'd increased the military presence at the train station, with orders to keep a strict watch.

'What's the point of having them keep watch?' Hihara said. 'You don't know who you're looking for.' He laughed. 'Even if you did spot him, it wouldn't make any difference, we can't arrest him yet. You've already given orders, I hope, that nobody should try to arrest him?'

'Oh, I have, I have,' Commander Zhang replied.

'Let him come.' Hihara was putting the handwriting samples in order as he spoke. 'Let him come. I'd be much more concerned if he didn't turn up. If K comes, that means he's taken the bait and doesn't know what's really going on here. It also means that you, Commander Zhang, are on the verge of a breakthrough! We just need to keep watch on their meeting place on Mount Fenghuang, wait for them to wander into our net, and we'll get the lot of them. First, though, let's hope that these tests will show us who our Ghost is.'

Naturally, Hihara invited Commander Zhang to join him in looking through the tests. As a well-trained and highly experienced agent, Colonel Hihara had made a study of handwriting; he knew that everyone's penmanship was different. However, a person's handwriting is not like a person's fingerprint. Fingerprints never change: even if you remove the skin, a fingerprint grows back just the same; it can't be destroyed, no matter how hard you try. Handwriting, on the other hand, is something you can change. It's true that there are certain handwriting traits you can't lose, but they're not always easy to spot, and with practice it's perfectly possible to acquire enough different styles to confuse anyone trying to identify them.

Today, the two men were in luck. The moment Commander Zhang looked at the second sheet, he called out excitedly, 'Colonel Hihara, look! Come and have a look at this!'

Hihara took one look and was as excited as Commander Zhang. He laughed in delight.

The two men examined each word in the four writing samples in turn, and on every occasion Commander Zhang said, 'It's him!'

Hihara didn't respond, but he was thinking the same thing. He could hardly believe that Ghost could have been forced out into the open in this way, and besides... And besides, it was even more difficult to believe that it was neither Li Ningyu nor Gu Xiaomeng.

So who was it?

Chief of Staff Wu Zhiguo!

Maybe he was just being cautious, or maybe he wanted as many people as possible to enjoy this unexpected result, but Hihara decided to call in both Police Chief Wang and Secretary Bai to see if they would come to the same conclusion.

Even with no advance warning about what to expect, they too came to exactly the same shocking conclusion.

'It has to be him!' Police Chief Wang Tianxiang said.

'It must be him!' Secretary Bai echoed.

Hihara looked at Commander Zhang. 'Well, that means it's him.'

Commander Zhang looked sombre. 'Arrest him!'

7

Chief of Staff Wu Zhiguo was arrested by Police Chief Wang Tianxiang.

The next step was to interrogate him. Given that they had cast-iron evidence against him, any questioning was just a formality. Colonel Hihara and Commander Zhang had been through it all before, so they took it in turns to attack him, asking the same questions again and again:

'When did you join the Communist Party?'

'Who is your superior?'

'Who are your subordinates?'

'Tell us everything you know.'

To begin with, Wu Zhiguo appeared very tough and clear-headed – he spoke carefully and approached the situation calmly. But when Hihara placed Ghost's original message in front of him, together with the four writing samples Wu Zhiguo had given that evening, the Chief of Staff was struck dumb with amazement. He looked as though he'd seen a ghost: his eyes were on stalks and his face went rigid. He must have been absolutely terrified.

Hihara was in the Japanese secret police; noticing how people spoke and observing their facial expressions was elementary for him. Looking at the sudden changes in Wu Zhiguo, he knew he was getting close to the end of his enquiries.

'You may as well confess, Chief of Staff Wu.' Hihara patted him on the shoulder.

'Didn't you hear what he just said? Confess!' Commander Zhang jabbed a dagger-like finger at Wu Zhiguo's forehead.

Hihara pushed Commander Zhang's hand away and continued with his more softly-softly approach. 'I seem to remember that there's a Chinese expression about how a clever man tailors his actions to the times. Right now, further resistance on your part would be very stupid.'

'A Monkey King can successfully change his appearance in seventy-two different ways, but clearly he can't change his handwriting!' Commander Zhang shouted.

'That's right.' Hihara pointed at the heap of paper on the table. 'Even if you don't confess, your handwriting has betrayed you. It's right there in black and white; we have rock-solid evidence against you.'

'You cannot put off the evil hour any longer.' Commander Zhang grabbed one of the pieces of paper and slapped it down in front of Wu Zhiguo. 'Just look at that – any idiot can see that it's your handwriting!'

'Commander Zhang is exaggerating,' Hihara said with a chuckle. 'An idiot would not be able to see that it's your handwriting, but we can. In total we have a sample of eighteen Chinese characters, three numbers, and one letter from the English alphabet. You wrote at least ten Chinese characters that were extremely similar to our sample of Ghost's handwriting, very similar indeed. And four of them were as identical as if they'd been made with a stamp. Perhaps with those, even a complete idiot would see that they were the same.'

But Wu Zhiguo simply refused to confess. He swore an oath that it wasn't him; he protested; he forcefully proclaimed his innocence and stressed the injustice of the accusations against him.

This infuriated Commander Zhang. The patience and sensitivity that Hihara had learnt from the weaklings he normally dealt with was also now sorely tested. He had imagined that when Wu Zhiguo was confronted with the evidence, the interrogation would proceed smoothly – he had expected to be able to wrap the whole investigation up quite quickly. He had not anticipated such stubbornness. From the looks of things, it would still be a while before he could pack up and leave.

In truth, Colonel Hihara hadn't expected to have a third party at the interrogation. He hadn't been able to say anything earlier, but now that their first round had gone so badly, he decided to make his position clear. He called Commander Zhang outside and suggested as politely as he could that he should leave. They couldn't possibly bother an important man like the Commander with such a minor matter! All the Commander needed to do was to give his orders, then he could go home and await news of their success, and so on and so forth.

Commander Zhang found himself relaxing. He issued a few final instructions, and left.

Hihara immediately ordered Police Chief Wang to take Wu Zhiguo away. Where to? To the eastern building. Why? For further questioning, of course.

The success of an interrogation depends on many things. You need to consider the location, the method, the language, the conditions, the atmosphere, the level of pressure, the sense of urgency, the stages, the process. All of these require careful thought and skill in their execution.

Hihara wanted Wu Zhiguo dragged over to the east building in order to gain control of the situation. He was hoping this would increase the pressure on him and force him into a state of collapse. Once he'd achieved that, he'd be nearly home and dry. Hihara could be there in the east building sipping tea while at the same time subjecting him to further questioning, intimidation, even torture – whatever he felt like. And when he got tired, there was a sofa in the sitting room or he could go upstairs and have a nap.

In the beginning, the interrogation was held in the sitting room. Hihara asked Wu Zhiguo to sit on the sofa and told Staff Officer Jiang to make him some tea. On ascertaining that Wu Zhiguo smoked, he brought out a packet of cigarettes and handed him one. There was nothing at all threatening in anything that he said; it was all very polite, and he even kept smiling at him. Anyone observing them would have been hard put to imagine that this was an interrogation – it looked like a meeting between a couple of old friends, or perhaps a reunion between two colleagues stationed a considerable distance apart. At least, that was the impression given to Staff Officer Jiang, who'd not been present in the other building and had no idea about what was really going on.

When you're interrogated, the whole point is to get you to talk – your interrogator wants you to tell the truth. If you don't confess, they consider you uncooperative. Hihara was a very patient man and he tried to persuade Wu Zhiguo to confess in every way he could think of:

'You've failed to understand where your best interests lie…'

'You've not grasped quite how insignificant you really are…'

'How about you take a long hard look at yourself?'

'Do you not understand how lucky you are?'

But in the end he'd had enough.

'Do you really imagine you're going to get away with this?'

He threw the teacup he'd been holding straight at Wu Zhiguo's face and cursed.

'Damn you! You're really annoying me now!'

Wu Zhiguo stood up to avoid the teacup and Police Chief Wang rushed forward and kicked him hard in the back of his knees. Since Wu Zhiguo had managed to dodge the teacup, the Police Chief was trying to recover a bit of authority for his boss. Wu Zhiguo was caught unawares and immediately fell to the ground and started moaning.

Hihara walked over and laughed derisively. 'I would have thought that a tough guy like you would refuse to kneel for anyone – what are you doing down there? Get up! Even if you don't care what you look like, you're a disgrace to your uniform.'

Hihara made one more attempt. 'Listen, this is your last chance. You need to face facts.'

But Wu Zhiguo was still unwilling to face these particular facts. Which meant he wasted this last opportunity. He refused to admit his guilt – he wasn't guilty! His protestations of innocence were different now. He still spoke in plaintive tones, still had tears in his eyes, but his professional spirit, his self-confidence, had been shattered.

Wang Tianxiang cursed. 'Stop pretending – you're nothing but a piece of scum now. Don't imagine that you can deceive us any more!'

Hihara waved away the Police Chief. 'What are you doing crying like that?' he said disparagingly. 'I really hate men that blubber – it makes them look like women. I don't want you to cry, I want you to talk.' He paused, took a step back. 'Okay, let's say that your tears have touched me. I'm going to give you one more chance, and that's the best I can offer you. You really do not want to test my patience any further.'

Wu Zhiguo wasted that chance too.

If the man could endure this, was there anything he wouldn't be able to endure? Hihara slapped the table and shouted, 'What the hell...? Well, it seems I've got a real nasty piece of work on my hands. I don't care how tough you think you are, if you're not prepared to cooperate when people treat you nicely, fine, we'll see how you feel after we've had you at our mercy for a bit.'

He turned to Police Chief Wang Tianxiang. 'It's your turn now. Let's see how hard he really is!'

He stomped off, but when he was halfway out of the room he looked back, glanced to left and right, then pointed to the room to the east. 'Do it in there, Police Chief Wang, but don't make too much noise.'

8

The room that Hihara had indicated was next to the main sitting room, right up against the east wall of the building. It was set up as another small guest bedroom, and right now it happened to be empty.

Police Chief Wang ordered the mattress and bedding to be taken away so as to clear the room. Then he had the fat staff officer bring his man in. The moment he entered, the Police Chief threw his cigarette stub at Wu Zhiguo's face, but the latter ducked.

'Your reflexes are still very good.' Wang Tianxiang smiled coldly. 'But you are also a nasty piece of work – we've had a ghost in our midst all this time.'

'Rubbish!' Wu Zhiguo glared at him angrily. 'You must be mad! How can I possibly be Ghost? It's Li Ningyu!'

'Oh my God, then I'm in so much danger!' Wang Tianxiang was pretending to be scared. 'When you prove your innocence, I'm going to be in real trouble!'

'So you'd better make sure that you have an out.'

Wang Tianxiang laughed unpleasantly. 'Well, this is your out!' he said, kicking Wu Zhiguo right in the stomach.

Wu Zhiguo screamed and fell to the ground.

The fat staff officer standing off to one side was so scared that he took a couple of steps back.

'Sorry about that.' Police Chief Wang didn't make it clear whether he was speaking to Wu Zhiguo or to Staff Officer

Jiang. Maybe he was even talking to Hihara upstairs, because judging by the volume of noise just produced and the direction of the screaming, Wang Tianxiang was quite sure that his boss would be able to hear it. Having been given strict instructions not to disturb him, he decided to bring one of the pillowcases and a sheet back in. He told the staff officer to help him gag Wu Zhiguo and tie him to the bed frame.

'Listen,' Wang Tianxiang said to Wu Zhiguo, once he was no longer able to make a sound, 'I'm now going to torture you the way you've always tortured Reds in the past. *Chief of Staff* Wu.' He snorted derisively. 'When you decide you can't stand it any longer and you're ready to confess, nod three times. Understand? If you nod three times, I'll let you speak.'

Wu Zhiguo was struggling violently, but he was making only muffled sounds. He looked as if he was cursing.

'I know exactly what it is you're trying to say,' Wang Tianxiang said with a sneer. 'You're trying to tell me that I'm shooting myself in the foot here and that when you get out and you have your old job back, you're going to make me eat shit for this. But I can tell you now, that's never going to happen.'

He straightened up and cracked his knuckles, right hand first, then left hand.

'If there was even the remotest possibility that you'd ever be in a position to get back at me, do you think I would dare to do this?' He bent down close to the bed frame. 'You won't be getting out of here alive. Didn't you hear what Commander Zhang said: even an idiot could tell that you're the guilty party here – and I am not an idiot. If anyone is an idiot here, it's you – despite all that's happened, you're still not prepared to admit it's you. You're the one forcing me to do this! Staff Officer Jiang, you agree with me, don't you? Are you happy to be punishing him like this? Of course you're not!'

He glanced over his shoulder, but Staff Officer Jiang was way too scared even to nod in agreement. He just stood there sweating and trembling and wishing he was anywhere but there. Police Chief Wang didn't appear to notice; he focused back on Wu Zhiguo.

'We've all worked together in the ECCC for a long time, obviously we want to be friends. But you've forced us into this situation and we don't have any choice – understand? You're making us do this. And since this is what you want, this is what you're going to get.'

As he spoke, he removed his handgun and then unbuckled its belt. This he handed to Staff Officer Jiang. 'Over to you.'

The torture began.

Even though Wu Zhiguo was gagged and so couldn't make a sound, Hihara could still occasionally hear what was going on downstairs. There was the sound of violent thumping; every so often the leather belt hit something hard – the bed frame or the wall – with a loud crack; there was muffled screaming from Wu Zhiguo; there were curses that Wang Tianxiang couldn't stop himself from yelling; and there were other strange and unidentifiable noises.

Whether it was the result of having been so angry, or because he was still tired after his exertions with last night's whore, Hihara was absolutely exhausted. His movements were slow, and he felt dizzy. He lay on the bed, thinking he would rest for a moment before going back downstairs to see what was happening, but he couldn't keep his eyes open and in an instant was fast asleep. Every now and then he was roused by the sounds from below. He thought idly to himself that these awful people were all just the same – they never admitted to whatever it was they'd done until you proved to them that they had no choice.

SIX

1

Just before dawn the following morning, when everyone else in the building was still asleep, Hihara was roused from his dreams by the sound of Wu Zhiguo sobbing. In his dream, he'd seen Chief of Staff Wu curled like a snake at his feet, begging for mercy, weeping piteously. On waking, however, he was struck by how dark and silent everything was. It was as if something had happened – as if someone had died.

The darkness right before dawn is the blackest of all; it poured through the window and sank heavily onto the bed: furry, powerful, hallucinatory… Because of the silence, he could almost hear the sound of the sunlight. It made him uneasy. He got out of bed as quickly as he could and pulled on his clothes. When he opened the door he had a gun in his hand, as if he expected there to be someone with a gun on the other side.

There was no gun, and no one was about. Soft noises were coming from the room next door, but the door was closed, so, not knowing who was in there, he didn't dare put down his gun. It was only when he saw through the corridor window the shadows of the guards watching the building opposite, carrying on as normal, that he finally relaxed and set down his weapon.

He knocked at the next-door room, to ask if anything was wrong; in fact, he wanted to see whether Police Chief Wang Tianxiang was in there or not. He wasn't there, and there wasn't anything wrong. Or at least, the two wiretap operatives in there didn't have anything important to say.

He went downstairs.

The fat staff officer seemed tired from having been up all night torturing Wu Zhiguo and was lying on the sofa snoozing. He looked very menacing with his gun resting against his thigh. He was the sort of person who was keen to maintain a good reputation no matter how many vile things he did.

Hihara coughed and he woke up immediately, getting to his feet in alarm. His knees were trembling slightly.

'Has he confessed?'

'No.'

What a pain, Hihara thought to himself. He's giving us so much trouble. 'Where is he?'

'In there.' Staff Officer Jiang nodded towards the small guest room.

Hihara had intended to go in and have a look, but that didn't happen because he suddenly felt terribly sick. When he got to the toilet, he realized this was no ordinary nausea. He was vomiting and had violent diarrhoea; in fact, he needed to go to hospital. Given how serious his condition was, he didn't have time to yank Police Chief Wang out of bed; he had to call to the fat staff officer to get him there in a hurry.

2

Although he'd become violently ill very quickly, treatment began so fast that his condition soon improved.

At ten o'clock he returned from the city hospital with Staff Officer Jiang. As their car drove into the rear courtyard, he happened to glance towards the western building and saw that one of the sentries was shouting at an old man to go away. The old man was carrying a bamboo basket on a pole, with a towel wrapped round it; he looked like a rubbish collector. He was very tall and very thin. As he walked, he held himself ramrod straight, but his arms and legs swayed loosely, which made him look quite bizarre and caught Hihara's attention. Hihara wasn't particularly concerned by his presence, though, and didn't think too much about it.

There was no sign of Police Chief Wang inside the east building, so Hihara asked the young soldier on duty to go and fetch him. Shooting a wary glance in the direction of Wu Zhiguo's room, the soldier moved closer to Colonel Hihara and whispered, 'Police Chief Wang has had to go out. Turtle has turned up and the Police Chief has gone to keep an eye on him.'

'Who's Turtle?' For a moment Hihara couldn't remember at all.

Staff Officer Jiang pointed to Wu Zhiguo's room and said in a low voice, 'His contact.'

Now Hihara remembered. He walked quickly to the door, from where he could see that Police Chief Wang and one of his men had taken their coats off and were pretending to do a bit of martial arts practice among the trees, all the while keeping their eyes trained on the old man.

Turtle had been forced to leave the western building by the sentries but was walking hesitantly, glancing from side to side, as if he wasn't quite sure where he was going – it looked as though he might be coming towards the east building but couldn't make up his mind.

Hihara summoned the staff officer. 'Go and ask Turtle if he's here to collect rubbish,' he said. 'If he says yes, tell him that there's a sack of waste paper here that we'd like him to take away.'

The paper wasn't actually waste at all – it was there for the people working the wiretaps to use – but they had to give Turtle something, and the sacrifice would be well worth it.

Thanks to this plan, Hihara was able to see and talk to Turtle, and with the assistance of the well-versed staff officer he was able to achieve two objectives:

One: although his conversation with Turtle was just an idle chat, with no concrete information discussed, it was conducted at a volume loud enough that Chief of Staff Wu Zhiguo would have heard every word from inside the other room. If Wu Zhiguo was indeed Ghost, he would have understood exactly what had happened – his comrades had come to find him! This ought to have made him desperate, and desperation made a person careless.

Two: when Turtle was collecting the boxes of paper, Hihara pretended to suddenly think of something and asked the fat staff officer if fruit had been taken over to the people in the western building yet. It didn't matter what the staff officer said – that the fruit had been taken over or not – the point was to give the impression that he was genuinely concerned about the people in the other building. This would ensure that Turtle was even more deeply entangled in the web of disinformation that they were spinning.

The first of these objectives was a laxative; it was to make sure that Wu Zhiguo (Ghost) could neither sit nor stand, that his every waking hour would be eaten up with anxiety, forcing him into making a misstep. The second was an anaesthetic; Hihara wanted his enemies to be unconscious – he wanted both Turtle and Tiger to be sedated, he wanted to drug them into imagining that they were safe. With one side kept wide awake and the other in a drugged slumber, they would fit together like a mortise and tenon joint – precisely, tightly, with no gap. The trap would be set. Now all they had to do was wait; sooner or later there would be a reckoning.

As he watched Turtle walk away, Hihara felt strangely affectionate towards the old man. Turtle had arrived at just the right moment, had given him the opportunity to set his trap. This absolutely guaranteed that K and Tiger and all their friends would be captured in a couple of days' time.

3

Hihara was still standing in the doorway, thinking, when Police Chief Wang appeared and filled him in on what had happened earlier.

'About half an hour ago,' he said, 'the sentries by the main gate phoned to say that they'd just let an old man in to collect the rubbish – the same rubbish collector we have on base. I assumed it had to be Turtle, so I went outside to keep an eye on him. The old idiot has no idea that his cover has been blown and that he's being followed by my people.' Wang Tianxiang smirked self-importantly. 'He fussed around the front courtyard for a bit and then he came all the way back here to the rear courtyard. That was pretty risky, seeing as no one normally uses this area – why would he even think to come back here and look for rubbish?'

'Did he go straight to the western building?' Hihara asked.

'Pretty much.'

'Don't say "pretty much" – yes or no?'

Wang Tianxiang hesitated. 'He stood at the entrance to the rear courtyard, looked around, and then went to the western building.'

'Did you give orders to the sentries not to let him into the western building?'

'Yes...' Wang Tianxiang said uncertainly, then hurriedly added, 'I didn't know that you wanted to see him, so I didn't dare let him in.'

'Of course not! There are far too many people over there and if you'd let him in, anything could have happened.' Hihara wasn't angry with him, but he did seem to be cross with himself. 'I summoned Turtle over here too soon,' he said out loud. 'Which means we can't be sure whether Turtle was intending to come over here anyway, or whether he came because I called him.'

'What difference does that make?'

'It makes a huge difference.' Hihara sighed. 'If I hadn't called him over and he'd just walked away, left the rear courtyard, I could have set one of our prisoners free straight away.'

'Who?'

'Gu Xiaomeng.'

Hihara explained that Turtle's appearance today meant two things: he was trying to find out whether the information he'd received was genuine or not, and he was looking for an opportunity to make contact with Ghost. 'He was lucky enough to find out,' Hihara said, 'via your cleverly planted disinformation, that Ghost is here working on an important mission. But that was just something he'd heard – he had no evidence, so he needed to see it with his own eyes. Now, supposing he'd only gone to the western building to have a look and hadn't come over here, what would you think?'

Seeing that Wang Tianxiang couldn't answer, he prompted him, 'The information you had him overhear – did it specify that Ghost was in the western building?'

'No.' Wang Tianxiang was quite sure about that.

'Well…' Hihara composed his thoughts. 'If he'd just gone to the western building to make enquiries and hadn't come over here, that would have meant that he knew in advance that Ghost was over there. You didn't tell him that, so how would he have known? Who told him?'

He began speaking much faster now. 'Ghost's family has been here, to the estate; they know that Ghost is here. But Turtle shouldn't have known that, so if he did, it means that one of the relatives told him. Why would they do that? Who pays any attention to an old rubbish collector? There would only be one possible explanation: Ghost's family are Reds too! As you know, the only person who came from Gu Xiaomeng's family was the housekeeper, and I got rid of her before she had a chance to join the dinner. She never came to the estate, so she can't possibly know exactly where Ghost is.' He sighed gloomily. 'Which means we would have had sufficient evidence to eliminate Gu Xiaomeng from our enquiries.'

Police Chief Wang tried to cheer him up. 'It doesn't really matter. We know that Chief of Staff Wu is Ghost, so there's no need for us to make any further deductions.' He had his own reasons for saying this. He'd thrown the worst possible insults he could think of at Wu Zhiguo, had cursed the man until he was blue in the face. He'd also tortured him. So Police Chief Wang was now absolutely terrified at the prospect that Wu Zhiguo might turn out not to be Ghost.

Hihara shook his head and inhaled deeply. 'I almost had the proof in my hands, but because I failed to take every angle into consideration, I messed it up. This is most unfortunate, it really is.' This seemed to be a matter of professional pride. 'I played a wrong move and I really shouldn't have done.'

He really was angry with himself. He sighed again. 'To go back to something you said earlier: we really need some more evidence. Wu Zhiguo is refusing to confess, which means that what we have on him isn't enough, or at least he imagines that he can still deny everything. If we had more on him, could he carry on denying it? Would he dare?'

'As long as he refuses to admit that he's guilty, he's

just bringing pointless suffering on himself,' Wang Tianxiang said.

'You tortured him last night?'

Wang Tianxiang nodded.

'Aren't you worried that he might not be Ghost?'

'What! You mean…? Has something happened?'

'No.' Hihara laughed. 'Whatever happens, he needed a thumping, and you had my permission, so there's nothing for you to be afraid of.'

'I'm not afraid.' And here Wang Tianxiang stuck his neck out stiffly. 'It has to be him, it must be.'

Just at this juncture, one of the sentries from the main gate phoned to report an astonishing piece of news: Turtle hadn't left the estate!

He'd handled the whole thing very cleverly – he'd gone to the kitchens to have a poke around and had got into conversation with someone who worked there. The two of them seemed very friendly, so it was possible they'd known each other for a while. Or maybe it was just fortuitous – the man worked in the bakehouse looking after the ovens and he also cleaned the dining hall, so they did similar jobs. They seemed to be getting on like a house on fire, and Turtle had decided to help him by chopping some wood. Chopping wood was really tiring work.

'He won't be going anywhere for a while yet,' Hihara concluded. 'He'll want to hang around until after lunch.'

'So he can make contact with Ghost?' Wang Tianxiang asked.

'Yes. He must have already found out from his pal that everyone goes to the front courtyard to eat.'

'So what are we going to do?' Wang Tianxiang gestured towards Wu Zhiguo's room. 'Are we going to let him join the others?'

4

Yes!

Of course!

The way Hihara saw it, Turtle was now the litmus paper that would reveal the presence of Ghost, the weathervane that would show the way the wind was blowing. They would drag Wu Zhiguo out, let Turtle get a good look at him, watch carefully for any sign of communication between them and then they'd know.

However, when he opened the door and saw what state Wu Zhiguo was in, Hihara knew that his plan wasn't going to work. Damn!

In the space of a single night, Wu Zhiguo had become unrecognizable. The ECCC's Chief of Staff was now a shadow of his former self. He was naked from the waist up: his jacket and shirt had been pulled up and wrapped round his head, and his back looked as if it had been flayed. Below the waist he'd been whipped with a leather belt. His trousers had been pulled down to below his crotch, and his underpants were clotted with blood – if he'd been a woman, you'd have thought he'd been raped.

Hihara immediately withdrew and ordered Police Chief Wang to tidy him up a bit and bring him out. He hadn't expected the Police Chief would have been so brutal.

When Wu Zhiguo finally emerged, he didn't look much better. He was bent over, stumbling, taking one slow step at a time. He looked like a defeated general snatched from a bloody battle in the nick of time. Thanks to Wang Tianxiang having wrapped Wu Zhiguo's jacket round his head before he set to work, there were no obvious wounds or bruises to his face (Wang Tianxiang had wanted to avoid seeing into Wu Zhiguo's eyes, and to muffle the noise and minimize the chance of disturbing Hihara). However, it seemed as though his jaw had been dislocated from having the pillowcase stuffed in it; he couldn't close his mouth properly and it hung open in an O, with a line of blood trickling from each corner.

It was an appalling sight. Hihara barely glanced at him before waving him away. He couldn't look at him, it was just too uncomfortable.

Wu Zhiguo struggled and shouted, furious at being denied this chance to protest his innocence.

Hihara walked up to him. 'Stop shouting,' he said lightly. 'If you yell one more time, I'm putting this back in your mouth.' He gestured at the staff officer, who was still holding the pillowcase.

Chief of Staff Wu shut up.

'You will have heard through the door that someone came to see you just now,' Hihara said.

'Who?' Wu Zhiguo appeared completely confused, or maybe he was just pretending.

'Turtle.'

'Who's Turtle? I don't know any Turtle—'

'Stop with this pretence!' Hihara snapped. He sighed. 'I was actually hoping to have you see him again, but given your… appearance at the moment, that would ruin everything. So you'll just have to go back to your room and wait.'

In the end, Hihara decided Turtle probably wasn't going to be much help. He'd had two opportunities to get something out of him, but neither had come to anything, and he'd been put to an awful lot of trouble over this. He hadn't even had time to get himself a glass of water. He was overstressed and thirsty, so he resolved to go upstairs and make himself a cup of tea. He also needed to take his medication.

He stood by the window in the upstairs corridor, looking out and sipping his tea. The sun was shining brightly on the western building opposite: the glass in every window glittered and the whole place seemed almost to be quivering slightly, as if countless ants were dismantling it one speck at a time. Everyone involved in this investigation must be wanting to go home, Hihara thought to himself. If only Wu Zhiguo would say the words 'I confess!'

Unfortunately, Wu Zhiguo didn't look at all like he was going to do that. He was prepared to die first. If he did die without making a confession, it would be impossible for Hihara to conclude the investigation. He'd have to widen the net; he might end up embroiled in a miscarriage of justice; he'd have to leave without ever finding out what had really happened… The more he thought about this, the more Hihara hated Wu Zhiguo. This focused his mind, and wave after wave of ideas began flooding in.

He headed downstairs.

5

Hihara held a meeting in the western building and announced that he had evidence to prove that Wu Zhiguo was Ghost.

'You will naturally all be wondering why you haven't been allowed to go home, even though Ghost has been arrested.' He smiled and continued affably, 'Well, there's no need to keep it a secret any longer. Despite all the evidence against him, Wu Zhiguo still seems to think that he can get out of this. He is refusing to confess.'

He shook his head and allowed himself to appear mildly irritated.

'Even with one foot in hell, he seems to imagine that he can escape into heaven. You Chinese have a saying along the lines of "when in Rome..." – he's going to have to pay for this stupidity, and I'm afraid he's unlikely to come out of it in one piece. The paperwork is done, but he just won't sign it, so we're all going to have to wait until he does.'

Having got this far, Hihara paused and looked around him. Gu Xiaomeng seemed to have something she wanted to say, but she was hesitating. He encouraged her. 'Come on, Miss Gu, if you have something to say, then go ahead.'

'What happens if he never signs?' she asked.

This was what everyone was worried about.

Hihara laughed. 'Is that likely? No, it's not. When a fox falls into the water, is it likely that his tail gets left behind on the bank? Of course not! It's just a matter of time. Wu Zhiguo is dreaming if he thinks he can get out of this, and now it's time for him to wake up – nobody can stay asleep forever. If we can't shout him awake, we can beat him until he comes to his senses. There's nothing to worry about, you just have to trust me. He's not going to get away with this – we will see to that, and so will you.'

Everyone sat there staring at their hands, desperate not to catch his eye. He was unperturbed.

'The reason I've called you to this little meeting is that I'm hoping you will join us in dragging him from his dreams, help us wake him up. The sooner he comes to understand the situation, the sooner you can all go home.'

When Hihara said this, he seemed sincere, as if he was speaking from the heart.

He carried on. 'Let me explain. We want you to tell us whatever you like and in as much detail as you can. Just see what you can remember, give me some evidence, and he'll crack.'

'What happens if we can't think of anything?'

'It doesn't matter. In many ways, that's to be expected. But if any of you do have suspicions about him, now's the time to tell us. It's natural to be cautious, and I fully understand if you've been protecting yourselves…'

In the end, nobody had anything of any value to contribute.

It was now time for Hihara to put his latest brainwave into action.

He sent everyone off to eat lunch – to eat lunch and to meet Turtle.

His thinking went something like this: if Turtle reacted in some way on meeting Ghost, that would be good, but what if he didn't react? Naturally, anyone he didn't react to couldn't be Ghost. There was an eighty to ninety per cent probability that Wu Zhiguo was Ghost, so if Hihara put the others right where Turtle could see them and Turtle did absolutely nothing, then wouldn't that prove that Wu Zhiguo was Ghost? This was a simple mathematical problem, which could be expressed in a series of equations:

Suppose that: Ghost is X

We already know that: X = 1/ABCD

Then: X ≠ ABC

Therefore: X = D

Or, to put it even more simply: if it's not this, then it must be that. A or B.

It was because he'd made this calculation that Hihara was in such a good mood. It made him feel that there was a point to what he was doing, that he was on the path to success.

He wanted everyone to be relaxed when they went in to lunch, because that would make it easier to get Turtle to react. Which was why he'd decided to be honest with the other three. There was no need to lie to them when telling the truth would be so much more effective. And he was still leaving room to attack them again.

Even though Wu Zhiguo was his chief suspect, Hihara couldn't be a hundred per cent sure of his guilt. What if he'd made a mistake somewhere and was now knocking at the wrong door? The likelihood of that was slight, perhaps as little as 0.1 per cent, but once an investigation has gone off track it's hard to be sure of anything, and a 0.1 per cent mistake could ruin everything. There were two possible ways in which he might have gone wrong:

One: X ≠ D, X = 1/ABC. In other words, Wu Zhiguo wasn't Ghost but someone else was.

Two: X = D + 1/ABC. Ghost wasn't one person but two.

Right now he didn't care whether he was knocking on the wrong door or not because telling the others the truth could only help him. If he was on the right track, then Wu Zhiguo was indeed Ghost (X = D), in which case he'd just shown his faith in the others (ABC), which they fully deserved. If he was wrong (X = 1/ABC or D + 1/ABC), then he still hadn't failed – this would make Ghost (1/ABC) feel secure, catch them off guard, make them feel safe enough to try and make contact with Turtle.

6

As they took their seats in the dining hall, Hihara continued being bright and nice, making a show of how friendly he could be. He came across as very approachable for a man of such high rank.

He'd designed everything to make it as easy as possible for Turtle to get close to them. He'd chosen a table right in the middle of the room, where they could be seen by everyone coming up and down the stairs and were easy to approach, and he'd also invited a couple of the girls from the officers' club to join them. Since he was trying to pretend that they were drinking to celebrate the successful conclusion of the investigation, he thought that having two whores pour drinks and sing was not a bad idea. Besides which, there were lots of girls at the club just waiting to be summoned.

To begin with everyone was very restrained, including Police Chief Wang and Secretary Bai. After all, Hihara was from headquarters, he was in the Imperial Japanese Army and he was their boss. But after a couple of songs and a few drinks, they came to life. They started raising their glasses repeatedly in toast after toast, the songs came faster and faster, and their voices got louder and louder.

Li Ningyu was left out of it all because she didn't drink, so she looked rather bored and lonely. But Gu Xiaomeng seemed determined to include her: if she didn't want to play the drinking game Guess-Fingers, they'd do something simpler, like flipping coins or throwing dice. They ended up playing Scissors, Paper, Stone, with Gu Xiaomeng drinking the forfeit for her every time she lost.

Evidently, Li Ningyu wasn't that lonely.

The more they drank, the more they enjoyed it, and the more they sang, the more they enjoyed that too; there was flirting and teasing, people drank toasts to each other, and then drank more just because it was there. Their table was so loud and lively that soon everyone else in the dining hall was staring at them in surprise and alarm. Among those watching in amazement were Police Chief Wang's men, some of whom were leaning over the upstairs banisters, while others were keeping an eye on them from elsewhere in the room.

Colonel Hihara and Police Chief Wang both frequently got up from the table. They went to answer the phone, to go to the toilet or to spit by the front door. The whole point was to make the three ECCC officers believe that what Hihara had told them was true: they were no longer suspected of being Ghost, nobody was watching them any more, they could do what they liked again – and if they wanted to pass on some secret message, it would be perfectly easy to do so.

Just as Hihara had expected, shortly after everyone had taken their seats, Turtle appeared. He came in through the door from the kitchen, headed towards the bar, where he asked for two toothpicks, and then went back out. Hihara assumed that this was just an exploratory move.

Seeing this, Wang Tianxiang glanced at a member of his team, who jumped to attention and went to the kitchen to deliver his message – a message that was intended for Turtle's ears – instructing the waiters that they should lay another place since Chief of Staff Wu was on his way. This was meant to prevent Turtle from worrying if he didn't see Wu Zhiguo.

About ten minutes later, Turtle appeared a second time. Strictly speaking, this didn't really count as an appearance, since he just came out into the corridor, craned his neck, then retreated. Again, Wang Tianxiang instructed a member of his team to go to the kitchen and let Turtle overhear him telling one of the waiters to prepare a packed lunch and take it over to Chief of Staff Wu – he was working on something urgent and simply didn't have time to come to the dining hall.

If Turtle were then to appear a third time, that would mean that Hihara might yet be knocking on the wrong door (X = 1/ABC); if he didn't, then they could be one hundred per cent sure that it was Wu Zhiguo (X = D).

In the end, Turtle didn't reappear. What was he doing? One of the surveillance team reported afterwards that he hadn't been doing anything; he just squatted down next to the oven and smoked a cigarette. He seemed worried and very disappointed.

★

A lot of important things happened during the lunch, but it was over in less than an hour. This was because once Hihara had decided that Turtle wasn't coming back, he lost interest in it; and also because Gu Xiaomeng had drunk more than was good for her and started cursing other people, in particular Wu Zhiguo.

'Damn him! It's all that bastard's fault that we've been locked up here for two days!'

Locked up…? They were supposed to be engaged in a top-secret mission! Gu Xiaomeng was going to ruin everything – they had to shut her up. Police Chief Wang quickly ordered someone to get her out of there, and everyone then started walking back to the rear courtyard.

Gu Xiaomeng clearly enjoyed a drink, but she didn't have a great capacity for it and she'd been drinking Li Ningyu's forfeits, so it was no wonder that she was extremely drunk. But at least she could still walk and wasn't shouting so everyone could hear – that really would have ruined all Hihara's plans.

After that lunch, Hihara began to feel quite fond of Gu Xiaomeng. At the fork in the path, he said goodbye to the rest of the party, who were returning to the western building, then began to chat with Wang Tianxiang as the two of them continued to the eastern building. 'Supposing that Ghost is one of them—' he nodded in the direction of Secretary Bai and the others '—bearing in mind what you just saw at the lunch table, what conclusion would you come to?'

Wang Tianxiang was puzzled. 'Why are you still suspecting them? It has to be Wu Zhiguo!'

'I'm not saying it isn't Wu Zhiguo. But just supposing it isn't, how would you analyse what happened just now at lunch?'

Oh, thought Wang Tianxiang, his boss was just doing this for fun; it was a test to see whether he'd grasped the essentials of the situation.

Unfortunately for Wang Tianxiang, he had not. He stammered out a reply of sorts, but he really had nothing to say.

'You don't think she's cute?' Hihara asked out of the blue.

'Who?'

'Gu Xiaomeng.'

'Cute?' Wang Tianxiang stiffened. 'Didn't you see what she did when she got drunk? She nearly showed us all up.'

'The fact that she dares to get drunk is proof that she's cute,' Hihara pointed out. 'You told me that she's a gourmet, that she likes to drink, so yesterday evening I invited them to have some wine, to see whether she'd dare to drink it or not; then Li Ningyu messed everything up and we didn't get to find out one way or the other. But then today, as you saw for yourself, she got drunk and talked all kinds of rubbish. If she was Ghost, there's no way she'd have done that. Which proves she's not the one we're looking for. I think you can stop having people watch her Mr Jian for us.'

Now that Gu Xiaomeng was no longer a suspect, Hihara could have set her free, but when he thought about what a loose tongue she had, particularly once she'd had a drink, he decided she'd have to suffer a bit longer.

Wang Tianxiang giggled. 'Quite possibly she'll be happy about that.'

'What do you mean?'

'Have you noticed how close she is to Li Ningyu?' Wang Tianxiang gave an inadvertent twitch of his nose. 'How she always comes to her defence, whether Li Ningyu is present or not. And then just now, when she got drunk, she looked very affectionately at her.'

'Are you trying to tell me that they're lesbians?'

'Girls from grand families like that get up to all kinds of weird things.'

'So do you know what lesbians get up to?' Hihara laughed.

Wang Tianxiang shook his head. 'Do you, Colonel Hihara?'

'That's an abstruse question,' Hihara said with a smile. 'What would I know about it?'

SEVEN

1

Both Hihara and Wang Tianxiang felt so much better after that lunch, and not just because they'd been able to eat and drink their fill. Mathematical formulae had allowed them to feel that they were in control of the situation, that they were going to get results. They were feeling confident, and they had planned what they were going to do next. So when they got back to their own building, Hihara had Wu Zhiguo brought to the sitting room; he was going to question him himself.

Wu Zhiguo's hands were manacled and his mouth was gagged – he obviously wasn't being a good prisoner. The fat staff officer said that he'd been shouting continuously and demanding to see Commander Zhang.

Colonel Hihara stepped forward and removed the pillowcase stuffed in his mouth. 'You want to see Commander Zhang? Right now, I am Commander Zhang, I represent him. If you have something to say, then go ahead.'

Wu Zhiguo couldn't speak right away. His mouth and

tongue were numb. Although he made several attempts, nothing came out.

'Okay,' Hihara said, 'then let us say something first.' He instructed Wang Tianxiang to tell Wu Zhiguo what had happened with Turtle during lunch. Then he had another go. 'So, tell me, what's your story now?'

Wu Zhiguo was now able to form a few words, though they came out hesitantly, as if he were only just learning to talk. 'I... really... don't... know... who... he—'

'If that's all you have to say,' Hihara interrupted, 'I don't want to know.' He turned to Police Chief Wang and Staff Officer Jiang. 'If you want to listen to him, go ahead. I'm leaving.'

Wu Zhiguo knew that if Hihara left, the beatings would resume. He lurched forward to block his path, glaring angrily, looking like he might attack him. Hihara dodged nimbly to one side, shoved the Police Chief out of his way, then slapped Wu Zhiguo twice across the face. 'Are you trying to get yourself killed?' he hissed.

Wu Zhiguo shut his eyes. 'Colonel Hihara, I had no idea... you were... such a fool... You actually think I... am a Red... when I am totally loyal to the Imperial Japanese Army...'

Hihara snorted. 'A full confession right now would be the best way to show your loyalty!'

Wu Zhiguo's tongue seemed to have got a bit better. 'You can... ask anyone in Hangzhou, ask... anyone in the Qiantang valley... Everyone... knows... how successful I've been in quashing rebel activities. I've arrested and killed plenty of Nationalist agents, and plenty of Communists. If I am Ghost, how could I have done that?'

'According to my information, you've arrested and killed plenty of Nationalists, but not many Communists.'

Wu Zhiguo was now able to speak without stopping. 'That's because we don't have many Communists round here, and those that are here are very slippery. Most are based in mountain areas, where it's difficult to arrest them.'

'No,' Hihara said with a laugh, 'it's because you're Ghost and you can't bear to arrest or kill fellow Party members.'

'No!' Wu Zhiguo shouted. 'Li Ningyu is Ghost!'

'So Turtle isn't a Red?'

'I don't know who Turtle is.'

'But he knows you.'

'That's impossible!' Wu Zhiguo screamed. 'Bring him here and let me confront him.'

Ah, well, once an officer, always an officer, Hihara thought wryly. Even in a situation like this, Wu Zhiguo still spoke like a Chief of Staff. 'You want me to bring Turtle here?' He chuckled. 'That's impossible, I'm afraid, since I need him to catch much bigger fish.'

He slowly walked away.

It seemed to Police Chief Wang that Hihara's patience was being sorely tested – or perhaps this was simply the calm before the storm. The Police Chief had been itching to show Wu Zhiguo where to get off, and now his chance had come. He grabbed him by the hair. 'Damn you, you motherfucking bastard, if you mention Li Ningyu one more time, I'm going to cut your tongue out by the roots! Are you telling me that she managed to copy your handwriting?'

'Yes!' Wu Zhiguo said. 'She's been practising my handwriting in secret.'

'Rubbish!' Wang Tianxiang punched him so hard that he nearly toppled over.

When he'd regained his balance, Wu Zhiguo moved a step closer to Hihara. 'Colonel Hihara, I'm telling the truth. Li Ningyu can forge my handwriting. She's been practising in secret.'

This was a most unexpected development, and it made Hihara laugh. Then suddenly he found that the idea wasn't laughable at all, but he still didn't believe it. 'Why not come out with all your dumb ideas at the same time?' he said darkly. 'This one is obviously ridiculous. Where's your proof? Produce some evidence and I'll release you immediately.'

Wu Zhiguo raised his head. 'My evidence is that the characters are too much alike,' he said excitedly. 'You think the fact that any idiot can see that the handwriting is the same is proof of my guilt, but actually it's evidence that she's been plotting against me. Look...' He pulled out a piece of paper that he'd prepared earlier and handed it to Hihara. 'I wrote all of these – do they look the same? Would any fool be able to see that they were written by the same person?'

Wu Zhiguo had written out the message over and over again. He'd done it after being untied so that he could eat his lunch. Perhaps an expert graphologist would have eventually spotted the signs indicating that they were all authored by Wu Zhiguo, but it certainly didn't jump out at you the way that yesterday evening's writing sample had, where even a fool could tell they'd been written by the same person.

While Hihara was studying the sheet of paper, Wu Zhiguo

grabbed his chance. 'If I was Ghost, I would have given you a quite different handwriting sample last night—'

'But when you were copying out the letter you didn't know it was a handwriting test.'

'If I was Ghost, I would have realized there was more to it. Why would you suddenly be making us copy out a letter to our families? Even I was sure you must be testing our handwriting in some way. If I was Ghost, I'd never have just used my usual handwriting, and absolutely no way would there have been a couple of characters so identical to the ones in the message that they could have been made with a stamp!'

He went on to say that if he was Ghost and was confronted with such cast-iron evidence, he could have avoided being beaten so badly by simply admitting to having written the message. 'I can't possibly be as stupid as you seem to imagine. On the one hand I'm supposed to be so idiotic as to blow my cover by giving a handwriting sample that reveals my identity, and on the other I am lunatic enough to risk getting beaten to death rather than admit that I am Ghost.'

As to why Li Ningyu would want to entrap him, he said it was because he'd arrested and killed so many Nationalist and Communist agents – they must all hate him. Since Li Ningyu was Ghost, she was determined to get rid of him, so she'd laid this trap for him. She must have practised his writing in secret and then written all her covert messages in his script.

'Secret agents often do that kind of thing,' he said, citing an example that made Hihara feel particularly pleased. 'I've heard that in Europe and America – and Japan as well

– secret agents are required to master two different styles of writing as part of their training, one of which they use only when sending intelligence.'

Of course, this hypothesis, plausible though it sounded, could be part of the conspiracy, Hihara thought. Yet another sting in the tail. When he'd heard what Wu Zhiguo had to say, he walked off without a word and went upstairs. His expression gave no clue as to whether he was persuaded by Wu Zhiguo's intelligent defence or whether he was furious that the man was still trying to deceive him.

2

As far as Police Chief Wang was concerned, the situation had taken a most unwelcome turn. He'd thought that this evening would see the conclusion of their investigations, and he'd in fact gone so far as to make arrangements with a prostitute at the officers' club. He'd been planning to really relax and enjoy himself tonight. But now circumstances seemed to have sent them down a completely different path. He found this hard to accept: it just didn't feel right. He wanted to get the investigation back on its old track, but that would have to be without Colonel Hihara's permission, and he didn't dare openly defy him. He would have to do it in secret, without anyone else noticing.

He locked Wu Zhiguo in his room, then went out to the front for a smoke. Having clarified in his own mind how to proceed, he came back in and closed the door, after which he began to interrogate Wu Zhiguo by himself. It seemed as though he had now set himself up as sole judge and jury.

To begin with, Wang Tianxiang kept his voice down, so even though Staff Officer Jiang was right there in the sitting room, he couldn't hear a word of what they were saying. Later on, their voices were audible from time to time, sometimes very loud indeed. Pretty soon, Colonel Hihara shouted down the stairs for Wang Tianxiang. Wang Tianxiang realized that he must have been yelling loud enough to disturb the Colonel, so he went upstairs sheepishly and tried to get his excuses in first.

'Colonel, he's just coming out with one lie after another. I don't believe a word he says.'

Hihara gave a cold laugh. 'So you're feeling angry and want to cut through it all as quickly as you can. But there's no need to be in such a hurry.' He gestured for the Police Chief to sit down. 'Commander Zhang is absolutely right – whatever it is that's been going on, we'll soon know all about it. Don't try and force it. We don't have to go into overtime on this interrogation. It's not worth it.'

Rather than complaining about the Police Chief's actions, he was actually showing concern for his subordinate. The thing that was really worrying Wang Tianxiang, however, was that Hihara might have been led astray by Wu Zhiguo's lies. The thought was like a bone stuck in Wang Tianxiang's throat; every attempt to swallow it had failed, so now he just had to spit it out. 'Do you think he's right, Colonel?'

Hihara considered this but didn't express an opinion one way or the other. 'Different situations call for different measures...' As he spoke, he handed the newspaper he'd just been reading to Wang Tianxiang. 'Where is she?'

He was talking about the concubine.

'In the city, under guard.'

'Bring her here.'

Wang Tianxiang hesitated.

Colonel Hihara glared at him. 'Don't tell me that she doesn't know who Ghost is, because I already know that you brought her out here behind my back the night before last, in the hope that she'd recognize her contact.' He clicked his tongue. 'You're always coming up with these little schemes, Police Chief Wang, but you really should learn to control yourself. One of these days you're going to ruin everything.'

Wang Tianxiang stared fixedly at the picture of the concubine in the newspaper. He couldn't begin to imagine what his boss was up to.

Hihara seemed to intuit this. 'Don't concern yourself with what I'm thinking, Police Chief Wang. Just go and get her and bring her here.'

3

The concubine was a young woman. For all that she'd been a concubine, joined the Revolution and experienced all sorts of life-changing events, she was still only twenty-two years old and very beautiful. Three years earlier, when she'd officially become Qian Huyi's concubine, she hadn't been particularly attractive – she was flat-chested and very thin, with a direct gaze, and her hair had been cut short by her fellow students, who held progressive ideas about women's rights; really, she looked like a boy in girl's clothing.

At that time she'd just finished senior school and her friends were encouraging her to take the entrance exams for the National Ginling Women's University in Nanjing. The problem was that her parents didn't agree, or rather they couldn't afford it. Even if they'd sold their house and all its contents, there wouldn't necessarily have been enough to pay her fees. Then one day this Qian Huyi came to meet her parents with a sack of money, saying that he wanted her for his concubine and that this was his gift to celebrate making it official. Her father calculated that the money was probably enough to allow his daughter to go to university, and he asked his wife to discuss it with her: was she willing to fund her undergraduate degree in this way? His daughter took the money, but in the end she didn't go to university. Her father was never able to work out whether she'd genuinely agreed to what happened of her own free will, or whether she'd been tricked into it somehow or forced to accept it by her mother. Be this as it may, she squandered her youth on Qian Huyi.

Young women can change a great deal in a very short time. Wang Tianxiang had watched as her body became curvier and her hair longer, to the point where more and more people would turn and stare when she walked down the street. People joked with Qian Huyi that he must have something really special in his trousers, since the women he pronged turned into such beauties.

What rubbish!

If anything, the opposite was true; he ruined this beautiful young woman's life by possessing and enjoying her. Fortunately, he didn't get to inflict himself on her for too long. The concubine was still young and still attracted men's attention as she walked down the road. As to her present occupation, she worked for a shipping company and was also one of Turtle's subordinates: a whore who often went to his stall to buy cigarettes. She had learnt how to make herself up in a way that inflamed men's desires. Her bag was full of make-up – rouge, lipstick, eyebrow pencil, perfume and so on – and with just a few puffs and sweeps of her brush she could create whatever effect she wanted.

When Police Chief Wang informed her that he was taking her to the Tan Estate, she assumed this was for another interrogation, so she got to work and made herself up to look like a real professional. That was her cover and it needed to withstand the most intense scrutiny. Under no circumstances was she going to admit that she was a member of the Communist Party or that she was Warrior. So what she said to Wang Tianxiang was, 'Hey, bastard, if you want to fuck me, you can – that's how I make a living nowadays, after all. I get fucked by bastards like you every day. But if you're trying to say that I'm some kind of Red, then you've seriously lost it, the Japanese really have screwed with your mind.' She almost spat in his face. 'What the hell are you thinking? I'm a whore, a whore that got her life fucking ruined by Qian Huyi. If that doesn't bother you and you still want a fuck, then go right ahead! But you'll have to take me to your house – I'm not going anywhere near the Tan Estate. I hate that horrible place!'

Wang Tianxiang laughed. 'I don't want to fuck you. There are plenty of girls I can fuck who are a whole lot younger and prettier than you.'

It was lucky that Colonel Hihara didn't get to hear that. If he had, he'd have cursed Wang Tianxiang for his stupidity and vulgarity.

When the Colonel caught his first sight of the concubine, he was immediately reminded of a line of poetry: 'as shining as gold, as soft as silver'. It was a line from one of his favourite Japanese classics, Murasaki Shikibu's novel *The Tale of Genji*; a line written by its hero, Prince Genji, about the Rokujō Consort.

The Rokujō Consort was both superlatively beautiful and also a woman of great refinement and intelligence. Unfortunately, these qualities brought her no luck in life and caused only jealousy; in the end, she had no choice but to take refuge in a convent, shaving her head and becoming a nun. But the Buddha's law proved no match for Prince Genji's powers of seduction. One glance from him was enough to arouse the Rokujō Consort's long-suppressed desires, and the two of them enjoyed a night of love at the nunnery, where she should have been living free from all human passions. Afterwards, Prince Genji sent her a poem:

You have proved as shining as gold, as soft as silver,
So for you there was a way to hell even from the gates of Heaven.

Hihara saw in his first encounter with the concubine an echo of Prince Genji and the Rokujō Consort at the nunnery. They were on opposite sides, and between them lay a gulf of a thousand fathoms, a mountain of knives, a sea of fire. But Prince Genji viewed the mountain of knives as little more than a molehill, and he leapt over the gulf as if he were merely crossing a bridge. No wonder he was considered such a romantic hero.

Hihara reminded himself that he had summoned the woman for a reason, so he put the poem out of his mind. No matter what his personal feelings were, he would not act on them.

There was only one reason for bringing in the concubine, and that was to see if she could identify Ghost.

So who would she be taken to see?

First she was to be confronted with Wu Zhiguo, and then she would meet with Li Ningyu.

From this it was evident that Hihara had found Wu Zhiguo's theory persuasive.

4

Which of them was guilty? Which of them was innocent? Hihara couldn't make up his mind.

He refused to believe that the concubine and Ghost didn't know each other; or to put it another way, even if the concubine didn't know Ghost, Ghost would definitely know her. And given that he would be using advanced interrogation techniques, it would be hard for Ghost not to react in some way. As the saying goes, a dog will always bark sooner or later, and a ghost will always fear the light. He wanted the concubine dragged there in chains to act as his dog, to test for the presence of Ghost.

The first to be tested was Wu Zhiguo, and every possible technique was tried on him. Traps were set, word games played; he was offered rewards, he was encouraged, he was threatened, he was beaten; they played good cop, bad cop on him; lies were told, promises were made. They tried everything they could think of, but nothing worked. He didn't react to anything.

Then they took the concubine to the western building, where their target was Li Ningyu. It was the same all over again – first dulcet words and then threats; they tried talking to her straight and then they tried lying, and then in the end there was violence and the concubine was all but beaten to death right there and then. Again, there was no reaction.

This was driving Colonel Hihara mad. It was hard to say whether Wu Zhiguo or Li Ningyu had shown less of a reaction. The real loser here was Hihara. He'd gone to all this trouble for nothing.

However, the concubine card still hadn't been played out – the woman was still alive. Hihara put it to her straight – 'Don't try my patience!' – but she paid no attention to that either. There was then no point in keeping her alive. He wasn't Prince Genji, to be so distracted by the sight of a beautiful woman that he would disregard all moral propriety. He was an officer in the Imperial Japanese Army. He decided to use the concubine's life as the final card in this game.

The concubine was dragged back from the western building to the eastern one and thrown to the floor in front of Wu Zhiguo. A gun was produced and Hihara asked, 'Shall I kill her or will you?'

'I'll do it.' Wu Zhiguo picked up the gun and pulled the trigger three times, aiming straight at the concubine's head, blowing her brains out.

'Very nicely done,' Hihara said admiringly, picking his way back across the floor, avoiding the globs of bloody flesh and clumps of hair. 'It reminds me of a saying you Chinese have about killing your closest relatives for the sake of your cause.'

Despite what he'd said, Hihara was now even more confused. The way that Wu Zhiguo had shot the woman three times altered the balance of probability: he now thought Li Ningyu was more likely to be Ghost.

So he came up with a new plan, to try and trap Li Ningyu.

He ordered Police Chief Wang to get him some paper and a brush, and then he ordered Wu Zhiguo to write a letter that he himself would dictate. The letter was to be written in blood. The blood was there ready for him, after all; it was flowing noiselessly from the concubine's head, coagulating, filling the room with a nasty rank stench.

Wu Zhiguo happily dipped the brush into the fresh, warm blood and wrote what he was told to in bright red characters. He pressed so hard that the words were visible on the back of the paper. It was a suicide note.

Commander Zhang,

I have killed myself in order to prove that I am no Communist – the Red here is Li Ningyu. Please believe me!

Be kind to my family.

Wu Zhiguo

With the bloody characters still dripping wet, Hihara said to Wu Zhiguo, 'Remember, from now on you're dead.'

'I can't die,' Wu Zhiguo protested. 'I have to see Li Ningyu brought down.'

Hihara smiled coldly. 'Don't celebrate too soon. I can tell you that if Li Ningyu proves not to be Ghost, you're going to suffer a much worse fate than this…' He nodded at the splattered brains of the dead concubine. 'And your family too.'

'I am positive she's Ghost!' Wu Zhiguo shouted.

Hihara glared at him. 'Then I will keep my promises.'

But in the end Hihara did nothing of the kind, because Li Ningyu outplayed him.

5

In the next act, not only did Hihara perform the opening scene himself, but he also involved a great many other people and included various props such as cars and so on in order to build momentum.

He began by escorting Li Ningyu out of the western house, on her own. Together they wandered the wooded slopes of the Tan Estate, apparently aimlessly, chatting about this and that, almost as if they were old friends meeting again after a long absence. Eventually, when they reached a pavilion, Hihara invited her to sit, as if he wanted to continue their conversation.

The Pavilion of Cooling Breezes was set in the lee of the mountains and had been built on a ridge, with high foundations. Not only was it refreshingly airy, with its widely spaced pillars but it also afforded impressive views. Tracts of lush, spring-green forest surrounded them, dotted with the sweeping black-tiled roofs and tiered towers of West Lake's temples and pagodas; they could even make out the bursts of pink plum blossom on the Su Causeway. Much closer in, there was also an excellent view of the entire rear courtyard of the Tan Estate.

Almost as soon as they had sat down, a white ambulance drove up and stopped outside the eastern building to take the concubine's body away. At the same time, Police Chief Wang rounded up the others from the western building – Section Chief Jin Shenghuo, Gu Xiaomeng and Secretary Bai – and drove them away in a green Jeep.

All of this was clearly visible to Colonel Hihara and Li Ningyu up in the Pavilion of Cooling Breezes. He explained to her – and every word was a lie – that it was Chief of Staff Wu Zhiguo's body that was being removed from the premises (not the concubine's), and he also said that Jin, Gu and Bai were going home.

'Why are they going home?' Hihara answered his own question. 'Because we're done here. We know exactly who Ghost is.

'And who is Ghost?' Again Hihara replied to his own question. 'Hmm, let's not get into that right now. First I want to carry out Chief of Staff Wu's dying wishes. Matters pertaining to the dead are so much more urgent than anything to do with the living, wouldn't you agree, Unit Chief Li?' As he said this, he beamed at Li Ningyu.

He wanted her to talk him through how she had revealed the contents of the top-secret telegram to Wu Zhiguo in the first place. 'You must understand,' he said seriously, 'that if you say something different from last time, if there are any mistakes, I will know exactly what to think.'

Li Ningyu thought about it for a while. Then she extracted a handsome mahogany comb from her pocket and began combing her hair. As she did so, she spoke quietly about what had happened: the time, the place, how it started, what happened next, what they said, what she'd thought, how he'd looked… Everything came out perfectly. Although she didn't use quite the same words she'd used last time, she made no mistakes.

'Very good! You've done very well indeed.' Hihara clapped. 'Well done! Of course, as Chief of Staff Wu said, if you can remember all your lies so well, all that proves is that you're a very tricky customer indeed.'

'I've told you the truth.'

'Really?'

'Yes.' Li Ningyu looked straight at Hihara. 'Colonel, do you really imagine that I'm a Communist?'

'I don't imagine, I'm quite sure. Why else would I have let the others go?'

Li Ningyu hesitated briefly. 'Colonel Hihara, why do you—'

Hihara cut her short. 'Stop pretending! The why is right here in front of you!' He produced Wu Zhiguo's blood letter and waved it at her, then put it down for her to read. 'Isn't this evidence enough of your guilt?'

At this point, the drama moved into its second act, but the climax was yet to come.

The blood-red characters against the white paper were a truly shocking sight. No matter how effective combing her hair was for keeping Li Ningyu calm under normal circumstances, it wasn't working now. She sprang to her feet in alarm and stood staring into the distance, as still and rigid as a statue. Hihara was genuinely taken aback. It seemed almost as if she'd lost her mind.

After a while, she appeared to come to a sudden realization, and she shouted in a panicky voice, 'Oh my God, Colonel Hihara, it's a trick! Wu Zhiguo… I think Wu Zhiguo must be Ghost!'

'What rubbish!' Hihara didn't want to hear that. 'Sit down and stop all this play-acting.'

'But… Colonel Hihara…' Li Ningyu shook her head painfully, as if she had a great deal to say and no idea where to start.

'Confess.' Hihara knew exactly what he wanted to say. In fact, he was just repeating what he'd said to Wu Zhiguo the previous evening. 'You Chinese have a saying about how a clever man tailors his actions to the times – if you confess now, you'll have the opportunity to atone for what you've done and you'll be able to start over. You're a clever woman, and as the saying goes, it's never too late for the lost sheep to return to the fold.'

He wasn't threatening her, he was trying to persuade her. Hihara was not a naturally violent man; he preferred to speak softly and behave civilly rather than resort to intimidation. Besides which, his many years as an interpreter had given him a lot of practice at playing with words, so manipulating people into making indiscreet remarks was one of his strong points.

Li Ningyu glared at him and said self-righteously, 'That's

what I want to say too, Colonel: it's never too late for the lost sheep to return to the fold! Go and get Wu Zhiguo's body – don't let them take it away.'

'Why?'

'He's using his own body to take out a message.'

'What? What are you talking about?'

Li Ningyu came over and stood right next to him. 'Did you search the corpse?'

Hihara narrowed his eyes. 'You're saying he's hidden a message on his body?'

'Yes.'

'Thanks for the reminder—' Hihara laughed '—but you're wrong. I can assure you that I searched his body from head to toe, from nostril to anus; no orifice was left unchecked. If it had been you instead, I would have looked inside your private parts and innards – something could be hidden in there, wouldn't you agree?'

Li Ningyu turned her head away in disgust. 'Come back to me when you've searched his body again. Perhaps there's something in his stomach.' She made as if to leave.

'Stop right there!' Hihara moved to block her exit. He waved his hand carelessly. 'We searched everywhere and there's nothing, nothing at all. Ha! Doing something like that would be childish – we're well aware of those kinds of games, so nobody tries to play them any more.' He began circling the inside of the pavilion, moving between the red-lacquered pillars as he talked to Li Ningyu in a slow, measured fashion. 'You're about ready to give up, aren't you? Why would you hold out any longer? The best thing you could do right now is to confess.'

Li Ningyu sat down abruptly on a stone bench. Before

she'd said a word, she was already in tears. 'Colonel Hihara, please believe me, I'm no Communist. If Wu Zhiguo says that I'm Ghost, then it means that he's the one who's been betraying you—'

'I don't believe the living; I can only trust the dead.'

Li Ningyu was silent for a while and then she said, loudly this time, 'Colonel Hihara, even if there turns out to be nothing in Wu Zhiguo's stomach, I'm still sure he was a Red. He killed himself out of fear of being punished, but you're treating it as if he died for a righteous cause – that's an insult to your intelligence! There are lots of examples of Communist agents doing exactly that after they've been arrested.'

Hihara came to a standstill and glared at her. 'Right now it's you who is insulting my intelligence, but you're not going to get away with trying to confuse me like this.'

Li Ningyu held his gaze. 'Then may I ask you to explain, Colonel Hihara, why Wu Zhiguo had to bolster his accusations against me by committing suicide? Couldn't he have used some other means to prove them?'

She paused, but this was merely to marshal her arguments.

'Look at it this way, Colonel Hihara: with Chief of Staff Wu dead, it's actually better for me. There's only one side of the story to tell, because all his evidence died with him. All I have to do is deny it. I can just keep my mouth shut and refuse to admit a thing. Therefore, if I really was Ghost, I'd be quite sure that Wu Zhiguo wasn't dead. But I'm not Ghost, so why does he say I am? There's only one possibility: that he was Ghost himself. He calculated that he wouldn't be able to survive this and if he was going to die anyway, he might as well use his death to trick you. If he succeeded in tricking you to the point where you arrested and killed me, then no doubt he'd be laughing long and hard in the underworld.'

Hihara laughed. 'If you've any other bright ideas, do share them.'

Li Ningyu stared briefly at a patch of forest caught in a shaft of evening sunlight, then carried on. 'I'm sure you must have found some evidence against Wu Zhiguo before you arrested him yesterday evening. But let's not talk about that right now. From my own point of view, if he wasn't dead, if he hadn't killed himself, I would never have considered that he might be Ghost. As I told Secretary Bai, lying about that telegram was just Wu Zhiguo trying to cover his back – I could quite understand why he wouldn't want to admit to that. But now that he's dead, his blood letter does make me think that he must have been Ghost. That's because I know it isn't me, so only Ghost would say that it was.'

Hihara tried to say something, but Li Ningyu didn't give him the chance. 'I can put it this way: if he died in order to prove his innocence, that you could believe. But he isn't just trying to claim that he's innocent, he's also wanting to drag in a scapegoat, he's trying to get me killed, and that means you can't believe a word he says. I'm the only one that can be sure that I'm not Ghost – you don't know that – and so he can trick you. I say that I'm not Ghost, but without any evidence, why should you believe me? Of course you don't. That's exactly what he wants, because now you're suspicious of all of us. He's using your suspicions against us, and it's a gamble, but it doesn't matter if he loses, because he was going to die sooner or later anyway. But if he wins, he's going to win big: he's going to have defeated you and got me killed, and that's great for him.'

She leant back against a pillar, increasingly sure of her argument. 'As to why he's accused me rather than any of the others, it's obvious – it's because what I said about him brought him into all of this. I hope you will do a full investigation, Colonel Hihara, and not let yourself be led astray by that bastard. If he knew I was Ghost, there's no way he'd be dead now – he'd be waiting to see me come to grief, to watch you arrest me and have his hatred of me bear fruit. How could he possibly kill himself when that would allow me to get the last laugh?'

'Have you finished?' Hihara clapped admiringly. 'What a fine speech! Everyone says that you're normally totally silent, but evidently you can be very eloquent when you try.'

Seeing that she was about to interrupt him, he stopped her. 'Now it's my turn to say something.'

He paused and fixed his eyes on hers. 'If I told you that, in fact, Wu Zhiguo is still alive, and, to use your own words, that I've been trying to trick you, what would you say to that?'

Li Ningyu appeared momentarily overwhelmed by this revelation. Her gaze seemed to lose focus and she had to steady herself against a pillar. A breeze whistled through and ruffled her hair. But within seconds she came to her senses again and replied, 'In that case, I take back everything that I've said.'

Hihara inhaled sharply. 'So you don't think he's Ghost?' he shot back, his tone aggressive. 'If it isn't him and it isn't you, then who? Section Chief Jin Shenghuo? Little Miss Gu Xiaomeng?'

'I'd need evidence before I could tell you that,' Li Ningyu replied thoughtfully. 'As I just said, I concluded that Chief of Staff Wu was Ghost because he'd used his suicide against me. But if he hasn't killed himself, my deductions are wrong. I still can't be sure that he isn't guilty, but I also can't say that someone else is. I've said right from the beginning that I'm not going to accuse anyone without concrete evidence.'

Hihara thought about that for a moment, then straightened up and stared down at the courtyard below. 'You've done very well up till now,' he said. 'I like you a lot, you're very intelligent and you can make a good case. But I'm going to have a lot more fun if I can arrest you, because I've always really enjoyed the sense of accomplishment that I get from arresting Communist agents, you know?'

He was telling the truth in this. He could see that there was no point in persisting with this particular role; it was time to bring his little drama to a close. If he could, he would have happily expunged all record of these events, since he had gone to so much trouble and put so many people out, and all to no avail.

Both Wu Zhiguo, locked up in the eastern building, and Police Chief Wang Tianxiang, waiting in the officers' club, realized that something had gone awry between Hihara and Li Ningyu.

After putting Jin Shenghuo, Gu Xiaomeng and Secretary Bai in the Jeep, Police Chief Wang hadn't even taken them as far as the estate's main gate – he simply parked in front of the main building, on the assumption that everything would be over pretty quickly. For a long time nothing happened, and then it was nearly dinnertime, so he allowed everyone to get out of the Jeep and go to the dining hall to wait. They waited and waited, until in the end Wang Tianxiang became so concerned that he put Staff Officer Jiang in charge of the three and went back to the rear courtyard to check for himself.

In the distance he could see first Hihara and then Li Ningyu walking down the slope from the Pavilion of Cooling Breezes, looking completely relaxed and at ease. It was obvious that nothing had happened.

Wu Zhiguo, who was cowering anxiously behind the shutters of the east building and peering out through a crack, was watching them too. When he saw that Li Ningyu was unconcernedly combing her hair, behaving as if she were by herself, the ground began to spin beneath his feet. He felt himself shrivelling up in terror, until he was no bigger than a single strand of hair, about to be snagged by Li Ningyu's comb and yanked out. At any moment he would find himself falling, discarded, lost in space and time.

The sun was setting just at that moment, and rays of golden sunlight bathed her beautiful mahogany comb, making it glitter and shine until you might imagine that Li Ningyu was invested with divine, superhuman powers.

6

In the event, it became apparent that Li Ningyu was not possessed of superhuman powers. At dinner that evening she was laid low, even before the hot dishes were served, by one of the cold starters, which contained only a tiny amount of chilli.

It was a stomach ache.

She was in such pain, she was curled up like a shrimp, contorted in agony, unable to sit up straight. Even if she'd been pretending that her stomach hurt, there was no way she could have faked the huge pearls of sweat beading her forehead.

Gu Xiaomeng demanded that Hihara take her to hospital. 'Even if she is Ghost,' she said, 'you can't just leave her to die.'

'Miss Gu,' Hihara said cheerfully, 'you've got it quite wrong. If she is Ghost, I need her alive more than ever.'

Of course Hihara needed her alive. But as to whether she should go to hospital or not, he left that to Li Ningyu herself to decide. If she insisted on going to hospital, then he would assume this was a self-inflicted illness. She might be claiming it was caused by a chilli, but she could easily have swallowed some kind of poison in order to create an opportunity to make contact with the outside world. And if she asked to be taken to a particular hospital, he could be sure that there would be other Communists working there undercover.

But Li Ningyu not only refused to go to hospital, she even made light of her pain. 'I'm fine,' she said to Hihara and Gu Xiaomeng. 'I've had this problem for ages. I'll take some pills and I'll be okay in a bit.' And indeed, just like anyone with a long-standing health problem, she knew exactly what to take for it: Dr Hu's Stomach Soothers and Hu Patent Stomach Pills. Both of these were produced locally and were widely available; they could be bought at any pharmacy or clinic. She didn't ask Hihara or Wang Tianxiang to lift a finger – she just asked Staff Officer Jiang to go and get them for her, which required nothing more than a short walk to the Gushan road.

Staff Officer Jiang took his motorbike, so he was back very quickly. When he returned, everyone was still eating, but Li Ningyu was resting to one side, waiting for her medication. Gu Xiaomeng went to the kitchen herself to fetch some hot water, and helped Li Ningyu up so she could swallow her pills.

The medication seemed very effective. Not long after she took it, Li Ningyu's forehead, which had been creased in pain, relaxed again, and the sweat mostly disappeared. By the time everyone had finished dinner, not only was she feeling much better, she could also walk. Although she couldn't stride out as normal with her head in the air, she was at least able to walk unaided. Even so, Colonel Hihara wanted Staff Officer Jiang to give her a lift back to the rear courtyard on his motorbike. But she refused.

'I'd better walk back with everyone else,' she said. 'I don't want to give you any more cause for suspicion.'

Hihara laughed. 'Is that why you refused to go to hospital?'

'Yes.'

'So proving your innocence is more important to you than your life?'

'It is.'

'Well then, let's go,' Hihara said with a smile. 'We can walk back together.'

EIGHT

1

A chill wind was blowing in from West Lake, through the all-enveloping darkness, bringing with it a curiously muddy smell. Ghost gazed out of the window in a mood as black as the night. Personal safety didn't matter any more – indeed, that had long been disregarded. What mattered was K's safety and that of the other comrades. It was becoming increasingly obvious that without a direct message from Ghost, the Party would not receive the necessary information. If Ghost couldn't get a message out, then the Gathering of Heroes would be ambushed and K and the others were doomed.

How to get a message out?

As an experienced undercover agent, Ghost was only too aware that in any mission the odds were stacked against a successful outcome. Having Turtle appear at the Tan Estate earlier had been a great boost. Even though in the end they hadn't been able to make contact, at least Turtle knew where Ghost was. Ghost was sure he would come back again tomorrow. It might then be possible to use their knowledge of each other to silently communicate that something was very wrong. Ghost was already fully prepared; what was needed now was for Turtle's steps to turn in the right direction.

2

'So who is it that you're now thinking is Ghost?'

'I don't yet have a definite answer to that.'

'I still think it's Wu Zhiguo. You don't want to be hoodwinked by him, Colonel Hihara...'

Commander Zhang was on the phone to Colonel Hihara, keen to get the latest on the investigation. In his view, there was no question that Chief of Staff Wu Zhiguo was Ghost.

'As I've said, when you review Wu Zhiguo's past in light of... ah... the current situation, it looks most suspicious.' The Commander cleared his throat and went on to reiterate what he had on the ECCC Chief of Staff.

As a young man, Wu Zhiguo had participated in the anti-imperialist May Fourth Movement; he'd then studied at the Whampoa Military Academy before joining the Nationalists and taking part in their Northern Expedition campaign to reunify the country. When the Communist Party split from the Nationalists and Chiang Kai-shek started to arrest and execute Communists, Wu Zhiguo disobeyed orders and deserted both his unit and the Nationalists. For a while he ran a business shipping freight along the Grand Canal, mostly in the Hangzhou–Jiaxing–Huzhou region. But then, not long after the Japanese had established their puppet government under Wang Jingwei in Nanjing, Wu Zhiguo assembled a unit of former soldiers, came to Hangzhou and joined the puppet regime himself, throwing in his lot with Qian Huyi, Commander Zhang's predecessor at the ECCC.

'To tell you the truth, Colonel Hihara,' Commander Zhang said, 'ever since he took charge of the ECCC's insurgent-extermination campaign, pretty much everyone he's arrested or killed has been a Nationalist – there have been very few Communists. That's really very strange, but I didn't take it nearly as seriously as I should have. The situation now suggests that he never actually left the Communist Party and that joining forces with Qian Huyi was a cover. He just wanted to make use of Qian Huyi and the ECCC to get his revenge. He's been using us to kill Nationalists, and what does that mean? He must be a Communist.' Commander Zhang was now quite worked up. 'I should have realized that long ago, but I was completely taken in by his display of loyalty. I have caused great trouble to the Imperial Army through my lack of care and attention.'

After the Commander had hung up, Police Chief Wang provided further corroborative evidence. At the start of the year, Wu Zhiguo had made it his mission to eliminate a small anti-Japanese militia unit active in the Huzhou region. 'They were a top team of Nationalist special agents,' he said. 'Wu Zhiguo could have eliminated them at any time, but he decided that this was the moment. Why? Because Chiang Kai-shek had just massacred thousands of Communist soldiers in the Wannan Incident. It's clear how it all hangs together: Wu Zhiguo targeted the Nationalist agents in revenge.'

It sounded convincing, but Hihara still couldn't quite

make up his mind. Sometimes he wondered at himself: why did he put so much trust in what Wu Zhiguo said and so little in the evidence against him? But if the ECCC's Chief of Staff really was Ghost and had been working secretly in their midst for years, he surely shouldn't have blown his cover so easily. Hihara had seen Ghost's shadow a number of times now, and from the clues he'd picked up, the traces he'd found of Ghost's modus operandi, Wu Zhiguo simply didn't seem to fit the pattern.

'From what we've seen in the last couple of days,' Hihara said to Wang Tianxiang, 'it's obvious that Ghost is no ordinary member of the Communist Party – whoever it is may well be extremely high up. But with the fuss that Wu Zhiguo's been making since he was arrested, he doesn't seem very senior at all.'

'But remember how he looked when he shot the concubine dead,' Wang Tianxiang pointed out. 'That's not the way some entry-level guy behaves.'

'I'm thinking,' Hihara said, 'that a really tough guy like him, who's also supposed to be senior in the organization, ought not to make a simple mistake with his handwriting. You saw the samples he gave us the second time – they were quite good enough to fool people.'

Wang Tianxiang seemed to have already given that plenty of thought. 'But might he not have done that deliberately? First he intentionally falls into the trap and then he gets himself out of it again. His aim from start to finish has been to eliminate Li Ningyu.'

Seeing that this line of argument had got Hihara's attention, he quickly added, 'And I've never believed what he said about the telegram, because Li Ningyu told us about that before any of us got here. At that point nobody knew what had happened yet, so why she would lie?'

Also, he went on to argue, the best way for Ghost to hide their identity was to make someone else a scapegoat. Right up until Wu Zhiguo wrote the letter in blood to accuse Li Ningyu, Li Ningyu herself hadn't made any accusations. Wu Zhiguo, on the other hand, had accused Li Ningyu right from the beginning. Again, making a silly mistake and then using that to get himself off the hook was an excellent plan. If it succeeded, he would find it easy to deceive people into believing him innocent and thus ignoring any later evidence against him.

So what with one thing and another, Police Chief Wang Tianxiang created a Ghost for Colonel Hihara, and that Ghost was Chief of Staff Wu Zhiguo.

'You're really improving, Tianxiang,' Hihara said when he'd finished. 'The way you've thought this through shows that you've been paying attention. You've also explained it well. Logically, it all makes sense, and I accept what you've said. However, I'm not completely convinced, because I also accept what Wu Zhiguo said when he accused Li Ningyu. One: she could quite easily have practised forging other people's handwriting. Two: if she is Ghost, she's going to be on constant alert, so when Commander Zhang suddenly asks her, just after she's passed the message on to her contact, if she's told anyone else about the telegram, what's she going to think? It would be pretty obvious that something must have gone wrong, so we shouldn't be surprised that she decided to bring in a scapegoat. Three: having produced her scapegoat, she has nothing to worry about, because in cases like this, sooner or later someone is going to think of testing everyone's handwriting. Then she can just sit back and enjoy the joke.'

As Hihara looked up at the Police Chief, his mouth twitched in an almost imperceptible smile. 'And there's the problem: you and I both have a great story, but I can't convince you to accept mine and you can't convince me to believe yours. If you're going to persuade me, then you need more evidence, and vice versa.'

There was an unnerving silence. Then Hihara made his decision. 'Therefore, we're not going to try and come to any conclusion right now. We're going to wait and see. We're going to go and find the evidence that we need. I want you to go immediately and search Li Ningyu's office back at ECCC headquarters. If you can find evidence that she has been practising Wu Zhiguo's handwriting, that would be wonderful.'

3

No such luck.

Half an hour later, Wang Tianxiang phoned Colonel Hihara from Li Ningyu's office back at base. He hadn't found a shred of evidence.

Hihara rushed straight over to the western building and had Li Ningyu brought downstairs to the conference room. He came straight to the point. 'Police Chief Wang has just been searching your office. Do you know what he found?'

'I have no idea.'

'Are you scared?'

'No.'

'No, that's not right, you are scared – you were brought here to the Tan Estate without warning, so you didn't have time to destroy the evidence. And Police Chief Wang tells me he found something. A really important secret. Do you know what it was?'

'I haven't a clue. But any secret in my office is going to be one of the Imperial Japanese Army's secrets.'

'Not true. Unless you're trying to tell me that the Imperial Army has been secretly forging Wu Zhiguo's handwriting?'

At this, Li Ningyu broke into a smile for the first time. 'I think Police Chief Wang must have gone to the wrong office.'

Hihara harrumphed, then gave Li Ningyu a thumbs up. 'I'm impressed! You've been doing really well. Should you manage to prove that you're not Ghost, you'll be an asset to the Imperial Army.' His thumb disappeared. 'But right now… I'm sorry, but I don't think you can prove it. I just don't believe your story.'

Li Ningyu sat in silence for a while. Then, quite out of the blue, she said, 'Colonel Hihara, I'd really like to know, is the letter written in Wu Zhiguo's blood that you showed me this afternoon real?'

'What do you think?'

'Well, I hope it is real,' she said, 'because then he's already proved that I am not Ghost.'

'And if it's fake?'

'Then there's something that you need to verify as soon as possible.'

She explained that just now she'd heard Section Chief Jin Shenghuo mention that Secretary Bai had been present when he handed over the top-secret telegram to Commander

Zhang. 'Section Chief Jin said that Secretary Bai read the message as soon as he got it.' Which meant that it was not merely four individuals who knew the contents of the telegram: there was a fifth, and that was Secretary Bai.

'How do you know we haven't been secretly investigating Secretary Bai all along?' Hihara said.

'When you asked him to draft our family letters,' Li Ningyu replied, 'I immediately realized that's what you were doing. You wanted him to write it out too so that you could study his handwriting. But placing him under secret investigation is unlikely to elicit good results.'

It seemed she had a lot to say about this. 'It's clear,' she continued, 'that, however you play this, you're not going to be able to force Ghost into making a move. Any action on Ghost's part would be like a moth flying into a flame, so they're not going to risk it. If they're not going to do anything, it's pointless spying on them. Then again, it's even more pointless if Ghost doesn't even know they're under suspicion, because they'll think they have nothing to worry about and so they'll just stay safe and sound where they are.'

So much for her reasoning. Hihara now urged her to get to the point.

'My point is: if Wu Zhiguo is still alive, then instead of wasting your time trying to trick me, you'd be better off trying to trick a confession out of Secretary Bai. I don't know, Colonel Hihara, whether you've been trying to deceive Section Chief Jin and Gu Xiaomeng the same way you have me—' Li Ningyu paused here, raised an eyebrow, waited for an acknowledgement, received none '—but I do know that Chief of Staff Wu would have been interrogated repeatedly, and eventually tortured. If Ghost really was one of us four, that alone would have forced them into the open long ago.'

Again, Hihara studiously avoided reacting to this.

Li Ningyu carried on. 'Ghost already has one foot in prison – give it another couple of days and the other one will join it. They must know that it's pretty much all over. Even if there's no confession, you'll see it in their face. They'll want to live, they'll be afraid of dying, and when they realize they've reached the end of the road, they're going to be terrified.'

'There are some people who look on death as the end of all their suffering,' Hihara said. 'I imagine you're one of them.'

'I have two young children,' she replied. 'Otherwise, I might well have killed myself over the way you've humiliated me.'

'Bearing in mind those two small children,' Hihara said, 'you really shouldn't hold out any longer. You're provoking not only me but also Commander Zhang. I would highly recommend that you acknowledge the gravity of your situation and confess as soon as possible. Then we can treat this as an isolated offence, and your family won't be involved. Otherwise,' he said with a menacing smile, 'they will all have to suffer the consequences of your actions as well.'

'Colonel Hihara,' Li Ningyu said, 'I suggest that you go and repeat that message to Secretary Bai. If Wu Zhiguo is indeed still alive, you may get some most unexpected results by threatening Secretary Bai.'

When Hihara heard this, he felt as if he'd been stabbed through the heart. But he wasn't going to admit that.

'Didn't you tell me that you wouldn't make any accusations without concrete evidence? Why have you changed your mind now?'

'I'm not accusing him of anything. I'm merely helping you analyse the situation. However, I want to make it clear that my recommendations only apply if Wu Zhiguo is still alive. If he really is dead, then I stick by my original theory: you don't need to waste any more of your time, Colonel Hihara, for he is Ghost, no doubt about it.'

Hihara was cursing inwardly: what do you mean, I don't need to waste any more of my time? You two bastards have already wasted plenty of my time, and now you're trying to drag Secretary Bai into it.

For all his cursing, Hihara was prepared to admit that Li Ningyu might have a point. But he couldn't decide how he felt about her performance. Was he now more sceptical of her story or the other way round? It was infuriating – there was no other word for it.

That evening, Hihara didn't go to the officers' club to find a prostitute. He wasn't feeling very cheerful and he couldn't summon the enthusiasm. Since he was irritable, he didn't sleep very well either, and his sleep was disturbed by dreams. Everything that he'd experienced during the day reappeared in his dreams: the questioning of Turtle, the drunkenness of Gu Xiaomeng, the deafening sound of a gunshot, the corpse of the concubine, Li Ningyu's logical exposition, Wu Zhiguo's letter written in blood. Images drifted in on the breeze and were then carried away into the darkness.

Dreaming is the twin brother of thinking. He was inspired by his dreams; now he knew exactly how he would play his next card.

The next morning, the first thing he did after getting out of bed was to hand Wu Zhiguo's blood letter over to Police Chief Wang. 'Go and tell Secretary Bai,' he instructed him, 'that there's to be a meeting immediately after breakfast. At the meeting he will show everyone this letter. Then he is to talk to them one at a time and see what they have to say.'

Wang Tianxiang wasn't sure what kind of trick his boss was trying to play. He thought it very unlikely that anything would come of it, since Li Ningyu already knew the letter was a fake.

Hihara was more sanguine. 'I never told her that Wu Zhiguo is still alive; it was just her guess.' Having thought some more, he added, 'Besides which, it doesn't matter if she does know it's a fake, because I'm not trying to deceive her this time. I want to see how she responds and whether or not she's mentioned it to anyone else.'

'What does it matter if she has?'

'It matters exactly how she explained it,' Hihara said darkly. 'If she has decided that Wu Zhiguo is actually dead, and that's what she's told the others, then that proves that she was just trying to cause trouble yesterday when she made allegations against Secretary Bai.'

'And if she hasn't said anything?'

'Then we can see how everyone else reacts.' Here Hihara spoke with conviction. 'There may be someone who has suspicions about Li Ningyu but hasn't dared voice them – because they're intangible, perhaps, and if they turn out to be wrong, that person will have made a serious enemy.

How could they possibly work together after that? But once everyone sees this letter, they'll have the confidence to speak up. And if Li Ningyu isn't Ghost, the real Ghost will see that we're focusing on the wrong person, so they'll be delighted. They'll be right there trying to throw oil on the flames.'

Clearly, Hihara was trying to play a complicated game in which he would bring down two birds with one stone.

Equally clearly, Hihara had no idea who to suspect any more – but he was still hoping this might prove to be the darkness before the dawn.

The investigation was now well past its midway point. The suspects had been held at the estate for three full days already, and the Gathering of Heroes was due to take place tomorrow night – less than forty-eight hours away! But still Hihara was without his result. And Heaven seemed now to be piling on the pressure, by sending down a shower of drenching rain.

4

Police Chief Wang Tianxiang ran through the rain to the western building and arrived soaked to the skin. Fortunately, however, the blood letter remained unscathed. He handed it to Secretary Bai.

Secretary Bai had seen the handwriting samples for himself and had thought it obvious that Wu Zhiguo was the guilty party – it had been there in black and white, after all. But on reading the blood letter, he now concluded that Colonel Hihara and Police Chief Wang must have somehow mixed up the samples so that Li Ningyu's writing ended up being confused with Chief of Staff Wu's. Really, it was too bad of them. He felt very sorry for Chief of Staff Wu.

He immediately summoned everyone to a meeting. When they saw the letter written in blood, they were naturally appalled. Section Chief Jin let out a series of shocked wails. He seemed enormously moved by Chief of Staff Wu's heroism and loyalty. His eyes were full of tears, and he glared angrily at Li Ningyu.

Li Ningyu should by now have realized that her head was on the block. She ought to have been frightened by the turn of events, but she seemed amazingly calm. That was not surprising, given that she'd already seen the letter. But Secretary Bai was clearly disgusted by her lack of response, and he made no attempt to conceal this.

Gu Xiaomeng's reaction was quite different. She didn't seem interested in the contents of the letter at all, nor did she show any anger towards Li Ningyu; instead, she focused on the circumstances of Chief of Staff Wu's death.

'So you think he was murdered?' Section Chief Jin asked, his voice hoarse, his bottom lip still quivering.

'Of course,' Gu Xiaomeng muttered dismissively. 'If he didn't commit suicide, then obviously it was murder.'

'So who killed him?' Jin Shenghuo asked.

'God knows.' Gu Xiaomeng pointed at something outside the window, and then in a quiet voice added, 'And so do I.'

'Who?'

'I'll tell you, but not right now.'

Jin Shenghuo wanted to ask more, but Secretary Bai waved him away irritably. 'Section Chief Jin, don't pay any attention to the silly things she says.'

The point of the meeting was to find out whether Li Ningyu had mentioned the letter to anybody and it seemed she hadn't, so proceedings were wrapped up quite swiftly. There was one other thing to say, and that concerned Li Ningyu's sleeping arrangements. She was to be moved out of the room she shared with Gu Xiaomeng and into the large bedroom formerly occupied by Wu Zhiguo. This was what the letter written in blood had bought her, and it was necessary to keep up the deception; they needed the others to see this.

After the meeting, Secretary Bai made Li Ningyu stay behind. With a cold, unpleasant smile, he began the interrogation, following the script that Police Chief Wang had prepared.

'Li Ningyu,' he said, 'I'm sure your feelings right now must be hard to describe. Chief of Staff Wu has informed us that you are the Communist agent. What have you to say for yourself?'

Li Ningyu was silent for a long time. Then she raised her head, glared at Secretary Bai, snapped, 'Go and ask Colonel Hihara,' and walked out, leaving Secretary Bai cursing furiously.

Over in the eastern building, Hihara listened to Secretary Bai swearing and the sound of Li Ningyu's retreating footsteps, and said to Wang Tianxiang, 'She must be on very good terms with Commander Zhang. When she's in the room, your Secretary Bai looks like an absolute clown.'

Next it was the turn of Section Chief Jin Shenghuo. This time he was completely open; there was none of the crying and wailing that he'd produced last time. He was in no doubt that Li Ningyu was Ghost.

Jin Shenghuo: I would never have guessed... Who could have imagined...? I've worked with her for years and it turns out she's a Red!

Secretary Bai: Can you provide any evidence?

Jin Shenghuo: Evidence? Oh, there's plenty of that...

He began disgorging a welter of pointless speculations and baseless suspicions. Listening to him, Hihara quickly concluded that he was kicking Li Ningyu simply because she was down. He joked to Wang Tianxiang, 'I really cannot understand why Commander Zhang has such a fool in charge of the most important section in the entire army. If Section Chief Jin turns out to be Ghost and I have to arrest him, I'm going to get no satisfaction out of that at all – the man is completely useless.'

'He is useless,' Wang Tianxiang said. 'It's an absolute embarrassment. I've seen him running round the base with his wife in pursuit, trying to give him a beating.'

'If that's the best kind of agent the Communist Party can get,' Hihara said, 'they're going to have to spend the rest of their lives hiding in those caves.'

Next it was Gu Xiaomeng's turn. Here, Secretary Bai made a mistake, and their conversation took a most unwelcome turn:

Secretary Bai: Why do you say that Chief of Staff Wu didn't commit suicide?

Gu Xiaomeng: Didn't you hear him screaming?

Secretary Bai: You mean...?

Gu Xiaomeng: He was beaten to death.

Secretary Bai: Surely not.

Gu Xiaomeng: That just shows you don't know anything about our wonderful Police Chief Wang and his men. They are happiest when beating people up. It's normal for them to kill people – the amazing thing would be if you survived.

When Wang Tianxiang heard that, he ground his teeth in fury.

As for the question of whether Li Ningyu was Ghost or not, Gu Xiaomeng had some very odd things to say.

Gu Xiaomeng: I don't know whether she's a Communist or not, but I hope she isn't.

Secretary Bai: And why is that?

Gu Xiaomeng: Because I love her.

Secretary Bai: What do you mean, you love her?

Gu Xiaomeng: That's none of your business.

Secretary Bai: Whether it's my business or not depends on quite how much you love her. If you love her to the point where you're passing top-secret information to the enemy, then it absolutely is my business.

Gu Xiaomeng: You aren't going to be able to interfere, for one, because your own position is pretty damn dicey. What a joke! You still think you're in charge round here!

Secretary Bai: I am in charge here. When I summon you, you come.

Gu Xiaomeng: And when I want to leave, I go.

Secretary Bai: Don't you dare!

Gu Xiaomeng: And why shouldn't I?

As she said this, she got up, ready to walk. Secretary Bai moved to stop her, but she pushed him away.

'Get out of my way! Who do you think you are? You're as much under suspicion for being Ghost as the rest of us.'

Secretary Bai laughed dismissively.

'It really is quite hilarious,' Gu Xiaomeng said. 'You carry on as if you're important, when you're nothing but a clown.'

'I don't care what you say about me,' Secretary Bai said, 'but I demand that you tell me about Li Ningyu.'

'Right now I want to talk about you,' Gu Xiaomeng said. 'I've come to the conclusion that you're much more likely to be Ghost than Li Ningyu is.'

'You lying little bitch!'

'Bastard!'

At the sound of the two of them shouting, the sentries burst in and intervened before they could start hitting each other. Gu Xiaomeng then demanded to see Colonel Hihara. Once he arrived, she made a bald claim, right there in front of Secretary Bai.

'Colonel Hihara, I think Secretary Bai Xiaonian is Ghost.'

5

Gu Xiaomeng wasn't joking.

'Why are we under suspicion?' she asked Hihara rhetorically. 'It's because we knew what was in the telegram. But Secretary Bai knew it too, so why isn't he a suspect as well? In what way is he more important than me?'

'Okay, there's no need to go on about it,' Hihara said. 'He isn't more important than you. You see this…?' He gestured at the walls and told her about the room being bugged and how he'd been listening in on their interviews with Secretary Bai from the other building. 'Didn't Li Ningyu tell you that we've had you all under surveillance?'

Gu Xiaomeng shook her head, clearly confused and shocked.

Hihara carried on. 'Right now, my main concern is how to get Li Ningyu to tell the truth. You've always been so close to her, have you really never noticed anything? Something that didn't strike you at the time but now seems odd, perhaps?'

Gu Xiaomeng did think about it, but all that happened was that she kept shaking her head. 'Either she's covered her tracks too well for me, or... I simply cannot believe that Li Ningyu is Ghost.' She paused and studied her expensively manicured fingernails for a moment. 'I can't help feeling there's something fishy about Wu Zhiguo's death. I don't think he died by his own hand.'

'So how did he die?'

Her theory was that Police Chief Wang had tortured Wu Zhiguo so badly that he died, and then, afraid that Colonel Hihara and Commander Zhang would punish him, he'd come up with this dumb suicide-letter idea. 'Which makes me even more suspicious of Secretary Bai,' she said.

'Because...?'

'Because if Police Chief Wang had to torture Wu Zhiguo so severely that it killed him, it must mean that Wu Zhiguo refused to confess, right to the last. Might he therefore have been innocent? In which case, who set him up? The only person who could have done that is Secretary Bai. He could have messed up the writing samples.'

'How so?'

'By swapping Wu Zhiguo's sample for someone else's.'

'And that someone else was...?'

'Secretary Bai himself.'

'But he didn't give a writing sample.'

'He could have prepared one in advance.' She gave Hihara one of her most winning smiles. 'As I recall, he collected all the samples himself that evening and then handed them over to you. That's right, isn't it?'

'Yes, you are right about that,' Hihara conceded. 'However, the fact is that before he died, Wu Zhiguo admitted to it being his handwriting, so your theory is actually quite wrong.'

Gu Xiaomeng wasn't going to give up that easily. 'If anyone succeeded in secretly practising Chief of Staff Wu's handwriting to the point of achieving a passable forgery, it wasn't Li Ningyu.'

'Why not?'

'Because she's a woman. It's really difficult for a woman to learn to write like a man.'

In the end, Gu Xiaomeng said quite frankly to Colonel Hihara, 'You must have noticed how, whenever Secretary Bai called me in for questioning, I talked all kinds of rubbish. Why was that? Because I don't trust him, and I wasn't going to be helpful. To tell you the truth, if Ghost really is right here in this building, I'm sure it's him. But I don't think Ghost is here with us.'

So where did she think Ghost was?

Colonel Hihara was not expecting that Gu Xiaomeng had now turned her sights on her ECCC boss, Commander Zhang!

Her tone was more aggressive now. 'As the saying goes: you should never drop your guard. Logically, anyone and everyone who knew the contents of that telegram is a suspect. Why is Commander Zhang being excluded? Is it just because he's a commander? People of much higher rank than his have proved to be traitors to the Imperial Japanese Army.'

Hihara was now distinctly uncomfortable; he was cursing inwardly as he got up to walk away. His anger wasn't directed at Gu Xiaomeng but at the facts. After all the trouble he'd gone to, Li Ningyu was still Li Ningyu, and Ghost was still hiding in the shadows. Gu Xiaomeng's comments had rendered Ghost's identity even more of a mystery. Although he felt that he could trust the Commander, logically what she'd said was quite right. It was this that infuriated him. He could no longer ignore how desperately he wanted Li Ningyu to be Ghost. For all that this was merely a suspicion, he had to face up to how unhappy he was, how furious, how abandoned and betrayed he felt when any evidence emerged that served to disprove the accusations made against her.

In truth, Colonel Hihara was very dissatisfied with his own performance with respect to Ghost. He'd set out thinking he'd be able to close down this investigation pretty quickly, but not only had he failed to do that, he was actually in a much worse position than before. It was as if they were right back at the start again, back at the afternoon three days ago when he'd only just arrived and was noting down their names for the first time in his little black book. But this time round he had virtually no cards left to play.

NINE

1

The situation was becoming ever more complex, and Hihara couldn't stop himself from wondering: have I been on the wrong track all along? You can know someone without ever understanding them, he reminded himself. Did that apply to Commander Zhang? For example, on the evening of the handwriting tests, the Commander had arrived apparently by chance and it was he who had then discovered Wu Zhiguo's guilt. And then, yesterday evening, Commander Zhang had phoned up to assert that Wu Zhiguo had to be their man.

After so many days of secret investigations and overt interrogations, the only person he believed to be innocent was Gu Xiaomeng. She was the one person he trusted, but she didn't agree with his analysis. In fact, she would rather accuse Commander Zhang than consider the possibility that Li Ningyu was guilty.

Thinking about it some more, Hihara remembered that Commander Zhang was a noted calligrapher, so if someone had forged Wu Zhiguo's handwriting, then – unfortunate as it was to have to admit this – he would be the obvious candidate. The more he mulled this over, the more uncomfortable Hihara became.

And so, just before lunch, he grabbed Police Chief Wang and together they paid an unannounced visit to Commander Zhang. First they sat and chatted in his office, and then Hihara insisted on going home with the Commander to meet his wife and join them for a family meal. Actually, of course, he wanted to see if he was spending time on regular calligraphy practice.

Given Commander Zhang's traditional education, it was unsurprising that in his library at home there were calligraphy brushes, ink, paper and ink stones. Hanging on the walls were works by various famous calligraphers, and a few of his own pieces that he was proud of, including a pair of couplets:

In the sky there is a constellation of stars,
while on earth men walk with upright steps.

In calligraphy there are hidden dragons,
while in paintings there are crouching tigers.

His calligraphy was most distinguished – the black strokes cut across the paper like swords. It was a style characterized by controlled energy, reminiscent of fifth-century Wei-dynasty stele texts.

In calligraphy there are hidden dragons... That was all too suggestive. Hihara gazed at that couplet until he managed to really worry himself. Of course he hoped that Commander Zhang was innocent, but, equally, the Commander often gave the impression that he was up to something that he didn't want anyone to know about.

After lunch, he rushed straight back to the Tan Estate and went to talk to Wu Zhiguo, which cheered him up a little. Wu Zhiguo was adamant that Commander Zhang was entirely honourable. 'Tomorrow evening, when you raid the Gathering of Heroes, everything will become clear,' he said with certainty. 'You will know for sure that Li Ningyu is Ghost. I swear it. I swear it not only on my life but on the lives of my family.'

Wu Zhiguo had a wife and three children as well as an elderly mother. He was prepared to risk the lives of these five family members – he was putting everything on the line. Would Li Ningyu dare do the same? With that thought in mind, Hihara prepared to cross swords with her again.

2

The rain had passed and the sky was clear, but the grass was still wet and very green. As Hihara came out of the front door of the eastern building, he looked up and saw that Li Ningyu was sitting on the balcony of Wu Zhiguo's old room. She was cross-legged and seemed to be enjoying herself. When he went over there, he discovered that she was painting; she had a very professional-looking easel set up, with paper and brushes that looked as though someone had prepared them just for her.

In fact, they were left over from the time of Qian-the-Dog.

Later, Secretary Bai told Hihara that Qian Huyi's daughter had studied painting and that her equipment had remained in her room (the bedroom now occupied by Jin Shenghuo) even after the whole family was murdered. At lunch, Jin Shenghuo had happened to mention this, whereupon Li Ningyu had immediately requested that he give it to her. She said that she too had studied painting when she was younger and that she'd like to take it up again now, since she was bored and had so much time to kill.

Li Ningyu's painting depicted a mountainside with two trees. 'That's very good,' Hihara told her. 'I can tell that you've studied painting.'

Li Ningyu didn't look up but carried on painting as she spoke. 'This must give you even more reason for suspecting that I forged Wu Zhiguo's handwriting.'

'Why's that?'

She painted a few blades of grass at the foot of her trees. 'Writing and painting both require good brush control, so if I can draw mountains and rivers, it would be easy for me to forge someone's handwriting.'

Hihara laughed. 'And next you're going to tell me that if you were Ghost and you had been writing your secret missives in Chief of Staff Wu's hand, you wouldn't now be revealing to me that you knew how to paint. Am I right? You know, I'm finding you more and more talkative – not at all how you were a day or two ago. What's that all about?'

She put down her brush and looked at him. 'You came to find me. If you think I'm talking too much, then I'll stop.' And with that, she retreated inside and lay down on the bed, where she continued with her painting.

Colonel Hihara followed her. 'Do you have much family?' he asked, lingering in the doorway, blocking her light. She ignored him, so he continued. 'We'll know for sure whether or not you are Ghost tomorrow evening, when we ambush the so-called Gathering of Heroes.' He moved further in, and the sunlight streamed past him. 'But if you confess now, you'll be the only one who gets punished. Otherwise, I'll have your entire family killed, every single one of them, including your two children.'

All Li Ningyu said to that was, 'Tomorrow you're going to find out that I am not Ghost.'

Li Ningyu had a husband and two children, a boy and a girl. Her son was seven and her daughter was five. She had also brought an elderly servant from her family home, someone who'd worked for them for many years and was obviously a devoted retainer. This was all explained to Hihara by Police Chief Wang after he got back to the eastern building.

'Her husband's a newspaper reporter,' Wang Tianxiang told him, 'a very scholarly and refined man to look at, but he's got a dreadful temper – he often beats his wife. One day this spring, he came to her office on the base and hit her till her face was a bloody mess. Something to do with her having fallen in love with another man, apparently. After that, she moved out of their house and slept in her office; later on, a room was found for her on the base, in the quarters for unmarried members of staff.'

'What about her children?'

'Oh, she goes back home to them every lunchtime.' Wang Tianxiang seemed to know an awful lot about her private affairs. 'Her husband works in the north part of Hangzhou, so he can't go home at lunchtime, it's too far. She goes every day to see the children.'

Hihara was about to say something when they both heard

the sound of Secretary Bai's voice challenging someone. It was coming through loud and clear over the microphone, from the western building. He was interrogating Li Ningyu all over again, yet again trying to force her to confess.

Hihara rolled his eyes. 'He's far too stupid to be able to play her.'

Wang Tianxiang cursed at the microphone. 'What does he think he's doing?'

Hihara laughed. 'Acting on your instructions, Police Chief Wang?'

'Why would I ask him to do that? Colonel Hihara, I really don't think it's Li Ningyu. It has to be Wu Zhiguo.'

Hihara stood up and walked over to the window. 'I know you're afraid of what'll happen if Wu Zhiguo is released, but there's no need. You work for me – he wouldn't dare cause you any problems. If you set aside your concerns, you'll see that Wu Zhiguo really doesn't look so guilty after all.'

Hihara thought that if Wu Zhiguo was Ghost, he would rather die than admit it. Fine. However, he would also try and produce a scapegoat, and the best person to fulfil that role for him would be Gu Xiaomeng. Her father being so close to President Wang Jingwei, that would make the Nanjing government look really bad, and it would alienate her father from the puppet regime. The next best choice would be Commander Zhang, and the third best would be Section Chief Jin Shenghuo. Both of them were much more senior than Li Ningyu, who was just a unit chief, after all, so there wasn't much point getting rid of her.

As he stared out of the window, Hihara muttered, 'This afternoon, I tried telling Wu Zhiguo that someone had accused Commander Zhang, but he rejected that in the strongest possible terms. If he were Ghost, he shouldn't have done that; he should either have kept completely silent or thrown his weight behind the accusation.'

Wang Tianxiang now said quietly, 'But if Li Ningyu is Ghost, when she was told that Wu Zhiguo had died in order to prove the truth of his accusations against her, she ought to have confessed. At the very least she would have done it to save her two children.'

'You're right.' Hihara turned and sighed. 'Which is why I can't make up my mind whether to torture her or not.'

'Let's do it,' Wang Tianxiang said. 'There are some people who don't give up until you torture them.'

'But it's so much more fun if you win by outwitting them,' Hihara said. 'So let's try another card.'

3

This card he played in a most odd fashion.

Just before dinnertime, Hihara informed Police Chief Wang that this evening they wouldn't be going to the front courtyard to eat. 'Even a cornered rat will bite you, and we only have twenty-four hours left. It's better to be safe than sorry, so we shouldn't let them leave the building. Turtle still hasn't reappeared, but I imagine he'll be back tonight. If he were able to make contact with Ghost in the dining hall without us noticing, all our hard work will have been for nothing.'

He arranged for the dining hall to send food over.

When they'd finished eating, Hihara demanded that everyone come to the conference room for a meeting. They assembled quite quickly, but Hihara wasn't there. When he finally turned up, he'd brought someone with him.

Who?

Wu Zhiguo.

The dead had come back to life.

Everyone sat there with their eyes like saucers and their mouths hanging open. And that included Police Chief Wang, who had no idea what on earth his boss thought that he was doing.

Of course, Hihara provided them with an explanation. 'Do not be so surprised,' he said rather solemnly. 'Chief of Staff Wu has not died and come back to life. He tried to kill himself but failed. In a moment of suicidal despair, he cut his wrists and used his blood to write the letter. He was determined to die to prove his innocence. However, he made an elementary mistake.' He gave a thin, wry smile.

What the others thought of this explanation was hard to gauge. There was no visible reaction; they continued to study the tabletop and kept their thoughts to themselves.

'It's not so easy to die by cutting your wrists,' Hihara said. 'You need to slash them and then put them in water – warm water, ideally. That way the blood will continue to flow and you'll bleed to death. Chief of Staff Wu cut his wrists and then lay down on his bed. He watched the blood dripping and shut his eyes, imagining that he was going to die. But once he'd shut his eyes, the wounds started to close up. Blood coagulates automatically – I'm sure that's something we've all experienced. If you are not destined to die, your attempts to kill yourself will fail.'

He turned to the Chief of Staff and nodded thoughtfully. 'You're a lucky man, Chief of Staff Wu. Anyone who survives something like that will enjoy good fortune in the future. Your good fortune will be seeing Ghost carried off in chains to face a firing squad.'

Having waxed eloquent on this subject for some time, Hihara informed them that they were also waiting for someone else to arrive.

Who could that be?

Commander Zhang.

'Our investigations here are coming to an end,' Hihara said. 'We have a mere twenty-four hours left. It is my fault that Ghost has still not been unmasked. However, this is a gamble that we were always going to win. Tomorrow night we're going to arrest K and the others, after which it will be impossible for Ghost, whichever one of you that is, to continue hiding from us.' Here he did a slow gaze around the room, lingering on each face as he went. 'I'm going to put it to you straight: when the time comes, I will have every member of your family killed – that's the price you'll pay for having refused to confess. I'm going to set a final time limit for this: midnight tonight. Until then, you'll be given every opportunity to turn yourself in, but after that, to use Commander Zhang's expression, you'll have only yourselves to blame for what happens next.'

At the mention of his name, Commander Zhang appeared. He had arrived under cover of darkness, which served to make the shadows in his face even deeper; he looked depressed and old, and he wore a cruel expression. He circled them slowly, eventually pausing to glare at Wu Zhiguo. It looked as if he was about to say something, but Hihara stepped in. Hihara was worried that the Commander didn't know what was really going on and might therefore get something wrong, so he jumped in to announce that he would now like to invite the Commander to open their meeting. He then proceeded to recount everything that had happened over the last few days.

It really was a comprehensive report, covering every twist so far: Section Chief Jin's baseless accusations of Gu Xiaomeng at the outset and his attacks on Li Ningyu afterwards; Li Ningyu's suspicions of Secretary Bai and her defence against the allegations made in Wu Zhiguo's blood letter; Wu Zhiguo's oath that he and his entire family would die if Li Ningyu turned out to be innocent; Gu Xiaomeng's continued defence of Li Ningyu; his own secret investigations into Secretary Bai, and so on. Everything that had been said in private, the group's secret denunciations, the details of their investigations, it all came out.

No, that's not quite right. Some things were still held back: their surveillance of Gu Xiaomeng's actor friend Mr Jian, Gu Xiaomeng's suspicions of Commander Zhang, and their secret search of the Commander's study – these, Colonel Hihara did not mention. This was quite understandable, because it was dangerous to suspect the Commander, and Gu Xiaomeng needed to be protected, since Hihara was now quite sure she had nothing to do with his case.

With their dirty secrets now out in the open, Gu Xiaomeng was the first to go on the attack. She cursed Section Chief Jin in the most vile terms. Secretary Bai wasn't far behind her. Although he didn't dare direct his anger at Commander Zhang or Colonel Hihara, he was quite happy to focus on Police Chief Wang, saying the most horrible things he could think of, threatening him at the top of his voice.

Chief of Staff Wu had had enough of Li Ningyu a long

time ago, and so he happily set about yelling at her. To begin with, she stayed calm, kept her temper well under control, but then something he said seemed to get to her and, exactly as before, she turned on him. This time it wasn't wine that she hurled but the comb she always carried with her. It went flying through the air like a dart. Perhaps because he was already badly injured, Wu Zhiguo wasn't fast enough to dodge it; the teeth hit his jaw, which started to bleed. He jumped up and rushed at her; he wanted to thump her, but to his surprise, Gu Xiaomeng picked up a stool to ward him off, heroically interposing herself between them.

'If it had been the Commander or Colonel Hihara saying Li Ningyu was Ghost, I wouldn't have interfered,' she said. 'But if a big guy like you thinks you're going to get away with hitting a woman right in front of me, you can think again!'

There was more to come. The grand finale was performed by Secretary Bai and Police Chief Wang Tianxiang. For props they used guns – real guns! The two of them had begun by quarrelling loudly, hurling abuse at each other, spittle flying in all directions, but eventually they reached for their weapons. Safety catches were released, and it needed only a finger to twitch and the pair of them could have ended up dead. It was all most odd.

When everyone had been screaming and shouting at each other, the Commander and Hihara had just sat and watched, but now that there was a real chance someone might die, they both leapt into action, each one hauling their own man off to one side for a talking-to.

This was no meeting; this was yet another of Hihara's nasty traps. Under the guise of recounting to Commander

Zhang everything that had happened, he had intentionally stirred up trouble between all of them. He wanted them to turn on each other, attack each other, reveal the most unpleasant aspects of their personalities. He also wanted to include Commander Zhang in his investigations, which was why he'd asked him to come along tonight. He was keeping his eyes open and listening carefully, hoping to spot some new clue as they fought with one another.

Besides which, it was a good way to pass the time.

4

It was very late.

One after the other, the lights in the rear courtyard went out, until the only lamps still shining were the ones in the conference room in the western building.

Suddenly, there was the sound of gunfire.

The sharp crackle of shots was interspersed with screaming and the noise of fighting and running footsteps… The people in the conference room had no time to react before two masked men burst through the window, shouting, 'Don't move! Put your hands in the air!'

Who could have imagined that the Red Army would risk everything to try and rescue Ghost?

Police Chief Wang thought about trying to reach for his gun, but then another two masked men came crashing through the door. He put his hands in the air obediently.

Everyone else did likewise. They were staring down the barrel of a black gun, and their lives were on the line.

'Ghost, come with us!'

'Let's get out of here! Tiger sent us to rescue you.'

Hihara seemed determined to find out who Ghost was before he was shot. As he raised his hands, he glanced round him to see who it would turn out to be. Most unexpectedly, everyone put their hands up as commanded – some raised them high and some kept them low, some held them up straight and some held them at an angle, but every single person obeyed. Hihara did notice, however, that only Li Ningyu seemed to be taking the whole thing as calmly as Police Chief Wang. She looked as if it had nothing to do with her, while everyone else looked terrified. Secretary Bai was so scared, he started drooling; it was really quite shameful.

'Ghost, you need to come with us. If you delay any longer it'll be too late!'

'Come away now! Enemy reinforcements will arrive at any moment.'

'Don't waste this opportunity – you can't delay any longer!'

But nobody stepped forward to join them.

Hihara now happened to notice that one of the masked men was wearing the special-issue steel-capped leather boots used only by the officers and men serving at Imperial Army headquarters. Which meant it was entirely possible that Ghost had seen through his little scheme. He was immediately overcome with embarrassment and rage. Before he'd even put his hands down, he was cursing.

'Bugger off! All of you, get the hell out of here!'

He was shutting the stable door after the horse had bolted.

He'd intended this to be the final show of the evening, and he'd taken a lot of care over it; it was the reason he'd held such a long meeting beforehand. Once it had got late, the 'Red Army' could risk appearing, and Ghost was supposed to blow his or her cover by trying to leave with them. But Ghost was not misnamed: he or she remained in the shadows, too experienced and intelligent to be fooled like this. They were all wearing regular-issue boots, they were carrying standard army-issue guns – how could anyone mistake them for Ghost's comrades? Ghost's comrades would be drawn from all over the country, they'd have weapons picked up here and there, and they'd speak with both southern and northern accents – how could they possibly all be identically kitted out?

Hihara had miscalculated yet again. Not only that, had he not also embarrassed everyone?

As for Commander Zhang, he couldn't remember when he'd last been so humiliated. He'd had to raise a pair of trembling hands in front of his own subordinates! Hihara had organized all this without saying a word to him. What on earth was going on? He was furious.

'Colonel, what do you think you're doing?'

'Do you need to ask?' Hihara shot back angrily. 'I was trying to lure the snake out into the open – to dig Ghost out of the woodwork. Is our little spectre not proving very hard to trick? But if you have a better idea, please don't hesitate to speak out!'

Seeing how livid he was, the Commander tried to mollify him. 'If I were you, I'd just wait until we've done the raid. By this time tomorrow, it's going to be obvious who K and Tiger and Ghost are.'

Hihara strode over to Li Ningyu and stood right in front of her. 'I think it's obvious now. What do you think, Li

Ningyu? You were totally calm just now. Can you tell me why that was?'

Li Ningyu didn't bat an eyelid. 'I can,' she said quietly. 'It's because being forced to live in such humiliating conditions, being suspected of being a Communist agent for no good reason and being continually tricked and lied to really is worse than death.'

Hihara chuckled. 'The fact is, Li Ningyu, I know you're Ghost.'

'In which case, why make so much fuss about it? Just arrest me.'

'I need evidence,' Hihara said. 'Of course, I could arrest you without any evidence, but I don't want to do that. I would rather play with you.' He clasped his hands behind his back, relishing the moment. 'Have you ever seen a cat playing with a mouse? It never eats the mouse immediately. No, it lets it go and then it catches it again; it catches it and lets it go. That's so much more fun than just eating it straight away. Right now I am playing with you because I want to see you caught in the traps that I've set. That way, you'll be furious with yourself and I will enjoy the whole thing all the more. Do you understand?'

Li Ningyu's scalp began to prickle and a red mist descended. Anger was forcing its way out; it was burning, it was exploding…

She lost control.

She darted forward and threw Hihara to the ground. Her hands gripped him tightly around the neck, throttling him. 'I am not Ghost!' she screamed. 'I am not Ghost! What gives you the right to say that I am? I've had enough of being tormented like this – I'm going to kill you!'

She'd gone completely mad.

Gu Xiaomeng and Secretary Bai tried to drag her off but couldn't. She'd thrown herself on top of Hihara and was squeezing his neck with hands that were like steel manacles. Trying to tug at her was making not the slightest difference. In the end it was Police Chief Wang who dealt with it. He quickly picked up a chair and smashed it down as hard as he could across Li Ningyu's back. She collapsed onto the ground.

Although Hihara was a small man and had quite a high-pitched voice, he'd practised martial arts since he was a child and was very good at self-defence. The whole thing had happened too suddenly; he'd had no time to prepare, and then she'd grabbed him by the throat, which severely limited his ability to counter-attack. Once Li Ningyu let go of him, he was able to breathe again. Then, with an elegant, fluid leap, he was back on his feet and standing firm.

Li Ningyu was lying on the floor and still hadn't fully regained consciousness. Hihara walked over, kicked her and ordered her to stand up. She staggered to her feet, and the moment she was upright, Hihara punched her full in the face. It was a fast, heavy punch, with a great deal of force behind it, and Li Ningyu immediately crumpled in a bloody heap.

'Get up!'

'Get up, I tell you!'

'If you've got the guts, get up again.'

Li Ningyu crawled back to her feet and Hihara punched her again. This time it was a left hook, then came a right uppercut. He hit her straight on, and he hit her at an angle – over and over again. He seemed determined to use her as a punchbag while he showed off his technique. He beat Li

Ningyu until her head was ringing, there was blood pouring down her face and she no longer had the strength even to drag herself to her feet. Since she could no longer move, Hihara ordered Wang Tianxiang to hold her up so he could hit her some more.

In the end she was beaten to such a pulp that she became like a rag in Wang Tianxiang's arms and he could no longer hold her up. Now even Commander Zhang was appalled, and he begged Hihara to stop, which he did.

By this time, Li Ningyu's face was appallingly swollen, and she couldn't really speak properly, but she tried nevertheless, demanding that Hihara hit her again.

'Hit me... Beat me to death... If you don't kill me, I'm going to take you to a military tribunal... How can you accuse me without any evidence? You're trying to torture me into making a confession... You'll pay for this in court... All of you are my witnesses.'

Hihara smiled coldly. 'You're going to take me to court? What court? A military tribunal? Who the hell do you think you are that you imagine you can take me to court! I don't care if you're Ghost or not, I can beat you to death as I would a dog. Nobody will care in the slightest.'

When Li Ningyu heard him say that, it seemed to cause her far more pain than his punches had. Her eyes filled with tears and she kept repeating to herself, 'I am nothing but a dog... I am nothing but a dog...' It was as if nobody else were present, and she looked completely numb.

Then, as if it were all more than she could possibly bear, the wooden repetition became a scream of agony and a flood of tears. 'If I'm a dog, then nobody cares whether I live or die. If I'm a dog, then let me die right now.'

As she said that, she wobbled to her feet and began smashing her head against the wall.

Everyone else in the room froze in horror.

5

Li Ningyu smashed her head repeatedly against the wall, but she didn't die. She didn't even have the energy to stand upright, so how could she kill herself that way?

Realizing this, she crawled over to Hihara and grabbed him by the legs. She spat a mouthful of blood at him. 'You animal! If tomorrow serves to prove… that I am not Ghost… you'll go to hell for this!'

Hihara shook himself free and walked off.

Li Ningyu now crawled towards the Commander, pleading her cause. 'Commander Zhang, I am not Ghost… Commander Zhang, I am not Ghost…'

Commander Zhang couldn't bear to watch any more. He gestured to Secretary Bai standing next to him and then walked off in the wake of Colonel Hihara. Even when he was outside the room, he could hear Li Ningyu screaming, 'Commander Zhang, I am not Ghost!'

Li Ningyu wasn't dead, but she wasn't far off it. There was a horrible open wound on her forehead, her nose had been broken, her teeth had been knocked out and she was bleeding from everywhere.

She had been their colleague for a long time. Even if she was Ghost, they weren't going to just stand by and watch her die. Besides which, from everything they'd seen, it didn't seem possible that she was Ghost. So everyone got busy: while someone went to the officers' club to call for a nurse, the others did basic first-aid on her, bandaging her wounds to staunch the flow of blood at least temporarily, and then helped her upstairs.

A nurse arrived quite soon, and Section Chief Jin and Secretary Bai used this as an excuse to leave. Only Gu Xiaomeng stayed behind to help the nurse bandage Li properly.

When the nurse had gone, Gu Xiaomeng got some water and washed the blood off Li Ningyu. Then she sat with her for a long time. Of the group, they were by far the closest. Despite the terrible ordeal they'd both been through, the two of them had never turned on each other.

Eventually, Gu Xiaomeng got up to leave. As Li Ningyu struggled to sit up, she thanked her. 'You are the only true friend I have,' she said. 'Even if I die, I will never forget you.'

The Tan Estate was pitch black and silent as the grave. Li Ningyu lay on the bed listening to the wind rustling the leaves of the trees outside the window. She couldn't sleep, and it seemed as though she wasn't even trying to rest – she just lay quietly on the bed with her eyes wide open, unblinking, shining, perhaps afraid that if she closed them she would never open them again. It was as if she were using her final sight of this world to pierce the layers of darkness.

The darkness gradually faded.

The sky slowly grew light.

Today was the last day for all of them. It was the last day

for Ghost and it was the last day for everyone else too. If Ghost wasn't exposed, the rest of the group would suffer the consequences of whatever secret instructions General Matsui had enclosed in his envelope for Colonel Hihara.

Having realized that he too had been under suspicion all this time, Secretary Bai hadn't slept at all well. He'd had one nightmare after another, and the sounds around him had seemed to slip easily in and out of his dreams: in one ear and out of the other. Just before dawn, he heard a sudden violent thud – brief, heavy – as if something weighty had fallen to the floor. In his semi-conscious state he thought something dreadful must have happened, and he forced himself to wake up.

He was awake for a few minutes before he realized that what he could hear was the muffled sound of Li Ningyu moaning in agony. He thought it only too likely that the Colonel was taking out his anger on her again. He relaxed and drifted back to sleep.

When he was woken again, in the early morning, by the warble of birdsong, the first thing he called to mind was the horrible sound of Li Ningyu in pain. He was now even more convinced that Hihara must have been beating her up again overnight.

He immediately went to find her.

The door to her room was ajar, and there was something about this that made him expect the worst. He didn't dare push it fully open straight away.

'Li Ningyu... Li Ningyu...'

He called her name twice, and when there was no response he gently opened the door and put his head in. The bed was rumpled, but she wasn't in it.

Taking two steps into the room, he saw her lying motionless on the floor, like someone who'd been beaten so badly they couldn't even crawl away, no matter how much they wanted to.

He called her name again, and stepped forward, intending to try and lift her back onto the bed, but then he stopped in horror. She was dead, and it looked like it had been a truly terrible death.

'There was blood all over her – her eyes, her mouth, her nose, her ears. Black blood. All over her face.' When Secretary Bai told Hihara what he'd seen, he seemed deeply traumatized.

'Blood trickling from every orifice?' Hihara replied. 'It sounds as though she took poison.'

6

Hihara was absolutely right: Li Ningyu had taken poison. Her suicide note explained that quite clearly.

She left three suicide notes: one addressed to Commander Zhang, one for Hihara, and one for her estranged husband. The notes were written on three sheets of paper torn from a notebook, and they ran as follows:

To the honourable Commander Zhang,

One year ago, when I accepted the heavy responsibilities that come with being Chief of the Decryption Unit, my superiors gave me a cyanide pill. I understood that if ever any of the secrets in my possession were threatened, it would be my duty to swallow that pill without hesitation. Today I have swallowed my pill, not because those secrets are under threat but because my loyalty to the Imperial Japanese Army and to you has come under suspicion.

Hihara has accused me – violently – of being a Communist. He treats me as a fly to be swatted or a dog to be beaten. This has been deeply painful.

This is the only way I can show my loyalty to the country. You know me better than anyone. I have been more loyal to you than anyone, and in this desperate situation, I am ready to die for you.

Any government official knows that danger lurks around every corner. You and I are both aware of the terrible things people can do. Hihara is blinded by his dreadful suspicions of me, and he is going to make an appalling mistake. Perhaps my death will expose his error, allowing him to distinguish between the truth and the lies. If I can achieve this by my death, then I have nothing to regret.

But this whole situation has come about because I've been wrongfully accused. I am being forced to commit suicide, and I am angry that I must die this way. I can only hope that you, Commander Zhang, will clear my name.

Your loyal subordinate,

Li Ningyu

Hibara,

You have treated me like a dog, and I am sure that you will not regret my death. However, even a cornered rat can bite, and the fact remains that I am neither a dog nor a rat but a lieutenant in the Imperial Japanese Army. I am not someone that you can just trample on when you feel like it.

You have forced me to commit suicide. I will not rest in peace. If I cannot get you in this life, I will get you in the next.

Lieutenant Li Ningyu

To my husband Liangming,

I hope you can forgive me for having fallen in love with another man, and for dying without saying goodbye.

I am dying of an infectious disease contracted while carrying out this mission. I have no regrets about dying in the performance of my official duties, but when I think about how young the children are, it's unbearable. I have painted them a picture. I hope you will bring them up to be strong and talented young people and that they will enjoy blessings and good fortune throughout their lives.

I will watch over you from Paradise.

Ning

Hihara was the first to see her suicide notes. He was on the scene immediately, prowling around, poking through her things. He read all three notes, not just the one addressed to him. After he'd read his, he did indeed feel as she'd predicted: there was nothing to regret about the death of a dog. How dare she threaten him! He ripped it to pieces. The other two notes he refolded, because it was important that he hand them over to the people for whom they were intended.

Next, he and Police Chief Wang collected all of Li Ningyu's possessions. These amounted to an English-style watch, a notebook issued by her work unit, a steel fountain pen with a white cap, a broken comb (missing three teeth), a leather wallet (containing the equivalent of half a month's salary), a hair clip, a tube of lip balm, a bunch of keys, a teacup, half a box of pills, a headscarf, a set of underwear and an ink painting.

The painting was now finished, and it depicted two trees standing strong and straight next to each other. Beneath them grew lush grass, and written to one side was the message:

Niu'er and Xiaoyu,

Mummy hopes that you will grow up to be like great trees and not like short grass.

She had obviously painted it for her children.

The painting was very simple; she'd done it all in black ink, without a speck of colour. But Hihara was worried there might be words concealed within the brushwork, so he examined it again and again: straight on, from behind, upside down, held up to the light, and through a magnifying glass.

Every item that she'd owned was carefully checked by the two men, piece by piece, including the painting, and only when all her things had been cleared were they put to one side to be returned to her family. The one exception was her notebook; she'd already filled about half of it, so it would take at least an hour to read from start to finish, and Hihara couldn't be bothered to look at it yet.

He next demanded that Police Chief Wang search Li Ningyu's corpse.

'Why?' Wang Tianxiang said crossly. 'You can't possibly still suspect her!'

Even so, the two of them then searched the corpse from head to toe, inside and out. They searched her hair, her nostrils, the gaps between her teeth, her ears, and then moved on to her anus and her vagina. Everything that she had worn or could have worn was searched as well: clothes, hats and shoes. In short, they checked everywhere that could hold a scrap of paper, everywhere that a message could be written. They searched and searched: first Hihara and then Wang Tianxiang, from the left and then from the right, upwards and then downwards, and then they started again from the other side. Nothing. There was nothing on her body. There was nothing in any of her things.

There was no message.

No secret message anywhere.

This was what Hihara had expected. He remembered how insistent Li Ningyu had been that he should search the corpse of Wu Zhiguo. If she was Ghost, she wouldn't have tried the same thing. Besides which, Hihara had to now admit that since yesterday night, when Li Ningyu had grabbed him by the throat, he'd decided that she couldn't possibly be Ghost. Such desperation, such rage, such hopelessness… It all went to prove that she wasn't guilty.

When she'd started smashing her head against the wall, Hihara had started to feel sorry for her. Or to put it another way, when Li Ningyu summoned all her strength to try and kill herself, Hihara finally believed she was innocent. The reason he'd just searched the corpse had more to do with professionalism than anything else; that and a strong conviction that it was better to be safe than sorry.

Had the head-smashing been a ploy to make him change his mind? If so, she'd achieved her objective. Why then had she gone through with the poisoning? You didn't need to do this, Li Ningyu, he found himself thinking. However, in the final analysis, he came back to his original starting point: there was nothing to regret about the death of a dog.

'She's dead. That's the price she paid for her own stupidity.' He was flicking through Li Ningyu's notebook and trying to cheer up Wang Tianxiang, who was still looking very upset. 'Do you know why she wanted to die?'

'To prove to you that she was innocent?' Wang Tianxiang's answer wasn't as naive as it sounded.

'No. She was afraid of what was coming next – she didn't want to pay for what she'd done. And of course I would have made her pay for attacking me like that. Really, what did she think she was doing? By dying like that, she's put an end to it all. It's over.'

Wang Tianxiang gestured at her corpse. 'What are we going to do about that?'

'You'd better get in touch with Commander Zhang and ask him to send some people to deal with it as soon as possible. It's nothing to do with us, after all.' He glanced at the body, taking in the bloody face, the wounds – he could hardly bear to look at it. 'And have someone tidy her up a bit and put her in a new uniform.'

By the time Commander Zhang arrived, Li Ningyu had been put into a brand-new uniform and post-mortem make-up had been carefully applied. This made her look rather proud, and she wore a slight smile, suggesting that she had passed away peacefully and without any regrets.

Despite all their efforts, however, when the Commander finished reading her suicide note, there were tears in his eyes, his voice sounded choked and he looked both angry and upset. He rushed forward and took hold of the dead woman's icy hand, bewailing her tragic demise, praising her loyalty, expressing the profoundest sorrow, speaking without the slightest restraint.

Hihara, who was standing to one side, felt more than a little awkward. 'You're surely not planning to treat her like a fallen hero?' he said.

Commander Zhang shot him a furious glance. 'So you think I ought to treat her like a Communist agent?' he asked, his voice arctic.

'Not necessarily.' Hihara smiled. 'But to honour her as a hero would be inappropriate in the circumstances.'

'Then how should I respond? Please explain, Colonel Hihara.'

'In her letter to her husband, didn't she say that she was dying of an infectious disease?'

Commander Zhang looked at the body with its broken nose and swollen face. 'She really doesn't look like it was a disease that killed her.'

Hihara couldn't be bothered to argue any more, so he turned away and said lightly, 'Do what you like! Whatever you decide is fine by me, but you cannot treat this woman as a fallen hero.' He was particularly concerned about this, because if she was deemed to have died a hero, his position might then become very perilous indeed.

He invited the Commander to join him downstairs in the conference room, but the Commander seemed quite unappreciative of his hospitality, saying rather pointedly, 'I'd prefer to stay up here with her for a bit,' and then sitting down next to the bed on which Li Ningyu had been laid out.

The hearse arrived just before noon, and once the corpse had been taken off the premises, it was time for lunch. Hihara asked Commander Zhang to join him, but the latter politely refused.

'There's no need for all that,' the Commander said. 'And seeing as Ghost is still out there somewhere, you really don't have time to have lunch with me. You'll need to get yourself into the city by early afternoon – you have a vital operation to organize for this evening, after all.'

Hihara cursed him silently. Who the hell did he think he was? How dare the Commander show such contempt

– what a bastard! The silent cursing hadn't made him feel any better, so he continued the cursing out loud as the car disappeared into the distance. 'One of these days I'll get you for this! How dare you treat me like this, when you're nothing but a piece of scum yourself!'

After lunch, Hihara and Police Chief Wang headed straight for where Wu Zhiguo was locked up. When Hihara thought about how he'd had cast-iron proof of Wu Zhiguo's guilt only to be led astray by the man's arguments and denials, he hated himself, but he hated Wu Zhiguo even more. He'd absolutely exhausted himself over this case. Now that all had been revealed, it was time for that bastard Wu Zhiguo to take the consequences. He was in for another round of terrible beatings.

Hihara also continued to stew over how Commander Zhang had disrespected him. He became even more enraged. When he walked into Wu Zhiguo's room, he didn't say a word. He just grabbed a whip and beat the Chief of Staff over and over again.

When finally his anger was spent, he started to interrogate him. It suited his mood much better to hit first and ask questions later. A way of working off his anger. He didn't want him to confess too quickly, after all. Now that Li Ningyu was dead, which effectively made her a witness to Wu Zhiguo's crimes, he was bound to confess. And once he'd confessed, Hihara would no longer have the chance to take out his rage on him.

What he could not have anticipated was that, even when confronted with all the evidence against him, Wu Zhiguo would refuse to confess.

They tortured him and he wouldn't confess.

They tortured him some more, and still he wouldn't confess. He died protesting his innocence.

This absolutely amazed Hihara: who would have imagined that a traitor like that could be so tough?

Chief of Staff Wu Zhiguo was beaten to death. This proved the truth of what Gu Xiaomeng had said, that Police Chief Wang and his men enjoyed beating people to death. It was normal for them.

7

Wu Zhiguo had refused to admit his guilt even in the face of death. This made Hihara lose confidence in himself. He worried that Ghost might still be in the land of the living, might still be in the western building. He was completely confused; in fact, Hihara felt that he would soon be driven mad by the whole thing. He now had two corpses on his hands, and Ghost had still not been conclusively identified. He felt half-dead himself – empty, black and broken.

Hihara would have liked to rip the hearts out of everyone around him, to find out who Ghost actually was, but he didn't have time for that right now because the car that would take him into the city was already waiting outside. Before he left, he ordered the guards to lock the western building and to prevent anyone from entering. They were to await his return. He needed to go into Hangzhou right now to organize the arrests that would be carried out that evening at the Agate Belvedere Inn. That was the point of the last few days, after all. The whole frustrating, confusing mess had been leading up to this moment. He would arrest K,

Tiger and the rest of that so-called Gathering of Heroes, and he would deal the Communist resistance a serious blow. And then he would discover who Ghost was.

The Agate Belvedere Inn was located on the slopes of Mount Fenghuang, beyond the suburbs of Hangzhou. It was a remote and very quiet spot, set amid the most beautiful landscape.

The inn was popular with writers and artists, who congregated there of an evening to drink and recite poetry, to gamble and fool around with whores, to discuss current affairs and hold debates. It was a place where people felt relaxed and at ease. The lights usually blazed bright and the sound of singing was often heard on the breeze.

That evening, however, all Hihara found was a dark and silent building. In the blackness of the mountainside, it seemed a mysterious and terrifying place. It was as if the inn had only just emerged from the gloom, as if nothing had started yet.

In fact, it was all over.

Colonel Hihara ordered his men to light all the lamps. The vast building began to take shape in the flickering light. The cavernous rooms glowed. In one corner stood a polished mahogany bar, its rows of bottles and cabinets of glasses glimmering; in another, a cosy arrangement of low tables, plump silk cushions and elegant scroll paintings. But all was silent. The moon continued its cloudy rise above this most beautiful mountain scene, but there wasn't a soul to be seen.

Hihara's men searched and searched but found nothing. There was nobody there; the entire place was empty.

Hihara didn't arrest anyone: not K, not Tiger, not Ghost. There was no sign of any of them, not a trace.

What on earth was going on?

He gazed out into the night, at the dark silhouettes of the encircling mountains. His knees began to quiver as realization dawned and blind panic set in. He had made a terrible mistake.

TEN

1

This final chapter is a kind of afterword. There are some important loose ends that still need to be cleared up, not least the identity of Ghost. Also, how did Ghost's message to the Gathering of Heroes get out? All of this has just been left hanging, unresolved.

I will explain, trust me.

However, first I want to say something about the story so far. How did I learn about all of this? Is it true?

To tell you the truth, most of my earlier novels are works of pure fiction. Kafka dreamt his plots, Borges was inspired by reading philosophy – there seem to be many different approaches. What I do is collect old maps, guidebooks and local histories and then imagine what it must have been like in a particular place at a particular time. At least, that's how I used to write my novels.

Because of that, I assumed that nobody could possibly see my books as anything other than works of fiction and that therefore I couldn't be held to account by anyone. The strange thing is that in recent years some of my better-known novels have been taken as fact, and people have contacted me in various ways, wanting to point out inaccuracies. When *In the Dark* was made into a television series (and I'm told it was watched by several hundred million people), there were even more people who wanted to discuss its rights and wrongs, and so I ended up having to go into hiding for quite a while. There were too many people trying to find out where I was; it was impossible to live a normal life.

Among their number was a very powerful general, as well as several individuals who had worked for or were currently working for organizations not dissimilar to the Unit 701 where my characters Abing, Huang Yiyi and Qian Zhijiang were employed. Some of them came on their own behalf or on behalf of their families; others were there to represent their work unit or organization; some had come to say thank you, others to complain. It didn't matter what had brought them, I still needed to make time to see them, to offer explanations and answer questions. Mostly, I was ending up repeating the same things over and over again, until I felt as if I were caught in an echo chamber. I felt a certain kinship with poor Sister Xianglin of Lu Xun's famous short story 'The New Year's Sacrifice'.

There was one person, though, who came not to thank me nor to complain but to tell me a story of his own. He came from the city of Hangzhou in Zhejiang province, his name was Pan Xiangxin, and he was a recently retired professor of chemistry. He told me that he'd read pretty much everything I'd ever written, that he'd watched the films and television series based on my work, and that he thought I was very good at constructing a story.

'However,' he said, 'real life is the very best storyteller.'

'Of course,' I replied. 'All kinds of things happen in real life.'

'I have a story for you,' he said, 'which happened to my father. It is absolutely true.' He asked me if I was interested in hearing it.

'I'm not interested in true stories,' I said. 'My novels are fiction. I like fiction.'

'Why not hear me out anyway,' he said. 'You might be interested.'

What he told me is the story that you have just read.

This story was handed to me on a plate; I didn't have to do a thing. But, hey, it's a great story.

I have to admit that compared with the fictional writings I produced in the past, the story that Professor Pan told me was more complicated, more bizarre and more perfect in its own way. I found it fascinating. Afterwards, I came to believe that the professor had told me the story for a very specific reason: he wanted me to reshape his father's image and experiences. And he certainly achieved that.

In order to get the full story, I visited Hangzhou three times in the days that followed, where I met face to face with Professor Pan's father and four other witnesses to the events concerned. They were all extremely elderly. Thank God they'd managed to survive that long and that they still remembered what had happened more than half a century earlier. In this case, the past had not been blown away on the wind. What surprised me, though, was that the story the five of them had to tell was amazingly similar, even though they were all interviewed at different times and in different places. It was an almost identical version of events in each case. So I was confident that it had to be true.

As you will have grasped, Mr Pan senior (Professor Pan's father) was able to clear up the remaining secrets; he was an important witness to much of what occurred. In this story, old Mr Pan was an agent in the Communist underground. His code name was Heaven and he was charged with maintaining wireless communication between the underground in Hangzhou and the Communist military. Radio waves travel through the sky, which is presumably how he got his code name. He was also responsible for transmitting all intelligence that came from Ghost.

So who was Ghost?

'It was Li Ningyu!' Mr Pan senior said.

Mr Pan senior was the Liangming that Li Ningyu mentioned in one of her suicide notes: her 'estranged husband'. 'But that was just our cover,' Mr Pan explained to me. 'We were actually brother and sister – comrades too, of course – and we pretended to be married to facilitate our work.'

2

In the earlier part of my story, when Li Ningyu herself said that her older brother had been murdered by Chiang Kai-shek's Nationalists, she was talking about Mr Pan senior. As a young man he'd been a Communist agent infiltrated into the circle around Generalissimo Chiang Kai-shek, but then his cover had been blown and he'd been condemned to death. He was lucky: the man charged with shooting him dead was one of his own comrades, and he was able to fake the execution. Mr Pan senior survived. After that he changed his name, went undercover, and moved around a lot.

When the puppet government headed by Wang Jingwei was established, the Communist Party sent Mr Pan senior to Hangzhou, to join his sister, Li Ningyu. She was already working undercover as an anti-Japanese agent at the ECCC. They were to pretend to be husband and wife, but to make it easier for them – so that they didn't have to do the things expected of a married couple, like going shopping together, going out for walks, taking the children on trips, and the rest – they made sure everyone knew their marriage was an unhappy one. Which was why Mr Pan senior turned up that time at her ECCC work unit on the military base and beat her up in front of everyone. She was then able to tell her colleagues that she'd fallen for someone else and that she wasn't going to be living with him any more, but at the same time she still had a reason to return to the marital home, to see the children and so forth.

'That's what we wanted,' Mr Pan said. 'Our house was a station from which a great deal of vital intelligence was transmitted.'

At that time, a lot of intelligence was coming from Li Ningyu. If she picked up something at the ECCC that needed to be urgently communicated back to her comrades, she would use Turtle to take it off base straight away. She and Turtle were able to meet regularly without causing suspicion, and there was a secret signal. If she dropped a piece of rubbish in his presence, that meant he had to go and collect a message immediately. But if Li Ningyu had intelligence that wasn't so urgent, she would just wait until lunchtime and take it home with her, ready for Mr Pan to transmit later that evening.

When Li Ningyu was being held at the Tan Estate, the cover story put out by Colonel Hihara and Commander Zhang was so plausible that from start to finish her comrades never discovered what was really going on. When he mentioned this, old Mr Pan became upset. 'The fact is that I was a little worried. It all seemed very strange. She was only going to be gone for a couple of days, but they were making such a fuss about it, inviting us relatives to eat at the Louwailou restaurant and then taking us out to the Tan Estate to look at them. It was as if they were afraid we might not believe them.'

He kept shaking his head as he told me this.

'And then Warrior (the concubine) happened to get arrested on the same day. There were holes in their story, but we didn't treat the situation as seriously as we should have. The main reason for that was because when Turtle went to the estate, Li Ningyu didn't signal to him at all. Turtle thought that if something really had happened, she would definitely have found a way to make contact – she always had before. He had no idea she was under such close guard that she simply didn't dare make the slightest sign.'

'But why, when Turtle came out of the kitchen a second time, did he simply leave?' I asked.

According to old Mr Pan, that was because he'd seen a steel fountain pen with a white cap in Li Ningyu's breast pocket. That was one of their signals. If Li Ningyu displayed a steel fountain pen, it meant Turtle mustn't approach her.

'That was a dreadful mistake,' Mr Pan said. 'He quite

misunderstood her signal with the pen. Li Ningyu undoubtedly meant that he should not approach her because she was afraid he'd be unmasked. But Turtle interpreted it as a simple sign that she had nothing to communicate. So he reported back that everything was fine. Tiger then took this to mean that Li Ningyu was indeed engaged in some kind of official mission for the Imperial Japanese Army and that there was no need to worry about her.' Emotion almost got the better of the old man at this point in his story, but he soldiered on nonetheless. 'I only realized that things had gone terribly wrong when they delivered her body to me.'

'But her suicide note claimed that she'd died of an infectious disease. How could you know that something had gone wrong?'

He sighed. 'Well, first of all, it seemed very strange that she'd died so suddenly. That didn't seem right at all. What disease could she have caught to die so quickly? And if she was dying like that, how did she manage to write a note? Also, she addressed her note "To my husband Liangming", when, given our true relationship, she could have just used my name – why did she need to stress "To my husband"? And another thing, she said, "I have no regrets about dying in the performance of my official duties." That was very odd. If she had died carrying out a mission for Hihara, how could she say, "I have no regrets"? The children were still so little, and the Revolution had not yet been accomplished – how could she rest in peace? It was that line that told me that she must have left a message to come out with her body. That was the only way she could say, "I have no regrets about dying in the performance of my official duties."'

3

But Mr Pan searched her body and everything with it and didn't find anything.

How could he have? Hihara had got there first, he'd been all over Li Ningyu's corpse and her belongings, and everything she was now wearing was brand new – of course there was nothing to find.

'But I was quite sure there must be something, so I didn't give up. I kept on searching, thinking about where it could be, trying to guess where she might have put it.'

Old Mr Pan frowned, as if confronting the conundrum all over again. 'I began to wonder if she'd used some secret method to hide it. If it were on her body, it would have to be in her stomach – she'd have swallowed her message. But there was nothing in her note to suggest that, and I didn't like the idea of trying to find out, so I left that for the moment. If it wasn't on her body then it had to be among her belongings. The only place she could possibly have concealed a message was in the painting, and she had mentioned her painting in her note to me. I studied it very carefully, hoping it would tell me something. But no matter how hard I looked, how many times I came back to it, whatever angle I tried, I didn't see anything.'

To this day, the painting hangs in old Mr Pan's study. It's been mounted on silk and placed in a brown frame. It's a monochrome ink painting, very expressive, with the trunks of the trees and their canopy of leaves depicted in broad brushstrokes. The effect is bold, dramatic. The grass is more simply indicated, with long and short strokes, very impressionistic. It's such a simple, straightforward picture and I felt sure there could be no message hidden there, even if I were to put it under a magnifying glass.

However, Mr Pan assured me that the message was right there in the painting. He asked me to guess where it was.

I began by remarking that the paper was comparatively thick, so perhaps it would be possible to peel apart the layers and hide the message between them. Then I said that the tree canopy looked a bit like a road map, so maybe that was it. And finally, I guessed that there might be something in the inscription Li Ningyu had written for her children.

Old Mr Pan shook his head at each of my guesses. When he saw that I had run out of ideas, he gave me a clue. 'Have you noticed the grass? Do you see anything special about it?'

I had already looked at the grass several times. There was a long line of it in the foreground, long and short blades, dense in some places, sparse in others. It looked to have been painted very casually, with only a stroke or two of the brush. If I'd had to say what was special about it, I'd have said that it was painted very freely. It would be impossible to hide something there.

Mr Pan senior laughed. 'You're going about this quite the wrong way. You're looking for something obvious, but think about the situation she was in – how could she possibly communicate something openly? Everything that was allowed off the estate would have been searched over and over again, so if you can see it, the enemy would have seen it too. That would never work. She would have put her message somewhere that only I would discover it. And what is different about me? Do I have some amazing superpower?'

His eyes twinkled mischievously at me.

'As I mentioned, I was a wireless operative. I was in charge of the radio station that maintained communication between the Communist underground in Hangzhou and our Communist military, the New Fourth Army, and Li Ningyu was a cryptographer, perfectly familiar with Morse code.'

Mr Pan stopped and asked me if I knew about Morse code.

Of course I knew about Morse code. If I didn't, how could I have written *In the Dark*? Abing was a surveillance agent specializing in the subject. Nowadays, there are lots of people who will tell you that I used to work in a top-secret department like his, and there's even a story that I was fired for writing *Decoded* and *In the Dark*. I have nothing to say to that, because I don't know what to say. It's not worth trying to argue. I used to imagine that people valued what I wrote, my books, and that my own circumstances were irrelevant. To me, it really is totally irrelevant whether my work unit fires me or promotes me. That's never been my main concern. I just want to write good books, for readers who appreciate my work. I want to allow my readers to imagine another world. To put it differently, what concerns me is holding on to my readers, keeping them interested, and that's harder than some people like to suggest. It's actually just thoughtless and ill-informed of people to say that being an author is easy.

4

Okay, back to the story. Let me tell you something about Morse code.

I've always thought that Samuel Morse was an amazing man to have come up with such a simple language. It's composed of two sounds, dot and dash, which you can write using just two signs: • and —. The relationship between the dot and the dash is set at 1:3. That means that three dot sounds together make one dash: three • put together make one —. And, what's more, Morse code can be used to transcribe every language in the world. It can be transmitted through the air, through the clouds, and out into space. As long as you're out there, you can use this language.

Thirty years ago, when I was in the second year of elementary school, my aunt's mother-in-law passed away. Her son was working in Beijing, and she needed to get in touch with him as soon as possible to have him come back for the funeral. My father took me to the post office. The person who sent off the telegram was another relative (I called him uncle), and that was the first time I had the privilege of seeing a Morse key and observing the process by which the message was transmitted.

I watched my uncle as he sat at the table, the middle finger of his right hand operating the steel key, filling the room with the sound of dots and dashes. In less than five minutes, he announced that he'd now sent the message to our relatives in Beijing and that they'd received it. It seemed incredible – how could such a thing be possible? He had to be lying! But that evening my uncle came round to our house with a telegram informing us that my aunt's son was already on a train heading home and that we were to delay the funeral until he got back.

I could already read quite well at that age, so I grabbed the telegram, but all I could see were numbers, line after line of them, and all of them in groups of four. I asked my uncle how he could understand what it said, and he told me that there was a book, but because he'd been doing the job for a while, he'd memorized pretty much all of it. He could read a message without having to look anything up.

In those days, when you went to the post office to send a telegram, you would always see a big book on the desk of the operative, sextodecimo, really fat, about the size of the Chinese–English dictionary that we had at home. In this book, every Chinese character and punctuation mark was given as a string of numbers. For example, China was 0022 0948; the United States was 5019 0948; and a comma was 9976. It was all done like that. In the hands of a telegraph operator, these numbers changed again into the sound of dots and dashes, so the number 1 became dot dash, 2 became dot dot dash, and so on and so forth:

1: dot dash
2: dot dot dash
3: dot dot dot dash dash
4: dot dot dot dot dash
5: dot dot dot dot dot
6: dash dot dot dot dot
7: dash dash dot dot dot
8: dash dot dot
9: dash dot
0: dash

That gives you the sounds, what you hear. When writing it out, it looks like this:

1: • —
2: • • —
3: • • • — —
4: • • • • —
5: • • • • •
6: — • • • •
7: — — • • •
8: — • •
9: — •
0: —

Now supposing we write dash (—) as a vertical stroke. Then the numbers 1234567890 written out in Morse code, will look like this:

• |• • |• • • | |• • • • |• • • • • |• • • • | |• • • |• • |
• |

This is a printed book, so everything is all the same size and very stiff; perhaps you can't imagine these symbols drawn out to look like grass. But as we know – in fact, as I mentioned above – dots and dashes are arranged in the proportion 1:3, so you could equally well describe them as short and long. Blades of grass can also be either short or long; indeed, as old Mr Pan said, the fingers on your hand are short and long, so why not grass?

Mr Pan senior pointed to the grass in the painting and said excitedly, 'Now you get it, don't you? This isn't grass, it's a message, a message in Morse code. The long blades of grass are the dashes (—) and the short ones are the dots (•).'

Of course I got it. There was no need for him to spell it out. Besides, with my knowledge of this code, I had already read off a string of numbers perfectly easily from the grass in the painting:

6643 1032 9976 0523 1801 0648 3194 5028 5391 2585 9982

As a specialist radio operative engaged in underground activities, old Mr Pan's professional abilities far outstripped my uncle's. Apparently, in the past a post-office telegraphist was required to remember the codes for five hundred words in common usage; Mr Pan said that when he was young, he had memorized the codes for two and a half thousand words. Which meant he didn't need to search his code book at all but immediately recognized what this message said:

For urgent dispatch!

Call off the Gathering of Heroes immediately!

I believe that thirty years ago it cost seven cents per word to send a post-office telegram; punctuation marks were charged at the same rate as a word. To send a message like this, the post office would have charged just over one yuan. But the price Li Ningyu paid to send her message was her life. Of course, to her, the contents were priceless.

Mr Pan senior could no longer remember with perfect clarity what happened that day, but fortunately he'd been interviewed some years earlier by Professor He Dacao for his book *Underground Paradise*, which was published in July 1995 by the Qingcheng publishing company, based in Chengdu. According to the account given there, on the evening of 2 May 1941, four days after the original date set, Zhou Enlai's special Communist Party representative K held a meeting in a house located at 108 Wulin Road in Hangzhou. Before the meeting began, all the comrades present observed a minute's silence in memory of Li Ningyu, a gesture of respect for a truly brave woman and heroic revolutionary who had died for the cause.

5

Now, finally, let us talk about what happened to Hihara and the others.

Colonel Hihara, of course, knew nothing of this. As you can imagine, when he stood in front of the Agate Belvedere Inn, he couldn't believe his eyes. His arrest mission had failed! Ghost had succeeded in getting a message out and calling off the Gathering of Heroes that night.

Who was Ghost? How had the message been transmitted?

Hihara wracked his brains, but he simply couldn't work it out.

Right then, however, he had no interest in pursuing his enquiries – he was too humiliated. He was much more interested in the secret orders General Matsui had given him when he'd left Shanghai. This was yet another top-secret message, and the key to its encryption was time. Before the time was ripe, he'd only been able to guess at its contents, but the moment to read it had now arrived.

Hihara opened the envelope containing his secret orders and read its lone sentence:

To have killed an innocent is no great matter, but to allow a single suspect to remain alive would be a terrible mistake.

In other words, his instructions were to kill every last one of his suspects.

There is no conclusive evidence to prove that Hihara actually killed anybody. According to testimony provided by Sentry A, one of the soldiers on duty at the Tan Estate that evening, all of the guards were dismissed, and Hihara arranged their immediate return to their original units. None of them were allowed to stay behind. Before they left, Sentry A saw Commander Zhang arriving in a great hurry, because he was supposed to be joining Hihara for a late dinner.

Back at base, Sentry A discovered that his wallet was missing, so he assumed he must have left it in his room at the estate. First thing the following day, he returned to the Tan Estate to look for it, only to discover that both the eastern and western buildings were now completely empty. As to when everyone left and where they went, nobody knew. Eventually, Gu Xiaomeng and Police Chief Wang Tianxiang both returned to work, but everyone else – Commander Zhang, Section Chief Jin, Secretary Bai, Staff Officer Jiang (the fat staff officer), the operatives who'd been in charge of the wiretapping – all of them vanished, never to be seen again. Sentry A believed that all of them were killed by Hihara, on the principle that allowing a single suspect to remain alive would have been a terrible mistake. He further speculated that when Colonel Hihara was himself murdered, that was the family or subordinates of the dead taking their revenge.

Old Mr Pan admitted that he didn't know much about Hihara, but when we spoke of his murder, his eyes glittered. 'That winter there were a lot of rumours circulating in Hangzhou about Hihara. At first it was said that someone had offered a guerrilla unit one hundred thousand silver dollars to kill him, then it was said to be two hundred thousand. And then one day it was all over the newspapers that Hihara had been murdered at West Lake and that his body and head had been dumped outside the main entrance of the Temple of General Yue Fei. His hands and feet had been chopped off and his eyes gouged out. It was a horrible death, but I'm so glad they got him!'

As to who killed him, there were all kinds of stories. Some said it was undercover agents sent by Communist headquarters in Yan'an; others maintained it was Nationalist agents sent by their headquarters in Chongqing. There were also theories that it was subordinates of either Commander Zhang or Chief of Staff Wu Zhiguo; or that Gu Xiaomeng had hired a professional assassin. There were many different stories, too many to recount in detail here. The murder of Colonel Hihara was so bizarre that it became a kind of local legend, to be handed down from one generation to the next. Even now, stories about it still circulate in Hangzhou.

I really regret not being able to get in touch with Gu Xiaomeng. I'm told that she is still alive, living in Taiwan, that she's done very well for herself and that she has a son who's an extremely successful businessman in Hong Kong. In the 1990s he was involved in many major business deals with the Mainland and invested heavily in industrial development as well as charitable endeavours. Thanks to that, he was able to establish positive relationships with a number of very senior members of the government. I did ask a friend of mine for help in getting in touch with his private secretary, since I hoped to be able to visit Madame Gu in Taiwan. The secretary hung up on me without even asking why I wanted to meet her, and such an outright rebuttal was very off-putting. According to my information, Madame Gu will be celebrating her eighty-fifth birthday next year, so I take this opportunity to wish her many happy returns. Long may she flourish!

First draft: 7.11.2006
Second draft: 3.12.2006

PART TWO

The Wind from the West

ONE

1

Gu Xiaomeng...

The old lady haunted my thoughts just as Ghost had, making it impossible to finish my novel. I did finish it, but then I had to start it all over again.

This was a very unhappy time in my life. Shortly before Chinese New Year, just as my new book (at that point entitled *The Code*) was going through the final production stages before being sent to the printers, the editor-in-chief, Abiao, suddenly phoned me one afternoon and informed me crossly that the book wasn't going to be published after all. I asked why not and he said someone had accused me of maliciously distorting historical facts, making deliberate mistakes and slandering them.

I thought he was joking. 'These things are like swearing that you're going to stop smoking,' I said. 'I've been through it many times before...'

That didn't seem to make him any calmer. In fact, he

sounded very worried. 'This is not the same – these people are serious. If we insist on going ahead with publication, they're going to take both you and us to court.'

I asked who 'they' were, and Abiao named a Mr X. I pointed out that there was no such person in my book. He explained that Mr X was Gu Xiaomeng's son. My head felt as if it were exploding because I knew that was the one weak point of my story: I hadn't managed to interview Gu Xiaomeng. I had imagined that, living as she did in Taiwan, she would never see my book, wouldn't even know that it had been published. But she was already off the blocks.

What on earth was going on?

It transpired that I had mentioned Gu Xiaomeng to Abiao at one point and I'd also happened to say that she had a son, Mr X, who was a famous businessman in Hong Kong and a member of the National Committee of the Chinese People's Political Consultative Conference. The CEO of the publishing company heard this and became worried; he felt the whole thing was too sensitive, and he demanded that my manuscript be handed over to the relevant departments for review. The people in charge of that review were equally unwilling to bear the consequences of any mistakes, so they cautiously suggested that the manuscript be shown to Gu Xiaomeng herself.

She decreed that it couldn't be published; she would see us in court if we tried.

Everything went black before my eyes... From the very first round of interviews to the completion of my manuscript, writing this book had taken three years. I was put in mind of something people say about track-and-field races, about how tragic it is when an athlete falls at the final hurdle. My fate seemed even worse than that of Li Ningyu! She died, but in doing so she ended up the victor – her death was worth it. I had spent years of my life working on this and all I'd got out of it was the sense that it had been a complete waste of time. I felt the urge to swear like a young person – bugger this!

2

Do not be in too much of a hurry, haste is of the Devil. Haste will make you do stupid things; it will make things even worse; it will push you beyond the point of no return. I consoled myself and forced myself to stay calm: I needed to adapt to these new circumstances, be patient and win over the old lady by showing her that my intentions were good. People become kinder and more tolerant with age; if I showed how sorry I was, maybe she would forgive me. So I wrote her a letter expressing my sincere apologies and gave it to the people who'd reviewed my manuscript to pass on to her.

One month went past.

A second month went past.

A third month went past.

Just when I was feeling that the situation was completely hopeless, I got a phone call from a stranger who introduced herself as Gu Xiaomeng's daughter. She said that she'd read my book and was hoping to be able to talk to me about it. She had no complaints; in fact, she was very happy with the first half of the manuscript, but she stressed that the second half contained serious inaccuracies. And then she said that her mother would very much like to see me and hoped that I could find time to go to Taiwan.

Perhaps she was afraid that I wouldn't go; during our conversation, she mentioned in a tactful way that she'd just been appointed to the National Committee of the Chinese People's Political Consultative Conference herself and was actually in Beijing right at that moment – that afternoon she was going to be speaking to various senior people in the government. The underlying message was that she wanted me to take her mother's request very seriously. What she didn't know was that this was exactly what I had been hoping for.

At long last, things were changing for the better.

I travelled to Taiwan as quickly as I could, to meet Madame Gu.

3

More than half a century had passed and I could find no signs of the erstwhile young beauty in the face of the old woman before me. She was now eighty-five: her silver hair had thinned, she wore full dentures, her eyes had dimmed and her gaze wandered. But the moment she opened her mouth, there was no doubting that this was the Gu Xiaomeng people had told me about. She spoke frankly and as if she was unquestionably in the right, and it was quite clear that she would never, ever back down. Indeed, she began by immediately telling me off.

'Why did you distort the truth like that? How could you write up Li Ningyu the way you did while maliciously making me out to be a traitor?' Her voice was sharp and angry; here was nothing of the kindness and benevolence that an old lady ought to show.

I tried to explain, but before I'd even started she waved her hand to shut me up. Clearly, she had a great many things she wanted to say, and it seemed as though she'd rehearsed them, because it all came out like a recording, an uninterrupted monologue in which she asked all the questions and gave all the answers. There wasn't a moment for me to get a word in edgeways. I was amazed by the extraordinary clarity of her diction and the logic of her argument. From the way she spoke and the care she took over her choice of words, it was as if she were at least thirty years younger.

'I know you claim it's just a work of fiction,' she began, 'but everyone will know exactly what you're talking about. The people, the names, the time and place are all quite transparent, and it's obvious that the Gu Xiaomeng character is me. It's me, but it's not the real me. I was never like that! You've got the facts quite wrong. For a start, it wasn't Li Ningyu who got the message out, not at all. It was me – you hear that?'

Gu Xiaomeng got the message out!

Do you believe that?

I certainly didn't.

Although I didn't voice my doubts, they must have been written all over my face.

'You don't believe me, do you?' the old lady immediately countered. 'You think I'm just trying to steal the credit for it, right? If I was trying to take the credit, what am I doing in Taiwan? I should have stayed on the Mainland to be feted as a hero! I don't care about credit, I want the facts to be known – I took the message out, and there it is. I am not having you messing this about!'

Now the old lady launched another salvo at me. 'Tell me, young man, why have you been slandering me like this? Who put you up to it? Let me guess, it was that old bastard Pan!'

I didn't dare deny it.

She snorted. 'Bastard! I guessed it was him. Everything has to be down to Li Ningyu, because then he can bask in her reflected glory; he's absolutely shameless! His whole family come out of this as heroes of the Revolution, and everyone else gets painted as traitors and running dogs. I ask you, how odious is that? He really is outrageous.' She leant forward, visibly agitated. 'Well, Pan, you old idiot, I'm not dead yet, and if you have the gall to go around lying to people about me, I'm going to see you in hell first! You're not going to get away with this! How dare you say such things about me?'

This was followed by a stream of insults and another bout of name-calling. Fortunately, her daughter was present and she now came forward to say a few soothing words, which calmed her down a bit.

The old lady thrust my manuscript at me.

'Do you really imagine that what you've written stands up to close scrutiny? Have you considered, given the circumstances, how Hihara could possibly have allowed Li Ningyu's corpse off the premises? In the hope of laying his hands on Ghost, he'd had all of us locked up, so why would he have been so kind as to let a body go? Even if he did think Li Ningyu had proved her innocence by dying, even if did then believe that she wasn't Ghost, he would still never have released her body. Why? Apart from anything else, he didn't have time! He was going to arrest everyone that evening at the Gathering of Heroes – he didn't have a moment to think about anything else. It was just a dead body, after all; it could wait a day or two.' She clacked her dentures impatiently. 'And you wrote about him searching the body – what would he do that for? It's quite implausible – you really shouldn't believe everything people tell you. And why would he send her body back to her family? It wasn't as if he'd incur any punishment if he didn't.'

'Well,' I said carefully, 'if her body was searched and they discovered there wasn't any kind of message hidden on it...'

'So they trusted to that?' The old lady laughed coldly. 'And how exactly are they supposed to have conducted this search? How you described it in your book? How could that possibly prove there was no message hidden on Li Ningyu's body? What a joke! There were loads of places where something could have been hidden – in her stomach, her womb, her intestines. A proper search would have required a full autopsy, and that would have taken longer than one day. Without a proper search there's no way they would have thought it safe to release the body.'

It was a good point, and I had nothing to counter it – nor did I get the opportunity.

'You're a writer, you ought to be able to think this through logically. If Hihara couldn't be certain she was innocent, how could he even consider handing over her body to her family? Supposing she was Ghost after all: if her comrades saw Li Ningyu's body, it wouldn't matter what the accompanying letter said – infectious disease, car accident, whatever – they would have immediately called off their meeting. In a situation like that, with such an important meeting about to be held, everyone would have been on edge; they would have called the whole thing off if the grass so much as rippled in the breeze. If what you wrote is correct, what on earth was that painting all about? She didn't need it – if her corpse was delivered to her family, that would have been quite enough. A perfectly healthy person suddenly dying at such a sensitive moment: that was surely going to set alarm bells ringing. Even if it turned out to be a lot of fuss about nothing, the meeting would still have to be called off; that's how it works with any underground activities.'

What the old lady said shocked me.

And the shocks kept on coming.

Over the course of the next few days, Madame Gu took me to her villa in the countryside (this was located some eighty kilometres from Taipei, and she kept some important evidence there), and we discussed everything that had happened in considerable detail. Time spares no one, and, given her age, it was impossible for her to talk to me for longer than half an hour at a time; sometimes she had to recline on a peach-coloured chaise longue, and at other times she felt strong enough to sit up in a lacquer-red cane chair. Some of the time she spoke with passion and sincerity, and at other times she spoke softly and courteously.

We went through every aspect of what had happened sixty-six years earlier. It was a story that I'd imagined I'd understood, but as the old lady made clear, I'd actually understood very little, and much had been carefully concealed from me. I decided then and there that I would rewrite my story. But now that I've done that, is someone else going to come forward, read the new version, and accuse me all over again of distorting the facts?

Sometimes I really do feel that I have no idea any more what's true and what's fiction.

Strictly speaking, everything that I've written in this chapter is simply an introduction to what comes next; perhaps it would be best to call it a preface…

TWO

1

Green creeper, dark bamboo, the sound of birdsong; an old lady, at the end of her life, living remote from the rest of the world…

These were my first impressions when I arrived, full of trepidation, at Madame Gu's villa in the countryside.

It wasn't a very big house, but it was quiet and elegant. You could smell the flowers and hear the birds singing, and the outside world didn't intrude at all; it really did seem like paradise to me. The villa was three storeys high, with a roof of black tiles; its red-brick walls were covered in green creeper and it was encircled by clumps of dark bamboo – you couldn't imagine a reinforced concrete building in such surroundings. The sitting room was furnished with a mixture of Chinese and Western pieces – she had a Louis XIV-style sofa, reclining chairs, oil paintings and bronze table lamps, but there was also a very Chinese household shrine, table and straw mats, and a rosewood armchair. A thread of incense rose from the shrine, which contained an image of Guanyin, the Goddess of Mercy; in front of the floor-to-ceiling window, two overgrown taro vines lent a greenish tinge to the blazing sunlight.

Although Madame Gu's face still bore traces of the anger I'd seen in it during our initial meeting the previous day, I noted that the delicate rattan table between us had already been laid with a traditional purple-clay tea set, so I realized that she had decided to go ahead with the interview. I was secretly thrilled, but I decided to make no reference to it. I understood very well that we were coming at this from quite different positions; no matter how deeply I went into this story, I would never be as closely involved as she was. She was a participant, a survivor, while I was merely an investigator, an observer. I needed to play down my own particular interest in the story and act like an ordinary visitor who'd come to talk to an important historical figure. But the reason I'd travelled all the way to Taiwan at very short notice was that I was determined to discover the secrets inside the riddle of what had happened more than half a century ago. I was looking forward to getting a new perspective and I quietly blessed the stubbornness in me that had brought me this far.

I got straight to the point. 'Madame, you said that it was you who took the message out. I would like to know how.'

'You ought to be asking me why!' the old lady fired back. 'Why I wanted to help Li Ningyu get the message out.'

'Okay… why?'

'Because I wasn't working for the puppet regime.'

'You were one of Li Ningyu's comrades?'

'Well, that depends. Insofar as we were both resisting the Japanese, we were certainly comrades-in-arms, but if it hadn't been for the Japanese, we would have been enemies.'

A light bulb suddenly went on in my head. 'You were sent by the Nationalists, by Chongqing?'

She laughed lightly. 'Oh, very clever – you've guessed. Yes, I was a spy sent by the Nationalists' Bureau of Military Statistics in Chongqing to infiltrate Wang Jingwei's puppet regime.'

I immediately realized that her wealthy father must also have been a secret agent working for the Bureau of Military Statistics, as the Nationalists' secret service was then known.

The old lady raised her head and looked at one of the framed photos on the wall; it showed a 1930s Japanese-made Zero fighter plane. 'That was the aeroplane my father gave to Wang Jingwei – it was the ticket that got the two of us into the very highest echelons of Wang's puppet government. The gift was actually arranged entirely by Dai Li, who was the head of the Nationalists' secret service at that point. That part was all done covertly, of course. All my father had to do was be the public face, put his name to it.'

'What year was that?'

The old lady stroked her blood-red bracelet with a gently trembling hand and then put her index finger slowly to her lips. Her gaze had drifted off into the distance, as if she were trying to catch at the last traces of events that she had remembered for more than half a century but that had almost been effaced by the passage of time.

2

It was the summer of 1939.

Gu Xiaomeng remembered quite clearly how she'd

come home all excited the afternoon after her graduation ceremony from the Qingpu Police Academy. Her father was sitting cross-legged on a red cane chair under the vine-covered pergola out in the garden, smoking a fat cigar and talking to another middle-aged man. Her father didn't normally smoke; he might occasionally take a few puffs, but that was just to make himself look like any other business tycoon. From the way he was blowing out huge clouds of smoke, Gu Xiaomeng could tell he wasn't happy about whatever it was he was discussing with the other man. He might even be angry; she noted the glacial expression on his face, the way his eyebrows were knitted, the way his gaze was fixed on the other man. It was very rare indeed for her father to look like that when he was at home. A couple of months earlier, a shipment worth several millions had been sunk by enemy fire and he hadn't been as angry as this.

He didn't even acknowledge Gu Xiaomeng. As far as she could remember, this had only ever happened once before, two years earlier, the day her mother was killed by a bomb dropped by the Japanese devils. Gu Xiaomeng had come home humming a popular song, having no idea what had happened, and her father had looked right through her, then turned around and walked away. His sombre back view had been like a black screen between them, breaking the strong bond that normally connected them.

The visitor was wearing a Chinese-style black serge suit and a homburg hat from the famous Shengxifu Company of Tianjin; the round sunglasses perched on the bridge of his nose gave him a mysterious, arrogant air. From the various official leather binders lying on the tea table, Gu Xiaomeng was able to pretty much guess who he might be – if he didn't represent the army, then he was from the police. Most likely the police, since she'd just graduated from the police academy; perhaps he was discussing her future with her father. In which case, it would be better if she didn't appear right away. So, after a brief hesitation, she slipped away quietly and went inside.

Mrs Wu, the housekeeper, greeted her warmly, and, seeing that her forehead was beaded with sweat, hurried off to get her a towel.

Gu Xiaomeng took the towel, patted her face dry and asked, 'Who's that man?'

Mrs Wu shook her head. 'I don't know… The master told me not to disturb them.'

'Has he been here long?' Gu Xiaomeng handed the towel back.

Mrs Wu checked the clock on the wall. 'More than an hour.'

Just as she said that, the wall clock and the bell of the church across the way both rang out. 'Ding… Ding… Ding…' It made it sound like the whole of Shanghai was preparing to hoist anchor and sail away.

Two years earlier, not long after his wife had been killed, Gu Xiaomeng's father had decided that in order to keep his daughter safe he would move the household out of Hangzhou, which was still being bombed by the Japanese, and up to Shanghai. Like many who could afford it, he chose the neighbourhood known as the French Concession, which, being under French control and home to many foreigners, was at that time largely immune from the Japanese. It was a comfortable and cosmopolitan place to live. Their house was opposite a Catholic church, and every time its bell tolled, a host of pigeons flew up from the roof with a noisy fluffing and rustling of feathers that you could hear all the way down the road.

Summers in Shanghai are hot and sticky. Gu Xiaomeng was feeling sleepy, so she washed her face and went upstairs for a siesta. But once she'd got into bed, she didn't feel like sleeping any more, so she lay there flicking idly through a film magazine, *The Viewer*. After a while, she got up and went to the window, just in time to see her father saying goodbye to his visitor. The man shook her father's hand and with his other hand patted him lightly on the shoulder. Her father looked helpless, as if he were being comforted by his visitor.

Even more disturbing was that when her father came up to see her, he wasn't wearing his usual cheerful smile. She asked who his visitor was, but he wouldn't be drawn and quickly changed the subject. Further surprises followed: at dinner that evening, rather than talk to her as he normally did, her father kept helping her to the most delicious dishes on the table. It was almost as if this were a farewell banquet, as if he expected never to see her again.

After her mother passed away and her two brothers went to study abroad, Gu Xiaomeng was the only member of the family living at home with her father. This had only served to increase the devotion and indulgence he showed his daughter, which had made her very spoilt and tiresome. As far as Gu Xiaomeng was concerned, her father was much less strict than Mrs Wu. She was very unhappy about her father's unusual behaviour and when he refused to give a straight answer to her questions, she was so furious she slammed her rice bowl down on the table and went back up to her room in a rage.

Later, her father came upstairs to find her. She was still furious. 'Who was that man who looked like a funeral director?' she shouted. 'He's made this place as lively as a morgue! Is he the God of Death or what?'

Although she was being very rude, her father wasn't angry with her. His head hung even lower than before. He sat down heavily opposite her and said dejectedly, 'I don't know how to explain.'

'Tell me what's going on!'

He took hold of her hand, then shook his head as if he wanted to speak but hardly knew where to begin.

Gu Xiaomeng had by now realized that something was very wrong, so she gripped his hand tightly. 'Daddy, what on earth has happened?'

He sighed and closed his eyes. 'It's the end of the world.' His voice became very serious. 'As you know, Xiaomeng, normally my money is enough to solve pretty much any problem we have. I've always assumed that if ever you happened to get into trouble, I'd be able to sort things out for you. But this time, your daddy… well, I can't help you. We don't have a choice – we're going to have to do what he says.'

Gu Xiaomeng leapt to her feet. 'You mean the man who came this afternoon?'

'Yes.'

'Who is he?'

'He's just a messenger. The important thing is who he represents.'

'So who does he represent?'

'Our country. Our wretched war-torn country.'

3

[Transcript from the interview with Gu Xiaomeng]
Well, my father told me that this man was called Song and was Deputy Chief of the Third Section of the Nationalists' Bureau of Military Statistics. He wasn't high up – he was only a colonel – but the documents he came armed with meant he had to be treated with the greatest respect. That's what the Nationalists' secret service was known as then: the Bureau of Military Statistics. Later on, when Dai Li really got into his stride as its top man, the Bureau became so powerful it could change day into night; it could raise you up, transform you into a dragon soaring high in the sky, or it could crush you, turn you into a worm consigned to boring through the earth.

As far as I know, my father had met Dai Li only once previously, before the war. The Nationalist Party was riven with divisions even then, and there was constant infighting, so the Bureau of Military Statistics was busily recruiting agents and placing people they trusted in positions of power. My father was in the armaments business and often had dealings with the military, and Dai Li wanted him to join the Bureau as an agent. Daddy was worried about that, he thought it could cause him serious problems, so he refused, though he had to pay a huge sum to the Bureau to get out of it. He was quite prepared to use his money for that, to buy his freedom, in a way.

As I said, the Bureau wasn't as important then, and Dai Li wasn't as powerful. Dai Li took the money and stayed on friendly terms with Daddy; if something important happened, he'd phone Daddy, but otherwise he didn't bother him. It was Dai Li who'd sent Section Chief Song to see my father; he'd phoned ahead to say he had something important to discuss and was sending someone for a face-to-face meeting. So Section Chief Song was there as Dai Li's representative.

My father thought he was probably coming to request either money or weapons. Because of the war, the treasury was now empty, but the Bureau had a very long arm and was able to extract a lot of private funds and material from ordinary people. What Daddy was not expecting was that Section Chief Song would bring a huge amount of money with him – that was most unusual.

Well, this gift came with some pretty hefty strings attached. To put it bluntly, this time Dai Li didn't want money from Daddy, he wanted him to put his life on the line for the Bureau. He wanted him to use the Bureau's money to buy an aeroplane, which he would then give to the traitor Wang Jingwei, in order to gain his trust. At that time, Wang Jingwei was in Wuhan, preparing to form his puppet government in collaboration with the Japanese, and the Bureau was trying to get one of their people into his inner circle. Dai Li decided that my father would be the perfect man for the job, so that's what he was trying to set up.

My father was the son of a blacksmith; he'd been able to make his fortune because the times were so troubled – troubled times give birth to great heroes! He was exceptionally skilled at maintaining good relations with those in power while at the same time making every use of his opportunities. If businessmen in China don't maintain good relations with officialdom, there's a limit to how far they can go; that's always been the case, and it's as true on the Mainland as it is in Taiwan. But if the relationship develops too far, then you stop being a businessman and start becoming a government official – there's no clear distinction between your activities. In the worst-case scenario, you end up failing in both arenas: your business interests collapse and you lose your government position, and it's one almighty disaster!

From start to finish, my father was a businessman, plain and simple. He was friendly to the right people but not too friendly. It was his business philosophy to keep everyone as happy as possible, so he could work with all sides. Now Dai Li was demanding that he serve the country and the Nationalist Party by going undercover and infiltrating Wang Jingwei's puppet regime, which was not something my father was ever going to be happy to do. But this time it was about his patriotic duty to resist the Japanese invasion; Daddy had to agree, there was no choice in the matter – money was not going to buy him a way out on this occasion.

My father had been through a lot over the years, and he was as good as anyone at working out which way the wind was blowing. The moment he realized that Dai Li had secretly prepared such a huge sum of money for him, he knew he wasn't going to be able to say no. That being the case, Daddy didn't waste his time – he agreed to do what they wanted without the slightest hesitation.

The problem wasn't Daddy, it was me. They had requested that I join the Bureau as well, to act as my father's subagent. I too would be found a position within Wang Jingwei's puppet regime. Of course, from a moral perspective, I was bound to accept their request – after all, they were spending an awful lot of money to put my father in place, so it made sense to get me in the door as well, at no extra cost. Two agents infiltrated for the price of one.

However, my father refused to agree to that. He didn't want me involved because he knew – everybody knew – that this would not be as straightforward as they were trying to suggest. It would be very dangerous, and we could both be killed at any point. I was my father's only daughter, we'd been very close ever since I was tiny, and my two older brothers were both abroad... Daddy treated me like a pearl in the palm of his hand – he wasn't going to let me do anything that dangerous! All that afternoon he'd been doing his best to persuade Section Chief Song to keep me out of it, but the Section Chief had insisted that they wanted me too, and that distressed my father a great deal.

He was torn between doing right by his country and doing right by his family. In reality, though, here was a huge secret organization pitted against a lone business tycoon – you can imagine the outcome. But Daddy didn't give up. After he'd explained to me exactly what had happened, he told me his decision. He was going to get me out of there right away.

[Transcription ends]

Mr Gu could never have imagined that his decision would meet with his daughter's refusal.

Having heard what her father had to say, Gu Xiaomeng

wasn't scared at all. In fact, she was smiling quite happily as she patted her father's arm and tried to comfort him. 'I don't understand why you're looking so miserable about this,' she told him. 'I thought something dreadful must have happened, whereas it's actually a wonderful opportunity. At the very least I can do something to avenge Mummy's death. To tell you the truth, I've been trying to find someone to get me into the Bureau – did you not know that?'

'You don't know what you're talking about!' her father warned her. 'You have no idea; that place is like a bottomless pit – once you're in, you'll never get out again.'

'So many people who want to join the Bureau get rejected,' Gu Xiaomeng said excitedly. She told him how the Bureau had come in secret to the police academy on numerous occasions, to recruit its top students, but their requirements were extremely high – the people they recruited were always the very best in their class. That made her even more determined to say yes: here was her chance and she wasn't going to let it slip.

'No, this time you have to listen to me.'

'No, I won't. This is my choice and you mustn't interfere.'

No matter what he said or how hard he tried, Mr Gu simply wasn't able to change his daughter's mind. It seems to be a rule that, whenever parents and children disagree on questions of love and marriage, or career choices, it's always the parents who lose in the end. And so it was with Mr Gu and Xiaomeng.

That evening, Mr Gu felt unusually weak and helpless for all that he was a vastly wealthy and successful businessman. He paced the quiet garden like a trapped beast, and the silvery light of the moon from time to time illuminated the tears that flowed down his haggard cheeks.

4

On another night, when the moon was again shining as bright as silver, Section Chief Song returned to the Gus' house. This time he brought with him a sheaf of documents, a Nationalist flag, and a portrait of the Father of the Nation, the late Sun Yat-sen. He was to induct both Mr and Miss Gu into the Bureau of Military Statistics. First they had to fill out their forms, one each, in triplicate. Having done that, they affixed their fingerprints and were each allocated a code number. Her father was 036, she was 312. Then they were formally sworn in. The two of them raised their right hands, made a fist and then swore an oath to the Nationalist flag and the portrait of Sun Yat-sen, as dictated to them by Section Chief Song:

'I swear that from this day forward I will live and die for the Nationalist Party. I will be loyal to the Nationalist Party in the face of all threats and temptations, and I will defend its interests at all costs. I will resolutely carry out every command issued by my superiors without any concern for myself.'

Section Chief Song was now their commanding officer, and he gave Mr Gu his first orders. 'You must inform everyone that your daughter is going to the United States for the holidays, to visit her two brothers.'

Mr Gu immediately understood that he and Xiaomeng were to be separated. 'You're taking her away?'

The Section Chief nodded. 'You need to be trained,' he told Gu Xiaomeng.

Shortly after this, Gu Xiaomeng boarded an ocean liner belonging to the Weiyuan Company and crossed the Pacific. She was to do her training as a secret agent in the United States. At that time, the Nationalist government had a secret military base in the suburbs of Washington DC. It was run by the Chinese ambassador to the US, His Excellency Xiao Bo, who was also the head of the American station of the Bureau of Military Statistics.

While she was doing her training in the US, Gu Xiaomeng read in the newspapers that her father had presented a plane to Wang Jingwei. This meant that for years afterwards both Mr Gu and Xiaomeng were regularly accused of being traitors who'd served as running dogs of the puppet regime. After the war was over, the Bureau provided evidence and witnesses to testify that they had merely been obeying orders, which restored their reputations. However, in the 1950s, concerns were again raised about their activities. By that time, both Dai Li and Section Chief Song were dead, so His Excellency Xiao Bo was now their best and most important witness. For many years, Madame Gu had treated his testimony as her most precious possession. I was lucky enough to be allowed to read it:

I can testify to the fact that Gu Xiaomeng was a secret agent working for the Nationalist Party.

In September and October of 1939 she received training at the secret base I had established in Washington for the Ministry of Defence. At that time she was one of seven agents specially chosen by the National Bureau of Investigation and Statistics (that is, the Bureau of Military Statistics). Miss Gu studied very hard and showed her determination to resist the Japanese and rescue the Motherland in both word and deed. This should be beyond doubt.

After she completed her training, she returned to our country, and on many occasions I heard members of the Bureau, including Dai Li himself, praise the patriotism that Miss Gu and her father showed towards our country, and the meritorious service they performed towards our organization.

After the end of the Anti-Japanese War, the Nationalist Party acclaimed the loyalty, bravery and patriotism of Mr and Miss Gu in the most conclusive terms; if anyone now tries to pervert the facts, it shows that they are deliberately trying to malign this family for the most sinister of motives. This should be considered a source of shame by one and all.

Addendum: Two copies of this witness statement have been prepared; one will be kept by the National Central Security Council, and one will be kept by Gu Xiaomeng herself.

This letter was printed on a single sheet of sextodecimo white paper and was the original document. Xiao Bo's signature in black ink, the red mark of his personal seal and his thumbprint at the foot of the page testified to its authenticity and its historical importance. With Madame Gu's permission, I took a photograph of it with my digital camera. When the old lady discovered that my camera had only a low resolution of four megapixels, she took another picture on her own nine-megapixel camera and forwarded it to me. I still have her higher-resolution image on my computer and every single part of it is clear and legible.

That was the end of my first interview. Madame Gu had by now completely changed her attitude towards me and very kindly offered to see me out to my car. When I politely declined, she insisted on at least escorting me to the door, where she shook my hand and said goodbye. It was the feeblest hand I'd ever felt – there seemed to be hardly any flesh on it, just skin and bone; it was as light as a feather, as if it might blow away at any moment, and there was no warmth or weight in her handshake. I couldn't help but think that it was just as well that her memory wasn't equally feeble. That her mind had not betrayed her was a source of silent delight to me, but I had no idea who to thank.

THREE

1

Even though it was only April, in Taipei it was as if spring had already been and gone; the streets were full of people in T-shirts and sunglasses eating ice creams as the sun beat down on them. Back home on the Mainland, my family would still be in their winter clothes. It occurred to me that coming from my home town to Taipei as I had was also like going straight from winter into summer.

Madame Gu's daughter told me that her mother couldn't stand air conditioning, so she always spent the summer out of Taipei, at her villa in the countryside. She normally moved there in the last week of April, but this year, because of me, she'd gone a week early.

There were two gardeners and a housekeeper who lived at the villa all year round, and Madame Gu also had a live-in carer, a Malaysian Chinese woman called Chen. She was about fifty, of middling height and slightly plump, and I addressed her respectfully as Mrs Chen. She could speak Mandarin, English and Cantonese; her family originally came from Guangdong province, and she'd been looking after Madame Gu for the last twenty years. Her monthly salary was about ten thousand RMB, which would put her in the upper pay bracket for a worker on the Mainland.

When I arrived to begin the interview the following day, Madame Gu had not yet come downstairs. Mrs Chen was in the sitting room, carefully arranging the old lady's special magnifying glass on the tea table, next to a printout of my novel *The Code*. The manuscript was held in place by a baton-shaped rosewood paperweight, a sign that my work was being treated with respect.

Mrs Chen helped Madame Gu downstairs, bringing with her a small and very shiny dark red lacquerware box, which was obviously an antique. When Madame Gu had taken her seat, she instructed Mrs Chen to open the box and show me what was inside. I could see a yellowing photograph and a comb with three broken teeth, a steel fountain pen (with a white cap), a tube of lip balm, two pills of some kind, three silver coins, and various other things – there was even a single strand of hair. The person in the photograph was a woman of about thirty, with her hair in braids. She was unusually good-looking, but her mouth was tightly closed and her eyes were cold – she looked as if she might have been through some terrible times.

'Do you know who that is?' Madame Gu asked.

Of course I knew. The moment I saw the photograph, I recognized Li Ningyu and assumed that those things had been hers. But what I didn't understand was the presence of the steel fountain pen with the white cap and the comb with the broken teeth. I'd seen them in old Mr Pan's house – how could there possibly be two sets?

When Madame Gu heard that, she cursed old Mr Pan roundly. 'The ones I have are the real thing – he couldn't possibly have them! Whatever he has is fake, he's been lying to you. The old bastard even maintains that Li Ningyu took the message out, so is there anything he wouldn't lie about? He's a cheat through and through – he owes everything to his lies, he claims credit for anything he thinks he can get away with. He's an absolute embarrassment, and I despise the way he behaves!'

I could see that she was getting worked up, so I hurriedly tried to calm her down. 'Yes, it would be easy enough to find similar-looking items in any antiques market. I'm quite sure that the real ones are the ones in front of me right now.' To get off the subject, I asked her, 'When did you first get to know Li Ningyu? Did you meet her when you came back from the United States?'

'Oh… not that soon,' she said evasively, gazing distractedly at the sofa.

I persisted. 'I've been told that when you got back from America, you worked for a time in the Shanghai police, is that right?'

'Yes…'

She told me that by the time she came back from America, her father was already firmly established in Wang Jingwei's good books, which meant he was also widely regarded as a traitor. He'd been made Deputy Director of the Shanghai Special Governance Committee and every time Wang Jingwei came to Shanghai the two of them would meet. Mr Gu could have got Xiaomeng whatever job she wanted, but as she'd graduated from the police academy, the Bureau decided it would look less suspicious if she worked at the police headquarters first, rather than joining a military unit straight away. Thanks to her father's connections, she was sent to Nanjing to study wireless telegraphy and decryption techniques. In fact, this was exactly what she'd been trained in while she was in the US, so she was just going through the motions, but once she'd completed her studies, it was straightforward enough to have her transferred into a key military division.

At that point the puppet regime was vigorously promoting reconstruction, and all enemy-occupied areas were busy setting up military units under the nominal control of the collaborationist Nanjing government. In particular, President Wang Jingwei had put enormous effort into creating the East China Counterinsurgency Corps, the ECCC, which consisted of four independent brigades, one of which was based in Hangzhou. It was intended to function as an umbrella organization ensuring the smooth establishment of the puppet regime in the present instance, and stable development in the future.

'If that region of East China was crucial for the enemy, it was also crucial for us.' Madame Gu gave a slight smile as she casually related the major decisions that had been taken all those years ago. 'It was imperative that we got our Nationalist agents into the ECCC. And who was best placed for that? Our superiors decided it should be my father and me.'

'Because your family was based in Hangzhou?'

'That was just an excuse.' The most important reason, she explained, was that thanks to her training in wireless telegraphy and decryption she would be seen by the puppet regime as ideal material for either their Telecommunications

Division or their Decryption Unit, both of which would give her access to top-secret information.

'And in the end you went into the Decryption Unit?'

'Uh-huh.'

'Was that how you got to know Li Ningyu?'

'And not just got to know...'

Madame Gu sighed and picked up the comb. She stroked it over and over again, as if that might help bring some order into her confused recollections of those long-ago days. It was quite clear that her fingers were no longer as nimble as they had once been, to the point where I worried that she might drop the comb at any moment.

After a long silence, she began.

'We will start with this comb. The first time I ever met Li Ningyu, this comb was there to witness it, and it was also present the very last time I saw her...'

2

One afternoon in December 1939, the then head of the East China Counterinsurgency Corps, Commander Qian Huyi, took Gu Xiaomeng to the office of Li Ningyu, the head of the unit that decrypted telegraphic communications. It looked as if Li Ningyu had just washed her hair; she was sitting there with her head down, reading a newspaper and combing out her dripping hair. Gu Xiaomeng was amazed at how beautiful her hair was, so black and straight, like a hank of shining silk hanging in front of her face, with the red comb repeatedly sweeping through it. It was like a scene from a fairy tale. In a very real sense, Gu Xiaomeng met the hair and the comb first, and only afterwards got to know the person.

When Li Ningyu straightened up, she didn't seem at all like someone out of a fairy tale; although very good-looking, and with beautiful pale skin, she didn't look pleased or smile at all. Her stony expression gave the impression that she would be difficult to get to know.

President Wang Jingwei himself had both written to the ECCC and phoned them to tell them of Gu Xiaomeng's arrival; when Qian Huyi introduced Gu Xiaomeng to Li Ningyu, he put special emphasis on this. You'd have thought that would have made Li Ningyu be a little more friendly, oblige her to offer her new colleague some warm words, but she remained as unsmiling as ever and simply said in an arctic tone, 'Welcome.'

This was no chatterbox. She seemed as hard as her comb, and her words were as stiff as if they'd been spoken by an automaton.

Gu Xiaomeng was also wanting to establish a reputation: she wanted everyone to know that she was a spoilt little madam from a rich family, superficial in her dealings with others, arrogant and tiresome, fearless in word and deed. So, faced with her immediate superior's disdain, she was rude in her reply.

'Why do I get the feeling that I'm actually not welcome at all?'

That was supposed to make Li Ningyu feel awkward, but Li Ningyu didn't bat an eyelid. She simply replied, in a loud, clear voice, 'Of course you're not welcome here. We don't have the time or space to cosset a little princess.'

[Transcript from the interview with Gu Xiaomeng]

That was how we started out, like enemies. You might think that I hated her for the way she behaved towards me, but you'd be wrong. Quite the opposite, in fact. I'd decided that I liked her. Strange, isn't it? Actually, it's not so strange. I'd spent my whole life surrounded by people who knew I had powerful connections and continually tried to cosy up to me – very few people dared to cross me. You value things more when they're rare, and she behaved in this extraordinary way, which was a challenge for me. It made me feel that she'd be fun. I was curious about her, I found it interesting. I knew that if she'd been just like everyone else, she'd let me get my own way every time, in which case we could never be really good friends. Of course, I had my own reasons for wanting to get close to her, since that would facilitate the mission I'd been given by Chongqing.

Let me tell you, it's very easy for enemies to become friends; opposites attract, and that's a fact. And Li Ningyu and I were completely different. I always say that she was like a polar ice cap: nothing grew in her vicinity, she led a colourless existence, she had a cold personality and nobody wanted to get close to her. As for me… well, I was Nanjing's very own Mount Zijin, always done up to the nines, always having fun, the centre of attention.

Li Ningyu would spend the entire day in her office and quite often whole days would go by without her saying a word to anyone – she just sat there in total silence. I, on the other hand, had ants in my pants; if there was nothing to do, I was out of the office straight away, in and out of other people's rooms, chatting or arguing with them, trying to persuade them to do this or that for me, taking nothing seriously. Of course, that was kind of my natural personality, but it was also a technique to deceive the enemy. Daddy once said to me that it's impossible to hide your natural personality for any length of time so you might as well show it right from the start; besides which, everyone there knew about my special status, so I figured I might as well exploit the fact that I was both young and very well connected. I wanted to give everyone the impression that I was a silly little brat from a rich family who thought it was all just a joke. I wanted people to think that I broke rules just for the hell of it, and that I larded my conversation with swear words no matter who was listening; I wanted them to think I was a complete idiot.

In our division at that time there were three units – Telecommunications, Decryption and Intelligence – with a total staff of about thirty. Within less than a week of my arrival, I'd managed to get to know all of them. It was easy. With the women, I'd take them out and spend money on them. We'd watch movies, or I'd buy clothes for them, or we'd go out to a restaurant together, or we'd go and have photographs taken of ourselves. With the men, it was the other way round. I let them take me out and spend money on me.

There was one time when I invited all my officer colleagues to my home for dinner and Daddy gave everyone a present. Afterwards, he privately analysed each one of them to me. When he got to Li Ningyu, he might as well have been a fortune teller: he said that in the future we'd become good friends. When I asked him why, he said that many of the things that we wanted to know we could find out from her. In other words, befriending her would help me carry out my mission.

So I kept trying. For example, if I'd bought some new clothes, I'd go and find her to ask what she thought about the fit and the colour. And I often asked her for help in my work. There would be telegrams that I could perfectly well decrypt by myself but that I'd pretend I didn't understand. I tried everything I could think of to get close to her, but I wasn't making any headway – she carried on being an ice cube and paying not the slightest attention to me. She talked to me about essential work matters and that was it. I really had no idea what to do next.

[Transcription ends]

This situation changed one day just after Chinese New Year, when Gu Xiaomeng turned into the corridor that led to her office and saw Li Ningyu quarrelling with a man. There was a crowd watching and whispering to each other, but Section Chief Jin was the only one trying to get them to stop fighting. There was nothing he could do, however. The man was absolutely furious; he was jumping up and down, calling Li Ningyu a whore, swearing that he was going to break her legs and would kill her if she ever set foot in his house again. He began beating her up, punching and kicking her until she was screaming in pain. Section Chief Jin was so frightened, he tried to run away and hide.

Seeing how serious it was getting, some of the onlookers sidled off to their offices, while others went downstairs to get the guards, but no one was actually helping Li Ningyu. Gu Xiaomeng ran forward, grabbed hold of her and refused to let go. She shouted at the man, hurling the worst abuse she could think of at him, until she was making such a racket that he decided to slink away.

3

I realized at once that this man must have been Mr Pan senior as a young man; he was pretending to have heard that Li Ningyu had taken a lover and he'd come to her office to kick up a fuss. That was the plan the two of them had come up with, the aim being to show everyone that she'd been thrown out of her home, that she couldn't possibly go back there every night and that from now on she'd have to stay at her work unit. That would make it much easier for her to keep an eye on what was going on. Later, senior management arranged for her to stay on the base in accommodation set aside for unmarried members of staff, and from then on she acted as if she were indeed a grass widow. She returned home every lunchtime, ostensibly to see the children but in reality so that she could take her intelligence out.

Naturally, Gu Xiaomeng knew nothing of this at the time, so she felt deeply sorry for Li Ningyu. On that first evening, it was obvious that Li Ningyu couldn't possibly go home, but she had nowhere else to go, so Gu Xiaomeng told her father's chauffeur to bring the car round and she took her home with her. Li Ningyu had to make her story as plausible as possible, so she accepted her kind offer.

Later on, the room her work unit arranged for Li Ningyu on the base turned out to be on the same corridor as Gu Xiaomeng's room, so they were now spending all their time together both at work and outside it. They would often go out together and they grew much closer; eventually, they seemed as close as sisters.

[Transcript from the interview with Gu Xiaomeng]
In those days I didn't go home regularly; if I had something to report, I would phone up and the chauffeur would come and collect me. But I did insist on going home every weekend, regardless of whether I had any intelligence to pass on or not, in order to get something decent to eat – the food in our canteen was quite dreadful!

Daddy had moved back to our Hangzhou house by then, which wasn't that far from the base and our ECCC office. If I was going home for the weekend, I would invite Li Ningyu too; she didn't always say yes, but more often than not she came with me. Gradually, she got to know my father as well. Even though she wasn't at all talkative, Daddy thought she could be very useful to us, so he suggested that I try and get her on our side, to see whether we could recruit her as a subagent. We obviously had no idea that she was a Communist agent working for Yan'an.

Of course, the reason she was so keen to make friends with us was precisely because she was working for Yan'an. At the beginning, when she'd been so cold to me, that was actually part of her plan to get close to me – she was paying out the line to hook her fish! She was hoping that my father and I would provide her with top-secret information about goings-on in the upper echelons of Wang Jingwei's puppet government! Working undercover is so exhausting, don't you think? If we'd known, we could have told her whatever she wanted to know – there was no need to make it all so complicated. After all, the

Nationalists and the Communists were of the same view when it came to the Japanese devils and their running dog Wang Jingwei. But that was impossible – we were all desperate to keep our masks in place, desperate not to give anyone even the slightest inkling as to who we really were; the tiniest slip and we'd have been killed.

As I just said, Daddy suggested trying to recruit her, but when he mentioned his idea to someone high up in the Nationalist Party, I was immediately summoned home and warned that under no circumstances was I to do anything of the kind. I wasn't to try and recruit anyone! Why not? The Bureau was afraid that its entire plan would be ruined if I failed. Daddy was an important agent and it had cost the Nationalist Party a lot of money to get him into Wang Jingwei's circle. They weren't going to risk losing him over such small fry. As for bringing anyone new on board, well, at that time we were surrounded by undercover Nationalist comrades, some of whom were totally reliable, but we were absolutely forbidden from making contact with any of them, and very few of them knew about Daddy and me. That was why so many people voiced their suspicions of us after Dai Li died and tried to bring us down – they didn't know anything about our mission, they'd never heard of us. They thought that my father must have bought Dai Li in the same way he'd bought Wang Jingwei. Fools! There were plenty among them whose lives Daddy and I had saved.

To get back to the story: if I'd been allowed to try and recruit Li Ningyu, I might have found out that she was a Communist agent long before I actually did.

[Transcription ends]

At this point, I naturally couldn't stop myself from asking Madame Gu, 'So when did you find out for sure that she was a Communist agent?'

'After we were taken to the Tan Estate,' she replied simply.

'So in spite of all the time you'd spent together up till then, you didn't notice anything at all?'

'What do you think?'

I didn't know what to say.

'Do you really believe that I was so useless I couldn't even decrypt one of our own cypher telegrams?'

She was talking about the top-secret, twice-encrypted message from Nanjing – the one about the Gathering of Heroes.

'As you know perfectly well, I received specialist training in decryption in the United States, and then after I came back I had further training in Nanjing. Handling something like that was perfectly straightforward. Or do you imagine that I completely wasted my time on my training courses? Am I that dumb? If I were that stupid, how on earth do you imagine I've managed to survive until now?'

It was obvious she was irritated and wanted to have a go at me.

She went on to explain that she'd decrypted the top-secret telegram quite easily and that the description given in my novel of how she'd struggled and then had to ask Li Ningyu for help was quite wrong.

'So if you'd already decrypted it, why did you ask Li Ningyu for assistance?'

She laughed coldly. 'Didn't you ask me why in spite of all the time we'd spent together I hadn't realized that she was a Communist agent? I've already answered your question.

Do you think I would have asked her for help if I hadn't realized that something was wrong?'

Maybe it was because she'd spent so long working as an undercover agent, but Madame Gu spoke in an unusually discursive manner – she'd begin a sentence and then leave it hanging, or she'd mention something but wouldn't explain its significance. It was very exhausting to listen to, and I felt as if I were taking some kind of intelligence test. Eventually, though, I discovered that she'd suspected Li Ningyu's true identity for a while, and that was why, when she read the top-secret telegram revealing that K and the other members of the Hangzhou underground were to be arrested, she'd pretended she couldn't decrypt it and asked Li Ningyu for help.

'I had absolutely no need of her assistance, but I was trying my luck – if Li Ningyu was indeed a Communist agent, then I was doing my good deed for the day.' She sighed. 'Of course, I was hoping that would prove for sure whether she was a Red or not. To tell you the truth, I didn't have any evidence for my suspicions at that point, not even a hunch. It was all because of something my father had said.'

4

What could Mr Gu have said?

Madame Gu seemed to be replaying the scene before her eyes.

By the time of the Mid-Autumn Festival of 1940, Gu Xiaomeng and Li Ningyu had been friends for more than six months. They were now almost as close as sisters – as evidenced by the matter of Mr Jian.

Mr Jian was a young man, very modern and progressive in his thinking and deeply committed to his career as an actor, but he enjoyed reflected glory too much and he would use people quite ruthlessly to achieve his ends. For example, he'd decided to give up his persona as a sensitive and modern young man in order to perform paeans to the Japanese devils and their puppet regime, appearing in a series of plays for them. The respect he showed the Gu family and his flirtation with Gu Xiaomeng was another manifestation of this – he took the Gus' apparent allegiance to the puppet regime at face value and had no idea that Gu Xiaomeng had joined the resistance and was secretly committed to a very different path.

Gu Xiaomeng's father immediately realized that Mr Jian could be very useful for them. As a famous actor, he was being promoted by the Japanese as a model for the younger generation of collaborators, so allowing him to get close to the family would show that the Gus were just the same – it would be an excellent cover for them. So Gu Xiaomeng started to act out a romance with Mr Jian. There were phone calls and love letters; they went out on dates. Everything was carefully arranged to look perfectly natural. This performance was very helpful as a cover, but it was dangerous for her personally, particularly once they started going out on dates together – she didn't want to get raped, after all. She needed someone to go with her.

Who to ask?

Li Ningyu.

Whenever she and Mr Jian were due to go out together,

she always asked Li Ningyu to come too. That's how close they were. And given that they were such good friends, was it likely that Gu Xiaomeng would leave Li Ningyu alone on base on public holidays? Of course not. At the Mid-Autumn Festival, which was the very last Mid-Autumn Festival that Li Ningyu lived to see, she joined the Gu family at home.

Like all the main festivals, the Mid-Autumn Festival is best celebrated with family, and Mr Gu wasn't one to stint on the traditions. The garden had been hung with strings of red lanterns and Mrs Wu had made mooncakes filled with red-bean paste, which they ate as they gazed up at the full moon. Even though Li Ningyu's story about not getting on with her husband and not wanting to live with him any more was a pretence, when they all stood there looking up at the moon together, she did miss her children, and she made them an excuse to leave early. Gu Xiaomeng had already decided to spend the night at home with her father, so she didn't go back to base with Li Ningyu, but she did see her off at the door. When she came back, her father was still looking up at the moon.

In an expressionless voice, he asked his daughter, 'Do you think your friend could be a Communist?'

That was a shock! Gu Xiaomeng was completely taken aback and asked him how he could possibly think such a thing.

'The Communist Party have a lot of their military forces in this region at the moment, so they'll be needing good access to inside information on the regime's plans.'

That made sense, but why would their insider be Li Ningyu?

'I'm not saying it's definitely Li Ningyu,' he said. 'I'm

just speculating. But if you think about it logically, the Communist Party will want to have infiltrated the key units, and there are only a few of those: your military division, Wang Tianxiang's secret police, and the front-line command. I've no idea which of them they've gone for, but if it turns out that it's your unit, then I'd have thought Li Ningyu would be the most likely candidate. I've met your other colleagues and none of them could possibly do it – they're just not right for that kind of work.'

Mr Gu had no real evidence for his theory, but Gu Xiaomeng could see the logic in it. She'd quickly got the measure of everyone else in the unit – you knew exactly where you were with them from the very first glance. The only exception was Li Ningyu: they'd known each other for a long time by then, but she was still a riddle to her. In the light of her father's analysis, however, it all made sense. Which was why, beginning on the night of the Mid-Autumn Festival, Gu Xiaomeng started to monitor Li Ningyu's activities in secret. Regrettably, however, as Madame Gu said, she didn't unearth anything and was still monitoring her right up to the day they were taken to the Tan Estate.

That afternoon, Madame Gu made one final comment to me as she looked up at the sky and sighed. 'She was dug in very deep!'

FOUR

1

Spring rains were falling – torrential rains – clearing the air of the oppressive heat. Out in the countryside, it was even fresher and cleaner. But because of all the rain the roads were slippery, and despite having the same driver and the same car and taking the same route, it was going to take twenty minutes longer to get there. I would be late and that was making me anxious; I was afraid Madame Gu would be angry. Even so, that wasn't enough to quash the flutter of excitement at what the day might hold. Madame Gu had dealt with the first chapters of my novel yesterday; today she'd be going more deeply into what had happened. I was prickling with anticipation for what I was about to find out, as if the person I was going to meet was not an old woman from the past but an alien who'd flown in from the future.

The good weather had made Madame Gu more cheerful, and because we'd already covered the basics in our previous interview, we were able to get on to our main subject straight away – the Tan Estate.

Given that she had actually been held there, and also because she'd grown up in a not dissimilar environment, Madame Gu was able to give a much better and more detailed account than Mr Pan senior and my other interviewees of what the Tan Estate had been like sixty years ago. She was able to describe quite precisely the architectural style of the buildings, the layout, and the trees and plants used in the landscaping of the gardens; she could even recall the stone statues arranged along the courtyard walls, and the pictures and ornaments in the corridors. She gave such a vivid account that it was almost as if the estate were right there before my eyes. If I wanted to, I could simply press play on my recording of that interview and copy exactly what she said into my manuscript. However, I came to feel that this would just be padding, that there was actually no need to include it. In the transcripts of the interviews given below, it's been necessary to occasionally trim some extraneous material.

Madame Gu explained that although she was very suspicious when Commander Zhang summoned everyone to the Tan Estate in the middle of the night, she could only guess at what might have happened. It was only once they'd decrypted the Commander's bit of doggerel that she began to seriously consider that Li Ningyu might be a Communist agent.

[Transcript from the interview with Gu Xiaomeng]

Ah well, although at the time I had no idea what was going on, when I sat with the others – 'Wu, Jin, Gu and Li, which of you can it be?' – I suspected it was her. Then when Commander Zhang explained that it was all because of the top-secret telegram from Nanjing, I was even more sure it was her – she'd fallen into my trap. I was feeling quite pleased with myself, because I'd finally got her. But it was also upsetting, because I had a sense that this time she wouldn't emerge unscathed.

To tell you the truth, it was a master stroke by Li Ningyu to get Chief of Staff Wu Zhiguo dragged into the whole thing. At the time I had no idea whether he'd gone into her office or not. I hadn't seen anything, and I hadn't been paying attention. But when she said that Wu Zhiguo came to find her because he wanted to know if the telegram concerned members of his staff, I was pretty sure she must be lying. Why? Because everybody knew how quiet and odd she was, and that she didn't like talking to people – if Wu Zhiguo had really wanted to know what the telegram said, he would have talked to me, not her. That was the first point. The second thing was that even supposing he had gone into her office and asked her about it, from what I knew of her, she would never have told him anything. At that stage, I was still copying out the message, it hadn't yet gone up to our superiors, so there's no way she would have said anything to anyone. She would just have said she couldn't talk about it until it had gone up. Anyway, I was pretty much one hundred per cent convinced she was lying, and that's why I was quite sure she had to be Ghost.

How did I feel once I knew that she was Ghost? You really want to know? Well, let me tell you, I didn't want her to blow her cover – that was for personal reasons and for the sake of the cause we were both devoted to. I wanted to help her. Even though there was very little chance I'd be able to do anything useful, at least I wanted to try – some good might come of it. But what could I do? To tell you the truth, if she'd asked me to denounce Chief of Staff Wu or Section Chief Jin, I wouldn't have dared. If I'd done that and the accusation didn't stick and it came out that it was Li Ningyu after all... well, I just couldn't take the risk. At best, I'd be in serious trouble too, and in the worst-case scenario, my father's position would be undermined as well. I didn't have the stomach for it; it was just too dangerous.

So what could I do? I did what you described in your book – I threw my weight around like a spoilt brat, I refused to be questioned, I spouted all kinds of rubbish to Secretary Bai. If he asked me something, then either I wouldn't answer or I flew off the handle – anything to divert attention. That lunchtime on the second day, I refused to eat anything, as you know, and instead chatted to one of the guards because I wanted him to contact Mr Jian for me. My motivation? I was muddying the waters; I wanted Hihara to suspect me. I had nothing to fear from being suspected, because I knew that I wasn't Ghost – you can't make something fake look real forever, and you can't make something real look fake. I just wanted to create a bit of breathing space for Li Ningyu, give her an opportunity to escape.

[Transcription ends]

Since her aim was to help Li Ningyu plot her escape, Gu Xiaomeng needed to discuss the situation with Li Ningyu, so they could lay their plans carefully.

What she was not expecting was that Li Ningyu would turn on her, despite her good intentions.

2

That afternoon, when Li Ningyu came back from lunch, she saw Gu Xiaomeng stretched out on her bed and asked her why she hadn't gone with the rest of them to eat.

Gu Xiaomeng sat bolt upright and glared at her. 'I was going to ask you about that! How can you possibly feel like eating in a situation like this?'

'You're too sensitive, Xiaomeng,' Li Ningyu replied. 'In a situation like this... well, we haven't done anything wrong, so I don't see what you're worried about.'

Gu Xiaomeng laughed coldly. 'I've certainly done nothing wrong!'

Li Ningyu smiled. 'So you have nothing to be afraid of.'

'And what about you?' Gu Xiaomeng stared pointedly at Li Ningyu.

'What about me?'

Gu Xiaomeng spoke with great sincerity. 'Ningyu, you don't need to lie to me, I know all about it...'

Li Ningyu was so furious that she opened her eyes as wide as they would go. 'What are you talking about? Are you trying to say that you suspect me of...? Are you out of your mind? We've known each other for ages, I thought we were like sisters – I must have been completely stupid!'

She stalked off in a rage, but when she got to the door, she turned round and said, 'Just you wait – we'll see what you have to say for yourself when the truth comes out!'

[Transcript from the interview with Gu Xiaomeng]

What was I supposed to think to that? I was so confused, and looking at her angry face, I wondered if I really had got it all wrong. But in my heart of hearts I knew I hadn't; she was playing a part and doing it very well indeed! I spent years working undercover and I never saw anyone who could hold their nerve the way she could.

It was much later that I found out that there were a number of reasons why she'd behaved so unkindly. One: she was sure that Hihara was going to test our handwriting, and once that happened she would have her scapegoat, so there was nothing to worry about. Two: she'd already realized that we were surrounded by plain-clothes police officers and guards, so there was no way we could escape, which meant the only way to deal with the situation was to deny all knowledge of it and keep on denying it, whatever they did. Plus she'd already discovered that the room was bugged, which was why she'd refused to say anything to me and had pretended to be so angry that she walked off. She was always so careful – impressively so. She could sum up a situation at a glance, and what she couldn't see, she could guess at.

Anyway, that evening there was indeed a test of our handwriting, and it ended with Hihara arresting Wu Zhiguo. When that happened, I thought I'd got it all wrong, that Chief of Staff Wu was Ghost, so I stopped trying to muddy the waters. In your novel you mention that the first person to be dismissed from Hihara's enquiries was me, and that's pretty much true. If it was Wu Zhiguo, I didn't particularly want to help him. Why should I? You see, a few weeks earlier, he'd killed about two dozen of our top Nationalist agents out in Huzhou. If he was indeed Ghost, that just showed that he didn't consider us Nationalists to be part of the anti-Japanese resistance; he was obviously using his position in the ECCC to kill us in circumstances where he wasn't going to get the blame for it. After the Wannan Incident, when the Nationalists killed thousands of Communist soldiers, there was a fundamental split between the Communists and the Nationalists, and there were plenty of examples of that kind of thing. The history of that period is too complicated; there are some things that are very difficult to understand, not just for you young people but also for those of us who were right there on the scene.

[Transcription ends]

I was afraid that she was trying to divert me from my enquiries, so while she was sighing over that, I jumped in with a question. 'Madame Gu, how did you find out that Li Ningyu was Ghost?'

'As I said, you can't make something fake look real forever, and you can't make something real seem fake.' She spoke nonchalantly, seemingly unwilling to get back on track.

But I wasn't going to give up. 'Indeed. So when did you realize the truth?'

'Oh, it was pure chance.' The old lady smiled bitterly. 'Or perhaps it was all meant to be and I was destined right from the beginning to help her.'

'So when did this happen?'

'Oh, it was that day…' She looked me in the eye and then said simply, 'The day she got that terrible stomach ache.'

3

Even though more than half a century had gone by, the old lady could remember quite clearly everything that had occurred that day. It was as if she were calling to mind the beginning of a real crisis in her life.

It happened on the way back from the dining hall. Li Ningyu had just had that terrible stomach ache and the pain had not yet entirely abated, so she was walking slowly. Gu Xiaomeng had been helping her along with a hand on her arm, but just before they got to a fork in the path, Li Ningyu moved her hand away with a smile. 'I'm fine,' she said. 'I can walk by myself.' As she said that, she happened to drop two of the plastic capsules that Hu Patented Stomach Pills were sold in. One of them rolled to the side of the path.

Gu Xiaomeng laughed and said, 'Your stomach medicine obviously really works – you've only just taken it and you seem much better already.'

'Oh yes,' Li Ningyu replied, 'I always take this for a stomach ache; it's very good.'

As the two of them chatted, they followed in the wake of Hihara and the others. They'd all been walking more slowly than normal for Li Ningyu's sake, but the pair of them still ended up falling behind: two or three metres to begin with, and then three or four.

Madame Gu informed me that Hu Patented Stomach Pills were a traditional Chinese herbal medicine. They came in the form of round pills, and one of the key ingredients was *ganlan* oil, which made the pills sort of moist. The pills had to stay soft and moist or they wouldn't work, so originally they were sold in waxed paper wrappings, but that wasn't very effective and over time they would still dry out. Later on, the Japanese designed a plastic capsule for them and sealed it with wax, which meant that pills could be stored for a year or two. The two halves of the capsule fitted together to form a complete shell and you just peeled off the wax to break it open.

'See, I have one here.' Madame Gu reached into the red lacquerware box and took out a plastic medicine capsule. As she waved it at me, she said, 'In those days it was quite common for people to take the medicine and then keep the capsule. I guess they didn't like the idea of just throwing the capsules away. But there wasn't anything you could do with them; people gave them to children to play with. So when she happened to drop the plastic capsules, I didn't pay the slightest attention.'

In fact, Li Ningyu hadn't 'happened to drop' them at all – she'd picked a spot that every visitor to the building, everyone going into or coming out of it, would have to pass, and she'd dropped them in the most eye-catching place. One capsule had rolled to the side of the path and as if by accident she kicked it into the middle. She had to do that – she had to put them in an obvious place so that if Turtle came again the next day he'd have no trouble spotting them.

Mr Pan senior had already told me that Turtle and Li Ningyu used various signals to communicate – the fountain pen being one of them. The plastic capsules from Hu Patented Stomach Pills were another.

[Transcript from the interview with Gu Xiaomeng]

Later on, Li Ningyu told me that she used to use three

different methods to send intelligence off base. The first method, which was the safest, was that at lunchtimes, when she visited her children, she would take the intelligence home with her. Mr Pan would then transmit it on to Tiger via the radio. That was safe, but it took time; Mr Pan worked at a newspaper and it would be past nine or even ten o'clock at night when he got back to the house.

If a dispatch was urgent or extra-urgent, it was usually Turtle who took it. An urgent dispatch meant it had to be in Tiger's hands by that evening. In such cases, Li Ningyu would hide the intelligence in a piece of rubbish, which she would then place in the rubbish bin for our office building on the base – she'd put a mark on the bag and then Turtle could see at a glance which was Li Ningyu's. He would collect the rubbish at around suppertime, six or seven in the evening, and then he'd go to the entrance to Lute Tower Park and pass it on to Qian Huyi's concubine – that was the agent code-named Warrior – and she'd take it to Tiger. It was an urgent dispatch that Police Chief Wang's people got hold of that evening – Li Ningyu's message to call off the Gathering of Heroes. Warrior had collected the message from Turtle, but she was arrested on her way to deliver it to Tiger.

If a dispatch was extra-urgent, it needed to reach Tiger in the shortest possible time. Given that Turtle had a fixed routine for collecting the rubbish, and he and Li Ningyu weren't able to communicate directly, how did they get round that? They used the plastic capsules from Hu Patented Stomach Pills!

Li Ningyu did actually have serious problems with her stomach. Hu Patented Stomach Pills were a standard treatment in traditional Chinese medicine: there were no side effects, they were produced locally and they were cheap, so she took them regularly. She had medicine capsules coming out of her ears!

As you can see, it's about the size of a marble, and black in colour; if you dropped it on the pavement, someone looking for it would spot it right away, but to everyone else it would just be rubbish – nobody would give it a second glance. Even if someone did notice, it wouldn't matter, because there'd be nothing in it – she'd put a bit of mud inside or a tiny pebble, just to give it some weight and stop it from being blown away by the wind. Anyway, the point is that there was no message hidden inside it; it was just a sign to tell Turtle: 'I have a message for you, you must collect it as soon as possible.' **[Transcription ends]**

And where would Turtle find that message?

Inside another medicine capsule. Not in one of the capsules strewn on the path, but in a capsule placed on the rim of the rubbish bin. The medicine capsules out on the path were just there to say: we're empty, but our fellow on the bin has what you're looking for.

4

As Madame Gu talked, I inspected the medicine capsules, now more than sixty years old, and I couldn't help but marvel at the strange and ingenious way Li Ningyu had chosen to pass on intelligence. There was a notch in the capsule to make it easier to open, and it then split into two hemispheres. When you closed it, the two halves fitted together perfectly, making it completely waterproof. It was just right for passing messages, and it would have been easy enough for Turtle to collect.

Every day when he started work, Turtle went first to check certain prearranged locations, and through the course of the day he'd go back and check them again from time to time. If he saw medicine capsules on the path, he'd immediately know to go and remove a message capsule from the bin. Since this was only done in the event of a very urgent piece of intelligence, he would then go straight away to find Warrior, or he might even phone his superiors directly, in order to get the information to Tiger as soon as possible. In a crisis, special measures applied.

When Gu Xiaomeng saw Li Ningyu drop the two capsules onto the path after dinner that day, she didn't think anything of it. She also didn't think anything of it when, after they'd walked a bit further, Li Ningyu pretended that her shoelace had come undone and went over to one of the bins and put her foot up on it to retie it.

'And what was strange about that?' The old lady answered her own question. 'She wasn't feeling very well, so she propped her foot up on the bin so that she didn't have to bend down. It was a completely natural thing to do.'

Gu Xiaomeng simply walked on. Then she happened to glance back – not because she was suspicious of Li Ningyu; she just chanced to look round. It was that glance that revealed to her what Li Ningyu was really up to.

'I saw a medicine capsule drop from her hand onto the edge of the bin,' the old lady told me excitedly. 'She did it very neatly – it wasn't like she went and threw it straight inside the bin; she just happened to drop it when she stopped to tie her shoelace. It seemed to be entirely accidental.'

But Gu Xiaomeng wasn't fooled. In a flash, she lost all faith in Li Ningyu.

'It was just too odd,' she said, a look of disdain on her face. 'It was just a couple of medicine capsules after all; what was she doing strewing them about the place when she could have put them all straight in the bin? And besides, this time she clearly didn't want me to see what she was doing.'

Which made Gu Xiaomeng all the more eager to find out what was going on. When they got inside the west building, she pretended she'd left their room key in the dining hall and went back to get it; on the way, she picked up the three capsules. She didn't open them immediately. She went back, unlocked the door to their bedroom, and let Li Ningyu in. She herself went straight to the bathroom. It was getting dark by then, and it was already pitch black inside the toilet, so she switched on the light and used her fingernails to open one capsule after the other.

The first capsule was empty.

The second capsule was also empty.

But inside the third capsule – the one from the rubbish bin – was a scrap of paper, which read:

For urgent dispatch!

K's movements are known to the enemy.

I am suspected and held under house arrest.

Call off the Gathering of Heroes immediately!

Ghost

Li Ningyu's secrets lay exposed before her, as bare as a newborn baby.

But that wasn't all. Even though the light was dim, Gu Xiaomeng was able to unravel yet another mystery. She immediately realized what must have happened with Chief of Staff Wu. Li Ningyu had framed him – it was she who had forged his handwriting on the original message. But now that Wu Zhiguo was apparently dead (Hihara at this point was still pretending that he'd committed suicide), she could no longer use his handwriting, so for this latest message she'd used someone else's.

Whose writing had she forged this time?

'Mine! My God, I could hardly believe my eyes – she was trying to use me as a shield!' The passage of time had done nothing to temper Madame Gu's shock or anger. She was shouting now, as if caught up in the nightmare of her past.

This was a real bolt from the blue for Gu Xiaomeng. She was stunned. She collapsed in a heap on the floor, unable to move. She remained there, practically comatose, until Li Ningyu came to the bathroom to find her. At which point Gu Xiaomeng regained her self-possession.

She was livid.

'So she'd been practising your handwriting?' I asked.

'Actually, I don't think so,' the old lady said. 'It was a spur-of-the-moment forgery, which is why it took me a little while to realize what she'd done. Of course she was familiar with my handwriting, and she'd studied painting, so it was still a pretty good imitation.'

'And if,' I said, 'that scrap of paper had ended up in Hihara's hands...'

'Then I would have been in serious trouble. Hihara would

have suspected me. If she'd managed to produce an exact forgery of my handwriting, it would have been better for me. But it was that similar-but-not-too-similar quality that would have caused the problems, because it would have looked as if I'd tried but failed to alter my writing, cover my tracks.' Madame Gu's hands were trembling now, but her gaze was steely. 'At that moment I truly hated her – she was trying to get me killed! What a bitch. She'd always said she thought of me as a sister, she made much of us being friends. Well, that was over now. I was going straight to the authorities to turn her in.'

Li Ningyu obviously realized something was wrong. She stopped Gu Xiaomeng as she headed for the door and asked where she was going.

Gu Xiaomeng cursed her and told her to go to hell. 'Don't touch me!' She pushed Li Ningyu's hand away. 'You're disgusting, you know that? I hate you! I want you dead!'

By now Li Ningyu must have had a pretty good idea of what the problem was. She held on to Gu Xiaomeng as tightly as she could, to stop her from going anywhere. She knew that the room was bugged and that if Gu Xiaomeng started to scream and shout, the people in the building opposite would discover the truth. She shut the door to the bathroom and locked it, turned the tap on so that the water would mask their voices, then asked Gu Xiaomeng what had happened.

Gu Xiaomeng made a dash for the door, but Li Ningyu held firm and wouldn't let her past. The two of them pushed and shoved and wrestled each other. Gu Xiaomeng started to scream, but Li Ningyu put a hand over her mouth and pressed hard. Rage had consumed Gu Xiaomeng's physical strength, and she couldn't escape. Short of breath, she collapsed to the floor, letting go of the medicine capsule and the scrap of paper she'd been clutching – right in front of Li Ningyu's eyes.

5

There was the evidence, in black and white.

There was no longer any point in Li Ningyu denying it. Denial would only provoke Gu Xiaomeng even more. Instead, she decided to admit everything. Of course, admitting everything wasn't going to be enough; she had to explain and beg for forgiveness. She said she'd forged Gu Xiaomeng's writing because she knew that Hihara wouldn't really suspect her, and even if he did, her father could get her off.

What kind of logic was that?

In situations like that, it doesn't matter so much what you say so long as you keep talking and coming up with excuses, lying if necessary, anything to make you seem helpless. Of course, the best way to make yourself look helpless is to cry, but not too loudly. Li Ningyu hugged Gu Xiaomeng tightly as she sobbed and whispered in her ear, 'We've been such good friends, I hope you can find it in your heart to forgive me. If you don't, then I'm dead – do you really want to send me to my grave? If I die, my two babies will be orphans, and they love you so much, they always make such a fuss about wanting to go and see their Auntie Gu… I didn't have a choice, Xiaomeng – I'm really sorry. Think of my children, you have to forgive me.'

She cried, she pleaded, the tears trickled down her cheeks, she choked down her sobs, and she begged Gu Xiaomeng to forgive her.

Her tears did make Gu Xiaomeng less angry, but she was still a very long way from feeling able to pardon her. So Li Ningyu tried a different tack: she started lying.

[Transcript from the interview with Gu Xiaomeng]
She thought that I was really in love with that creature Jian, so she lied to me and said that he was one of her comrades.

To begin with I didn't believe a word of it, but she was very convincing – she knew a lot about his family and his background, about how we met, and other things that hardly anyone else knew, so she made it sound good. I certainly got the impression that she knew him very well, even better than I did.

Some of what she said I'd never heard before, but there were a few things she mentioned that I knew to be true – like that he'd gone to Chongqing in secret. That I knew to be a fact. And it was also true that he read a lot of progressive books and magazines, like *Threads of Talk* and *Fiction Monthly* – that kind of thing. He bought them on the quiet, but I knew he read them.

Jian was a big star in Hangzhou in those days, famous in the arts world for his pro-Japanese performances, so the newspapers often carried stories about him, and there was plenty of gossip doing the rounds too. So she could have got some of her information that way. The other source would have been me – I'd forgotten what I'd told her, but she hadn't.

She even claimed that the reason he'd become so friendly with me was that he wanted me to become a comrade too. Later on, I found out for a fact that he wasn't a member of the Communist Party and never had been, but she felt confident in plucking all this out of thin air because she knew I couldn't check her story with him. She was prepared to lie herself blue in the face if it might get me to calm down and stop me from turning her in.

Ha! She had absolutely no idea that there was no point in talking like that to me – I never had the slightest affection for Jian, and I was never going to be one of their comrades. It wouldn't have made any difference if that Jian creature had genuinely turned out to be a Red.

And then she tried to recruit me into the Communist Party, right there and then, because she wanted me to take her message out. She tried everything: summoning up every patriotic martyr, right back to the twelfth century, to General Yue Fei; listing the horrors the puppet army was guilty of; describing the vile behaviour of various collaborationist traitors; trying to make out that she and her comrades were the only people doing the right thing in the face of all the outrages that were happening in our country.

I listened to what she had to say, but it disgusted me. I swore at her and made fun of her in the worst way that I could think of. I don't remember exactly what I said, but I'm sure that in order to demonstrate that I was not the shameless traitor she thought I was, I must have made some very pointed remarks. And that was when she started to suspect who I really was.

[Transcription ends]

When Li Ningyu realized, thanks to all the curses and sarcastic comments, that Gu Xiaomeng might be working undercover for the Nationalists, she tried another tack – blackmail!

'Okay,' Li Ningyu said, 'you don't need to say any more. I understand. In fact, I understand everything. So, we ought to help each other, since, after all, you Nationalists and we Communists are really on the same side.'

'What do you mean, you know everything?' Gu Xiaomeng asked, stalling, appalled at the possibility that she might have blown her own cover. 'How are we on the same side?'

Li Ningyu went on the attack. 'Why won't you admit what you've been up to? You should be given credit for your patriotism. But you also shouldn't try and make me take the blame for everything. If you turn me in, I'll say that you wrote the message – I don't care if they kill both of us!'

'Well, off you go then,' Gu Xiaomeng shot back defiantly. 'Go and turn me in right this minute!'

Li Ningyu gave a hollow laugh. 'You might be fine with that, but what about your father? You and I are mere minnows in this particular pond – Hihara won't get much satisfaction from arresting and killing the two of us, will he? But think how he'll enjoy being able to catch a big fish, someone who managed to get so close to the traitor Wang Jingwei.'

Gu Xiaomeng was out of her depth. After a couple of rounds of this, she was already on the back foot, unable to extricate herself. She didn't know what it was that she'd said – how could Li Ningyu have discovered her father's real identity?

In fact, she hadn't said anything; at the most, she'd given a few pointers as to their real opinions, but Li Ningyu was very alert to that kind of thing, and she'd understood immediately. She grabbed hold of what she had and then without the slightest compunction forced Gu Xiaomeng into a corner, using a mix of veiled threats and lies. In the end, Gu Xiaomeng had to throw down her weapons in surrender, and Li Ningyu came up with the terms for a temporary truce: Gu Xiaomeng wouldn't betray Li Ningyu to the authorities, and Li Ningyu wouldn't make Gu Xiaomeng help her get the message out.

The fact that Gu Xiaomeng agreed to this meant that Li Ningyu was even more convinced that she'd guessed right.

Having got this far with her story, the old lady became very emotional. 'Li Ningyu could steal things right out from under your nose; she was a very crafty character. She could also make you believe whatever she said, and as for trying to work out what she was up to – well, that was impossible. Any ordinary person would have been flummoxed in that situation, but she counter-attacked on nothing at all really – it was the flimsiest of hunches – and managed to knock me off balance. I didn't know what to do, I had no idea how I was going to get out of it. I really didn't know which was worse: turning her in or not! That's why she was perfect as an underground operative – she was the sort of person who planned her actions from every conceivable angle, and whatever happened, she never panicked. No matter how dangerous things became, she never showed the slightest fear.'

I felt that the story was now unfolding in much the same way that a flower bud unfurls its petals. The old lady was very much enjoying her recital of the events of so long ago and seemed oblivious to the fact that our time was up, so I encouraged her to carry on talking. However, Mrs Chen was too professional to allow that; she immediately noticed that the corners of Madame Gu's eyes were drooping, which she said was a sign that she was getting overtired. She told me that I would have to leave. When I hesitated, she said, in a rather teacher-ish fashion, 'When a child gets overtired, they recover after a short rest; if you get overtired, you can take a nap and you'll be fine; but if she gets overtired, it will be a couple of days before she's back to normal.'

What she meant was that I had to consider the bigger picture.

That evening I went back to Taipei in a fever of speculation. I didn't sleep all night because my mind was in such a ferment.

I now had two important questions.

One: given the circumstances described (the two women having become enemies), what happened to make Gu Xiaomeng eventually decide to help Li Ningyu?

Two: how did Gu Xiaomeng get the message out?

Regarding the second question, I had a strong feeling that the very best way would have been to simply put the three capsules back where Gu Xiaomeng had found them and then wait for Turtle to collect them the following day. The first question, however, was a lot more complicated. The two of them were now sworn enemies, and Gu Xiaomeng wasn't the sort who could be easily persuaded to change her mind. In addition, her agreement with Li Ningyu that neither of them was to turn the other in had been forced upon her; it wasn't the result of any sincere desire to assist her.

So what could have happened to change her mind?

That question caused me a sleepless night. My eyes burnt with the unbearable pain of insomnia.

FIVE

1

Insomnia is a state of mind in which the darkness of the night torments you.

The following day, Madame Gu noticed the shadows under my eyes and asked me what the matter was. I told her the truth: I hadn't slept all night. She laughed cheerfully. 'What on earth could be keeping you awake? If anyone should be losing sleep, it's Li Ningyu.' That took us straight back into our conversation.

As you can imagine, Li Ningyu had not been sleeping at all well. She knew better than anyone just how bad the situation was – she'd realized that even before they'd all been rounded up and driven to the Tan Estate. When Commander Zhang phoned that evening to ask her if she'd told anyone about the top-secret telegram from Nanjing, she immediately understood that something must have gone badly wrong. Her message about the Gathering of Heroes must have been intercepted. A couple of hours earlier, she'd put it in the rubbish bin on base, and now here was Commander Zhang suddenly asking about the telegram.

Straight away she decided to drag Chief of Staff Wu into the imbroglio. As the old lady said, that was a master stroke on Li Ningyu's part.

Li Ningyu had long been determined that, at some point, Chief of Staff Wu should pay for his actions in support of the puppet regime. She had practised several people's handwriting but had paid particular attention to mastering Wu Zhiguo's – every line, every stroke – and it really did look like his. She wrote most of her secret dispatches in his handwriting, in the hope that if intercepted they would get this hero of the anti-insurgency campaign into serious trouble; if she could trick people into believing that he was a Communist, that would get him executed.

This had always been the plan, but she was now obliged to put it into action earlier than she'd wanted. Her original idea had been to create some false intelligence, allow it to be intercepted, and entrap Wu Zhiguo that way; if the intelligence was false, the underground wouldn't be compromised and she herself would never be suspected. But what had now happened was the worst of all possible scenarios. The intelligence that had been intercepted was real, which meant that her comrades had no idea what was actually going on, placing K and the others in extreme danger. And she'd been unable to avoid being caught up in it too.

Even though she was taken to the Tan Estate with the others, she wasn't frightened to begin with because she knew – she'd planned right from the start – that Wu Zhiguo would get the blame. What worried her was being under house arrest; there was no way she could get a message out. So, that morning, when she realized that

Turtle had come to find her, she was absolutely delighted. She thought she might be able to get her intelligence to him. However, she had no idea quite how many things would happen that afternoon.

[Transcript from the interview with Gu Xiaomeng]

First of all, she had no idea that Hihara was going to keep such a close eye on her. Judging by what she told me later, at that time she wasn't sure whether Chief of Staff Wu was alive or not, but she thought it most likely he was dead – she couldn't imagine how he'd have persuaded Hihara to suspect her instead without actually killing himself. In this, Li Ningyu made a mistake, and that's why, later on, Hihara was so determined to pursue his investigations into her activities.

Secondly, she was even less prepared for the fact that I would cause her so many problems. She hadn't expected me to work out the truth, and that made it very difficult for her to decide what to do for the best. Although I had said too much myself, which had allowed her to discover my true identity and so get me to promise not to turn her in, she had also seriously upset me, so she had to be afraid that in the end I would betray her. We'd been friends for a long time, so she knew me very well; she knew that I was stubborn and competitive, that I hated to feel that I'd lost out on something, and that if I got angry, there was no saying what I might do. So, as you can imagine, she needed to make sure that I would stay on her side, and that I would remain completely silent.

To tell you the truth, I had no intention of reporting her to the authorities, because I was afraid she'd then just turn round and denounce me. But nor was I going to forgive her, and as for helping her… no way. I hoped that she would confess, because that would be best for both of us. But she said she'd never do that – at least, not until after the message had been smuggled out. Unbelievable, isn't it? She was trying to set conditions: she said that if I helped her get her intelligence out, she would confess. I told her to stop dreaming. She said that there was no point in her still being alive if the message didn't get out – she'd rather be dead. So I told her to go right ahead, she could hang herself or take poison or swallow razor blades, whatever the hell she wanted. Anyway, I was very hard on her – I really didn't want to say another word to her ever again. As far as I was concerned, I'd already done enough by not turning her in; under no circumstances whatsoever was I going to do anything else to help her.

However, I was nowhere near as tough as she was. She kept on at me, on and on, and in the end I agreed. **[Transcription ends]**

2

That proved to be a very special evening. The usually silent Li Ningyu spoke from the heart and told Gu Xiaomeng many things.

Madame Gu told me that when they left the bathroom and went back to their room that evening, she went straight to bed, without even washing her face and hands. Li Ningyu did likewise. At first, the two of them behaved as if they were complete strangers; each lay in their own bed without saying a word to the other, and the only sound in the room was of them tossing and turning. The sound of insomnia.

During the latter part of the night, Gu Xiaomeng dozed fitfully. At one point she thought she heard Li Ningyu getting out of bed and feeling her way around the room for a good long time. She had no idea what she was up to.

In fact, she was dismantling the bugs.

After she'd disconnected the listening devices, Li Ningyu woke Gu Xiaomeng up and started to talk to her. Every detail of her life, everything that had happened – it all came pouring out.

[Transcript from the interview with Gu Xiaomeng]

To cut a long story short, Li Ningyu was born into the gentry in Hunan province, into a well-educated and forward-thinking family. At sixteen she went with her older brother – that old reprobate Mr Pan senior – to study in Guangdong. He went to the Whampoa Military Academy and she went to the Women's Medical College. While they were away studying, the Revolution came to their home town – landlords came under attack, land was redistributed to the peasants, and their father was targeted by the Red Army for being the richest landlord in the area. He ended up being shot.

Li Ningyu and her brother swore that they would avenge their father's death, so after they graduated they both joined the Nationalist Party's National Revolutionary Army. They were sent to the front line in Jiangxi and Hunan provinces, and both of them participated in the Nationalists' encirclement campaign against the Red Army there.

It's hard to believe, but a few years later, her brother joined the Communist Party in secret. And then so did she. In time, Li Ningyu fell in love with the man who'd brought her brother into the Party. She married him and had two children with him, but then he died in 1937, during the Battle of Shanghai. He was killed at home, hit by a stray bullet while he was reading the newspaper – can you imagine! Apparently, nobody ever found out who was responsible. Li Ningyu was pregnant with their third child at the time, but, unsurprisingly, the shock of seeing her husband die like that caused her to miscarry. Her baby went to join its father in paradise.

When she got to that part of her story, Li Ningyu started to cry. It really was sad, and I was moved too, but I was still so furious with her that I refused to give her any sort of reaction. I stayed completely quiet and still, in the dark there. The silence was quite oppressive. **[Transcription ends]**

Eventually, Li Ningyu regained her self-control. She wiped away her tears and continued. 'Let me tell you the truth, Xiaomeng. I've shared all of this with you not because I want you to feel sorry for me, but so that you understand my position. You hold my life in your hands. If you so much as open your mouth in Hihara's presence, it wouldn't even matter if I were a cat with nine lives, I'd be off to meet Marx regardless. But we've been such close friends, I don't want to die without you understanding how I got to this point.'

'There's no need to go on about it!' Gu Xiaomeng said.

'I've already told you I'm not going to turn you in.' That was the first thing she'd said all night.

Li Ningyu reached out and tried to take her hand. 'Thank you, Xiaomeng. If you can forgive me, it shows that we're still friends.'

'Stop that!' Gu Xiaomeng brushed her aside. 'We aren't friends – we just have a deal.'

At the mention of a deal, Li Ningyu said that she'd be willing to do pretty much anything if Gu Xiaomeng would help her get the message out. 'Even if we're not friends,' she said, 'we're still comrades-in-arms in our fight against the Japanese devils. You can't be wanting our comrades to get arrested and killed by Hihara, can you?'

Gu Xiaomeng harrumphed at that and said with a sarcastic laugh, 'I nearly found myself suffering the same fate as Wu Zhiguo, and yet you still have the gall to say that we're comrades-in-arms? I know exactly what I think of the way you treat your so-called comrades – you've been trying your best to get me killed!'

'But I didn't know then that you were one of my comrades…'

'Who are you calling a comrade? Don't fool yourself!'

'If I can't get the message out, I might as well be dead.'

'That's up to you,' Gu Xiaomeng countered. 'It has nothing whatsoever to do with me. Go to hell!'

'In that case,' Li Ningyu said, 'if I'm going to hell, you're coming with me!'

Li Ningyu showed her hand now: unless Gu Xiaomeng helped her get the message out, she would tell Hihara exactly who Mr and Miss Gu really were.

She was overturning their original agreement and upping the stakes.

Gu Xiaomeng was so angry, her entire body was shaking. 'You bitch!'

Li Ningyu was perfectly calm. 'I'm not a bitch – it's you who's forcing me to do this. It wouldn't cost you a thing, but you're refusing to help me – you seem to want me to sit by and do nothing while my comrades are arrested and killed by Hihara. Quite frankly, I would rather be dead, so why don't you go and turn me in? That way I can die with honour!'

That's the kind of logic only a criminal would come up with.

Gu Xiaomeng couldn't think of a thing to say.

Li Ningyu had already planned all of this and now everything came out smoothly, exactly as she'd scripted it. 'You're already helping me by not going to the authorities, so why not go the whole hog and help me take the message out. Just helping me a bit is no damn good! As I said, it will be even worse for me if I survive this and my comrades don't – why should I be grateful to you for that? It would be perfectly straightforward for you, but you won't even consider it – if that's going to be how it is, then we might as well not bother.' As she said this, Li Ningyu climbed onto a stool and started to reconnect the wiring on the bugs.

'What are you doing?' Gu Xiaomeng asked.

'What do you think I'm doing? If we're both going to die, we don't need to worry about people listening in – let them hear us, I say!'

The knife was now at her throat. Gu Xiaomeng pulled Li Ningyu away and started to cry.

[Transcript from the interview with Gu Xiaomeng]
Oh yes, I gave in. I didn't have any choice – I had to do what she said. She had power over me because she knew who I was. She could cause us a lot of damage. I'd be put under surveillance, people would start analysing everything we'd done in the past and testing us over every little thing from then on – even if we were able to cover up our past activities, how could we possibly continue with our mission? I was terrified. So I just had to swallow my rage and let her lead me around by the nose.

It turned out that what she wanted me to do was actually just as straightforward as she'd claimed: I was to put the medicine capsules back where I'd found them, so that Turtle could pass on the intelligence when he returned to the estate the following day. I thought that if it really was that simple, she ought to be able to do it herself – why did she have to blackmail me into doing it? – but she said Hihara was already watching her too closely, so it would be too dangerous for her.

That explanation was obviously only half the story. I later discovered it was actually just a test so that she could find out for sure whether or not my father and I were really working undercover for the Bureau. If my father and I weren't working for the Nationalists, I'd probably have slapped her across the face when she broke our deal. But because I'd acquiesced, she knew exactly where she was with me.

Ah, Li Ningyu was an angel, but she could also be a real devil. She always worked out everything in advance, considered every possible angle – there was absolutely no way I could keep up with her.
[Transcription ends]

The experienced agent won out; Gu Xiaomeng was still far too young to be any sort of match for her. Li Ningyu had already spent years in the underground, honing her skills; even a long-serving counter-intelligence operative like Hihara could get nothing out of her, so Gu Xiaomeng, who was after all only on her first mission, had no chance.

Time and experience are needed to build a successful agent; when people talk of natural ability, what they mean is the person concerned has been through a lot to get to where they are.

3

The next day was the blackest of all for Li Ningyu.

She and Gu Xiaomeng had only finally got to sleep just before dawn. They were both exhausted, so they only woke up when Secretary Bai knocked on their door to call them to breakfast. They got up as quickly as they could and rushed downstairs, but as they went out of the front door Gu Xiaomeng realized she'd forgotten to bring the capsules with her. It was infuriating! When Li Ningyu discovered this, she wondered if Gu Xiaomeng was trying to trick her – but she was also furious with herself for having made a mistake at such a critical moment. It would have been easy enough to remind Gu Xiaomeng. Sometimes even the best-laid plans go wrong.

When they'd finished breakfast and were walking back, Li Ningyu demanded that Gu Xiaomeng make up a story so she could go out again and return the capsules to where they were meant to be. Gu Xiaomeng agreed. But as soon as they reached the west building, they were all called into the conference room for a meeting, and she didn't even have time to go upstairs – how could she possibly have slipped away?

This was the meeting that began with everyone being shown the letter Wu Zhiguo had written in blood. Gu Xiaomeng knew better than anyone that Li Ningyu was indeed Ghost, as the letter stated. She didn't dare accuse Li Ningyu outright, but now she could just stand back and watch her squirm; it would be nothing to do with her.

Li Ningyu was as quiet as ever. She was under terrible pressure. After so many days in captivity, this was the first time that she thought she might crack. She had not expected that Hihara would bring out Wu Zhiguo's blood letter and let everyone know that she was under suspicion. She didn't know whether this was just another ruse on Hihara's part or whether she'd made a mistake somewhere. Or perhaps Gu Xiaomeng had betrayed her?

As always when faced with a crisis, she picked up her comb and started to comb her hair.

This annoyed Secretary Bai enormously. 'Why don't you say something, Li Ningyu?' he said sharply. 'Even the dead have made their opinions known. Or is it that you have nothing to say?'

'Everything that I want to say I have already told Colonel Hihara,' Li Ningyu said. 'I have nothing more to add. But if I have to talk to someone, then I would like to ask Gu Xiaomeng a question, since she's the only one who hasn't made her opinion clear.'

'What do you want to know?' Gu Xiaomeng asked.

'Do you think I'm Ghost too?' Li Ningyu said.

That was what she was like – for her, attack was always the best form of defence.

Gu Xiaomeng was both impressed and furious. She was impressed by Li Ningyu's acting skills, by the fact that her expression hadn't changed, not even in the face of such intense antagonism, and by the way she'd held her nerve until she'd managed to regain the initiative. But Gu Xiaomeng was also furious because she didn't know what to say: should she keep silent or tell the truth? She couldn't afford to fall out with Li Ningyu under any circumstances, and yet she still felt a powerful urge to fight back – she was genuinely worried that she might actually tell them the truth just for the momentary pleasure of seeing Li Ningyu brought down. She wished she could just run away and avoid all this torment.

How could she run away? Li Ningyu was staring at her fixedly, as if she had staked everything on this final roll of the dice.

Gu Xiaomeng raised her eyes and met Li Ningyu's gaze squarely. 'And what if I say I think that you are Ghost?' she asked rudely.

Li Ningyu's words conveyed a hidden warning: 'Given what you know about me, I am sure you won't do that.'

Gu Xiaomeng was cursing inwardly. Given what I know about you, that's exactly what I ought to tell them! But...

She glared at Li Ningyu and said threateningly, 'And what if I say it anyway?'

Without hesitating, Li Ningyu replied, 'That would just go to prove that this is hell, and everyone here is lying like the devils they are.'

Gu Xiaomeng burst out laughing at this, howling like a lunatic. 'Yes, everyone is lying, and this is a hell that the devils have constructed for us – a hell!'

When she stopped laughing, she turned to Wang Tianxiang.

'To tell you the truth, Police Chief Wang, I find it impossible to believe that Unit Chief Li is Ghost. And I should also tell you that I don't believe Chief of Staff Wu is the kind of person who would happily martyr himself to show his loyalty to the Imperial Japanese Army.'

As soon as she heard that, Li Ningyu's biggest worry evaporated. As long as Gu Xiaomeng was on her side, as long as she kept her promise, even if Li Ningyu was arrested that instant, there was still hope that her message might yet be taken out.

4

Although Li Ningyu wasn't placed under arrest, she wasn't far off it. From then on, she wasn't allowed to leave the building, her food was brought to her by the guards, and she was moved into the room originally occupied by Wu Zhiguo. It was a bigger bedroom and now she would be on her own. That was the special treatment she received because she'd been named in his letter written in blood. Hihara had to do this in order to prove his bona fides – to convince Section Chief Jin and Gu Xiaomeng that the letter was real.

[Transcript from an interview with Gu Xiaomeng]
At that point we had no idea that Wu Zhiguo's death had been faked, so I thought Li Ningyu had had it. If someone commits suicide to prove their allegations against you, how on earth are you going to get out of that? To tell you the truth, at first I was quite pleased to see her get into trouble; even though I hadn't been able

to turn her in, somebody else had. But then she started attacking me and I realized she thought I'd betrayed her – which was obviously going to be very bad for me. The more danger she was in, the worse it was going to be for me too. That's why I kept saying that she couldn't possibly be Ghost; I was showing her that whatever had happened was nothing to do with me.

But I knew that wasn't going to be enough to convince her, because she might think that I'd planned it like that with Hihara and the others: stabbing her in the back and then pretending to be on her side – just an act, you see? So how could I convince her? I decided I would help her return the capsules to their original location. That way she'd have to trust me.

So the minute the meeting was over, I'd have to slip out. But right then I couldn't think of a reason to leave, and she'd reconnected the wiring for the bugs, so we couldn't say anything.

Li Ningyu then suddenly hugged me and started to scream and cry, yelling that Wu Zhiguo was maligning her, trying to get her into trouble; at the same time, she whispered me my instructions. She told me to go to Secretary Bai and say that we'd been sharing one tube of toothpaste, so now that we'd been moved into separate rooms, I needed to go to the officers' club to buy myself another tube.

That was how I got out of there and was able to put the three medicine capsules back where they needed to go – and it was not even ten in the morning by the time I had finished.

[Transcription ends]

By the time that Gu Xiaomeng was heading out of the door to buy herself some toothpaste, Li Ningyu had already been moved into Wu Zhiguo's old room. As she stood out of sight beside the window and watched Gu Xiaomeng walk away, a strange sense of excitement and anticipation wound its way through her heart. Her main concern was the medicine capsules, but she was also happy that Gu Xiaomeng had kept her word and was willing to take risks for her. She might be tiresome and stubborn in the ordinary way of things, but when it came to the crunch, she was very cautious and obedient.

Li Ningyu was amazed that despite all the time they'd spent together, she'd never discovered that Gu Xiaomeng was working undercover for the Nationalists; she was even more amazed that, even though Gu Xiaomeng had worked her way in so deep, she had still made that tiny mistake that blew her cover. Li Ningyu was suddenly grateful for her own ability to keep quiet and remain calm, because it was that which had allowed her to notice Gu Xiaomeng's slip – and when she'd tested her hypothesis, she'd got the evidence she needed. That really was a great discovery. A victory like that, she told herself, ought to mean that in the end their side would triumph.

Gu Xiaomeng disappeared behind a clump of bamboo. Li Ningyu knew that the bins would be directly ahead of her now – all she had to do was walk over and drop the first capsule, the one with the message inside, and then keep going until she got to the fork…

As she thought about this, she moved away from the window as if in a daze and sat down on the bed. Having sat for a while, she realized she was absolutely exhausted and had to lie down. The bed was so huge, so soft, that, lying there in the middle, she felt as if she'd shrunk; she seemed much smaller and lighter than usual. The embroidered coverlet smelt of cigarette smoke – in fact, the whole room stank. That was down to Wu Zhiguo. If he was really dead, that would mean that the smoke from his cigarettes had outlasted him. She smiled. The year or more she'd spent struggling to perfect his handwriting had finally paid off.

Outside the window, a bird wheeled through the empty sky, flashing past her eyes like an apparition in a dream. The bird led Li Ningyu to thinking about what was happening beyond the estate, in downtown Hangzhou, to Turtle.

Over the past year and more, she'd seen Turtle at regular intervals and in set places, come rain or shine, in summer heat and winter cold. It was as if Turtle were one of the scenic spots on base: if you went to the right place, there he would be. But they had never once spoken to each other; if they met face to face, they communicated in silence, with glances. Once, when she'd been late leaving work and had missed Turtle's collection, she'd had to give him her rubbish directly. Their hands had accidentally touched and it was as if she'd got an electric shock; she'd moved quickly to one side, her whole body shaking.

She was having a similar sensation right then. It was as if she'd become a flash of lightning, as if she were spinning through space, as if she had disappeared into the sky above the Tan Estate…

A little while later, Gu Xiaomeng returned looking pleased with herself; out in the corridor, she mimed that she'd done as asked. A wave of happiness surged through Li Ningyu; she felt almost light-headed, as if she were floating. When

Turtle made his next round of the estate, he would be sure to notice the two black capsules lying on the path and then he would know exactly what to do. It was a huge estate, but there weren't that many rubbish bins; he wouldn't have any difficulty locating the right one.

As she thought about this, Li Ningyu unconsciously curled her knees under her until she was kneeling on the bed, then she put her hands together and closed her eyes. She was praying that Turtle would come to the Tan Estate right away.

She was pinning all her hopes on this. When she'd seen Turtle yesterday, it had been impossible to signal clearly to him that he needed to come back again today. But she kept telling herself that the Gathering of Heroes was now imminent, and so her superiors would be desperate for news from her – Turtle ought to be trying to stay in regular contact, he ought to come and see her every day. She even imagined that he would have made arrangements to this effect yesterday – perhaps he had left something behind, or maybe he'd agreed to help one of the servants at the officers' club to clean the toilets.

All she needed was for Turtle to show up, even if just for a few moments. That would be enough.

5

If Turtle had turned up, none of the rest of it would have happened.

But Turtle didn't come. He never appeared. The hands on the clock ticked on; morning became afternoon became evening. For Li Ningyu, expectancy became worry became reluctant acceptance. Even so, she found it very difficult to believe that at such a critical juncture, Turtle would go a whole day without coming to see her.

[Transcript from the interview with Gu Xiaomeng]

She had no idea what had happened. Turtle and that old idiot Pan had completely swallowed Hihara's story – they thought that Li Ningyu was there carrying out some kind of ECCC mission.

I met Turtle once, later on. He'd been arrested by Police Chief Wang and was in prison; I went to see him on the sly, to find out if I could help get him out. But one of his legs had been broken, so he couldn't escape. In the end he couldn't stand the torture any longer and he killed himself.

When we met, he told me all about it – he thought I was a comrade. Why? Because it was me who'd taken the message out and given it to him. But that was later…

Getting back to our story, Turtle told me that if the weather had been good that day, he might well have come out to the Tan Estate one more time. But that morning it was raining; the weather gods were against us. He decided that it would look too obvious if he came out in a downpour. The Gathering of Heroes was just about to happen, and everyone was on high alert, so he didn't dare do anything that might draw attention. It stopped raining in the afternoon, but the base was in a bad state, with fallen leaves all over the place, so he had no time to go anywhere else. Of course, if he'd realized that Li Ningyu had intelligence for him, he would have made time to go to the estate regardless, but the crucial thing was that he had no idea. Nobody knew! Even my own father didn't realize that I was under house arrest at the time. What can you say? It was Heaven's will – the rain ruined everything. In our line of work, that happens from time to time: something quite beyond your control can spoil everything. You can plan as carefully as you like, but in the end it all comes down to chance.

[Transcription ends]

Li Ningyu was in a ferment of anticipation, but her patience was severely tested as the rain passed and the skies cleared into a gloriously sunny afternoon. By the time it got to four o'clock, she was almost at the end of her tether. She knew that Turtle always headed off to collect people's household rubbish at about five thirty; if he still hadn't appeared by then, he wouldn't be coming to the estate today. The Gathering of Heroes was due to take place tomorrow evening, so she had very little time left. At the very latest, her message would have to be taken out by noon tomorrow. But without Turtle, how was she supposed to manage that?

Li Ningyu wracked her brains. She kept asking herself: how do I make contact with my comrades? In her confused state, the faces of her comrades floated before her eyes: first Turtle, then Warrior (Qian Huyi's concubine), and then her brother, Mr Pan senior. Even Tiger appeared. Strictly speaking, she had never met Tiger, she'd just seen him once in the distance – it was dark and he was moving, so she only got a very vague impression. Her brother had met him, though, and described him as being as slim as a girl, narrow-waisted, and with the long, slender fingers of a surgeon. It had been difficult to imagine such a person as a successful killer, but she knew from her brother that once the campaign to eliminate collaborators and kill the Japanese had got started in Hangzhou, it was Tiger who'd killed the most people – hundreds, if not more. If she didn't get her message out, both Tiger and someone even more important – K – would be killed by the Japanese devils. The prospect was terrifying.

Fear coursed through her like a fever. Her limbs had no strength, her heart was pounding and her mind was a complete blank. She had never felt like this before in all the time she'd worked in the underground; fear and helplessness were crippling her. She was unable to make any attempt to establish contact with her comrades – all she could do was lie on the bed, quite shamelessly.

It was this realization that prompted her to get up and walk around the room; perhaps she was trying to prove to herself that she could still do something.

The room, like the bed, was extravagantly appointed and very big – so big, in fact, that she wondered whether she'd be able to make it to the other end. She was feeling faint; the stress of recent days had utterly exhausted her, her knees started to give way and with a thud she fell to the floor. Having been forced to her knees, she couldn't stop herself from bursting into tears.

Squatting down and hugging her knees, she sobbed like an abandoned child.

[Transcript from the interview with Gu Xiaomeng]

She was crying so violently, you'd have thought she'd been raped or something. She made so much noise that nobody in the building could remain undisturbed. I think to begin with she was crying for real, but afterwards she was putting it on. She was making such a racket because she wanted everyone to come. If everyone else came, then so would I, and that was exactly what she had in mind. She wanted to see me. She had to see me! She wanted me to do something for her.

The first person on the scene was Secretary Bai, and then Police Chief Wang – they were there to take charge, to complain about the noise. Then came Section Chief Jin, who just wanted to see what was going on. I was the last to arrive. To tell you the truth, I really didn't want to go because a sixth sense was telling me that she was going to ask me to do something for her.

Just as I'd expected, the moment she saw me, she rushed over, threw her arms around me and hugged me. She was crying and sobbing all over me, screaming that she was innocent, she hadn't done anything, and cursing Wu Zhiguo. Then she dragged in Colonel Hihara, Section Chief Jin, Secretary Bai, Police Chief Wang and had a go at all of them too. When they heard the kinds of things she was saying about Hihara, and about them too, everyone left. Which was precisely what she wanted – she was hurling abuse at them because she wanted them to piss off. Once they were gone, she could talk properly with me.

What did she want? She wanted me to get her some paper and brushes to paint with. She kept crying and cursing, and at the same time she quietly told me what she was planning. I said I had no idea where I could get such things for her. She said that the officers' club would have them and that I should get them when I went for dinner that evening. But if all else failed, a large piece of paper and a pencil would do. She told me she was going to paint a picture to take her message out.

It was quite unbelievable. Think of the situation she was in: she couldn't set foot out of doors, she couldn't phone anyone, she was under continual surveillance, and yet she still hadn't given up, she was still trying to think of ways to get her message out. I told her that I didn't think a painting would work, that they were bound to think of that, but she assured me that she knew what she was doing and as long as I could get her the paper and brushes, she could get her message out. I wanted to see exactly what she was capable of, so I agreed to help her. **[Transcription ends]**

It was entirely by chance that when Gu Xiaomeng went back to her room and started turning things out, she found a piece of paper in one of the cupboards, hidden under the spare blankets. In fact, this was no ordinary piece of paper, it was a movie poster, but the back was white and completely unmarked. Gu Xiaomeng showed it to Li Ningyu and she decided that it would do. A pencil wouldn't work, though, because the paper was good quality and very glossy, so on the spur of the moment Li Ningyu decided to do her drawing with a fountain pen. She used her own pen.

When Madame Gu said that, I was amazed. That had to mean that the painting I'd seen in Mr Pan senior's house was a fake! I immediately found the photograph I'd taken of the picture on my computer and showed it to her. 'Are you saying that Li Ningyu didn't paint this?'

'Of course not!' Madame Gu spoke without the slightest hesitation. 'I'm afraid you've been taken in by a complete fraud. The old man has been lying to you from start to finish. In your book you said that the paper and brushes that Li Ningyu used were left behind by Qian Huyi's daughter – how could that possibly be true? You know perfectly well that after Qian Huyi and his family were murdered, the building was completely refurbished. How could her paper and brushes still be there? Someone would have walked off with them long before.' She shook her fist at the audacity of the man. 'I was right there – remember! And he knows bugger all about it.'

'But—' I looked at the picture on my screen and then asked a truly pointless question '—who painted this?'

'I have no idea. That tricky old bastard must have found someone to do it for him. All I can tell you is that I've never seen it before.'

She looked at the photograph and pointed out various things. 'You see that? It's obviously a fake. They've painted the blades of grass far too regularly, there's not the slightest attempt to conceal the pattern. It really is quite laughable! I saw what Li Ningyu actually drew, and it was a whole lot more realistic. Unfortunately, I didn't get to keep it. Hihara took it away.'

However, Hihara hadn't been able to take away the old lady's memory of the picture. She began listing the various similarities and differences between the fake one and the real one. Some of the differences were tiny, but she could still discuss them in great detail – the painting seemed to be engraved in her memory. While she was doing this, Mrs Chen was constantly glancing at me and making signs to tell me that my time was up.

SIX

1

'This must be about it,' Madame Gu said with a smile when I turned up again the following day. 'I'm sure we'll be finished today.'

It's true that there wasn't much left to talk about. Just the events of that last evening: the final struggle between Hihara and Li Ningyu.

The old lady's account was pretty much as I'd recorded it in my novel. There were only two things that I'd got wrong: Chief of Staff Wu Zhiguo wasn't actually present that evening, and the people dressed up as the Red Army didn't just attack the western building, there was also an attack on the eastern building, in which they set fire to one of the garages. It was a much bigger operation, and made a lot more noise, than I had described.

'That bit when you have Wu Zhiguo coming to the meeting is too bizarre,' Madame Gu said. 'Hihara had told everyone categorically that he was dead, so how could he possibly come back to life then?'

I disagreed, but I put it as politely as I could. 'If Hihara was still considering the possibility that Wu Zhiguo might be Ghost, he'd surely want him to run the gauntlet of the fake Red Army as well.'

Madame Gu laughed. 'And you think he wasn't being tested? I told you, both buildings were attacked at the same time.'

I thought about that and had to agree that Chief of Staff Wu's reactions would therefore also have been closely monitored. However, Madame Gu said that was all secondary; the most important thing was what happened later, and I hadn't got my account of the fight between Hihara and Li Ningyu right at all. I hadn't managed to capture Li Ningyu's spirit. The old lady kept emphasizing one point: the reason Li Ningyu behaved the way she did that evening, including trying to strangle Hihara, was because she'd already decided to kill herself.

'Other people might not have realized that,' she said, 'but I immediately saw what she was up to. She was going to use her own death to prove that she wasn't Ghost, and then, just as you said, she was hoping that the enemy would hand her body back to her family, along with her few possessions, including the painting. I hadn't yet seen the painting, but I was sure that was where she'd hidden her message.'

'When did you first see the painting?' I asked.

'After Hihara beat her up. It was after we got her upstairs.'

2

At that point, Li Ningyu barely looked human – there was a huge open wound on her forehead, the bridge of her nose had been broken, knocking it out of shape, she'd lost some teeth, both cheeks were badly swollen, and she was bleeding all over the place.

As the nurse bandaged her up, Gu Xiaomeng began to feel nauseous with the horrible smell of blood and disinfectant. She went over to the window for a breath of air and saw that the picture Li Ningyu had done was lying on the table there. She was curious – and nervous – so she took a look.

It was such a simple picture, it didn't seem possible that it could be hiding a secret message. She presumed the message must be on the back, on the movie-poster side, so she waited until the nurse had left, then immediately turned it over to check. She examined it from a distance and close up, she examined it from every angle, she turned it this way and that, but she still couldn't find anything.

As she flipped the poster to and fro, the paper crackled quite noisily, and it was this that alerted Li Ningyu. When she saw what Gu Xiaomeng was doing, she motioned to her to bring the picture over, and then told her in a whisper exactly where the message was.

[Transcript from the interview with Gu Xiaomeng]

When she told me that the grass was a message in telegraphic code, I was amazed!

Oh, you have to admit, it was a good idea, a very neat trick, something nobody else had thought of before or since – she was a kind of genius in her way. That was Li Ningyu for you. As I said, she was the best underground agent I ever came across – she outclassed everyone else. I have no idea how she thought of it, but I am sure, I can swear to it, Hihara would never have found it in a million years. Nobody who didn't know where to look would ever have discovered it.

The problem was that we couldn't be sure the enemy would return her body and all her things to her family. And even if they did, this was the last day of the investigation; so as far as the enemy were concerned, there was no urgency. If they didn't return her possessions right away, then Li Ningyu would have died in vain.

When I started whispering all this to Li Ningyu, she made a massive fuss about needing to go to the toilet. I knew she was worried about bugs, so I helped her in there. As a matter of fact, by that time the enemy had stopped listening in on us – it was the last evening, after all, and Hihara was in such a rage that he'd abandoned all of that, he wasn't bothering with trying to trick us any more. He was just keeping us under lock and key, waiting for the moment he could issue his instructions and have us all put to death.

[Transcription ends]

Once they were safely inside the bathroom, Li Ningyu explained her idea to Gu Xiaomeng.

'If I had the slightest hope that I might be able to get a message out in my picture,' she said to Gu Xiaomeng, 'why would I tell you about it?'

As Madame Gu told me, 'Li Ningyu was always several steps ahead – nobody had a hope of following her thought processes.'

Li Ningyu told Gu Xiaomeng about the notes she was

going to leave for Hihara and Commander Zhang, the aim being that this would look as if her suicide was an attempt to prove her innocence and show them that she wasn't a Communist and couldn't possibly be Ghost.

'Do you think Hihara will believe that?' Li Ningyu asked.

'No.'

'I agree. That won't allay his suspicions. He'll search my body, search all of my belongings, and when it comes to this drawing, he'll be sure there's something hidden in it somewhere, so he'll pay it particular attention.'

'But he won't crack the code.'

'Do you think anyone can crack it?'

'No.'

'You could.'

'Me?'

'Yes. Haven't I already told you what it says?'

'Don't worry about that. I'm not going to tell him.'

'Oh, but you must!'

'What?'

'That's the only way. You have to betray me, you have to show that I am indeed Ghost. That's the only way that he'll be able to trust you completely, and then you'll be able to get out of here…'

Outside the window, an owl hooted a brief warning. The all-enveloping darkness could no longer conceal the shadows of the impending death. Inside the room, Li Ningyu explained in an undertone exactly what should be done after she died. Gu Xiaomeng listened intently. She could feel the hairs on her scalp prickling, because it seemed as if she were talking to a ghost.

3

The next day, everything happened exactly as Li Ningyu had planned it. At just after six in the morning, Secretary Bai was the first to discover her body curled up on the floor with blood trickling from every orifice. In his wake came Section Chief Jin and Gu Xiaomeng. Half an hour later, Colonel Hihara and Police Chief Wang hurried to the scene. Gu Xiaomeng was wiping away her tears while at the same time putting Li Ningyu's possessions in order.

Hihara immediately ordered them all to leave the room, and he and Wang Tianxiang then conducted a basic search. About ten minutes later, they came out to have breakfast. Hearing them approach, Gu Xiaomeng rushed out to intercept Hihara on the stairs; this time she didn't look upset at all. Glancing quickly to left and right, she slyly made her report. She said that when she was collecting Li Ningyu's things she'd found a drawing and she thought there was something odd about it and would like to have another look. Hihara had already been studying the picture and was bothered by the fact that he couldn't make anything of it, so when he saw that Gu Xiaomeng might be able to help him, he was very happy to agree.

After breakfast, Hihara went to get Gu Xiaomeng and ask her what she'd found. Gu Xiaomeng was careful to appear unhurried.

'Colonel Hihara, I've made the most amazing discovery. You're not going to believe it!' She was spinning it out, playing her fish on the end of her line.

'Oh really? Do tell.'

'I know who Ghost is.' Hihara opened his mouth to

respond, but Gu Xiaomeng got in before him. 'You're not allowed to ask anything yet. You have to promise me something first and then I'll tell you.' She was being deliberately provocative and arrogant – an act that she'd become very good at.

'Okay, what do you want?'

'If I tell you, you have to give me a reward.'

'Of course, what do you want?'

'I want you to let me go, I want to get out of here.'

'That's fine. No problem. We'll let you go.'

Of course, making promises came easily to him. But Gu Xiaomeng wasn't going to let him get away with just empty words; she crooked her little finger and wanted Hihara to hook his own around it in a pact.

Why not? Would it bother him – an officer in the Imperial Japanese Army – if he broke his word?

So they hooked their little fingers together, he swore to keep his promise, and their deadly compact was reframed by Gu Xiaomeng as a children's game.

Only then did Gu Xiaomeng point to the grass in Li Ningyu's drawing and gently explain what it meant. As her beautiful lips formed the words, a shocking secret stood revealed. As if by magic, the grass transformed itself into a string of Arabic numbers:

6643 1032 9976 0523 1801 0648 3194 5028 5391 2585 9982

It was written in standard international Chinese-language telegraph code, in plain text. Transcribing this was easy enough for Gu Xiaomeng; it was what she did for a living, after all, so she could read it off straight away. The numbers metamorphosed into this message:

For urgent dispatch!

Call off the Gathering of Heroes immediately!

To prove that she wasn't lying, Gu Xiaomeng recommended that Hihara bring in Section Chief Jin to check the message. Jin Shenghuo had been a Section Chief for many years, so he'd lost the familiarity that comes from daily practice and he couldn't just read off the message at first glance the way that Gu Xiaomeng could. But he could decrypt it one word at a time, a little more slowly. The message he got was exactly the same as Gu Xiaomeng's.

'Oh!' Hihara sighed in amazement. 'What a genius. Li Ningyu really was a remarkable woman to think of something like that. Thank God I had your sharp eyes to help me, Xiaomeng, or I might never have discovered the identity of Ghost. Who could have imagined it? She really was dug in very deep.'

He gripped Gu Xiaomeng's little hand tightly. He was bubbling over with delight and excitement; he was so grateful, he hardly knew how to express it.

'That's really amazing, Xiaomeng. I'm so impressed that you realized what she was up to – that takes a kind of genius too! All I can say is that I am proud, Xiaomeng, to have someone like you working for me.'

He would have been only too happy to do Gu Xiaomeng's packing for her. He sent her on her way, just as he had promised.

4

There was no need to be in such a hurry; Gu Xiaomeng had no intention of leaving.

Although she'd earlier demanded to be released, when the time came, she didn't want to go.

Madame Gu asked me to guess why she refused to leave. I really had no idea and every guess I made was wrong. In the end, she had to explain. She said that Li Ningyu had instructed her that she should only leave if Hihara also released everyone else. If Gu Xiaomeng was the only person allowed to go and that evening the enemy failed to arrest K, then there was every chance that Hihara would suspect her again.

So Gu Xiaomeng told Hihara, 'Now that you've found Ghost, we can all leave. I'll go with the others.'

'No, you can go now,' Hihara said. 'Have you considered that Ghost might be more than one person?' The old fox liked to think of every possibility. He patted Gu Xiaomeng's hand, smiling gently. 'Maybe I'm reading too much into all of this, but it never hurts to be careful. You're too young to know how dangerous this world can be. Did you know that your Unit Chief Li was Ghost? No, you did not! So you will get to leave first – that's your reward, just as I promised.'

'I really appreciate how open and honest you've been with me, Colonel Hihara,' Gu Xiaomeng said, 'but I can't leave like this. I'm not that stupid. I'm not prepared to run silly risks just so I can leave a few hours before the others.'

'What do you mean?' Hihara asked.

'Colonel Hihara, have you considered that if I leave ahead of the others and by some chance the Communists change the time or place of the Gathering of Heroes on the spur of the moment, what a difficult position that would put me in? How would I explain? How would I clear my name? Even if I jumped into the Yellow River, I could never wash myself clean!'

'But you have me on your side,' Hihara said. 'There's nothing to be scared of, I can vouch for your innocence.'

'But you're leaving in a couple of days. You can speak up for me now, but what about later? I'm not going anywhere, Colonel Hihara; you're just going to have to put up with having me around for a few more hours. By spending a little bit longer here, I'll be able to prove my innocence for the rest of my life – as far as I'm concerned, that's worth it.'

When she said that, I was completely confused. 'So you didn't leave? How did you get the message out then?'

The old lady chuckled happily. 'Who says I didn't leave? Of course I got out of there, but I wanted to leave on my own terms. When I told Hihara I wasn't going anywhere, I also asked if I might be allowed to phone my father, and of course he agreed. My father and I had various code words set up in the event of one of us needing to call the other, so the minute he picked up, I pretended that he was telling me I had to go and do something for him. I deliberately raised my voice: "What am I supposed to do? I've got important things to do here, I can't possibly leave." My father immediately played along, telling me I had to leave right away. I refused and he insisted, so it was stalemate.'

Hihara was standing right next to her when she made her call; he understood what the problem was and started to make conciliatory gestures at her before she'd even put the phone down. He told her to tell her father she would do what he'd asked, that she'd be on her way immediately.

So what was it that was so important?

She told Hihara that her father needed the phone number of a certain official in Nanjing; she had his private number in her address book, but the address book was in her office. So Gu Xiaomeng had to go back to her work unit.

'I'll be right back; at most it will take me an hour,' Gu Xiaomeng said.

Hihara laughed. 'There's no need for you to come back, it's a waste of your time. Do as you're told and get out of here.'

Hihara quickly arranged a car for her.

'No, it's not enough just to get me a car, you have to send someone with me.'

'Why?'

'To prove that I'm not involved in your case, what else?'

She insisted that he send Police Chief Wang with her. Then she'd be in the clear.

Hihara said that wasn't necessary, but Gu Xiaomeng was adamant. Curling her lip, she announced in a high-pitched voice, 'Colonel Hihara, you just said that the world is a dangerous place and it never hurts to be careful. I have no intention of messing things up for myself now, so I will be coming back, and I insist on having Police Chief Wang go with me; otherwise, I'm not going!'

'All right, all right, go then.'

That morning, just after nine o'clock, Wang Tianxiang got behind the wheel and drove Gu Xiaomeng off the Tan Estate.

As you can imagine, she did not forget to take three

medicine capsules with her. Not the original three, of course, but others that Li Ningyu had given her the night before.

As you can also imagine, Li Ningyu had reminded Gu Xiaomeng exactly how she should get the capsules to Turtle. She should either drop two empty capsules at one of the intersections on the main road through the base and then place the third, the one containing the message, on the edge of the rubbish bin in front of their building; or, if she saw Turtle in person and the situation allowed it, she could simply drop the third capsule right in front of him. The second option was much safer and simpler, as well as quicker, but she would have to be lucky.

That day, Gu Xiaomeng's luck was in. As the car drove onto base, she could see Turtle sitting smoking on the steps of the auditorium; they had to turn past him in order to get to her office. It was all so simple – she just dropped the tiny medicine capsule to the ground without making a sound; it was only rubbish anyway. Even if Turtle had been surrounded by people keeping him under surveillance, he could have picked it up and taken it away without anyone thinking twice about it. After all, who could have imagined that a message of such importance would be hidden inside an ordinary medicine capsule?

SEVEN

1

The final round of interviews took place on a very special day – it was Declassification Day for Madame Gu's former work unit. Her daughter told me that whenever anyone stopped working there, they were obliged to hand over everything that they'd written while they were in that unit, including their personal diaries and so on. These were kept by the work unit until the time for secrecy was past, then returned to their owners in an annual practice that had begun in the 1980s and was known as Declassification Day. Every year Madame Gu's daughter would go to the work unit on behalf of her mother to see whether anything belonging to Madame Gu had been included. This morning she had gone as usual, and she'd collected something for her mother.

It was in a blue silk bag and appeared quite heavy. Because it had already been declassified, Madame Gu was quite happy to open it in front of me. There was a framed cabinet photograph and a handful of letters. The photo was of a man of about sixty wearing gold-rimmed spectacles. You could tell he was someone important.

Madame Gu looked at the picture and muttered, 'He must have died.'

Her daughter nodded.

'He was eleven years younger than me,' the old lady said.

'They said he got terribly sick and passed away,' her daughter replied.

The old lady shook her head. 'Oh well, he's gone. That's fine, everyone's dead, I'm the only one left now.' She got up, tottered off and headed up the stairs.

Her daughter seemed to be under the impression that Madame Gu wouldn't be coming downstairs again, so she carefully asked whether I'd finished my interviews or not. I said no, I still had a couple of minor questions.

When the old lady heard that, she turned around and waved me away. 'No, it's all over, I've said quite enough. I regret having said as much as I did. Our interviews are finished, everything is finished. It's all over, so you don't need to disturb me any more. Go away now – my daughter can take you back.'

She deliberately didn't say goodbye, just wished me a good journey home. I decided that the quite unnecessary care with which she chose her words had to be a kind of professional disease.

2

I was born in the 1960s and grew up in Zhejiang province, on the east coast, right by the sea, so when I was a child, if there were strange lights in the night sky, we used to imagine it was secret agents being parachuted in by Taiwanese planes. Taiwan was the first place in China that I became aware of – I learnt its name even before that of Beijing or Shanghai. I assumed it was very close by, just out of sight over the horizon, and I was certain that when I grew up, I would go and see it for myself. But for my generation it was to prove a great deal easier to go to other parts of the world than it was to go to Taiwan; if you wanted to go to America, or Argentina, or Iceland or Australia, that was fine, but going to Taiwan was not, for all that it was supposed to be a province of China.

Since it was so difficult to get there, I was of course determined to see as much as I could during my visit to Madame Gu. I arranged a five-day tour that would take me to some of the big sights: the museums and pagodas of Kaohsiung, the cities of Hsinchu and Taoyuan, Alishan's scenic mountain railway, the human rights memorial on Green Island...

However, it didn't matter where I went, nor how beautiful the scenery was, I just couldn't get the old lady's voice out of my head. When I came back after my few days away, I had five major questions noted down on my pad and a number of minor queries. The five major questions were as follows:

1. *How did Turtle pass on the intelligence to his superiors? He was under round-the-clock surveillance and the whole situation had blown up because Warrior had been arrested with a message that he'd passed to her, so how could he guarantee that this new piece of intelligence wouldn't be intercepted?*

2. *The old lady had repeatedly stated that when she discovered that Li Ningyu had forged her handwriting she was absolutely furious, and the only reason she decided not to turn her in was because she was afraid Li Ningyu would expose her in retaliation. But by this time Li Ningyu was dead and couldn't blackmail her any more, so why did she still help her?*

3. *After it was all over, Hihara took everyone who'd been under house arrest at the Tan Estate away, together with Commander Zhang and some of his staff. Where did they go? None of them were ever seen again, so what happened to them? Were they all killed?*

4. *Who killed Hihara?*

5. *Why did Madame Gu hate old Mr Pan so much? Had there been some sort of quarrel?*

These questions just wouldn't let me rest; they obsessed me. Thanks to them, I had no interest in sightseeing; all I wanted to do was go and talk to Madame Gu. I got in touch with her several times, and each time she refused my request for a further interview. But I wouldn't give up. I was determined to have another go. On the fourth day, feeling pretty desperate by now, I decided to get a taxi and make my way out there uninvited. Even though I knew it was wrong, I did it anyway.

Madame Gu was resting after lunch in a shady nook in her garden. Having me turn up unexpectedly like that was such a shock that she couldn't quite summon the energy to get rid of me. She just shook her head and sighed, muttering complaints to herself.

I didn't apologize, because I knew that would make her wonder what I was up to. It wouldn't get my questions answered. Instead, I seized my opportunity and took control of the conversation.

'I've come back because I think some of what you said doesn't stand up to close scrutiny.'

'What?'

My challenge had worked. Madame Gu was hooked.

'I told you the truth.'

I pressed on.

Just as I'd hoped, she took my questions very seriously; she answered each one of them, large and small, very carefully. But when it came to the final one, on whether she was angry with Mr Pan senior for some reason, she got very cross and refused to respond. All she said to that was, 'Don't mention him – it just annoys me!'

I was convinced that the two of them must have fallen out, but what could it be that even after all these years she could neither forget nor forgive? As a middle-aged man, I had come to believe very strongly in the words of the philosopher: time will erode every human emotion, even the deepest and most elemental feelings of love and hate. Perhaps I should have shared those words with her, and perhaps she would have felt better for telling someone about it. But in the end I didn't have the heart to put more pressure on her. In many ways, I was only too happy with how far I'd managed to get with those interviews, and something told me that certain things were probably better kept under wraps and not exposed to the light of day.

3

Other things, however, did need illuminating, and my first and second questions fell into that category.

Regarding my first question, Madame Gu said that when Hihara failed to arrest K and the others that evening at the Agate Belvedere Inn, he decided that Ghost must have had an associate and Commander Zhang was the prime suspect. So he had Turtle arrested and he interrogated him that same night, hoping to find out who Ghost's contact was. But Turtle would rather have died than reveal his secrets (and in fact had nothing to say about this, since he didn't know who had dropped the capsules for him), so Hihara probably never found out exactly what had happened. Hihara then went back to Shanghai. Turtle remained under lock and key, and Gu Xiaomeng eventually managed to smuggle herself in to see him. By that time, Turtle didn't have many more days to live. It was at that meeting that he told her many things, including how he had managed to pass the message on.

Turtle always proceeded according to the level of urgency indicated in the message. This sometimes required that he go to the nearest post office and phone his superior directly. 'That was risky,' Madame Gu explained, 'because it might give the enemy the phone number of his contact, which would then blow the cover of that entire string of agents. But sometimes there was no alternative. In this instance, Turtle didn't have a moment to waste; he had to put his head in the noose. And he was lucky: the enemy hadn't stationed their people too close, in case Turtle spotted them, so although they saw him making the call, they didn't hear what was said. That was how the message got out, and how we made sure that Li Ningyu didn't die in vain.'

I immediately moved on to the second question. As Madame Gu listened to me, her expression changed; she was clearly deeply moved and very upset. When she started to speak, she couldn't keep the sobs from rising in her throat, and that made me feel bad for having brought it up. But once she'd rubbed her face with a hot towel and had a sip or two of water, she calmed down. She then recalled once again for me everything that had happened on Li Ningyu's last night.

The two young women were in the bathroom. Li Ningyu had finished explaining to Gu Xiaomeng about the suicide notes and the code in the painting and was now trying to make her promise to take the message out for her. She knelt down on the bathroom floor and handed Gu Xiaomeng the three medicine capsules. But then she refused to get up again.

'She said that I had to swear I'd help her get the message to Turtle, and until I did so she would stay on her knees.'

The old lady shook her head vigorously, as if she were right there, caught up in those long-ago events, as if she could still see Li Ningyu kneeling in front of her.

'Every time I pulled her to her feet, she knelt down again, and that happened a good few times. I really didn't want to swear that I'd help her – why should I? She was begging me for help and then asking me to promise I would actually do it. What the hell...? She was absolutely insistent. She kept falling to her knees, and her kneecaps were getting more and more scraped, until in the end there was blood everywhere.'

Madame Gu picked up the hot towel and gave her face another dab.

'It got to the point where I just couldn't stand it any more, so after a while I said I would. I promised her I would do it.'

She paused, fiddled with her dentures. Out of regret, or irritation, or something else, it was impossible to tell.

'You want to know why she did it like that? By the next day she wouldn't be able to blackmail me any longer. She'd be dead and I'd be free to go back on my word. If I didn't help her get the message out, then her death would have been in vain. So she had to move me, she had to arouse my sympathy, because that was the only way to get me to help.

'To tell you the truth, afterwards I did hesitate, because it was dangerous. But when I hesitated I remembered what she'd looked like kneeling on the floor and refusing to get up, her face wet with tears, the blood soaking through the legs of her trousers. It was so awful, so distressing. In the end, we're all emotional beings, and sometimes that's just how it happens. My memory of those moments proved more important than my earlier hatred and fear of her. I decided to do what she'd asked of me because I felt sorry for her.'

Madame Gu made a point of emphasizing that she'd acted as she did because she felt sorry for Li Ningyu and not because she'd been won over to her cause. She seemed determined not to aggrandize her own role in what happened.

'I felt sorry for her, but there was also a kind of professional respect at play. Nobody on the inside could get out, nobody on the outside could get close to us, and we were being watched constantly – how would you get a message out? I thought it was impossible, but she had found a way, an amazing way to do it! That wasn't just a question of bravery, it took intelligence. I was so impressed. There's an expression, isn't there, about helping people achieve their ambitions? Well, in the end, that's why I helped her. She'd come up with an extraordinarily ambitious plan and I wanted to carry it out for her. She'd done all the hard work, she'd managed to get it ninety-nine per cent realized; all I had to do was carry out that final step and a new legend would be born. It's often said that people working in the same business are slow to appreciate their peers, but if you really do make it to the very top, it's those same peers who'll be your biggest admirers. That was certainly true for me; I admired Li Ningyu enormously, and I wanted to help her bring her plan to completion.'

When I heard her say that, I suddenly wanted to hug Madame Gu.

She was so open, so honest and so even-handed that I found I had no reason not to believe what she was saying. By contrast, when talking to old Mr Pan and my other interviewees, I'd come to feel that there were holes in their stories: sometimes because they were frightened, or because they were wallowing in reflected glory, or because they benefited from a particular version of events being accepted or had some other selfish motive. I could understand that; after all, it's perfectly natural to want to get something out of it or to try and protect your own position. But in the face of the rare honesty shown by Madame Gu, I realized how ordinary the rest of them were.

As to my third question, she told me that Hihara, unable to decide who had been conspiring with Ghost, took everyone off the Tan Estate, including her. They were all sent to Shanghai for questioning. When they got there, she was separated from the others, and she had no idea where the rest of them went next. Eventually, both she and Police Chief Wang were allowed to return to their units, but nobody ever knew what happened to the others.

'Nothing good will have befallen them,' she said. 'If they weren't killed outright, they would at the least have suffered appallingly.'

There now remained only one question. Who killed Hihara?

'Oh,' Madame Gu said, 'that was me. I had him sent down to hell!'

She told me the time and place of the murder, and explained very clearly who was involved and what they did at each stage, with full details. I am quite sure she wasn't making it up.

According to her, it cost her four gold bars to hire two professional assassins to kill Hihara. At her request, they dismembered him and dumped his body by the side of the road. I asked her why she'd spent so much money to have him murdered, and in such a horrible way, with his corpse chopped into pieces. She stared at me in silence for a long time, before closing the subject down. 'There are some things that people spend a lifetime trying to forget – it's not very kind to keep asking about them!'

From a myriad of small signs, it was clear that Madame Gu had complicated feelings about the whole experience of being interviewed by me. On the one hand she wanted me to know the truth about what had happened, but on the other hand she also wanted everyone to forget all about it. She had hoped that these events would remain secret for all time, but the decision to talk about them had been forced on her. People were rewriting the history of that period and changing the facts, and that included me. The best way to stop that was to come forward herself and tell the truth. I think that must have been pretty much what Madame Gu felt. She kept reminding me that she was the only person with the right to explain what had gone on, and she warned me that I shouldn't listen to gossip, that I had to believe that she was telling the truth.

Just before I said goodbye, she emphasized this to me yet again. 'Young man, I am eighty-six years old now and I am going to die soon – in fact you could say that I am half-dead already. Do you think I got you to come all this way in order to lie to you, to concoct a story that would make me look good? What for? I'm past all of that now. What I want is the truth. Aren't people on the Mainland always supposed to seek truth from facts; isn't that the slogan we always hear? Well, that's what I want, I want you to seek truth from facts – I want you to say what really happened. If I hadn't got you to come here, if I hadn't told you all this, you'd be able to distort what happened out of all recognition once I'm dead. You would then be responsible for creating a lie.'

I believed what she'd told me, but I was still a little puzzled. In my opinion, Madame Gu came out of this very well; in fact, we all owed her a debt of gratitude, so why had she tried to keep it all a secret?

It's true that by then I'd already learnt something of what lay behind her reticence from Police Chief Wang's family, but I decided not to reveal that. There were things that she wanted nobody ever to know and she was determined to take those secrets to the grave. I was prepared to keep them too, and I have no regrets about that decision. After all, in this world, there are always many more things that are kept secret than there are things that you are allowed to know.

First draft: 5.6.2007
Final draft: 1.7.2007

Conclusion
Dead Calm

'Dead calm' is a term derived from meteorology, and in lay terms it means that there is no wind at all. In fact, there is always some kind of wind, because as long as there's an air current, you will have breeze. It's just that when airflow is below a certain level (<0.2m/s), we can't feel it. People's perceptions are very limited. There are many things that we cannot see, cannot hear and cannot feel, but they are still there, lurking around us, and may have a greater influence on us than the things that we are fully aware of.

I have entitled this section the 'conclusion', but I should explain that the story of Li Ningyu is already over; what I am going to talk about next has nothing to do with her. So what is it about? That's hard to say. Although this part of my story is not directly connected with what's gone before, it's still important, for all that it is very confused. Just like life, all sorts of things are going to come up that do not fit within the neat structure of beginning, middle and end.

Some people say that the plot is the positive side of a novel. In that case, this is the negative side.

For superstitious reasons, I chose to write every word of this section either at night or on dark and rainy days, and I chose to reread my work in similar conditions, which may have had some unexpected results. There is supposed to be a book, the *Dictionary of the Khazars,* published in 1691, that will bring disaster on anyone reading it after midnight. I promise you that reading my book will not cause you any trouble, whatever time of day you choose for it.

ONE

1

After the wind from the east there came the wind from the west. A cross-straits war of words seemed inevitable.

When I got back from Taipei, I avoided Professor Pan. I don't know how he found out that I'd gone to Taiwan to interview Madame Gu, but within the space of a few days I received a letter, two phone calls and a dozen text messages from him asking where I was and saying that he really wanted to see me. I was staying in the countryside, working on my manuscript (this is a fact; I was busy writing the section entitled 'The Wind from the West'), and I really didn't have time to talk to him.

It might seem as if I'd been influenced by Madame Gu and was now at odds with the Pan family too, but that wasn't the case. My reasoning was purely practical – I was trying to protect myself. It was quite easy to imagine what would happen if we met. Sooner or later the conversation would turn to Madame Gu's story, and once he heard what she'd said, he would marshal his forces for a counter-attack.

Old Mr Pan would obviously spearhead this; flanking me on either side would be the elderly Mr Xin (one-time head of the Hangzhou underground, who appears in this book under his code name, Tiger) and Chen Jinming, the eldest son of K, the senior Communist official at the Gathering of Heroes; and Police Chief Wang Tianxiang's daughter, Wang Min, would bring up the rear along with Sentry A. They would have a whole bunch of researchers working on Party history cheering them on. A year earlier, it had been the recollections of these five, and various research papers, that had allowed me to write 'The Wind from the East'. Now that someone had come forward to challenge their veracity, was it likely that they would just stand by and let all their hard work count for nothing?

Of course they would get together and launch a counter-attack!

If their counter-attack was ineffectual, that would be one thing, but I was worried lest their efforts actually dampened my enthusiasm for writing 'The Wind from the West'. Writing can sometimes be like falling in love in that once you've discovered every lump and bump, you may find yourself in love no longer. What you're talking about then is real life, and real life can make you feel really uncomfortable. I didn't want to be on edge, gritting my teeth while I was finishing work on 'The Wind from the West'.

So I decided to hide somewhere Professor Pan couldn't find me. I would deal with him and the others after I'd finished writing. I would give them my manuscript and then they could say whatever they liked. I didn't want to be partisan. I would do my very best to convey their views accurately, and having provoked the two sides into a war of words, I would report both what it was each side wanted to say and what it was they wanted nobody to know, their truth and lies, and let my readers decide for themselves. I have never believed what people say about crooks being able to hide among honest folk. I'm quite sure that crooks are crooks and honest folk are honest folk – if they get mixed up, it's not difficult to separate them out again.

2

In the countryside, you can slow down.

Just as these days it's no longer considered beautiful for a woman to be fat, it's also not considered acceptable to go about things in a slow, relaxed manner. You're supposed to move ever faster. If you were to travel to New York by boat, it would be taken as proof that you're either off your head or poverty-stricken. Likewise, it's no longer unusual for a couple to go to bed together pretty much straight away; that's effectively a lifestyle choice and is not something to make a big deal about. But the fact that I'm still using the mobile phone I bought ten years ago is seen as worthy of comment and strikes some people as absolutely amazing.

I get countless comments about my not having adapted to the headlong rush of modern life; some admire this, others are snide or mocking. Even so, we are all caught up in this obsession with speed, we demand it, we won't be satisfied without it. But hastiness is something that clever people have always tried to avoid; it's a monster born from the wind, it's a pirate ship that once it has you aboard will keep you captive. Unquestionably, it's now easier to own a mobile phone than not, and easier to get a new phone than stick with your old one. We are racing ahead in desperate and dangerous pursuit of ever greater speed and we cannot slow down, since slowing down would mean swimming against the current and expending twice as much effort.

That's the real reason I chose to go to the countryside to write. In the countryside I'm like a prisoner released from his shackles. I'm free; I have no other claims on my attention; I can go to work when the sun rises and rest when it sets. My energies are consumed in the slow process that is memory and waiting.

Waiting is also a desire for speed.

In other words, whether you choose to view this subjectively or objectively, the pace of my writing accelerated, and so I had reason to write proudly to Professor Pan: *I am sure that I will finish this manuscript with all due haste, and I hope that after you have read it you will respond at the earliest possible moment.*

The words 'earliest possible moment' imply hurry; they lifted their wings, speeding past in a flash, whistling as they went.

3

Eventually, an answer arrived from Professor Pan. Strictly speaking, it wasn't a reply but notification of a death. Mr Pan senior had passed away and the Professor hoped I would be able to attend the funeral.

I was suddenly worried in case it was my manuscript – Madame Gu's version of events – that had caused a crisis and led to his death. If that was what had happened, then I really ought to attend the funeral, no matter how awkward I felt.

When I spoke with Professor Pan about this, he responded with his usual gentleness. 'I am afraid that your manuscript did indeed cause my father's death, but that doesn't mean he passed away in anger – it's quite possible that he was overcome with shame. If what you wrote is true and my father was still lying to everyone, even at his age, that really was… what can I say? I'm ashamed of him. My father was in hospital for seven days after his heart attack and there were several occasions when he tried to speak to us, but we couldn't understand what he wanted. We really have no idea what exactly it was that upset him so much. That would be entirely typical of him, of course, to die with his secrets untold.'

I didn't know what to do with myself. I felt as if I had killed a child and had no idea how to even begin to atone for what I'd done.

Professor Pan was a lovely man; not only did he not blame me, he tried to comfort me. He spoke very carefully. 'A man of ninety has to face the fact of his mortality every day – after all, even a sneeze could carry him off. Your role in this is nothing more than that of a sneeze; there's no reason to feel responsible. I am my father's only child and I can promise you that the Pan family will not go after you for what's happened. If you want, I can give you an official statement to that effect.'

He seemed so open-minded, so honest and friendly, but I wondered whether that might be a ploy to get me to suppress Madame Gu's testimony and support old Mr Pan's version instead. Was he being nice to me for selfish reasons? I decided to take the initiative. I told him that if Madame Gu was wrong in anything she'd said, all he had to do was tell me and I would respect his opinion. If necessary, I was even prepared to destroy my manuscript.

I was quite wrong. That was not what happened, not at all. Professor Pan explained quite clearly that with his father dead, he had nothing to say. 'It's not that I don't have an opinion about all of this but that I don't feel the need to express it. I'm sure the Party has already decided what contribution my father made, so whatever anyone else says now, they'll just be wasting their time.'

It was because of this that Professor Pan was particularly conscious of the wording of the eulogy that the Party had provided for his father. He repeatedly proposed amendments, to the point where it seemed like he was quibbling. But that doesn't mean that he got his way. Indeed, the fact that he refused to allow me to reprint the text of the eulogy here suggests that he wasn't happy with the final wording determined by the Party hierarchy.

4

As the last surviving representative of that generation, Mr Pan senior was given an extremely formal memorial ceremony. He had previously been employed at Unit 701, and they had a committee responsible for organizing funerals, which made sure an obituary was published in the papers. Vast numbers of people came to express their condolences, including three very senior Party leaders, which meant that the whole thing had to be done on an even grander scale than originally planned.

The memorial ceremony lasted for three full days. The first day was for family members and old friends, and the entire place was awash with tears. On the second day it was old Mr Pan's former comrades-in-arms who came, together with colleagues and representatives from each division of Unit 701, and the current leadership. They were all very solemn and everyone was pretty much silent. On the third day it was representatives of the local government, together with anyone who'd been unable to make it on the previous two days. There were also some people who just turned up uninvited. Of course, old Mr Xin (Tiger) came in person, together with K's son, Chen Jinming. Police Chief Wang Tianxiang's daughter Wang Min was there, and so was Sentry A, as well as their families. All of them came with wreaths, and in the end there were so many that it must have taken half a dozen trucks to remove them.

On the very last evening, Professor Pan came to see me at my hotel. He brought me two things: my manuscript and a CD. I had sent him the manuscript by email, and there was no reason for him to give it back to me, so I assumed that this must represent some kind of emotional closure for him – what the eye doesn't see, the heart doesn't grieve over.

I took back my manuscript and asked, 'Are you sure you don't want to offer an opinion?'

He shook his head. I was hoping that he would say something. His silence implied that a mistake had been made, that maybe Madame Gu was in the right.

But as I renewed my attack, he suddenly turned on me. 'Did you notice, on the second day, when so many people came from Unit 701 where my father used to work, how many people cried? Not one. Nobody shed a single tear. Why not? Because none of them believe in tears.'

'What are you trying to say?' I asked.

'In your manuscript it says that in the end Madame Gu decided to help my aunt, Li Ningyu, get her message out because she was moved by her tears. Do you really think that can be true? You ought to know by now that these are very special people: they don't trust emotional displays of any kind. Speaking as my father's son, I've already said that I have nothing to say about your story. But speaking as a reader, particularly as a reader with knowledge of the kind of people that feature in your book, I feel that... this is something that deserves further consideration. Because, as it stands, the key to your plot rests on very dubious foundations, and I'm not sure that's a good idea.'

I thought the counter-attack was now underway. But in the blink of an eye it was over. Other than recommending that I rewrite that crucial scene, he made no further suggestions – in fact, he refused to say another word. There was definitely something going on there. His silence was making me very curious.

'What aren't you telling me?' I asked.

He shook his head and walked off.

Four hours later I received a text message from him. It was clear from both the time he sent it (three in the morning) and what it said that he couldn't sleep. I imagine that insomnia broke his determination to keep silent, which was lucky for me:

Why have I kept quiet?

Because Madame Gu is my mother.

As with atoms in a molecule, external pressures forced them apart... What can you do when your parents quarrel? Leave them to speak for themselves. I feel I have no choice but to stay silent.

That was a shock! All thoughts of sleep were driven from my mind.

Two hours later, I was still awake, too excited to sleep, when I received another text message from him:

Please don't ask anyone what happened between my parents. I really want it to stop here. Tomorrow I'll arrange for someone to take you home.

5

I wasn't going anywhere.

I felt that my investigations had only just begun.

I made the excuse that I still had a lot to do and then changed my hotel, after which I went in secret to speak to Mr Xin and the others. Professor Pan had obviously anticipated this, since he'd already got them to agree not to tell me anything. Not one of them was happy to see me, and when I pointed out that they kept avoiding the subject, all of them said the same thing: 'There's nothing to know...

Don't ask... I've told you as much as I can... I never really knew what happened, you'll have to ask Professor Pan. It's his family, after all...'

It was as if they had gone back in time and were being interrogated by the enemy; none of them was prepared to say a thing. In the end it was Police Chief Wang Tianxiang's eldest son, Wang Min's older brother, a man named Wang Hanmin, who explained the mystery to me. He had suffered a terrible stroke four years earlier, which had robbed him of motor control over half his body. Confined to hospital as he was, with very few opportunities to speak to other people, it was possible that Professor Pan didn't think I would contact him and so hadn't made him promise not to say anything. It was equally possible that, having been in hospital for such a long time, Mr Wang was feeling terribly lonely. He was certainly very friendly to me and answered all my questions.

Mr Wang informed me that for a certain reason (here I have to apologize, but I want to keep my promise to Madame Gu that I wouldn't reveal this particular secret) Gu Xiaomeng had long refused to marry. However, after the War of Resistance against the Japanese occupation finally ended in 1945, Mr Pan senior renounced his membership of the Communist Party and rejoined the Nationalist Party, and he and Gu Xiaomeng got married. Mr Pan senior, don't forget, was Li Ningyu's brother, and they had been born into a landowning family, to a father who was killed when the Revolution came to their home town. The two siblings had sworn to avenge his death and had fought for the Nationalists' army; it was only later that they both went over to the Communist Party.

In actual fact, old Mr Pan hadn't really renounced his

membership of the Communist Party – that was done to trick Madame Gu, so that he could use her connections to infiltrate Nationalist Party headquarters and continue his undercover activities. After the wedding, thanks to the strings pulled by Gu Xiaomeng's father, the two of them were moved to Nanjing, which was now once again the seat of the post-war Nationalist government. Gu Xiaomeng was employed in the Nationalist Party's Intelligence Bureau, and Mr Pan senior became a Unit Chief in the Administrative Department of the Nanjing Garrison. The following year, Gu Xiaomeng gave birth to her first child: Professor Pan.

The civil war between the Communists and the Nationalists intensified and by 1949 the Communists' People's Liberation Army had the upper hand. Mr Pan senior was very aware of how risky it was for his family to remain in the Nationalist city of Nanjing, especially as Gu Xiaomeng was now pregnant with her second child. And so, that spring, one month before the PLA's planned liberation of Nanjing, he got permission from his superiors for them to relocate to an area of the country that was already under Communist control. He made up a story to explain their journey to Gu Xiaomeng and he managed to get the family all the way north to Beiping (as Beijing was then known). By the time they got there, Nanjing had been liberated by the PLA, the Nationalist Party was on its last legs and the evacuation to Taiwan was underway. Old Mr Pan decided that, given the circumstances, there was nothing Gu Xiaomeng could now do, so he told her who he really was and encouraged her to join the Communist Party so that they could start a new life together. He had not anticipated Gu Xiaomeng's determined refusal. She immediately went for an abortion. Then, abandoning her husband and child, she fled. After a very circuitous journey of several thousand kilometres, she finally made it to Taiwan.

When I heard this story, I felt profoundly sorry that I'd been told it by an outsider and not by Professor Pan himself. But that would have been impossible. We all have our limits as to how much we're prepared to share with other people. I knew that Professor Pan was already regretting that he'd ever come to see me. He told me he felt he'd allowed me to open a Pandora's box.

TWO

1

I wrote these lines at the Tan Estate. Nowadays, it's a guest house operated by some government department or other – meetings are held there, and rooms are rented out to tour groups. The fixtures and fittings are pretty old, it retains its communal toilets and bathrooms, and if you want hot water you have to take a thermos to be filled in the boiler room. The rooms are designed for two or three people to share, so I booked a two-person room, which cost me a modest hundred RMB a night. It was my fifth visit to the Tan Estate but my first overnight stay.

Thanks to its location right beside West Lake, the Tan Estate escaped both wartime damage and subsequent demolition and has retained its original features: the buildings in Ming-Qing architectural style, the huge old trees, the cobbled paths, the clumps of emerald-green bamboo, the upright dawn redwoods... One difference would be that the high walls surrounding the estate have today been replaced with iron railings.

As I wandered around, I had to admire its setting – to the

west you have the Temple of General Yue Fei, to the east is the stone arch of Xiling Bridge, there are green mountains behind and the clear waters of the lake in front. Here you might imagine you are deep in the hills, there you might feel as if you're floating on the misty surface of West Lake, but at every point you're struck by how beautiful the landscape is; it seems far removed from the hubbub of the city. You'd think that the person who built this house must have been a great man.

Not so.

From what I've been told, the original owner of the Tan Estate started out as a gangster. At the beginning of the twentieth century there was a great deal of fighting in Zhejiang and Jiangsu provinces, and the city of Hangzhou was in a state of virtual anarchy. Old Mr Tan took advantage of this to put his criminal career behind him. He used the money he'd stolen to buy this land and build himself a mansion, and he also bought himself a position of influence. So this man not only worked for the notorious Green Gang, with its connections to people in both politics and organized crime, and continued to be involved in murder, robbery and other violent activities, but was now also a salaried government official.

His legal and illegal activities together brought him great wealth and he very quickly became a major figure in Hangzhou's criminal underworld. He was rich enough to be able to satisfy his every desire, no matter how extravagant – so rich that it would have taken him half a dozen lifetimes to spend what he'd stolen. He was also notoriously cruel, and it was the degree of violence he brought to his activities that eventually got him killed.

One night early in the winter of 1933, Mr Tan went to Shanghai with his wife, his youngest son and a maid to see the celebrated actor Mei Lanfang perform at the opera; on the way back, they were all killed by a group of black-clad assassins. This was shocking news and it made the front pages of the newspapers in both Hangzhou and Shanghai. But when it came to the police investigation, there was a lot of argument over jurisdiction, and what with one thing and another the killers were never caught. The old man had committed plenty of murders in his time, for which he had never been brought to book, so this was a kind of poetic justice.

I call him an old man, but in fact he wasn't particularly elderly; he was in his fifties when he was killed, and his children were still teenagers or in their early twenties. He had six children in all: three surviving sons and two daughters. His elder daughter was living in Japan with her husband and couldn't return to organize the funeral. Eldest Brother was twenty-three, a very handsome young man, and though he seemed capable enough, he had no idea how to deal with this crisis. Second Brother wasn't right in the head; for all that he was twenty years old, he was completely useless in this situation. With the murders having thrown the household into chaos, two of the servants turned to crime themselves and carted off all the paintings and calligraphy in the house that were worth anything. Fortunately, the estate's head butler proved loyal and helped Eldest Brother take charge. However, the real headache remained: his father hadn't left a penny in the bank.

As with any former bandit, the old man didn't take banknotes seriously – he wanted to see gold and silver, jade, gemstones and the like. He often used to say that in a war zone, banknotes weren't money, they were waste paper. Once you set fire to them, they went up in a puff of smoke, and then you had nothing. The man may have been a career criminal, but he wasn't stupid. It was likely that before he died he'd converted all his wealth into gold and silver. In fact, his family and servants had seen him bringing back gold bars and silver ingots on numerous occasions. The problem was that nobody knew where he'd put them.

What to do?

Search!

Even the completely cretinous Second Brother knew that if they could find where their father had hidden his wealth, they'd be the richest family in all of Hangzhou. In other words, if the next generation of the Tan family wanted to continue enjoying the same kind of lifestyle, working wasn't going to do it for them. They needed to find their father's hoard. At least, that was how Eldest Brother saw it, as he began what was to prove an endless hunt. He searched during the day. He searched at night. He did the searching himself and he hired other people to help. He kept searching for years, but he didn't find a thing.

From everything I've read on the subject, and the many stories people tell, it seems that Eldest Brother was just not a lucky person. He was well educated and perfectly intelligent, but fortune was never on his side. He's a tragic figure. The search for his family's lost wealth consumed his entire life, right up until the moment the Japanese devils occupied Hangzhou and took forcible possession of the Tan Estate. All that effort for nothing. The treasure remained hidden; it existed only in his imagination, in his dreams;

it was separated from him by a sheet of glass; it was to be found only in his castles in the air.

2

The Japanese took possession of Hangzhou in December of 1937. The defending forces had withdrawn, leaving the city entirely at the mercy of the enemy. The Battle of Shanghai had only just finished and it had been terrible for Chiang Kai-shek and the Nationalists. He'd lost huge numbers of officers and men, and there'd been serious damage to morale, so he was no longer capable of a frontal assault. All that was left to him was an orderly withdrawal. Retreat. In order to secure that retreat, he even ordered that Hangzhou's Qiantang River Bridge, which had only recently been completed, be blown up.

Boom!

Boom!!

Boom!!!

Those were the only explosions heard when the Japanese took Hangzhou.

Before the Japanese devils entered the city, the rich and powerful had already fled in terror, leaving their properties empty. That was what happened at the Tan Estate. And when the Tan brothers eventually came back, they found the Japanese ensconced there.

In point of fact, there were plenty of grand mansions around West Lake in those days, and there were many – the Liu Estate, the Guo Estate, the Mansion of Lord Yang, the Willow Garden – that were much grander and better known than the Tan Estate. Just next door was the Yu House, which might not have been as big, but it was the retirement home of the late Qing scholar Yu Yue and was thus quite as famous as his Quyuan Garden in Suzhou; given its historical and cultural importance, it should have been a prized asset for the Japanese. All of these mansions, thanks to their privileged location in the vicinity of West Lake, had been lucky enough to escape the Japanese bombing raids unscathed. The mansions were all still standing, each one more magnificent than the last, but the Japanese weren't interested in any of them, they only wanted the Tan Estate. Now why was that?

The problem for the Tan Estate was the treasure it harboured – treasure that nobody had found yet. The longer the treasure went undiscovered, the more people there were who knew about it. Word had spread. One person told ten, and ten told a hundred, until in the end pretty much anybody with friends had heard about it. If that many people knew, how could the Japanese not know? Where there were Japanese devils, you would find their Chinese collaborators, and these Chinese collaborators were endlessly trying to think of ways to curry favour. And so it was natural that they would try and make a good story out of it, adding details from their own imaginations, until the Japanese were convinced that the Tan Estate was a veritable gold mine, which they needed to secure as soon as possible.

To put it bluntly, when the Japanese took possession of the Tan Estate, it was because they were treasure hunting.

When everyone around you is being made to suffer, you just have to put up with it, but if it's only your family that's been singled out, how can you let that pass? It was completely unacceptable! Eldest Brother came out fighting. How dare the Japanese bully the Tan family like that! He went to complain at the headquarters of the puppet regime. However, not only did he fail to win his case, but they also caught him on the back foot.

The Japanese devils had plenty of traitors helping them and they easily found out all they needed to know about the Tan family. They came up with two very plausible explanations as to why they had requisitioned that particular property. Firstly, old Mr Tan had built his mansion with proceeds from thuggery and robbery, so the government was fully within its rights to confiscate it. That which he had taken from the people would now be returned to them. Secondly, the subsequent owners had been engaged in illegal activities on the estate, leading to a decline in public morals and serious social problems.

This was all perfectly true, and the Tan brothers had no grounds for appeal. Particularly on the second point – everyone in Hangzhou knew that they'd been peddling flesh out at the Tan Estate. The place was nothing but a brothel. However, the Tan family weren't actually responsible for that; they'd only been in the business for a couple of months, but the brothel had existed for years.

This is what happened: in the front courtyard of the estate there was a teahouse, with accommodation attached. This had been originally set up by old Mr Tan as somewhere he could meet his gangster cronies without generating comment, a place where the occasional discreet murder of a rival could be carried out, and where further illegal acts could be planned. In calling it a teahouse and guest house, I am being polite – it was a rat's nest. But it had been in operation for years, it was known about, and it was located on the road right next to the lake, so it would have been perfectly possible to turn it into a legitimate business if anyone had been prepared to do the necessary work. However, thanks to the fact that the two servants had stolen all the family's valuables, the Tan brothers simply didn't have the money for that. And Eldest Brother was fixated on the missing gold – he had no interest in sorting out anything else. Someone proposed renting the teahouse from them, but Eldest Brother initially refused, since he imagined he'd be unearthing the treasure any moment now, and how embarrassing to have to rent out part of their property! But the gold was never found and their financial problems got worse and worse, until in the end they had to sell some of their belongings to pay their debts. At this point, Eldest Brother swallowed his pride and agreed to rent out the teahouse.

The man renting the property bore the surname Su, and he was a typical thug. His mother had died young and his father fled, so Su was brought up by his maternal grandfather, who worked in the kitchens at the Louwailou restaurant. Even as a tiny child, Su had worked as a gambler's runner and tout, and he was famous for the way he could spin a yarn and extort money from the unwary. His companions called him Su-the-Arsehole, because he was the kind of person who'd do the dirty on you just for the hell of it.

Su-the-Arsehole wasn't going to work at anything legal for his money – in the blink of an eye he'd turned the teahouse into a brothel offering all kinds of exotic services, and every kind of criminal found their way there, until the place was notorious throughout Hangzhou. Locals took to calling the hookers 'chickens' and their clients 'wolves' and pretty soon the reputation of the Tan Estate stank to high heaven. The more its reputation stank, the more people flocked there. Su-the-Arsehole was making money hand over fist and soon he started wearing a little moustache and dressing in a Western-style suit. Now that he'd become a man of substance, he wanted everyone to forget his past as a petty crook.

In a most unexpected move, a couple of years later Su-the-Arsehole proposed buying the whole of the Tan Estate – quite possibly he too was interested in doing a bit of treasure hunting. This only served to alert the Tan family to quite how much money he must be making: why not cut out the middleman? They decided to terminate his tenancy.

How was that going to work? By now Su-the-Arsehole was rich and powerful; he wasn't going to be taking orders from any little brats! 'Dream on! You might want to kick me out, but I am determined to stay – if you've got the balls, you can try and force me out!'

Eldest Brother had the balls, but having thought through the matter carefully, he decided that he didn't dare touch him. Second Brother was useless; there was no point even asking him. Third Brother was hopeless too, an effeminate little creature, pale and delicate, and so cowardly that he didn't even dare kill a chicken. That was how Eldest Brother saw it: of his two brothers, one was little better than a dunce and the other might as well have been a girl. The family's economic situation was going from bad to worse and they didn't have money to waste on trying to recruit supporters. Eldest Brother had schooled himself in patience and learnt how to swallow humiliation, so even when he was faced with a bastard like Su-the-Arsehole, he rarely showed his true feelings.

Nobody was expecting that Third Brother would grit his teeth, flush bright red and announce to Eldest Brother, 'We've got to get rid of him!'

3

Third Brother wasn't like the rest of the Tan family. He was cut from different cloth. A changeling.

According to my information, Third Brother was born immediately after an elder sister had fallen sick and died at only three years old. Everyone agreed that the two of them were very much alike; they were both very small and sickly, and, strangely, they both seemed much closer to the servants, with whom they spent all their time, than to any members of their own family. The little girl died because she'd been infected by a consumptive servant. Third Brother couldn't even take milk from his own mother's breast. It made him sick, it might as well have been poison to him, and very nearly killed him.

Having no other choice, the family had to find him a wet nurse, and this was another odd thing: once he started being fed by the nurse, he wouldn't stop. They simply couldn't wean him – they tried smearing chilli oil on her nipples, so hot that his pale little face went bright red and his tongue swelled up, but he still hung on. They drew horrible images on her breasts, shocking enough to make him scream and give him nightmares, but in the end when he got hungry enough, he would latch on. It seemed as if he would pay any price to stay on the breast. When they weaned him forcibly, he would respond by getting terribly sick, to the point that they worried he might die: he would be running a high temperature, covered in ulcers, and vomiting bile. Since this happened time and time again, he was still breastfeeding at the age of seven. By that time he was too big to be held in his wet nurse's arms, so he had to stand up to feed. His nurse's pale breasts had been tugged on until they hung down like limp sacks. Those who saw him at it just wanted to laugh. At eight he was sent to a school in the city, but he ran away because he couldn't cope without his nurse.

He had almost no primary schooling, but later on he did go to middle school, where his grades were consistently appalling. However, when it came to painting (which was not part of the regular curriculum), he did remarkably well. Everyone who saw his art agreed that he had an amazing natural talent, so he was sent to the Academy of Fine Arts. His father was still alive then and didn't know whether to laugh or cry at the prospect of his own son becoming a painter. He treated Third Brother more or less as if he were a girl and held out no particular hopes of him ever achieving much. The money he'd spent on his upbringing had clearly been wasted, but it didn't really matter.

Since he'd been almost entirely brought up by his wet nurse, Third Brother wasn't particularly close to the other members of his family, and even the servants saw no reason to respect him. Otherwise, why did everyone call him Third Brother, when they ought to have been calling him Third Young Master? There was a reason for that, too. When his parents were killed and the rest of the household were all weeping and wailing, he – then aged sixteen – was the only one who didn't shed a tear; he seemed more like a world-weary sixty-year-old than a teenager. At first, everyone said that he hated his parents for having treated him so badly, but then he decided to let his hair grow, apparently as a mark of respect, as if he really missed his parents. Nobody understood what he was trying to do. He'd always been quite effeminate-looking and with his longer hair he seemed more girlish than ever, until it got to the point where they started to worry. However, what he really most resembled was one of the new breed of art student, with his long hair swishing about his face, his starry-eyed expression, and a portfolio under his arm. He attracted a lot of attention from modern young girls with progressive ideas.

Eldest Brother didn't enjoy the sight of his arty sibling. It annoyed him every time they saw each other; it was quite stomach-churning to look at him. He often muttered to himself as he looked at his two younger brothers, just as he did whenever he thought about having to deal with that bastard Su-the-Arsehole, but what could he do? When a tiger loses its claws, it is helpless. He just had to accept that he was out of luck. However, Third Brother refused to accept anything of the kind; he wanted to call time on Su-the-Arsehole and get rid of him, and he began to act as if it were a revolver he held in his hand and not a portfolio of drawings.

Eldest Brother found his attitude quite laughable. He glared at him and stomped off. What was the point in talking to him? It would just be a waste of breath.

Third Brother launched himself forward and said through gritted teeth, 'We've got to get rid of him!'

Eldest Brother did his very best to suppress his irritation

and said lightly, 'How? Are you planning to draw a tiger that'll make him run away?'

'I'm going to join the army,' Third Brother said.

Eldest Brother looked at him with his shoulder-length hair blowing in the wind and suddenly found it impossible to contain his rage. 'Just stop annoying me, why don't you!' And he walked off without another word.

Eldest Brother didn't see Third Brother again until a couple of evenings later, and it gave him a terrible shock, as if he'd seen a ghost. Third Brother had indeed gone and joined the army, and the long jet-black hair he'd been growing out as a sign of mourning had all been shaved off. He was now wearing a peaked cap and an army uniform – and he looked quite dreadful in it. Even in that garb he managed to look effeminate! On the one hand, with his close-cropped head, he looked like a thug, and on the other, with his eyes swimming in tears, he looked like a poor wretch. Even worse, perhaps because of the inordinately long time he'd spent on the breast as a child, he had particularly fair skin, which made him look like a bookworm, a weakling, a coward.

Seeing someone like that with two revolvers strapped to his waist did not comfort Eldest Brother one bit. He was furious, he was red with rage, he could not have been angrier! Over the last few years, the family had sold off their remaining bits and bobs to see Third Brother through his studies, and he was now nearly ready to graduate. Eldest Brother had already gone to the trouble of making representations on his behalf and spending money to see him placed in a good position. He'd thought that at long last he was about to get Third Brother off his hands. And now he'd gone and done this...

'You must be off your head! How could you do something like this! You're sending us all to rack and ruin!' Overcome with rage, Eldest Brother slapped Third Brother across the face and cursed. 'From now on, I wash my hands of you!' This scream echoed through the night, as if someone had died.

4

I should perhaps explain that, as a soldier, Third Brother received a salary from the state, and his basic needs were taken care of. But he had cut Eldest Brother to the quick and embarrassed the Tan family in front of everyone. How could a Tan become a common soldier?

In fact, there was no need to be so concerned. Third Brother was soon promoted to platoon commander, serving under Qian Huyi in the Zhejiang Garrison of the Nationalist Party's National Revolutionary Army. A platoon commander wasn't very important, but at least he was an officer, and it was a stepping stone.

In the past, if he'd wanted to move on up the ranks, to become a company, battalion or regimental commander, a gold bar or two would have been all that was required. His father, after all, had bought himself the position of Chief Inspector (which would be equivalent to Chief of Police nowadays). But that was then and this was now. Third Brother had no such means for securing his promotion, so in the end he came up with a particularly low ploy – he got the young niece of the family's loyal head butler to sleep with Division Commander Qian Huyi and that got him a position as a company commander.

No matter how you looked at it, Third Brother's behaviour was an embarrassment, and it certainly confirmed the general impression that the Tan family was on its last legs. But his actions had made Su-the-Arsehole uneasy, and he began to worry that he might actually have to give up his tenancy.

Sure enough, one afternoon, Third Brother turned up at the teahouse, barged his way into Su-the-Arsehole's room upstairs, and without mincing his words revoked the tenancy. Su-the-Arsehole had by that stage put quite a bit of effort into getting Qïan Huyi on his side, so was he likely to be scared of some company commander? In a scornful tone he said, 'If you want a bit of money to piss off, you can have it, but you're not getting this teahouse back. If you don't believe me, you can go and ask my pal Qian Huyi. Hey, you only gave him one woman, but I gave him twelve – buxom and skinny, pale and dark, all kinds – so what do you think he's going to say when you try and get rid of me?'

If Su-the-Arsehole thought that would be the end of it, he was wrong, because Third Brother now reached for his knife. It was a throwing knife with a very short blade, quite thick and shaped like an enlarged protruding thumb. He'd been carrying it under his uniform belt.

Third Brother began flipping the knife backwards and forwards in his hands. It was as if the knife were alive: the blade glinted with a cold light, its point trained on Su-the-Arsehole.

Su-the-Arsehole leapt back, shocked. 'What do you think you're doing?' he yelled.

'I only want what's fair,' Third Brother said coolly. 'Give us our property back.'

'Give it back?' Su-the-Arsehole was trying to be polite. 'I never stole it! I'm just renting the place from you, and when the tenancy is over, of course you'll get it back.'

'I want it back now,' Third Brother said.

'And if I refuse?'

Third Brother waved his knife. 'Then I'll just have to make you give it back.'

Su-the-Arsehole quickly picked up a chair to defend himself with, and Third Brother burst out laughing.

'What are you so scared of? You're a pal of Division Commander Qian – I'd get cashiered if I hurt you. Anyway—' here, he patted his holster '—if I wanted to hurt you, a gun would be a lot easier.'

'You wouldn't dare!' With the mention of Qian Huyi, Su-the-Arsehole had calmed down slightly.

'Of course I wouldn't. Or rather, it's not that I wouldn't dare but that it wouldn't be worth it.' Third Brother gave Su-the-Arsehole an appraising look. 'If I shot you dead, I'd be a murderer and then I'd be up in front of a firing squad. Why should I have to risk my life to bring you down? It's a fairly petty disagreement after all, and there's no reason we should both have to die to resolve it. That really would be a waste.'

Third Brother moved across to a nearby table, held out his left hand and playfully clenched all his fingers bar the little one. Narrowing his eyes, he said. 'This little finger is nothing, but it is mine and not yours.' He raised his knife then lowered its curved blade to the top joint and held it there, pinning the finger to the edge of the table as if he were about to slice a bamboo shoot. It really was a terrible sight.

Su-the-Arsehole was not a clever man, but he got the

message. Third Brother was acknowledging that Su-the-Arsehole was more important than he was; he had more money than he did; and even his little finger was worth more than that of Third Brother's. It would be nothing for Su-the-Arsehole to return the estate to Third Brother.

All this while, Third Brother's little finger was sticking up, all by itself, against the edge of the table.

With a single sharp snapping sound, Third Brother sliced off its top joint.

The fingertip didn't twitch in the way stories would have you believe; it just lay there resembling a bamboo shoot, motionless, and there was very little blood. Third Brother seemed a bit disappointed. He stared at it in disgust, then with the tip of his knife he flicked it at Su-the-Arsehole, as one might flip a cigarette butt.

Su-the-Arsehole was quite short and he managed to duck it. But his face had turned a sickly green, his voice was shaking and he began to scream like a fishwife who'd just been groped. 'Help! Help!'

A servant came thudding up the stairs, but Third Brother got in first and, showing him his bloodied little finger, shouted loudly, 'Bring wine!'

The servant quickly rushed away to find some.

Third Brother dipped the stump in the alcohol and felt a stab of pain as if it were being fried in oil. Sweat immediately beaded his forehead, but other than that, he didn't react at all; he didn't grit his teeth, or moan, or furrow his brow or close his eyes. In fact, he joked with the servant, 'Mr Su and I are going to seal our agreement by swearing an oath in blood.'

The servant congratulated his boss, which annoyed

Su-the-Arsehole mightily, so all he got for his pains was a command to bugger off. The servant picked up his feet and removed himself.

Third Brother let the servant leave, but he stopped his master from going anywhere. 'If you just walk out, I'll have cut off my finger for nothing. Do you really think I'm going to allow that?'

Su-the-Arsehole didn't pay the blindest bit of notice, just tried to dodge past him. Third Brother whipped out his pistol, pointed it at the back of his head and said, 'If you set foot outside this room, I'll shoot your nasty little legs out from under you, and then I'll gouge out both your eyes. I'll make sure that the rest of your life is a misery. If you don't believe me, then give it a go!'

Of course he wasn't going to give it a go. The man was a lunatic, far more frightening than even a rabid dog, and Su-the-Arsehole was scared witless. He tried to get Third Brother to put his gun down, to see if they could discuss the matter in a civilized fashion.

Third Brother did put his gun down, but somehow it wasn't so easy to discuss the matter in a civilized fashion. He decided to get the whole thing over and done with as quickly as possible. 'If you aren't out of this teahouse by the end of today, I will kill you!'

At that time, Third Brother was still only eighteen years old. He was slight and thin and he had a reputation for never raising his voice, never getting angry. His eyes always seemed to be swimming in tears and he looked like an innocent child – how could he be this unpleasant? It seemed impossible, absolutely impossible. But as Su-the-Arsehole stared down the black barrel of Third Brother's gun, it was as if the young man's father had come back to life.

A bastard may not care in the slightest what other people say about him, but he is liable to be very concerned about his own survival. When Third Brother cut off his own finger, it was to show that from then on Su-the-Arsehole's life would be on the line, and he was scared just thinking about it. That evening he collected his ill-gotten gains, did a lot of cursing and took himself off in humiliation. He went to find his pal, Division Commander Qian Huyi, but the latter refused to even see him. The fact was that Su-the-Arsehole was just a cheap and nasty criminal like everyone said, and nobody was prepared to give him the time of day. Besides which, the Division Commander had the niece of the old head butler at the Tan Estate with him, and she'd already put a word in.

This all took place in the February of 1937, just after Chinese New Year, when the winter-flowering plum trees that stood proudly on the slopes behind the rear courtyard of the Tan Estate were giving off a delicious perfume, heralding the arrival of spring. It seemed that even they were delighted to finally see the back of Su-the-Arsehole. That time of year is always a quiet period for the flesh trade, so on the Tan Estate they focused on preparations for their reopening of the teahouse. By the time the spring flowers began to bloom, everything was ready: the front courtyard was once again wreathed in lights and busy with the pouring of wine. At first, business wasn't as brisk as it had been under Su-the-Arsehole, but it got better night after night, and by the summer it was pretty much back to normal.

If this state of affairs had continued, the Tan Estate would have gradually become financially more stable. But the good times didn't last long. In August, the Japanese started their bombing campaign, and when people are being blown to bits left, right and centre, who has time to go to a brothel? You're too busy trying to survive! By the end of the year, the Japanese devils had occupied Hangzhou and requisitioned the Tan Estate. So Third Brother had cut off his finger, but all he got was a couple of months of good times and an awful lot of humiliation. He was abused and ridiculed – there was nothing he could do. As the old saying has it, when luck is against you, even a hero will find himself helpless.

Third Brother had cut his finger off for nothing.

5

After the Japanese devils occupied the Tan Estate, outside the front door and up on the roof there hung the usual baboon-arse red flags, and yellow-uniformed sentries guarded the entrance. But this huge estate wasn't taken over by a division of the Imperial Japanese Army in need of suitable accommodation, and nor did an important official move in. Instead, a very respectable-looking Japanese couple came to live there, with just a handful of servants. There were less than ten members of the household, and even with the guards, that barely brought it up to two dozen.

Once they'd taken up residence, the couple had very little to do with the outside world, but occasionally they would stroll to some of West Lake's most scenic spots, taking in its sweeping willows and shady pavilions, its arched stone bridges and yellow irises. The master of the household was in his thirties, bespectacled and always carrying a fan, quite handsome, and elegantly dressed. He was extremely polite and refined in his manners, and he seemed very knowledgeable about both poetry and painting. He would often pause to look at hanging scrolls, seemingly lost in admiration for the work of art or calligraphy in question. Sometimes he appeared overwhelmed by the beauty of the scenery and he would stand gazing out at West Lake, reciting a snatch of verse, standing tall with his robe billowing in the wind. He seemed highly civilized, in a way deserving of respect.

Compared to him, his young wife was a piece of work, parading about in her sun hat, dragging a huge Alsatian dog the size of a small pony around with her, and glaring at anyone who had the temerity to walk past, snorting with irritation, as if she were quite the colonial memsahib. No wonder people went out of their way to avoid her.

Where the pair of them had come from, who they were and what they were doing there, nobody knew, and it was hard to find out. Nobody from the outside was allowed in, and whatever was going on inside the estate was done very quietly, as if it wasn't happening at all, so it was impossible to know what was afoot.

In fact, for all that the work took place in silence, the Tan Estate had been completely dismantled. In particular, the two little Western-style buildings at the back had been smashed to smithereens.

Why?

They were searching for gold!

The reason the Japanese devils had requisitioned the Tan

Estate in the first place was because they were looking for treasure, but that they'd put a scholar in charge of proceedings seemed more than a little odd. Perhaps they were hoping he would be a decoy. Who would suspect a scholar of having turned treasure hunter, a loving couple of being thieves, silence being used to cover up a robbery? No one. Which was what the Japanese wanted: to stop people from putting two and two together. After all, everyone knew about the gold and silver hidden on the Tan Estate, so if the Japanese turned up openly to steal it, it wouldn't look so good for their self-styled Greater East Asia Co-Prosperity Sphere.

Day followed day, months passed, the seasons rolled by and they'd searched everywhere they could think of. Even the gardens had been excavated to a metre or more. They had no idea where to look next. Everything that could be smashed had been smashed; everything that could be dug up had been dug up; the grounds had been thoroughly gone over, every room had been searched inside and out, the pipes and drains had been checked, the walls and trees too, every nook and cranny… They had looked everywhere and found nothing.

It seemed as if horrible old Mr Tan had taken his gold with him to hell – and now he was about to drag the young wife after him.

That happened the following year, immediately after the Duanwu Festival. Whether or not the couple had been out to see the dragon-boat racing during the festival or had eaten the traditional sticky-rice dumplings has not been recorded. You'd have thought the scholar would have enjoyed the sight of those handsomely painted longboats honouring the memory of the poet Qu Yuan. We do know, however, that the weather was already hot by then, and that the scholar and his young wife had got into the habit of taking their Alsatian out for an evening runabout beside the lake. They would go out as the sun was setting and return once the moon was high in the sky.

That evening it was really hot and they headed for where they could be sure to catch the breeze, out on West Lake itself, across the Su Causeway and all the way down to Prince's Cove. By the time they turned back for home, it was already dark. As they retraced their steps, four men in black, wielding swords, suddenly leapt out from a covered boat anchored by the shore and attacked them.

The woman and the Alsatian were slashed to death before they could make a sound. The man, for all that he seemed so scholarly and refined, had clearly had a lot of training in martial arts. Armed only with his fan, he was able to dodge and parry so that the four assassins found it impossible to touch him. He was also screaming for help at the top of his voice, which made his attackers nervous. Eventually, he retreated to the water's edge and dived beneath the surface of the lake, disappearing into the darkness. Thus he was able to escape with his life.

It was later discovered that none of the woman's gold jewellery had been taken, so it obviously wasn't a robbery. The attackers had carefully cleaned up the scene of the crime before they fled, leaving no clues as to their identity. A chunk of flesh was extracted from the jaws of the dead Alsatian, but that too proved unidentifiable. How could the police solve the crime? There was nothing they could do.

The murderers were still out there – what if next time they used guns? The more the scholar thought about it, the more unbearable it became. His martial arts skills were good, but he couldn't stop a bullet. He wasn't going to risk his life in pursuit of this gold. He'd been lucky to survive that first attack and he had no intention of risking his neck a second time.

Enough!

That was the end of their hunt for the gold; they left in silence, just as they had come. The Tan Estate had been in beautiful condition when they'd arrived, with its gardens in bloom, but now the entire place was a ruin, inside and out, as if it had been butchered.

Even though the Japanese devils had now left, they weren't going to allow anyone else to take possession of the Tan Estate. Plenty of powerful people from within the puppet government came to look at it, but when they saw how badly damaged it was, nobody was interested in taking it over. In the end it was a couple of dozen horses that moved in, stabled in that beautiful place before being sent to the front line, to injury and death.

The horses didn't care about the treasure, they just cared about the grass. Within a few months they'd grazed the garden down to bare earth and shat it out. Yet again, the Tan Estate stank to high heaven, but this time nobody bothered to complain, because everyone expected stables to be filthy. It was becoming increasingly difficult to call to mind how lovely the place had been in its prime.

6

In March 1940, the collaborator Wang Jingwei established his puppet government in Nanjing. A few months earlier,

Division Commander Qian Huyi of the Nationalist Party's National Revolutionary Army had become famous; every newspaper carried his name and new title, for he had just been made Commander of the puppet regime's East China Counterinsurgency Corps. People in Hangzhou called him Qian-the-Dog, because he had sold himself body and soul to the Japanese and was nothing but their running dog. Third Brother had deserted at that point. He robbed Qian-the-Dog's armoury, blew up what he couldn't take away, and then disappeared with a dozen or so trusted soldiers from his old unit.

Whether it was because he was Third Brother's former commanding officer or because he was an old friend of Su-the-Arsehole, Qian Huyi (Qian-the-Dog) knew all about the treasure that was supposed to be hidden on the Tan Estate. He was also quite sure that he'd be able to find it – he had Su-the-Arsehole to help him, after all. After Qian Huyi went to work for the Japanese, more than half of his soldiers deserted, so there was no point in being picky, he took everyone he could get, even dyed-in-the-wool criminals like Su-the-Arsehole. Anyway, the latter had thumped himself on the chest and sworn until he was blue in the face that he would definitely find the Tan Estate treasure. So, soon after he took office, Qian Huyi got rid of the stables and had a works division of the ECCC placed at the Tan Estate, with a budget for renovations. This was to facilitate their treasure hunting: they could 'renovate' after each area had been searched, and that would prevent anyone from realizing what they were up to.

It turned out that Su-the-Arsehole didn't know what he was talking about. All his promises came to nothing. The treasure was never found, and the scope of the renovations grew and grew, until in the end it was all-encompassing; even the glazed tiles on the roof were removed and smashed, one by one, and then had to be replaced. The trees were all uprooted, only to be replanted in a new location; the front courtyard was moved to the rear courtyard, and then vice versa.

Once everything had been rebuilt, it had to be used for something, didn't it? Of course it did. The front courtyard could be an officers' club for the ECCC. After all, the teahouse and accommodation were there already. As for the two little buildings at the back, the Commander wanted to keep them for his own use. The western building would become his private residence, where his family could live, while the eastern building could be used for other purposes: upstairs could provide accommodation for his staff, while downstairs would be perfect for secret meetings with like-minded officials, or indeed for sex. The sex was all about keeping colleagues on board by giving them a free trick with a whore. A couple of minutes was all it took, and the girls were right there at the officers' club anyway.

Opening a guest house on the site of a famous brothel was always going to mean that sooner or later it would be business as usual once again. And indeed, pretty quickly the girls were back, strong wines were being poured for eager customers, and people were partying. The only real difference was that the whole place had been militarized; the men who came for the whores were now all in uniform and carried guns, so most outsiders didn't dare set foot in there. Even so, there was still a hierarchy: those with rifles had to give way to the men who carried pistols; those in the puppet forces had to give way to members of the Imperial Japanese Army. The officers and men in the Imperial Army weren't saints: when it came to murder, robbery, rape or pillage, there was nothing that they wouldn't do.

Qian-the-Dog was happy to see members of the Imperial Army coming here; if they hadn't come of their own accord, he would have invited them – that way he wouldn't need to worry even if the Tan brothers took their complaints to the central authorities in Nanjing. So he threw himself into the business of making his brothel a success and felt sure that the Tan Estate would bring him everything that he wanted in life.

However, Qian-the-Dog just didn't have the personal qualities required to sustain such a position for any length of time. In fact, for him, the good times lasted exactly one hundred and twenty-one days, and they came to an end in a massacre late one night.

What happened that night on the Tan Estate is recorded in many accounts of the history of Hangzhou. I've seen dozens of these records and they are all basically the same. The description given in the *Gazetteer of Hangzhou* is as accurate as any and has a certain literary quality to it. I have excerpted this account:

> On the 22nd June 1940, on a stormy night when the moon was obscured by clouds, the eastern and western buildings in the rear courtyard of the Tan Estate were the site of a series of murders. Qian Huyi and his entire family were killed, nine persons in all, together with two pro-Japanese officials with whom Commander Qian had secret dealings, and the three prostitutes he had hired

that night to entertain them. In total, fourteen people lost their lives.

In both buildings, the blood of the dead poured from the upper floors down to the lower ones, overflowing the lintels of the doors and soaking into the ground outside. For the longest time, the air of the rear courtyard was saturated with the metallic stench of blood and gore.

Who on earth could have done this?

On the wall, there was a message written in blood:

Those who surrender to the Japanese for personal gain deserve to die!

Those with shamelessly corrupt morals deserve to die!

Kill! Kill! Kill!

Clearly, this was the work of resistance fighters.

Those words were written on the wall of a guest bedroom in the eastern building, using the Commander's blood – red characters on a white wall and thus exceptionally eye-catching. The corpse of a naked woman was found in the same room as Qian-the-Dog – he had obviously been with a whore that night. The two stark-naked bodies, one male and one female, were at different ends of the room, but their blood had pooled together: it was a shameless sight. Compared to them, the bright red words seemed honourable; not only was their content admirable, but the characters were written in a strong script, by a practised calligrapher – this was not the work of some common criminal.

I don't know who first suggested that the words had likely been written by Third Brother – he had, after all, studied painting and he wrote a good hand. Given that he'd been involved in the art world for many years, it wasn't difficult to find samples of his calligraphy. An expert was asked to check them and duly confirmed that the words had been written by Third Brother.

Overnight, Third Brother became famous. Even the events of two years earlier, when the foreign couple had been attacked at West Lake and the wife killed, were now ascribed to him. But nobody knew where Third Brother was or what he was trying to do. Some people said that he'd taken over from his father, that he was nothing but a gangster who made no distinction between robbing ordinary people or fighting against the Japanese, that he would do anything for money, like some kind of demon. Some said that he was still in command of his old Nationalist unit, that he appeared from time to time in the mountains of western Zhejiang province, attacking the Japanese devils and the puppet army, and that he was a national hero. There were others who said that he was a member of the Nationalist Blueshirts and that he was often to be seen in the Shanghai/Hangzhou region, dressed in signature blue shirt and trousers, murdering Japanese devils and Chinese traitors. In other words, he was a secret agent working for the Nationalist Party's Bureau of Military Statistics. There were also people who said that he was a member of the Communist underground... Well, there were a lot of stories, and the only point of consensus was that Third Brother was a mysterious figure.

7

For all that I have been trying my best to conceal it, I am sure that by now my more intelligent and attentive readers will have guessed that Third Brother was Tiger, otherwise why would I have written about him in such detail here? You are quite right, Third Brother was indeed Tiger; today he is an elderly gentleman called Mr Xin, but at that time he was in charge of the Communist underground in Hangzhou.

And Police Chief Wang Tianxiang started life as Su-the-Arsehole.

Both of these men changed their names. In the case of Third Brother, it was necessary for his work in the underground. For Su-the-Arsehole, it was because he wanted to escape his past as a cheap crook; he was hoping everyone would forget what a nasty piece of work he was. As to why he changed his name to Wang Tianxiang, it was because he thought it sounded Japanese. Some people really are cheap and nasty through and through. I am happy to say that his children are quite different; they are really lovely people and very patriotic. His daughter, Wang Min, told me that she still won't have a Japanese object in the house, and the reason she gave for this behaviour (which might otherwise seem a bit excessive) was that this was how she could atone for what her father had done. When I asked her why she didn't change her surname back to Su, she said she wanted to remember the humiliation her father had caused them and become a proper Chinese person. Her brother took the name Wang Hanmin, the character 'Han' meaning 'Chinese', so his feelings on the subject could not be clearer.

Wang Tianxiang was executed for treason in 1947; the shame of what he did affected not only his children but all Chinese people.

As my more intelligent and attentive readers will also have guessed, the niece of the Tan Estate's loyal head butler, who was 'given' to Commander Qian Huyi by Third Brother and became Qian Huyi's concubine, ended up as Warrior. Old Mr Xin confirmed that, so it must be true. The years had turned the delicate, rake-thin and pale-faced young art student into a fat and balding old man, but his memories of Warrior had not faded.

Old Mr Xin told me that neither he nor the head butler was in any way involved with Warrior's decision to become Qian Huyi's concubine – that was entirely her choice. At that time, Qian Huyi's Nationalist forces were moving to surround and exterminate the Red Army on the border between Zhejiang and Jiangxi provinces; for the Communist Party, the situation was critical and they were desperate to infiltrate Qian Huyi's headquarters as quickly as possible and gain access to intelligence about this mission. Warrior was already a member of the Communist underground in Hangzhou, having been recruited by a teacher at her school. She now took the initiative and proposed that she get close to Qian Huyi. As a result, she was instrumental in the Red Army being suddenly able to break through the encirclement and move to a place of safety.

Old Mr Xin said that when the Japanese devils occupied Hangzhou, Qian Huyi led his Nationalist troops into the mountains and announced that he would regroup and launch a counter-attack against the Japanese at the first opportunity. Shortly afterwards, however, Qian Huyi surrendered to the puppet government, which prompted Third Brother, as he still was, to desert; Third Brother took his soldiers back to Hangzhou and formed an anti-Japanese resistance group, unaffiliated with any political party, its aim being to kill the Japanese devils and their Chinese collaborators.

Soon after Third Brother had murdered Qian Huyi and his family, Warrior came to see him. Thanks to the old head butler, Warrior and Third Brother had always been friendly; over the years, she had repeatedly encouraged him to join the Communist Party, and now finally he agreed. His unit was immediately enrolled into the Party's New Fourth Army, but he himself remained in Hangzhou to engage in covert missions. Eventually, as Tiger, he assumed responsibility for the entire Communist underground in the city.

When he spoke about Warrior, old Mr Xin at times became very emotional. He said that they all owed quite as much to her as to Li Ningyu – both of them were totally loyal to the Party, and in their achievements, in their revolutionary mindset, in their convictions and their fearless self-sacrifice they were models for every underground operative at that time. Of course, 'Warrior' was merely her code name in the underground; in real life she was called Lin Yingchun. Her family came from Fuyang in Zhejiang province, and in fact she grew up by the banks of the Fuchun River. She was born in 1919, and when she died she was just twenty-two.

Today, Mr Xin is eighty-nine years old; he has used countless names throughout his career, but the name he goes by now is the one he adopted after the end of the War of Resistance: Xin Chunsheng. He told me that he chose it specifically to honour the memory of Warrior – a way of telling others, and reminding himself, that all the glory he enjoyed today had come to him through her. As for the treasure hidden by his father, old Mr Tan, Mr Xin told me that it still hadn't been found. He was sure that it was out there somewhere, but he had no idea where; the only thing he could be certain of was that it was nowhere on the Tan Estate.

THREE

1

This chapter is about Hihara: his past, his family and his story. I will explain it in the simplest terms, though at the same time I am very much aware that it will make a long chapter. That's because he was a far more complicated character than I can really begin to understand or imagine.

To be honest, there's an enormous difference between what I knew at the outset and the impression I developed later on. I came to fear him, even to hate him, because of the contempt with which he responded to events. In trying to get to grips with this character, I felt as if I were walking into a maze of endless twists and turns, of illusions created by smoke and mirrors. Here my knowledge and intelligence were profoundly tested.

There are many historical records that speak of Hihara; there is more information available about him than all the other characters in this story put together. He's an important protagonist in the histories of twentieth-century China and Japan, and if you go to any library with a modern Chinese history collection and start reading, you will find references to him all over the place.

The foreign scholar who went to the Tan Estate to look for treasure? That was Hihara. It was he who stayed at the estate some years prior to the events of this book and not only found nothing but also lost his wife to murderous assassins. Twenty years before that, Hihara had been a journalist stationed in Shanghai, working for the Japanese newspaper the *Osaka Mainichi Shimbun*. Under the pen name 'Nakahara' he wrote a travel diary and occasional column introducing Chinese culture and customs to his Japanese readership, and this had a great impact on the intelligentsia at the time.

In fact, Hihara came from a family that had a long and deep interest in Chinese history and culture. This went all the way back to the seventeenth century, when Zhu Shunshui – a Chinese scholar who had failed in his attempts to raise an army and get the deposed Ming dynasty restored to power – was forced to flee to Japan. He became friendly with the Hihara family, who were powerful nobles and were at that time based in the city of Mito. The Hiharas were great admirers of Zhu Shunshui's scholarship and they invited him to live in their household as a sort of private tutor; he taught them history, literature and the art of classical Chinese poetry and remained there until his death in 1682.

The Hiharas' passionate interest in Chinese history and culture continued through the generations. In the time of our Hihara's own great-grandfather, several members of the family visited China for themselves and returned with boatloads of books, paintings and other works of art; they subsequently founded a school in Kyoto that specialized in the Chinese language. The entire family was famous in Japan for their knowledge and understanding of China.

Hihara's grandfather travelled three times to China and was an eminent authority on Japanese studies of Tang-dynasty poetry. In 1914, he was sailing home to Japan from China when his boat sank, drowning everyone on board. When his friends in the Japanese Concession in Shanghai heard this news, they bought a plot in the cemetery there and erected a tombstone for him. The following year, Hihara's father took his son to Shanghai to perform a tomb-clearing and soul-summoning ceremony for his grandfather. Although his father subsequently went back home to Japan, the young son was left behind on the banks of the Huangpu River, to comfort the soul of his deceased grandfather. He was only thirteen years old, just an ordinary middle-school student. He lived with the family of one of his late grandfather's friends, speaking Chinese, reading Chinese, wearing Chinese clothes and learning Chinese poetry; he was more Sinicized than many a Chinese person, to the point where people didn't realize that he was actually Japanese but thought that he was a Chinese person who had lived for a time in Japan.

In the spring of 1921, just as Hihara was about to graduate from Shanghai's Fudan University, the famous Japanese short-story writer Akutagawa Ryūnosuke arrived in the city as a journalist for the *Osaka Mainichi Shimbun* and Hihara went to pay him a courtesy visit.

Since the beginning of the twentieth century, Japan's attitude towards its vast Chinese neighbour had been quite clear. In 1905, Japan had won the Russo-Japanese War, a victory that had given it an authority and freedom of action in north-east China that would eventually, in 1932, lead to it establishing its puppet regime of Manchukuo in that part of the country. Extreme right-wing ideology was gaining traction across Japan and by the late 1920s its adherents were calling for the country to expand its army and prepare for war. The aim was to incorporate by force China, Korea and other countries into the Japanese realm as part of the so-called Greater East Asia Co-Prosperity Sphere.

Hihara was violently critical of this fascist movement, and Akutagawa admired his stance enormously. The two of them became friends immediately.

Akutagawa needed an interpreter on his assignments in Shanghai and Hihara was the perfect man for the job. They became constant companions, wandering round the city's sophisticated foreign concessions, visiting the wharves and international trading houses of the waterfront Bund, interviewing people at home and journeying out to the countryside. They also toured scenic spots like Suzhou, with its many lovely formal gardens, and Hangzhou for its West Lake vistas, temples and pavilions. Akutagawa published a series of essays about these journeys after his return to Japan, including *My Shanghai Travel Diaries*, which contains an account of the young Hihara:

> Although not yet twenty, he has the wisdom and experience of a much older man. He is gentle by nature, but when the conversation turned to the strong support shown in Japan for the plans set out by the Imperial Army, he became righteously indignant. For people of his age, righteous indignation is often nothing more than

a fit of enthusiasm; they get excited, they tear into the topic, they will say anything to prove their point and don't care that they cannot justify the position they have adopted. But the young man sitting opposite me was not only emotionally engaged, he also brought his intelligence to bear; he was motivated by affection for his adopted country and by reason.

The breadth of his reading had honed his wits and he was able to quote chapter and verse. He defended his position so strongly that his opponents felt themselves beaten back against the barricades; he spoke fluently and with passion. If our own people were to hear him, they would curse him as a traitor and say that he had lost his Japanese soul.

It was as if he were living in the golden age of the Tang dynasty, and he repeatedly expressed his great admiration for the glories of Chinese civilization. What he said made perfect sense. He acquired and processed new information at speed, weaving it into a web of visible and invisible threads, expertly choosing what to reveal of his learning, and when.

Some Japanese people may feel like cursing him, but we cannot laugh at him for the simple reason that he is not blindly enthusiastic: he has evidence for what he says.

This was just an introduction; it was followed by a whole string of stories and examples, all described in great detail and very enthusiastically. Akutagawa wrote several thousand characters on the subject, unstinting in his praise of Hihara.

The kind of person who would write such things would naturally recommend his protégé to all and sundry. Not long after Akutagawa returned to Japan, Hihara received a letter of appointment from the *Osaka Mainichi Shimbun*. It could not have come at a better moment. Hihara had just graduated and he needed a job. Akutagawa's recommendation landed him the position of his dreams; it was the best graduation present he could have imagined, and he never forgot it.

Some years later, on 24 July 1927, Akutagawa committed suicide by overdosing on sleeping pills. When Hihara got the news, he rushed over to Japan to offer his condolences to the family. This was the first time he'd been back home in more than a decade; he'd not even returned when his grandmother had passed away a few years earlier.

But by then Hihara was no longer the person that Akutagawa had known, and by the time he left Japan again, he had changed even more, in much more profound ways. He was now an utterly different person.

When Hihara returned to China after Akutagawa's funeral, he was no longer just a reporter but a top-level secret agent working for the Imperial Japanese Army. He was part of a secret organization, bound by strict rules and with a clear mission to gather intelligence concerning the Chinese military and blaze a trail for the Imperial Army as they expanded their territory into the heartlands of China. To achieve this he was prepared to risk everything, even his own life.

What a loyal subject of the empire!

It was just as well that Akutagawa was dead by then, because Hihara's betrayal of all that he stood for would have destroyed him. The change that Hihara underwent from this point onwards was as significant as that which occurs when you move from life to death.

2

Akutagawa's move from life to death was achieved by two dozen sleeping pills. The changes that Hihara underwent were achieved more gradually, but in many ways they were only made possible by his accreditation as a journalist, which he owed to Akutagawa. Hihara started out living only in the world of books, and that is how Akutagawa found him:

> He had a detailed plan for his future studies. He wanted to read one thousand Chinese books before the age of twenty-five, and then he would select the very best of them and devote five more years to studying them. In his thirties he planned to work on translations, while also writing and publishing his own works.
>
> Golden mansions are to be found in books.
> Beautiful women are to be found in books.

That was Hihara's plan, and Akutagawa had nothing but praise for it. But his accreditation as a journalist changed him; he was no longer part of the world of books but found himself in the world of men. Although Shanghai remained his primary base, Hihara began to travel to towns and cities all over the country. Whether he spent just one day in a place or stayed there for weeks or months, he would always make an effort to meet people from all walks of life, trying to get to know them and to listen to their concerns. He really did travel round half of China, and because of this he developed a deep understanding of the political and economic situation and learnt a great deal about the culture. He was told about local customs, about natural disasters and man-made problems, about people's joys and sorrows, about life and death, yin and yang, bandits and whores, heroes and villains... all sorts of weird and wonderful things.

He wrote reams of notes and worked up this information into a series of articles. He also had a fortnightly column in the *Mainichi Shimbun* called 'Travelling Around China'. A complete account of his experiences would fill a fat book.

Having begun his travels, Hihara found that he couldn't stop. He continued tirelessly, watching, thinking and recording. He became overwhelmed, caught up in an undertaking from which he could not extricate himself, and it was impossible now for him to stick to his reading plan.

He kept on moving.

He kept on observing.

He kept on thinking.

He kept on writing.

He never, ever stopped.

If he were to have given up one aspect of his work, it would have been the newspaper columns. But he didn't stop writing them, he just changed the publication in which they appeared. From the *Mainichi Shimbun* he moved to the *Asahi Shimbun*, then he changed again, and again, moving from one publication to the next, before finally ending up at the *Jiji Shimbun*. In other words, 'Travelling Around

China' was like a baton in a relay race, being handed from one periodical or newspaper to another; as soon as one publication dropped it, another picked it up and carried it forwards.

Each time the column was dropped, it was a goodbye. A goodbye to that newspaper. A goodbye to those readers. A goodbye to the old Hihara from the new one. His first paper, the *Mainichi Shimbun*, was the most left-wing in Japan; the very last paper he wrote for, the *Jiji Shimbun*, was its most right-wing – in the 1920s it was quite notorious for the way it beat the drum for an invasion of China. Hihara was becoming more and more right-wing and extreme in his views. In the end, none of his old friends recognized him any more. He didn't recognize himself.

For his first column in the *Jiji Shimbun* he wrote:

> The Chinese today are a worthless race, but perhaps this is because in the past they were so impressive. China now is nothing but a toothless tiger, a phoenix plucked of all its feathers, and all that is left is an empty reputation. Fundamentally, these weakly superstitious and pitifully obedient people deserve neither our love nor our hatred; this place will collapse at the first nudge.
>
> It is only by destroying it and then establishing the Greater East Asia Co-Prosperity Sphere that these people can be reborn as worthy heirs to five thousand years of history.

This was quite different from the kind of thing he'd been writing a few years earlier, in the *Mainichi Shimbun*. In fact, it could hardly have been more different. His earliest columns had been pure travel diaries, and he hadn't held back in expressing his admiration for China or his contempt for the handful of small islands that made up the Japanese archipelago:

> After Penglangji you arrive in Pengze County. It is located on the south bank of the Yangtze River, amid high peaks and steep cliffs. Between the mountains and the river, reed beds flower as far as the eye can see – all along the course of this great river you have islands and sandbanks where the reeds grow thick. It is a wonderful sight.
>
> It was the first month of winter and willow-floss was everywhere, like frost or snow, creating a beautiful scene. Sometimes I could look into the distance and see the clouds dancing in the treetops; sometimes the water and the sky seemed to blend and become one.
>
> Such majestic scenery can only be found in the heartlands of China, and those of us familiar only with the refined and exquisite landscapes of Japan will find them impossible to picture; we can only look up at the sky and sigh.
>
> The longevity of China rests in its vastness, its grandeur, its vigour, its sturdiness, its adaptability, its quiescence, and we savour it in the way we might a piece of sugar cane, allowing the full flavour to gradually burst on our palate. The landscapes in our own country are indeed lovely and elegant, but the experience of seeing them is like tasting molasses: your whole mouth is overwhelmed with the sugariness of it all. To my mind, molasses is just too sweet; when you continue eating it, you get nothing

from it. It may be very refined, but it lacks the sensory depth that you find in raw nature, and the sheer sense of enjoyment.

Now, just a few years later, on another trip through central China, his tone was quite different:

If you look ahead, you see the bare mountains and muddy rivers, with clusters of hovels and huts here and there; it is just one eyesore after another. There is a constant stream of refugees along the road, and beggars are everywhere, you cannot take your eyes off them. Every face is shrouded in the shadows of tragedy and hopelessness, as if an appalling famine has struck. And yet hidden behind high walls, in the mansions of the rich, you have bevies of wives and concubines, with crowds of maids in attendance, and pampered pet cats and dogs, and they gorge themselves on the finest delicacies. Here the rats can eat their fill until they are a match for any cat outside.

Even worse, officials here care only about holding on to their positions and do no real work; they merely quarrel over the vast profits from corruption. The military does not concern itself with training soldiers to defend the nation, and they consider that the funding they receive puts them under no obligation to protect the civilian population. So various generals have carved out territories, with the result that civil war has now spread throughout this land and those in power abuse everyone else, showing themselves to be no different from gangsters.

In an even greater tragedy, the intelligentsia have proved foolish and ignorant, thinking only of what will benefit them, showing themselves to be without the slightest social conscience.

The glory days of China under the Han and Tang dynasties are long past and yet these people have failed to advance; they have isolated themselves and become stick-in-the-muds, indescribably arrogant and yet also sycophantic, obsessed with the past, greedy for pleasure, unchanging over the centuries, and all the same. As a result, their vitality has withered away, corruption increases day by day, and the whole system is rotten: it is a society without cohesion.

Some readers complained about the contradiction, since the things that had been described so positively before were criticized so severely now, and they didn't think they could trust his account. He responded with a confession:

When I was a scholar, I was steeped in literature from dawn till dusk and I judged real life by what I had read in books, thinking that they were one and the same. However, they are in fact two quite separate realms, as different from each other as black is from white.

Recently I have begun to regret having left the world of books. If I had not come to understand what is really going on, I could have remained happily muddle-headed, enjoying my books, appreciating their superlative literary qualities, loving every minute spent amid their pages. That would probably have been best for me. So I do regret that my gaining accreditation as a journalist has resulted in my having travelled widely and seen the world for what it really is.

However, what's done is done. Having seen the truth, having felt it in my very bones, am I supposed to pretend that I have heard nothing, seen nothing? That is impossible. It would be quite wrong. I simply cannot do it; I cannot sell my soul that way.

His meaning is clear: he used to love China because he learnt about it from books. He paid no attention to what was going on in the real world, so he was misled. But now that he found himself confronted by real life, for all the pain that this caused him, he could no longer remain blind to the suffering around him.

As Akutagawa said, he was very quick-witted and good at presenting a case, and in this instance he was fighting his own corner, so naturally he wanted to show himself in the best possible light. His argument seemed flawless, and, as always, totally plausible. There were people in the Imperial Japanese Army who had noticed that his writings were becoming increasingly right-wing. They saw him as a potentially valuable asset: he could be presented as a prodigal son who had returned to hearth and home. If they could recruit him, he might be just the person to carry out certain important missions for them.

An agent of the Imperial Japanese Army sought him out at Akutagawa's funeral and gave him the nod. He didn't refuse; in fact, he felt as if he had finally come home. Someone appreciated him! At last he'd have the chance to show what he could do. He was happier than he could have said. He felt no pain at all in giving up his old life and taking his first steps down to hell, just as his mentor Akutagawa had calmly and painlessly moved from this world to the next.

It seems almost unbelievable. Akutagawa thought Hihara was like him, but in fact he turned him into his opposite. Hihara's accreditation as a journalist, and his column, eventually led to him joining the secret service, and this was all the unintentional outcome of Akutagawa's encouragement. That's the way of the world, but once you're dead, you're dead – there's nothing more to worry about. Later on, there would be people who made a connection between Akutagawa's despair and Hihara's betrayal; they said that by turning his back on everything Akutagawa stood for, Hihara caused his mentor's death. This is just gossip. In all fairness, Hihara didn't betray Akutagawa, their paths simply diverged. They had very different perspectives on the world and so their paths led them further and further apart.

3

As his friend and mentor, Akutagawa paid close attention to Hihara's 'Travelling Around China' columns and often mentioned them in interviews with journalists. To begin with he was very admiring, but later on he became highly critical. A couple of months before he died, he was interviewed by a reporter from the *Jiji Shimbun* and was even more cutting than normal. I don't know whether this was because he'd already made up his mind to commit suicide or because he so fundamentally disagreed with the extremely right-wing tone of the *Jiji Shimbun*. Whichever it was, their conversation ran as follows:

Akutagawa: I realized about six months ago that today would happen.

Journalist: I'm sorry but I don't understand what you mean by 'today'?

Akutagawa: Today, right now, the situation that we see before us. That 'Travelling Around China' would migrate to your paper, and therefore that you, or someone like you, would come and ask me the questions that you've just asked.

Journalist: And can we discuss them? I'm sure you have something to say on the subject.

Akutagawa: I've already said everything I want to. I answered all these questions a few days ago when I was interviewed by another journalist from your paper.

Journalist: I've seen the notes from that interview. You said that some people are on their way to heaven, while others are heading for hell. So I'd like to ask where you think Mr Hihara is going: to heaven or to hell?

Akutagawa: To hell, of course. In my opinion, your paper is a kind of hell, since only people who live in eternal darkness, surrounded by demons, could write the kind of articles you want. As I see it, he's just right for you.

Journalist: And for the majority of our country. Our newspaper represents the majority view of the Japanese people.

Akutagawa: Then I am in the minority.

Journalist: Mr Hihara used to be one of the minority, which

is why you got to know him. Can you see yourself joining the majority, as Mr Hihara has done?

Akutagawa: No. Never. And I refuse to believe that I'm in the minority. We at the *Mainichi Shimbun* have just as big a circulation as you at the *Jiji Shimbun*.

Journalist: But you have lost Mr Hihara.

Akutagawa: You win some, you lose some. Everyone has their own ambitions – there's nothing surprising about that.

Journalist: So you admit that Hihara's ambitions have changed?

Akutagawa: They haven't changed, they've regressed... been corrupted.

Journalist: If they have regressed, have you thought about why?

Akutagawa: I have very little time to waste, and there are many more important matters for me to think about.

Journalist: I feel that this is a very important question, one that deserves careful consideration. In my personal opinion, Mr Hihara has indeed been travelling through hell. I just came back from China last month, where Mr Hihara took me on a two-week tour of the cradle of Chinese civilization, the Yellow River, and the whole way I felt as if I were in fact on a journey through hell. The people were all in rags, reduced to skin and bone, and beggars outnumbered everyone else on the streets. When they caught sight of us they'd rush over, kneel down in front of us and beg for money or food. I'm convinced that Mr Hihara is writing the absolute truth, and we ought to give him credit for that.

Akutagawa: I too have been to China, and more than once. I too travelled with Hihara, and we saw exactly what you've just described. But that is their business and it has nothing to do with us.

Journalist: I remember that you once said writers should be humanists; why would you say that their suffering has nothing to do with us?

Akutagawa: Are you telling me that sending soldiers to invade their country is an expression of humanism?

Journalist: What invasion? So far, all we've seen is a civil war there. As far as I know, our Imperial Army hasn't gone into battle against Chinese government forces.

Akutagawa: Just because it hasn't happened yet doesn't mean it won't. You're still young; if things carry on the way they're going now, I think you'll live to see the day when Japan goes to war with China.

Journalist: And if that day does come, I'm sure the Imperial Japanese Army will be victorious.

That day did come; in fact, there were a succession of such days, beginning just four years after that interview:

- 18 September 1931: the Japanese invasion of Manchuria, north-east China, and subsequent establishment of the puppet state of Manchukuo.
- 28 January 1932: the Japanese bombing of Shanghai, followed by the stationing of Japanese troops in Shanghai.
- 7 July 1937: the Marco Polo Bridge Incident (a fight between Japanese and Chinese troops near Beijing), after which the Imperial Japanese Army invades northern China, including Beijing and Tianjin.
- 13 August 1937: the Battle of Shanghai begins and the various branches of the Chinese military join forces to

create an enormous army; this subsequently crumbles in defeat, resulting in the Japanese occupation of Shanghai, Nanjing and Hangzhou.

In short, after 18 September 1931 there were many such days in China, and they happened all over the country – first on one side of the Great Wall, then on the other; north as well as south of the Yangtze; both inside and outside the capital. On all too many of these days, the Imperial Japanese Army did indeed win, just as the reporter from the *Jiji Shimbun* had anticipated. And, just as Hihara had predicted, the place collapsed at the first nudge.

4

As I have said, there were many such days, and in August 1937 yet another one came to pass, this time for Hangzhou.

On this day, one hundred and twenty-seven planes with red circles on their sides took off from Unryū-class aircraft carriers anchored in the Wusong River and flew directly to Hangzhou, where they dropped countless bombs. West Lake was in terrible danger. The people of Hangzhou have always had great affection for their West Lake; even as they were running for their lives, they thought about how it had nowhere to go, and they worried about it – there were many whose escape route took them right past it or who made a special detour to visit it for what might be the last time. An endless stream of people, young and old, men and women, gathered by the lake shore, praying to whatever gods there might be to protect it. If they could have carried West Lake with them instead of their gold and silver and household treasures, I am sure they would have.

Since they couldn't take it with them, they gazed intently at it so that it might be engraved in their memories. They knew that even if they escaped, even if they were to come back alive one day, West Lake would have been blown to pieces. And so they would not return to look at it again; they would rather not see it at all than see it in ruins.

But as everyone now knows, the bombing eventually stopped and West Lake had been left completely unharmed. It was as lovely as ever. Its three hundred hectares of wetland and dozens of beautiful vistas and scenic spots were untouched. The mansions were still there, the formal gardens were still there, the pretty stone bridges and blossom-filled causeways were still there. Not a single tree had been knocked over, and every flowerpot was still in its place; you could say that not a hair on West Lake's head had been harmed. It seemed almost miraculous.

What kind of magic had worked such a miracle?

The people of Hangzhou were determined to get to the bottom of this because they wanted to thank whoever was responsible. However, the person behind this miracle turned out to be a demon, and there was no way they could do anything to repay the unexpected kindness. The demon had a name, Matsui Iwane, and at that time he was the senior general in command of the Japanese army in the Battle of Shanghai. This was no ordinary demon but the devil himself! That summer, he sat in an Unryū-class aircraft carrier anchored at the mouth of the Wusong River as a massacre began that was to claim the lives of hundreds of thousands of Chinese soldiers and civilians. A few months later, he was directly responsible for orchestrating the tragedy known as the Rape of Nanjing.

It seems hard to imagine that a devil of this kind would be interested in saving West Lake. But it's a fact. According to historical records, the evening before Matsui brought together the hundred-plus aircraft in preparation for the bombing of Hangzhou, a famous Japanese journalist came to see him. The result of the secret conversation between this individual and General Matsui was that the latter gave orders that a thick red line delineating a no-bombing zone be drawn on the maps of Hangzhou given to the air force. This red line seemed to follow the winding shores of West Lake, and it incorporated not only the whole of the lake itself but also all the major beauty spots surrounding it. General Matsui also wrote an instruction inside that red line:

> This blue area is an imperial beauty and must not be destroyed. Anyone who contravenes this command will be dealt with according to military law.

Of course, it was this hand-drawn red line that saved beautiful West Lake, just like a fairy ring.

That sinuous red line separated heaven from hell. Outside the red line the flames leapt high in the sky and bodies were blown to pieces; inside the line, the waters flowed peacefully and fish played in the shallows. Hangzhou in August 1937 was a very strange sight – it was bizarre, unnatural, even a little ridiculous. But what is entirely clear is that the famous journalist who turned up to talk to General Matsui was none other than Hihara. So when it comes down to it, the people of Hangzhou had much cause to be grateful to him.

Ever since he'd first visited Hangzhou with Akutagawa, Hihara had been obsessed with the place. He'd developed deep feelings for it. He particularly loved West Lake with its mountainous backdrop. He once wrote an article in which he compared West Lake to a moon that had descended to the human realm, filled with clear waters. *You can travel all over the world and you will never find the like; you can read ten thousand books and you still won't have discovered all there is to know about it.*

After he was employed by the Japanese military as a secret agent, he would bring his young wife to Hangzhou every summer and they would rent a room somewhere beside West Lake and stay for a week, reading and walking and enjoying the landscape. Even then he would be carrying out his official duties, since he might, after all, see or hear something that constituted intelligence, which he could either pass on to the authorities to show his loyalty or sell to the highest bidder; it really was a wonderful job.

When the Battle of Shanghai broke out on 13 August, Hihara and his beloved wife were at West Lake, escaping the summer heat. He soon received word from his superiors that they should leave Hangzhou, and he immediately guessed that the city would shortly be attacked. When he got back to Shanghai he was distraught to learn that General Matsui Iwane had already given orders to prepare for the bombing of Hangzhou.

Hihara was convinced that as soon as Shanghai was taken, Hangzhou would simply surrender without a fight. Every month he wrote a 'Strategic Analysis Report' for his superiors, and he'd given this as his opinion on numerous occasions. But it seemed that General Matsui was paying no heed to his advice.

General Matsui was himself an old China hand and had lived there for more than a decade. He had headed up a regional secret-police force, been Deputy Commander of Japan's prestigious Kwantung Army and served as the military attaché at the embassies in Guangdong and Shanghai. His knowledge of the country was entirely comparable to Hihara's. Which was why, on the outbreak of hostilities in Shanghai, he'd been summoned back and given the position of Commander-in-Chief, even though he'd already retired from active service on the grounds of old age.

Nevertheless, Matsui's experience had been gained many years earlier, so when it came to the current situation in Shanghai and Hangzhou, and the various new organizations and up-to-date connections, Hihara was in a much stronger position. The latter had great confidence in his own judgement and insisted on meeting Matsui to try and bring him round to his own point of view.

And so Hihara and Matsui had their historic meeting on the deck of an Unryū-class aircraft carrier.

5

What I'm going to say next falls largely within the realm of gossip and should not be taken too seriously.

It is said that the first meeting between Hihara and General Matsui was very dramatic, and so were its results. To begin with, Matsui refused to meet Hihara; he was a secret agent and the general was very familiar with the arrogance of such men, and anyway he didn't think a meeting was necessary. He furrowed his brow and said to his staff officer, 'If he has some intelligence to report then let him write it down.' But when he heard that Hihara was the author of 'Travelling Around China', he changed his mind.

It transpired that Matsui was a loyal reader of Hihara's recent essays in the *Jiji Shimbun*. Both men were convinced that China was on the brink of collapse, and now they found themselves in complete accord. One was a true believer, the other was the man tasked with actually carrying out the policy.

Matsui had repeatedly informed the Japanese parliament that as long as the Nationalist government remained in power in Nanjing, Japan's territorial gains in China would be just a flash in the pan and the Greater East Asia Co-Prosperity Sphere would never be established. His many years as a military attaché had given him a deep understanding of the Nanjing government, but it had also fostered in him an inexplicable hatred of the city and everyone in it. Not long afterwards it was he who orchestrated the Rape of Nanjing, so horrific that it shocked the entire world.

Hatred made him into the devil himself and destroyed the last vestiges of his humanity. On 23 December 1948, Matsui Iwane was hanged as a Class A war criminal by the International Military Tribunal for the Far East, because of his direct involvement in the Rape of Nanjing.

In the summer of 1937, as he issued orders from the Unryū-class aircraft carrier, he was able to correctly predict much of the outcome of the battle he was commanding, but he was unable to anticipate what would eventually befall his own person.

Matsui invited Hihara to join him on board. They paced the decks together, enjoying the breeze as they analysed the situation and discussed future plans. Both of them very much enjoyed their conversation, each man feeling that he had found his complement.

It was only when Hihara brought up the precise reason for his visit that their views diverged: Matsui laughed at his idea that Hangzhou would simply surrender once Shanghai had fallen. He took Hihara into his office and pointed to a large, three-dimensional, multi-coloured tabletop model of the battleground. Reports detailing conditions on the ground were pinned to the wall opposite and he encouraged Hihara to look at them.

From these, Hihara learnt that there were more than three hundred Chinese aircraft at Hangzhou's Jianqiao Airbase and that these planes were continuously patrolling the Bay of Hangzhou, appearing at regular intervals in the smoke-filled skies above where the Battle of Shanghai was being fought. Far from surrendering, Hangzhou and its planes were greatly limiting the operational effectiveness of the powerful Japanese air force.

That was in the skies. On the ground, three major divisions of the Chinese army were advancing on Shanghai via two separate routes and would join the battle any moment now. A further nine divisions were advancing via three other routes, and soon they too would arrive in Shanghai. All of which meant that the Chinese forces stationed in Hangzhou could determine whether the Japanese won the Battle of Shanghai. The point wasn't whether Hangzhou would surrender if Shanghai fell; it was that Shanghai wouldn't fall unless Hangzhou was bombed into submission first.

The scales now fell from Hihara's eyes. He swallowed his long-standing advice. But when he thought about the imminent destruction of beautiful Hangzhou and paradisiacal West Lake, the place he always chose for his summer holidays, he felt a soft clutch at his heart. It was a kind of blind sadness, genuine regret at the loss of a treasure.

His feelings showed clearly on his face, even though he didn't say anything. As their discussions continued, Matsui finally realized how upset Hihara was about his plan. With a laugh, he asked, 'Is there a gorgeous girl in Hangzhou that you have your eye on?'

It was a joke, and Hihara responded in kind. 'Oh, I think about her day and night.'

When Matsui heard that, he ordered his staff officer to fetch a 1:3000 military map of Hangzhou and spread it out in front of Hihara. 'I have the finest air force in the world under my command,' he said, 'equipped with the most advanced overhead positioning system. If you can pinpoint the girl's address, Hihara—' he chuckled and raised his eyebrows in a humorous manner '—specifying such-and-such a house on such-and-such a road, I will tell my men that her home and an area measuring a certain number of metres all around it must be left untouched.'

Hihara had an inspiration. Since West Lake was more important to him than the most gorgeous of girls could ever be, he took his cue from the long line of the lake's Su Causeway and drew an irregular circle. 'This is the home of my beloved.'

He imagined that Matsui would just take it as a joke and laugh. He was not anticipating that the general would pick up a pen and draw a thick red line following the outline he'd made, and then write his message inside it. From start to finish, Hihara never knew whether Matsui understood what he was doing or not.

There are many stories about how West Lake came to escape being bombed by the Japanese and I don't know if this one is true or not. In my opinion, like so many Chinese folk tales, it seems short on plausibility. All I can say is that I personally do not place much faith in any of these stories about the meeting between Hihara and Matsui.

Anyway, General Matsui gave orders for the bombing of Hangzhou and Hihara visited him at about this time. Since the latter was such an admirer of West Lake, it was able to escape destruction – this seems to be a fact. The *Gazetteer of West Lake* quotes an article that Hihara wrote about this:

> The Japanese Empire is strong, but China is weak, too weak to withstand the slightest assault; it will collapse at the first nudge. Because of this, it's possible for us to show mercy, to hold back. Just as when a man beats a woman, if it's appropriate to show restraint on account of her gentleness and beauty, then he should. The key is to understand that some things should never come under attack. West Lake in Hangzhou is one such example, a place as lovely as the moon descended to the human realm; the softest of beauties. To damage it in any way would be a terrible shame. Let us preserve it, and then in the future we may enjoy it ourselves. Is that not a delightful prospect?

6

From the time of their very first meeting, General Matsui had become a second mentor to Hihara; he admired him enormously. He used his great skill as a writer to praise the old general to the skies, and he was always putting in a plug for him, licking his arse, singing paeans to his glory and finding excuses for anything that went wrong. The two of them became close friends.

One day, the general invited Hihara to join him on a sailing trip along the Huangpu River. The Imperial Japanese Army was celebrating yet another victory and the two men raised their glasses in toast after toast, congratulating each other on their success. Matsui asked an officer to fetch a tourist map of Hangzhou, then informed Hihara that their forces had occupied the entire area the previous night. 'So you can go back there whenever you choose,' he said, his eyes twinkling, 'and reunite with your lovely lady.' He pointed at the map. 'We didn't touch a thing in the blue area, so I'm sure she's safe and sound.'

Hihara wondered nervously whether he would now have to tell the general the truth, but to his surprise Matsui didn't pursue the matter any further; he seemed to be purposely avoiding the subject. References to the 'lovely lady' ceased entirely as he instead pointed to a spot on Beishan Road, on the edge of West Lake. The conversation now turned to the Tan Estate.

Hihara knew it well – it was the site of a famous whorehouse. He'd been a regular visitor up until a few years ago, before he was married. But now Matsui told him something he didn't know. Specifically: 'There are ten thousand gold bars hidden on the estate!'

Hihara could see why Matsui was intrigued by this, but he was surprised that the general hadn't simply sent in military engineers to dig for the treasure. Why go to the trouble of telling him all about it?

Because Matsui wanted to keep the gold for himself.

There were two reasons he chose Hihara to go and get it for him. The first was that Hihara went regularly to Hangzhou and knew the situation on the ground there. The second was that Hihara would be a good decoy. Who would suspect a scholar? He would tell everyone that Hihara was there to collect historical materials about West Lake; that would make a decent enough cover story.

Victory comes to those who use surprise – in this respect, life is like a battleground. And so it was with the Battle of Shanghai. Fighting had been going on for three months already, involving more than a million combatants and with each side suffering tens of thousands of casualties, but still neither side had managed to seize the advantage. Then General Matsui suddenly pulled a truly unexpected trick: he dispatched a small group of soldiers to circle round and make a surprise attack on the Jinshan Garrison south of Shanghai in the Bay of Hangzhou. Attention was still focused on the front lines further north, so the Chinese forces were not expecting to have to think about what was going on at some insignificant little place behind them. They may not have been thinking about it, but General Matsui was. If someone knifes you in the back, it's still going to kill you, right? Unless you've managed to hide your heart somewhere else.

Sending Hihara to the Tan Estate was done on the same principle. He wasn't the obvious choice and that meant he was the best choice. And he wouldn't be too greedy, so he counted as cheap labour.

Just as the general had anticipated, Hihara didn't demand his fair share; in fact, he said he'd do it for nothing. All the gold would go to General Matsui. Hihara merely asked that if possible he'd like to be given an official position afterwards. He seemed tired of his life as a mole; it was time for him to come out into the open and get some credit for the work he did.

What was wrong with that? Nothing! Matsui was happy to promise him everything he wanted and even said that when he got his hands on the gold they would split it eighty-twenty. They looked like two honest, upright gentlemen coming to a mutually acceptable agreement. But the thing that they were agreeing on was filthy, a robbery, a crime that needed to be kept secret and must never see the light of day.

As we know, the gold was never found. Not only did Hihara not get anything out of it, he also lost his wife. He'd expected the mission to be perfectly straightforward, but it turned into one damn thing after another. He came to feel that the mission had been a complete nightmare. And that nightmare had ended with another nightmare.

In fact, Hihara was very lucky that his wife was murdered, because otherwise he would never have been able to get out of there, not without finding ten thousand gold bars first. He'd have had to keep looking. And if he still hadn't found them, would they have let him go? Would General Matsui have believed him? When it comes to money, morality goes out of the window, and here we're talking about ten thousand gold bars.

To put it bluntly, everything that Hihara went on to acquire – his good reputation, his freedom of movement, his official position and the power this gave him over others – he owed to his wife's untimely demise. That being the case, how could he forget her? Of course he couldn't. He would remember her forever. Her shadow followed him wherever he went. He sometimes seemed to see her in broad daylight and he often encountered her in his dreams. Sometimes she came drifting in on the wind, at other times she seemed to emerge from the bowels of the earth; an object might call her to mind, or she might appear out of nowhere. In a word, he was haunted by her.

When it comes to matters of the dead, you can't find the answer in books; not even Hihara, the number two man in Japan's secret police, could find a solution to this haunting. The only option was to find a religious expert, someone who could mediate between this world and the next, who could communicate with ghosts and stave off disaster.

Eventually, Hihara found a pro-Japanese Taoist master at the Jinshan Temple in Zhenjiang and had him perform a ceremony to summon the soul of his late wife and direct it on the right path. The master said that the reason her soul couldn't rest in peace was that her body and blood had been separated. For her to find peace, the best plan would be to reunite the two. However, it was now more than six months since the murder, and the body had already been cremated and sent back to Japan for burial. Reuniting it with her blood would be impossible, harder even than trying to bring the dead back to life. Or to put it another way, when his wife's body was cremated, the best plan went up in smoke too.

So they turned to Plan B. That was quite simple and straightforward. Hihara was advised to go back to the scene of his wife's murder and pile up the earth where her blood had been spilt into a tomb mound, to comfort the soul of the deceased woman. This is exactly what he did, on the shore beside West Lake. Every year thereafter, at the Qingming tomb-sweeping festival of the ancestors, and in Ghost Month, when the deceased return to visit the living, he made a special trip to the tomb mound to perform the traditional memorial ceremony, offering prayers, lighting incense and burning ritual spirit money. And when he found himself back in Hangzhou or its environs for other reasons, it was like coming home – he could go and tend the tomb, walk round it, remember his late wife and light a candle for her.

To return to our story, that evening when Police Chief Wang Tianxiang accompanied Hihara to the lake and watched him hold a memorial ceremony by a tomb, it was the grave of his late wife, Yoshiko. The fact that his wife had been murdered by the Chinese was not something to be proud of, so naturally Hihara didn't go into that.

I think that the reason Hihara was so eager to take charge of the investigations into the ECCC officers at the Tan Estate (he received his orders in the morning and arrived that afternoon), quite apart from his love of West Lake itself, was bound up with his complex feelings towards his dead wife. That assignment allowed him to mourn her at public expense.

Even after the investigations into Ghost were closed

down, Hihara continued to take every opportunity to visit Hangzhou, walk round the lake and hold a memorial ceremony for his late wife. Which was all to the good, because when Gu Xiaomeng bought his life with four gold bars, his killers knew exactly where to find him.

7

This isn't some story that I've just made up; you can find reports about it in the newspapers of the day, with photographs too.

According to all accounts, on the evening of the Mid-Autumn Festival in 1942, Hihara, together with his new wife, their baby daughter and a maid, boarded a skiff with the intention of sailing out across West Lake to drink some wine and enjoy their moon-viewing from the water. They did not come back. By the time they returned to shore, all four of them were dead. The skiff was ruined too, since it had been sunk to the bottom of the lake and then had to be raised.

The rescuers did the best they could by the light of the moon but managed to salvage only three bodies. The wife, the baby and the maid were there, but there was no Hihara. Once it got light, a passer-by discovered Hihara's dismembered corpse dumped by the entrance to the Temple of General Yue Fei.

It surprised those who saw the bodies that all four corpses looked just as the corpse of the cuckold Wu Dalang did in the classic historical novel *The Water Margin*: their faces had turned completely black. It was obvious that they'd been poisoned. When the skiff was brought ashore, the police discovered that a hole the size of a fist had been carefully bored through the bottom of the boat in advance – it could not have been accidental.

All the evidence indicated that these murders had been planned and carried out most carefully. The killers had put poison into the wine, the snacks and the sweet-bean mooncakes provided by whoever had rented Hihara the skiff, in order that the four would die immediately they consumed them. The murderers then swam across the lake under cover of darkness and removed the bung in the hole they had bored earlier, which caused the skiff to sink. Their swimming skills were clearly quite as exceptional as those of the Ruan brothers in *The Water Margin*, since they were able not only to clean the scene of the crime by sinking the boat but also to drag Hihara's corpse through the water and up onto the shore.

According to one of the investigating officers, a line of footprints stretched for some seventy metres along the shallow lake bed. The footprints had made deep impressions because the killers would have been manhandling the dead weight of a corpse as they headed for Beishan Road. Once they reached dry land, the footprints disappeared.

Because the prints had been made in soft mud, they were of little evidential use and did not help crack the case. The investigative team eventually gave up. As to who the murderers were or what they looked like, probably only West Lake could tell you.

Given that Hihara had saved West Lake from destruction, I don't know if the lake was sad when Hihara was poisoned and had his body chopped into pieces. But I think I can say that there was poetic justice in Hihara ending up the victim in an unsolved murder; after all, there were plenty of people that he'd had killed but where the crime was never laid at his door. The mills of the gods may grind slowly, but they grind exceedingly small. As the saying goes, he who lives by the sword will die by the sword. There is a mysterious logic in all things: as you use your right hand to gouge out your enemy's left eye, your enemy uses his left hand to put out your right eye. That is how the world is, though cause and effect are never so direct or so obvious. They are like an elusive perfume or a fleeting shadow, like deeds carried out under cover of darkness, for this is a private, underground world.

First draft completed in Chengdu: 31.7.2007
Final revisions completed in Hangzhou: 10.11.2013

A SELECTIVE CHRONOLOGY

1911–1912: The Revolution of 1911 results in the founding of the Republic of China under Nationalist Party leader Sun Yat-sen and the abdication of the last Qing emperor.

1921: The Chinese Communist Party is formed; its leaders include Mao Zedong and Zhou Enlai.

1925–1935: Chiang Kai-shek takes over as leader of the Nationalist Party, moves the capital from Beijing to Nanjing, and breaks with the Communist Party. Civil war breaks out as Communist uprisings are suppressed by Nationalist forces. Mao leads a 10,000-kilometre retreat of Communists in a 'Long March' to the new Communist Party base in Yan'an in northern China.

1931–1932: Japanese forces invade Manchuria, north-east China, which becomes a puppet state, Manchukuo. Japanese forces bomb Shanghai, then station troops in the city.

1937: The Nationalist and Communist parties nominally agree to suspend the civil war and unite in a War of Resistance against the Japanese occupation.

July 1937: The Imperial Japanese Army invades northern China, including Beijing and Tianjin. The Second Sino-Japanese War begins.

August–December 1937: During the Battle of Shanghai, the Japanese army carries out extensive bombing of eastern China, including Hangzhou, resulting in the occupation of Shanghai, Nanjing and Hangzhou. Chiang Kai-shek relocates the Nationalist Party headquarters to its wartime capital, Chongqing, in the unoccupied south-west.

March 1940: The Japanese install Chinese politician Wang Jingwei as the head of their puppet government in the capital Nanjing.

January 1941: In the Wannan Incident, Communist and Nationalist forces clash in southern Anhui province, resulting in the deaths of thousands of Communist soldiers and the fracturing of the united front against the Japanese occupation.

August 1945: Japanese forces surrender, bringing an end to the Second Sino-Japanese War and the War of Resistance against the Japanese occupation.

1949: The civil war ends in victory for Communist Party forces across mainland China. The People's Republic of China is founded under Chairman Mao, with Beijing as the new capital. Chiang Kai-shek retreats to Taiwan and establishes a Nationalist Party government there.

ABOUT THE AUTHOR

Mai Jia's first novel in English, *Decoded*, was published by Penguin Classics in 2002, and has been translated into over twenty languages. His novels have sold over 10 million copies and Mai Jia has won the Mao Dun Literature Prize, the highest literary honour in China. *The Message* was first published in 2007 and has sold over a million copies in China. Mai Jia was born in 1964 and spent many years in the Chinese intelligence services.

ABOUT THE TRANSLATOR

Olivia Milburn is professor of Chinese language and Literature at Seoul National University, South Korea, specializing in the cultural history of early China. Her award-winning translations of modern Chinese literature include two of Mai Jia's earlier works, *Decoded* and *In the Dark* (with co-translator Christopher Payne).